SMALLER
AND SMALLER
CIRCLES

SMALLER AND SMALLER CIRCLES

F.H. BATACAN

Portions of this book were first published by the University of the
Philippines Press in novella form under the same title in 2002.

Published by
Soho Press, Inc.
853 Broadway
New York, NY 10003

Library of Congress Cataloging-in-Publication Data

Batacan, F.H.
Smaller and smaller circles / F.H. Batacan.

ISBN 978-1-61695-398-0
eISBN 978-1-61695-399-7
International PB ISBN: 978-1-61695-527-4

1. Teenage boys—Crimes against—Fiction. 2. Serial murder
investigation—Fiction. 3. Priests—Fiction. 4. Forensic
anthropologists—Fiction. 5. Catholic Church—Fiction. 6. Payatas
(Philippines)—Fiction. 7. Quezon City (Philippines)—Fiction. I. Title.
PR9550.9.B35S66 2015   823'.92—dc23
2015001668

Printed in the United States of America

10 9 8 7 6 5 4 3 2 1

To Tess and Frankie, for all that I am.
To Coke, for all that I cannot be.
To Jamie, for all that I will yet become.

"A man who has depths in his shame meets his destiny and his delicate decisions upon paths which few ever reach, and with regard to the existence of which his nearest and most intimate friends may be ignorant; his mortal danger conceals itself from their eyes, and equally so his regained security. Such a hidden nature, which instinctively employs speech for silence and concealment, and is inexhaustible in evasion of communication, desires and insists that a mask of himself shall occupy his place in the hearts and heads of his friends; and supposing he does not desire it, his eyes will some day be opened to the fact that there is nevertheless a mask of him there—and that it is well to be so."

FRIEDRICH NIETZSCHE

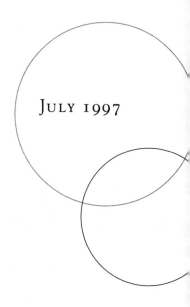

JULY 1997

Some days I just can't seem to focus. It's hard to concentrate on what's going on around me, on what I'm doing.

It's been getting worse lately. Sometimes I feel overwhelmed from the moment I wake up in the morning, as though something bad is going to happen. I can't breathe right; my hands and feet are cold. My head hurts.

I feel like everything I do from sunup to sundown is just to keep this bad thing from happening. And every day I have to do more and more. It is exhausting. Nothing that I do is ever enough.

I feel like I'm always being watched.

I hate being watched.

Prologue

EMIL IS RUNNING after his slum kids, panting in the noonday sun, loosening the high collar of his shirt as he goes.

The children urge him on, their voices shrill with agitation.

"Not much further, Father Emil!"

"Over here, this way!"

"Just a little more!"

His fear grows with each step. It tastes like rust, feels gritty like dirt in his mouth.

The stench from the sea of garbage around them is overpowering. It rained last night, and now that the sun is out, the dump site is steaming. Awful vapors rising lazily with the heat: wet paper and rot and excrement mixing in a soup of odors around them, above them.

You'd think by now you would be used to this, he tells himself, *but you're not. One never gets used to this.*

At last they come to a small space about five feet in diameter, where the garbage has been cleared away to expose the older, compost-like layer beneath.

"There." One of the children points.

Even before he looks in the direction indicated by the thin forefinger, he detects it, a new note of putrescence among all the putrescences mingling in the unwholesome air.

A small, thin, pale hand protrudes from beneath the garbage.

"Mother of God," he mutters under his breath. He turns to the children. "Quick, get me a long stick."

Three children immediately come forward, offering him the digging sticks they use to poke through the garbage. He takes one and walks grimly toward their discovery.

He is about to begin when a flash of concern for the children stabs through the grey, slow-moving haze of fear. He stops, turns around and tells them to leave.

"No, Father Emil," they say, first one voice, then many voices. "We will stay with you," and in their faces there is a kind of quiet determination and sympathy so grown-up it startles him.

Secretly he is glad of the company. He does not repeat the order and returns, face set, to the business at hand.

All right. Here we go then.

He begins to root through great clumps of garbage, and slowly the thing begins to emerge. He won't look at it yet—although he already knows what it is—not until he has more or less cleared away the refuse above and around it.

When he is done, the body of a child emerges. It is a boy about eight to ten years old, though it is difficult for Emil to tell the age accurately. Even at fourteen or fifteen, most of these kids are small, very small, owing to malnutrition and disease.

It is lying face down in the muck and completely naked.

The smell of it—now the dominant note in the vile broth of rot smells; it hangs heavy and horrible in the air.

Flies like fat, shiny blue-black beads, buzzing around the body insistently.

Emil cannot see any marks or wounds on the back or on the back of the head. Afraid to touch the corpse, he slides one end of the stick underneath the body, just beneath the chest, and uses it as a lever to turn the body over. The deadweight almost breaks the stick in two.

The sudden silence among the children is odd. In fact, the whole world seems to Emil to have fallen silent. The neighborhood sounds and the sounds of the traffic from the highway have faded to a strange, low rumble in his ears.

The front of the child's body seems to be moving, and it takes the priest a few seconds to comprehend that there are maggots in it, thousands of them. Gaping wounds—no, holes—in the chest and stomach.

Emil realizes the heart has been removed, the child eviscerated. The genitals are missing.

He looks at the face. *Please, God, let the face remind me this used to be a human being.* Another few seconds and he realizes the face is gone, as though it has been scraped off, leaving a mess of jellied eyeball and bone protruding here and there through muscle.

Hard to make sense of what is missing, what is left.

Purple-brown scabs on the child's knees, probably from an afternoon's rough play.

The spell abruptly broken now, the children running, screaming, from the clearing, leaping goatlike over the garbage in terror.

Emil turns, staggering away from the body, and throws up until his stomach feels completely empty. It does not seem enough; he still feels sick, and he forces his throat to constrict several times, to no avail.

Through the tears that stream from his eyes, he sees that three of the older children have remained. They come toward him now, wordlessly take him by the hand and lead him out quietly, gently, through the garbage.

It rained last night. Heavy rain from a blood-red sky, crashing down for hours without stopping.

I like the rain. Sunny days and their heat make me listless, sluggish, depressed. Isn't that strange? Shouldn't it be the other way around?

But when it rains I feel powerful.

The rain sends everyone running for cover. But while they scurry like rats for the nearest shelter, afraid of the wet and the thunder and the lightning, I come alive.

The rain makes it easier to do the things I have to do.

1

"Horrible weather."

Gus Saenz looks up. Water is running in rivulets off Jerome's wet umbrella. Between the beating of the rain on the roof and the steady thump of the music blaring from the stereo component system, Saenz didn't hear the other man come into the room.

Jerome folds up the umbrella, props it up against the wall in a corner beside the door, looks around. "Where's Tato?"

Tato Ampil is Saenz's young autopsy assistant, a med school dropout who decided in his fourth year that he really wanted to be a musician of some sort, although after nearly two years, he hasn't quite figured out what sort yet.

"You just missed him," Saenz says. The surgical mask he wears over his nose and mouth muffles his warm, deep voice. "Hot date."

"Lucky guy. At least he's someplace warm."

The air-conditioned room is inhospitably cold; colder, of course, because of the weather outside. The high-ceilinged laboratory is a study in white: white walls, white floors, white ceiling. Almost all the equipment and furnishing in it is shiny stainless steel, from the shelves suspended from sturdy brackets fixed to the walls to the two gurneys pushed to one corner.

Mounted on the wall opposite the door is a large whiteboard about four feet high by six feet wide. Close by stands a do-it-yourself workstation, incorporating a computer table, bookshelves and cabinets in honey-colored wood.

A spanking new computer sits in the middle of the station, with a very large monitor. Saenz bought it with grant money from a Japanese foundation. It is used, among other things, to construct three-dimensional skull-photo superimpositions, which help in the identification of the dead—a tedious task

for forensic anthropologists before advances in computer tech-
nology made it simpler.

Gray's Anatomy; works by Boas, Coon, Lacan, Malinowski;
Darwin's The Origin of Species; Landsteiner's The Specificity of
Serological Reactions; and Coleman and Swenson's DNA in the
Courtroom: A Trial Watcher's Guide share the bookshelves with
a complete set of Asterix comic books, yellowing reams of clas-
sical guitar scores. Glossy, full-color volumes on the works of
Magritte, de Chirico, Modigliani. The exhibition catalog from
the 1995 Monet Exhibition at the Art Institute of Chicago.

On hanging shelves and wall cabinets scattered throughout
the room are odds and ends of equipment and supplies Saenz
uses in his work. Plaster casts of skulls and teeth with paper
tags dangling from them on bits of string. Sealed specimen jars
of several sizes, with or without sundry discolored bits of
unpleasantness floating in them.

Most visitors find it unsettling to talk to the priest in plain
sight of this particular collection. The jars demand attention
and usually get it, no matter how strong the outsider's resolve
to ignore them.

Depending on what type of case he happens to be handling
at the moment, Saenz will often wrap his long fingers around
a particular jar, prop it up on his chest and stare into its contents, meditating on vein and muscle and membrane for hours
on end.

On a small table, Telesforo—Saenz's prized tempered-
ceramic model of a human torso with removable, vividly
colored polyurethane organs—stands upright on his cut-off
thighs, a navy-blue New York Mets baseball cap perched rak-
ishly atop his headless neck. He, too, was purchased with
grant money, this time from a Baltimore firm that specializes
in casting anatomical models for use in medical schools.

A clothesline stretches across another wall, garlanded with
strips of photographic negatives processed by Saenz himself in
the small darkroom off to one side of the laboratory.

On other walls hang huge, glass-framed reproductions of four of Leonardo da Vinci's anatomical studies. The organs of the thorax. The heart and the main arteries. Profile studies of a skull facing left. The principal female organs.

Jerome looks at Saenz, listens briefly to the music and rolls his eyes. "R.E.M.?"

Saenz smiles, and the crow's-feet fan out from the corners of his eyes, the eyes of a man who smiles often. "Ah, there's hope for you yet."

Gus Saenz is tall, a little over six feet—the metal autopsy table at which he is working has been adjusted so that he won't have to bend too far over it—and he has the wiry muscularity that comes with zero body fat. He has angular mestizo features, thick, wavy hair greying at the temples. *Rock star hair*, Jerome often teases him.

Jerome fiddles with the volume control knob until he is satisfied. Even after nearly two decades, he has yet to get used to Saenz's performing autopsies to very loud music. "You're too old for this."

The stereo component system is surrounded by stacks of CDs and cassette tapes: András Schiff and Glenn Gould playing Bach partitas, Julian Bream and Manuel Barrueco on the guitar. A large collection of Gregorian chant recordings from way before Gregorian chants became hip. And The Clash, The Doors, Jimi Hendrix, the Sex Pistols, the Grateful Dead. R.E.M. is a recent addition to his postmortem repertoire.

Saenz raises his head; he's grinning under the surgical mask. "Don't knock it. It's the closest either of us will ever get to sex."

Jerome feigns shock with open mouth and bug eyes. "Reprobate."

"Why, thank you. Coffee in the pot if you want it."

The younger priest shakes water from his hair and then busies himself with getting a cup of coffee.

Father Jerome Lucero is about five foot nine, of a physical

type that is usually described as "compact" or "solid." Beefy arms, broad shoulders tapering down into a slim waist and hips. Wavy hair tamed in a severe crew cut; wide, dark eyes. He has an intensity, a seriousness about him that makes him seem older than his thirty-seven years.

Only the keenest observer would note that he walks with an almost imperceptible limp.

He sips the coffee, then makes a face. "Oooh, that's bad."

Saenz pulls his mask down beneath his chin, his hand encased in a stained surgical glove. "Cost cutting."

Jerome notices that the older priest is lisping a little. "How's that tooth?"

It is the other man's turn to grimace. "Don't talk to me about it."

Jerome laughs quietly. Saenz has an impacted tooth in the left side of his mouth that has been due for extraction for several months; it has now nearly rotted through. Whenever the subject of dental work comes up, Saenz is transformed from open-minded, logical man of science to fearful, petulant child.

The older priest scowls at Jerome's amusement. *"Vos vestros servate, meos mihi linquite mores."*

Jerome nods in mock solemnity. "'Keep to your own ways, and leave mine to me.' Yes. Well. I'm quite certain Petrarch wasn't talking about tooth decay. You realize, of course, that putting that off could be bad for your heart?"

"I'll tell you what's bad for my heart. Pain and terror. *That's* what's bad for my heart." Saenz straightens up with a groan. He hunches his shoulders to relieve the tension in the muscles there and then relaxes them again before surveying his work, now in the final stages. "Looks like number six to me."

Jerome walks over to the metal table, where the remains of a child's body lie. Its back rests on a rubber block, pushing the chest up and out for better examination.

"Viscera gone?"

"Pretty much. Heart missing. Face peeled off."

"Neat bladework." Jerome bends at the waist, tilting his head to one side to look obliquely into the chest cavity. "Skull?"

Saenz nods. "Heavy blow. From the fracture lines, it looks like—"

"It came from the right." Jerome straightens up. "About how old?"

"My guess, about twelve or thirteen."

Jerome picks up a pair of surgical gloves from the stainless steel trolley and pulls them on, the rubber snapping against the skin on the underside of his wrists. He quickly surveys the other injuries. "Genitals removed." He leans forward and runs the tip of his forefinger in a straight line beneath the child's exposed chinbone. "Face flayed, just like the others."

Saenz nods. "Clean horizontal slit under the chin from ear to ear."

Jerome looks up at him. "What do we know about the knife?"

"Again, very likely a small blade, about six inches long, no more than an inch wide. Something easy to handle for close, detailed work. Very sharp, no serration. And we've got the same grooves on the chinbone."

Saenz peels off his gloves and drops them into a bucket reserved for medical waste. He walks to a drafting table to one side of the room. The table is a cast-off from the university's Mass Communications Department; it was originally used by film students for drawing cartoons. In the center of it is a translucent circle of hard, movable plastic, with a lightbulb underneath. He flips on the switch and slides two sets of photographic negatives onto the plate, motioning for the other man to look.

Jerome follows him, stripping his own gloves off as he goes and dropping them into the same bucket. He squints into the magnifying glass Saenz holds over the first set of negatives, black-and-white photos of thin, scratchy marks gouged through flesh and into the child's chinbone.

"They're a bit difficult to see with the flesh still clinging to the bone, but they're there if you look closely."

Unlike this boy, most of the other victims were examined by Saenz either weeks or months after they had been killed. By then much of the flesh that had remained after the flaying had decomposed, revealing far more of the bone surface, and any instrument marks that had been made on it, than with this victim.

The younger priest stares down through the glass for a few moments. "Long marks, and deep. Think it was the same blade used on the torso?"

"No, the blade notches on the ribs are slightly thicker." Saenz moves the magnifying glass over the second set and waits while Jerome examines them. This second set of negatives was taken from the sternum and some of the ribs exposed after evisceration of the body.

"Could have been the tip."

Saenz frowns and shakes his head. "Still too thick. No, I don't think it was even a blade at all." He switches off the light as Jerome moves back toward the body. "Ask me about the teeth."

"Father Gus, what about the teeth?"

"Pitting."

"A mouth breather. Just like some of the others."

The front teeth of three of the five other victims they'd seen had minute pits, invisible to the naked eye. This showed that they had breathed often through their mouths—a sign of chronic respiratory disease. Their families could rarely afford meat or fish, and so the children were raised on diets short on protein, long on carbohydrates and other soft, mushy, insubstantial food. The lack of protein in their diets also partly explained how small they were as they hit their teens.

"Sexual assault?"

"Nope."

Jerome nods. "But the excision of the genitals . . . I still can't fully account for that." He thinks back to previous case reports and clinical assessments that he had come across during his studies in abnormal psychology. "Some sexual conflict in there somewhere." He thrusts his hands deep into the pockets of his jeans. "Time of death?"

"When he was found, he was a mass of maggots. The weather's been both humid and wet. I wouldn't put it at more than two, three days. Four at most, but highly unlikely."

Saenz walks over to his desk and puts on his reading glasses, then picks up a clipboard and squints down at a document typed in smudgy carbon on a sheet of onion skin. "Like the others, there was very little blood found around the body."

"Suggesting . . ."

"That he killed them elsewhere. Wherever he does it, there's going to be a lot of blood. So it must be fairly well hidden. Or at least somewhere easy to clean, easy to flush out—a bathroom, a garage. He would have had to change clothes too before he dumped the bodies, to avoid suspicion."

Jerome runs a hand over his face and holds it over his mouth for a few seconds before walking to the whiteboard. Saenz joins him there.

Six is the heading of a new column on the extreme right of the board. Down the leftmost column, marking out the rows, is a series of categories: *age, sex, date found, approximate date of death, mutilations.*

"The body was found on the seventh of this month," Jerome says. He picks up a marker, stares at the blank space at the end of a row titled *approximate date of death* and starts tapping the board, as though counting. Then he glances over his shoulder at Saenz. "So we're looking at, what?"

"Medicolegal officer says the fifth, most likely."

Jerome turns to the whiteboard again and writes *July 5* in the space. He caps the marker, puts it on the whiteboard ledge and steps back. That's when he notices Saenz staring hard at the board, his brow furrowed in concentration.

"What's wrong?"

A light seems to go off in Saenz's head. "We've been look-ing at the *dates* all this time."

"Right."

Saenz is now a flurry of long limbs and motion as he darts away from the board and back toward his desk. He shuffles through the piles of papers, folders and paraphernalia until he finds what he is looking for. "Maybe we should have been look-ing more closely at the *days*." He holds a desk calendar aloft.

Jerome immediately sees where he is going with this. "Got it." He turns back quickly to the whiteboard. "Okay. First boy found February second. Medicolegal says approximate date of death was the night or day before."

"February second was a Sunday. Approximate date of death was Saturday."

Jerome pens the days in below the dates. "Second boy—found March third. Date of death, the first."

"The third was a Monday. Date of death—Saturday."

Jerome writes, then goes to the next row down the line. "Third boy—found April sixth. Date of death, the night or day before."

"Sunday—and Saturday."

"Fourth—May fifth. Date of death, the third."

"Monday—and Saturday." They pause a moment to absorb this. Then Saenz says: "Go on."

"Fifth boy—found June tenth. Approximate date of death, the seventh."

"Tuesday—and Saturday."

"And this one—the seventh and the fifth."

"Monday—and *Saturday*." Saenz looks up from the calendar to study the new information on the board. "That's the first Saturday of every month since February."

EMIL SITS BY himself in Father Saenz's faculty office.

In the chill of the room, he can feel acutely the wetness of the socks inside his shoes, the dampness of the legs of his trousers from the knees down. He crosses his arms over his chest, keeping his fingers tucked into his armpits.

A storm is raging outside, and the government has hoisted typhoon signal number 2 over several parts of Luzon, including Metropolitan Manila. The branches of the trees on the campus whip back and forth with every shift in the direction of the wind. The rain lashes against the windowpanes. Occasionally a plain or flowered or patterned umbrella bobs up and down just outside the glass—someone caught in the fury of the elements.

The door opens. It's Gus Saenz, struggling with a soaking wet umbrella that has been turned inside out by the wind. Jerome Lucero follows close behind, his umbrella in somewhat better shape.

"Oh, Emil, I'm sorry you've had to wait so long," Saenz says, moving forward with both hands extended to grasp the parish priest's in a warm, if wet, handshake.

"It's okay, Father Saenz. Father Lucero."

Saenz takes the umbrellas and leaves them to drip dry inside a plastic bucket in one corner of the room. "Coffee?" he asks Emil.

"Yes, please."

A cup is poured and gratefully accepted. Emil takes a sip, then blows on the surface of the coffee to cool it down.

"Nice day for a super typhoon," Jerome says, pulling up a chair. "Have classes been suspended in your district, Father Emil?"

Emil nods. "Early this morning. Half of the students had already turned up."

Jerome grunts in disapproval. "Huh. You'd think they would have learned to suspend classes early enough after all these years. It's not like they didn't know the typhoon was coming until this morning."

Saenz sits behind his desk and turns to Emil. "So," he prompts.

Emil sets down his coffee cup and begins wringing his hands, trying to calm himself before asking questions. "Is it one of our boys?"

Saenz pauses a moment. "We can't be absolutely certain yet. But it's definitely the same set of mutilations."

"My God." Emil crosses himself. "Why is he doing this?"

Jerome stands, pulls up the blinds to allow more grey daylight into the room. *And if I knew the answer to that question, Emil,* he says to himself, *we might actually be able to stop him from doing it again.* He keeps his eyes focused on some vague spot outside the windows, looking but not really seeing, and does not respond. For a moment the room is still and silent save for the sound of the wind and rain outside.

Saenz clasps his hands together on top of his desk. "We don't know yet. Honestly, we may never know. But you can help. You can tell your parishioners to keep an eye out for suspicious characters. And warn the kids about staying out in the dump late."

Jerome nods. "Do it discreetly—try not to create a panic. Whoever it is, we want to be careful not to alert him to the fact that the authorities are already looking for him."

"So—we wait for him to make a mistake?" Emil frowns.

"I know it sounds contrary to common sense, Emil," Jerome says. "But if he feels threatened, he may go into hiding, and there's a chance we'd never find him again. And there's nothing to suggest that he'd stop doing this if he were forced to flee to another place."

Emil chews on this a moment. "All right, Father Gus. I'll do what you advise. I just hope you manage to find him soon. The people aren't stupid; they're already asking questions; the fear is growing. It's a poor community, and they're used to being ignored by the powers that be. If that fear turns to anger—well, you know very well what can happen."

"I know, Emil. And I can promise you, this situation is not being ignored." He glances at Jerome. "Certainly not by us."

⌣

THIS IS HOW it happens in Jerome's dreams.

Always it begins with him standing in the dark, in the rain. He is alone, dressed as if for sleep in loose-fitting shorts and a T-shirt, rubber slippers on his feet. Always it is very cold.

And then he hears it, a child's voice screaming for help.

He starts running, first this way, then that, slipping in the mud and the slime, losing first one slipper, then the other, leaving deep, gouged tracks where his feet slide. Dirt lodges deep under his toenails and fingernails when he claws the mud to regain his balance. He runs until his heart can pump no more and his lungs give out and his legs ache, shouting for the child.

Tell me where you are; talk to me. I'll find you.

And then he realizes his voice is no longer his own. It is small: a child's voice.

And again he stumbles in the mud and the garbage, legs failing him, arms failing him, and then the hand on his shoulder, rough and hard, shoving him down. He can smell the muck—warm, moist, sweet with rot—as his face is pushed into it.

Then he turns—he tries to turn—and he can almost see the man's face, and then the hot breath on his cheek and words, words he can't understand, spoken in a whisper that seems like a thick, slow churning of blood in his ears, the man's spittle falling on his face like tiny shards.

Always the rock first and then the blade, sharp and slim and cold.

When he awakes in the safety of his own bed, he's bathed in sweat. He shakes his head to clear his mind and waits in the stillness for his labored breathing to return to normal.

He untangles his legs from the blanket, swings them over the edge of the bed and feels in the dark with his feet for his rubber slippers. He goes into the bathroom, switches on the light.

Jerome reaches for the tap. Cool water rushing. He bends forward and splashes it on his face.

When he is done, he looks into the small mirror on the medicine cabinet. His eyes seem to have lost their whites. They are round and deep and dark, black holes full of unanswered questions. His face, still dripping water, is pale and thin, paler and thinner than it has ever been since this whole ugly business began. In the quiet spaces between his clinical practice and counseling, his teaching and his religious duties, these killings have consumed him, occupied his thoughts, filled him with dread.

Yet they call to him, as they call to Saenz. And neither of them can turn away.

"And he said to them, 'Well did Isaiah prophesy of you hypocrites, as it is written, "These people honor me with their lips, but their heart is far from me; in vain do they worship me, teaching as doctrines the commandments of men." You leave the commandment of God and hold to the tradition of men.'"

Mark 7:6–9

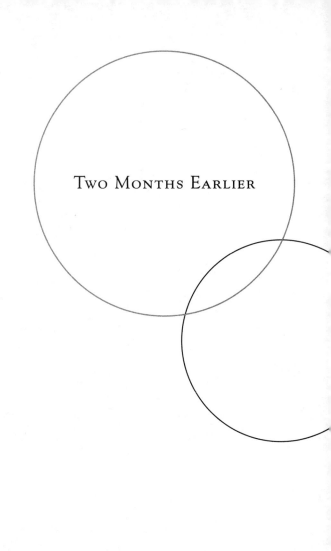

TWO MONTHS EARLIER

2

When Jerome opens the door to Saenz's office, he sees Saenz standing by an open window, lost in thought.

"Hey," he says, but Saenz doesn't turn. Jerome glances at the desk and sees a letter lying open on it. It's creased in several places, and he can imagine Saenz crushing it in one of his large hands, anger coursing through the long fingers, before smoothing it out again.

Jerome stands there for a while, waiting for Saenz to say something. When he doesn't, the younger priest quietly volunteers, "I'm sorry."

Saenz keeps his eyes fixed on a cluster of coconut trees on a stretch of campus lawn visible from the window.

"Bud rot," he says, finally.

Jerome looks up at him, confused. "Excuse me?"

"Bud rot," Saenz repeats. "I've told the head of facilities management about the bud rot on those trees. He won't listen to me. It started with one tree. Now three others are infected."

Jerome moves toward the window, glances out at the trees, then back at Saenz, puzzled. "You're thinking tree mortality at this moment?"

"The first tree is too far gone. Some days, when the wind blows in the right direction, you can smell it: decomposing tree tissue."

"Okay." The end of the word curls upward, like a question, and Jerome stares at him, frowning. "I'm afraid I don't understand."

"It's a fungus, you see. *Phytophthora palmivora*. It attacks the heart of the palm. I knew that's what it was when I saw that the topmost leaf was dead. The fungus eats its way down and through the tree."

"Right." Jerome takes a deep breath. Before long he, too, is staring at the trees. Cars and students go up and down the small road that borders the lawn. One student, seeing the two priests at the window, smiles and waves at them, but the men fail to notice, and she continues on her way. "Are there others?"

"There will be." Saenz moves away from the window, toward the desk, looking grimly down at the letter. "That's the nature of any kind of rot. If you don't stop it, it keeps going. It will keep going until it destroys the very organism that feeds it."

Jerome folds his arms across his chest and leans against the window frame, observing Saenz. "You know the cardinal won't change his mind. The matter's closed as far as he's concerned."

Saenz's face darkens with a tightly controlled fury. "It is not closed. It will never be closed. Not until Ramirez is made to answer for what he's done."

Jerome is startled by the phone ringing, the sound loud and shrill in Saenz's small office. When the older priest doesn't move to answer it, he asks, "You want me to get this?"

Saenz nods, and Jerome picks up. "Yes?" It's Susan, an administrative officer in the Sociology and Anthropology Department where Saenz teaches and his de facto secretary. "Yes, he is. Hang on a moment while I ask him." He claps a hand over the mouthpiece and whispers, "Susan's asking if you want lunch."

Saenz shakes his head, waves the offer away, not once looking up from the letter.

Jerome hesitates, then returns to the call. "Hey, Susan, thanks, but he's not hungry just yet, and he has a pile of things to attend to. He'll probably pop down to the cafeteria when he's starving. You know how he is." A pause, a chuckle. "He'll scarf down something from the pastry case on the way to his afternoon class. Don't worry about him; he's a big boy now." He wonders if Susan can detect the artificial cheer in his voice. "Okay. See you."

When he sets the receiver down, he realizes that Saenz has not moved. "Look. You've been chasing him through the system for more than a decade. The cardinal just moves him around. The children won't talk because they know nothing will happen. He's made powerful friends. What else can you do that you haven't already done?"

Saenz sighs. "I honestly don't know, Jerome. But I have to do *something*. This can't go on."

Father Isagani Ramirez is a diocesan priest serving under the Archdiocese of Manila. For many years he served as a parish priest at a parish in Quezon City, until rumors of inappropriate conduct with minors began to surface. Saenz became involved when one of his former pupils, a quiet, intelligent young man who had been struggling to get through university, attempted suicide. When Saenz tried to find out why, he learned, among other things, that he had been molested as a child by Ramirez.

Saenz sought help to verify the young man's claims and later found reason to believe them true. But a report to the archdiocese was met with silence. Months after that, Saenz received news that Ramirez had merely been transferred to another parish.

Saenz was incensed, but he was advised to think carefully about taking any further action. So, like any good Jesuit, he reflected, he prayed, he sought guidance and discernment. In the end, his conscience told him to continue to press for further investigation of Ramirez's misconduct and information on the decision to move him to another location.

In his new parish, Ramirez—a charismatic speaker who could keep a crowd enthralled and whose charming, easygoing, even gossipy manner endeared him to people—quickly found wealthy backers to help him set up what was supposed to be a charity shelter for orphans and street children in the area. *Kanlungan ni Kristo*—"Refuge of Christ"—had twenty beds initially, but soon expanded to thirty, to forty, and now seventy beds.

Saenz watched all this from afar, unhappy that his pleas

went unanswered for years, even more unhappy that Ramirez was now in a position of even greater access to and power over children and preteens. But just when it seemed completely hopeless, a nun, Sister Miriam Taguibao, came to him out of the blue with suspicions of her own. She had been helping out at the shelter for two years and been disturbed by certain things she had seen and by the atmosphere of secrecy and unease that had been evolving slowly there. Her disclosures—credible to Saenz as well as to other experts whom he consulted, including Jerome—seemed to confirm Saenz's worst fears about Ramirez's involvement in *Kanlungan*.

It was with Sister Miriam's help that Saenz brought forward a set of fresh complaints against Ramirez; and this time he argued strongly for a criminal investigation rather than a Church inquiry. But Ramirez had powerful friends within the Church hierarchy and in society, and Saenz was shut out of the ensuing Church investigation. One by one, the children and teenagers who had been willing to testify dropped out, fearful and intimidated. Saenz himself had by now earned a reputation for being a bit of a troublemaker, and Sister Miriam was mysteriously reassigned to distant Cotabato City.

The outcome of the slow, secretive inquiry arrived today, in the form of a letter from Cardinal Rafael Meneses. It is, as Saenz had feared, yet another transfer of parish—and Ramirez, while instructed to minimize contact with *Kanlungan*'s wards, remains executive director of the charity.

"He'll keep doing the same thing, no matter which parish he's rotated to, no matter what project he takes on. And this charity he runs—he's just using it as a way to choose and groom more victims."

"But Gus"—Jerome puts a gentle hand on his forearm—"without the children's testimonies, how much further can you go?"

"I've already told you, I don't *know*." It's extremely rare for Saenz to raise his voice. When he sees Jerome flinch, he quickly pulls back. In a calmer tone, he says, "But I have to think of something."

Jerome glances at his wristwatch. "Look, I've got a class in half an hour."

Saenz waves his large hands in the air. "Yes, go, go." He returns to the window, staring out at the dying trees once again.

"We end at three. Then I'm seeing patients till around, oh, six thirty." The other man seems not to be listening anymore, so Jerome speaks louder, a bit more firmly. "Why don't I swing by for you around seven? I'll buy you dinner. Someplace cheap," he jokes.

"You won't have time," Saenz says. "You haven't packed for your trip yet, and your flight's tomorrow."

Jerome is off to Chicago the next day to attend an academic conference. He knows Saenz is right, and that there's no time to discuss this further over dinner tonight.

"We'll make it quick," he says, but Saenz shakes his head, and that's the end of that.

Jerome had already expected that Saenz would take the cardinal's decision hard, but seeing him like this worries him. He stands there, not certain what to do, what else to say. After a few moments, he reluctantly decides to move on with the rest of his day. "Well, I'd better get going."

"Hmmm."

"You'll be okay?"

"Hmmm."

Jerome waits, but Saenz's mind is too far away. So, without another word, Jerome leaves the room. He begins to close the door behind him and then remembers that it's nearly time for Saenz's student consultations, so he decides to leave it open. He walks briskly down the corridor, but just two or three steps after he turns a corner, he bumps hard into someone.

"I'm sorry," Jerome apologizes, and then finds that he has to tilt his head up to look up into the man's face, he's so tall. But he's also rather old, and Jerome finds himself laying his hands gently over the man's forearms, almost skeletal beneath the long sleeves of a *barong Tagalog*, to steady him. "So sorry. I'm afraid I wasn't paying attention. Are you all right?"

The man gestures toward a brown envelope that has fallen to the floor, and Jerome quickly stoops to pick it up, handing it back to him. "Yes, thank you." The voice is deep, quiet, roughened by age. "I'm all right." It's only when he speaks that Jerome recognizes who he is—he heard the voice at a news conference that aired on television just a few nights before. "I am looking for Father Saenz's office."

"Yes. Yes, of course." Jerome's curiosity is piqued. He briefly considers accompanying the visitor to Saenz's room and hanging around to find out why he's here. But he knows that if he does, he'll be late for class. "Down the corridor to your left, third room after the fire extinguisher cabinet."

The man glances down the corridor in the direction Jerome is pointing, then turns and looks straight into Jerome's eyes.

"Thank you, Father Lucero."

Of course you would know who I am, Jerome thinks as the man disappears around the corner.

SAENZ IS TRYING to decide whether to feed the letter into the shredder or to file it away as a reminder of his continuing failure when he sees the tall, thin man framed by the open doorway. He looks at Saenz, waiting to be invited in. Although he is standing in the dim light of the corridor, Saenz can tell that the cloth of the man's *barong Tagalog* is fine, the embroidery finer.

"Yes?" Saenz stands.

"Father." The man makes no move to enter the office.

"May I help you?"

The man's eyes narrow, but his expression is quizzical. "May we go for a walk, Father? It is a nice day for a walk."

The man steps back into the corridor, the gesture an invitation, the light of one of the fluorescent lamps in the ceiling falling upon him.

Saenz sees him more clearly then: hair almost completely white; thick eyebrows also going to white; pale, deeply lined skin drawn over the fine bones of his face; sharp eyes; a nose curved like a parrot's beak. Saenz is tall, but this man is even taller, about six feet five inches; in his *barong* and khaki-colored trousers, he seems like a long, pale ghost. A flat, brown envelope is tucked under one arm. He stands motionless, with a slight stoop—he looks like an old man, really, except for the small, black, watchful eyes.

Now Saenz recognizes him: the director of the National Bureau of Investigation, Francisco Lastimosa.

"Of course, sir. Give me a moment."

THE SUN HAS dipped behind a bank of fat, grey clouds, and the branches of trees are swaying in a strong breeze. The two men walk, unhurried, along a narrow path lined with greenery on either side, with the old man in front of Saenz, setting the pace. The path takes them farther away from the building that houses the Anthropology Department, toward a grassy open space on the campus, dotted with trees. Farther ahead it forks at various points; depending on one's business, one might choose to head to other departments and buildings on campus or, by a roundabout way, to the residence halls.

Saenz is beside himself with curiosity as to why the director has come to see him so unexpectedly. He already asked minutes ago, when they first emerged from the building, but he received no answer. Saenz decides to wait respectfully for the director to talk, but the man seems in no particular rush to get down to business.

When he finally speaks, it's to say, "You'll get him yet, you know."

Saenz stops and stares at the back of the man's head. "Excuse me?"

Director Lastimosa likewise stops and then glances at

Saenz. "Your Monsignor Ramirez." He watches in mild amusement as the blood drains slowly from Saenz's face. "You seem
surprised, Father Saenz. Did you not think anyone else knew?"

"Certainly no one else seems to care," the priest says, and it
comes out angrier, more bitter than he had intended. "And
he's not *my* Monsignor Ramirez."

The old man shoves his hands in the pockets of his trousers
and begins walking again. "I'm reminded of Ecclesiastes three,
Father. Surely you know it?"

Saenz takes a deep breath. "To every thing there is a season,
and a time to every purpose under the heaven."

"A time to keep silence, and a time to speak," the man
continues.

"What are you trying to tell me, sir?"

"Perhaps you've forgotten verse seventeen, Father."

"I said in mine heart, God shall judge the righteous and the
wicked: for there is a time there for every purpose and for
every work." Saenz reflects on the verse for a moment, then
sighs. "I've been at it for years, sir."

"You're a man of God. You of all people must have faith in
the possibility of a satisfactory outcome. Even if, sadly, long
delayed."

"Faith in God, yes. Faith in man—to be honest, I sometimes . . ." Saenz's voice trails off.

"Ah. Faith in man." He sighs. "You and I both, Father."
They walk again in silence for a minute or two. "While you
await God's time for the monsignor, Father, I ask you to
devote some of your time and your considerable intellect to a
problem that I have brought to you." When he smiles, it is a
sad and weary smile. "I believe, in light of your recent disappointment, you will find this a suitable undertaking."

"I'm listening."

3

"We have the remains of a boy, Father Saenz. He was found this Monday in the Payatas dumpsite. The injuries are quite . . . horrific." Director Lastimosa shakes his head vigorously, as though by doing so he can rub out the memory of what he's seen. "Most of the internal organs have been carved out. The penis, severed. The face, mutilated beyond recognition."

They both look up when they hear voices coming from the opposite direction. Two seminarians, one with a breviary in hand, are coming down the path, talking and laughing. When they see Saenz, they smile and nod respectfully, extending the same courtesy to the director. The path is narrow, so the two men step aside to allow the seminarians to pass.

When he's satisfied that they're out of earshot, the director continues. "The case comes to us from the local police. Apparently they found another corpse in February with very similar injuries. In both cases, they could not find any witnesses who had seen anything unusual that might have been related to the killings."

"Let me guess. That's as far as the investigations went."

The director nods. "Life is cheap in that part of the city. Just yesterday, a market vendor was stabbed to death in a fight at Litex. He took up a prime selling spot on the roadside that somebody else wanted." Litex Road, along Commonwealth Avenue and not far from the dumpsite, has a teeming flea and wet market whose vendors spill over onto the avenue, sometimes occupying two to three lanes and hindering the flow of traffic. "Between the lack of policing skills and the sheer volume of criminal activity that goes on there—the drugs, the rival gangs, the rapes, the random violence . . ." The director lifts up both hands in a gesture of resignation.

"Have the victims been identified?"

"The first boy has been. Ryan Molina. The killer left part of a shirt near the body that the boy's parents were able to recognize."

"And this second boy?"

"Hasn't been identified yet." The director hands the envelope that has been tucked under his arm all this time to Saenz. "I know you've seen terrible things before, Father, but this is . . . different."

Saenz opens the flap, removes the contents, and then studies them. *It's surreal*, he thinks—the horror in the photographs set against the peace and quiet in this pocket of green, against the normal flow of everyday life along Katipunan Avenue bordering the campus: the jeepneys, the school buses, the private cars ferrying their human cargo to and from their destinations in the city.

He's aware of the director's eyes watching his reaction.

"If you need a moment, Father," he says.

Saenz shuffles the photographs together and puts them back in the envelope. "Thank you, sir. I'm all right." He returns it to Director Lastimosa. "But I'm not sure what I can do that your own people at the bureau can't."

"Father Saenz, I don't believe you can look at those photographs and think that we can do it on our own. My people can recognize a drug deal gone wrong, a carnapping that turns into rape and murder." The director holds out the envelope to him again, his hand shaking slightly. "This is different. Whoever did this is talking to us. And I believe you can help us understand what he is trying to say." When Saenz takes the envelope, the director grasps one of his hands firmly. "And you and I both know, Father. If there is a second one, there could very well be a third. Or perhaps there already has been, and we just don't know it yet. We must find him."

Saenz looks down at the director's pale hand, its green veins bulging up beneath the thin skin from the tension in his grip. It's at this moment that the man appears to realize how tightly he's holding Saenz's hand. He loosens his grasp and steps back, taking a moment to compose himself.

"Forgive me, Father." He clears his throat, then fishes a handkerchief out of a pocket of his trousers and wipes his now-damp forehead with it. "I'll be honest with you. I'm shaken by this. I know you are too—aren't you?" He searches Saenz's face for an answer.

Saenz gives him a look that tells him, *Yes.* "But what exactly are you proposing, sir? I have classes at my department here. I have administrative work and religious duties. I have research projects."

"Look, I know you're a busy man. And frankly, we can't pay you for anything other than expenses. But if you have any time at all to spare to consult on these murders, I must appeal to you to lend us that time."

"It's not just a question of spare time, sir." Saenz thinks back on all the cases he has consulted on that involved the bureau. In most of them, he had been part of an independent panel of experts convened at the order of the president to investigate the crime. In all of them, he had found strong cause to question the bureau's work methods and investigative practices and, ultimately, their findings. "You must know that I'm not very popular with some of your people. I'm not sure they would appreciate my wading into their turf, even at your invitation. You could become very unpopular very quickly."

Saenz can tell from the man's lack of surprise or hesitation that the director has already considered and dismissed this. "I'm not interested in popularity contests, Father. I will talk to my staff. They can agree or disagree with me, but at the end of the day, it's my call. In the eighteen months that I've been at the head of the bureau, I have not been wasteful with resources or cavalier in hiring outside expertise. I think I can fully justify bringing you on board."

"Now I know you've worked with some of our better boys before," the man is saying as they retrace their steps back to Saenz's building. "Rustia in SOCO speaks very highly of you."

Saenz nods. "Ading is a good man." The National Bureau of Investigation has precious few good men, and Fernando Rustia—Ading for short—at scene-of-the-crime operations is one of them. A lower-level supervisor with some twenty years of largely unrewarded experience under his belt, he and Saenz had met nearly a decade before through Saenz's work with human rights organizations involved in the search and identification of *desaparecidos* or "salvage" victims under the Marcos dictatorship.

"Yes, he is. I'm trying—" and here the man stops, as though struggling to remember the words he wants to say, and reaches out to touch Saenz's arm, his long fingers bent with arthritis, resembling claws. "I'm trying to get them . . . to stay. The good ones. I'm trying to stimulate them. To remind them why, you know—why it is they came to us in the first place."

Saenz nods. Like most other intelligence and investigative bodies in the country, the NBI is understaffed, underfunded and in dire need of upgrades to its facilities, equipment and human resources. But it also suffers trust and integrity issues, going all the way back to the dark days of the dictatorship— from technical questions over the proper recording of crime and custodianship of evidence to accusations of inefficiency, corruption and collusion with criminal elements. The bureau has good people, to be sure. But many of them, like Rustia, are underpaid and burned out and have few avenues for advancement in either pay or position within the bureaucracy.

The two men start walking again, the director a few paces ahead of Saenz.

"I've not been with the bureau long, and I don't imagine I'll be staying in my post very long either. I'm an old man, and there are a lot of young guns who would love to take my place."

Saenz nods again. Francisco Lastimosa had been a trial lawyer, then embarked on a long and remarkably untarnished career in the judiciary. When that part of his life was over, he served on company boards, government panels, committees of inquiry, but always somehow failed to land the high-profile posts, the juicy appointments. That ended about eighteen months ago, when his predecessor stepped down in the midst of corruption charges. The president had plucked him then out of semiretirement and, in a confluence of gumption and good judgment rare in Philippine politics, appointed him to the post despite protests from many quarters that he was a nobody—and an old nobody at that.

"Now, Father, it must be clear by now that I know a lot about you. Your work for *desaparecidos*, for victims of disasters. I have great admiration for you. And without any arrogance, I must assume that you know a fair bit about me as well. Perhaps you will agree that you and I share a somewhat similar view of the world. And while I've never had the chance to work with you, I guess there's a first time for everything." He faces Saenz now, his expression both grim and earnest. "I need your help."

IT IS DARK by the time the director returns to the bureau. He walks slowly down the corridor to his office and finds his middle-aged secretary still in the outer room, tapping away at the computer on her desk.

"Luz. It's late."

"Evening, sir. I had to finish filing some of these expense reports. They're due on Monday."

"Monday is next week. Tonight you have dinner with your family. Go home."

She smiles. She types a few more lines into what looks to be a spreadsheet, saves the file, then begins tidying up the reports. "Oh, by the way," she says, "Attorney Arcinas dropped by earlier looking for you."

He stands straighter now, shoulders back, as though bracing himself for a small violence. "What a coincidence. I was just about to go looking for him."

Luz turns off her computer. "Would you like me to send him up to see you on my way out?"

When he speaks, his voice is quiet. "I don't suppose I have a choice." So quiet that she can't hear him.

"Excuse me?"

"Yes, Luz, do send him up."

She nods, gathers up her things and heads to the door. "Good night, sir. See you tomorrow."

"Good night."

He stands there until the door closes, then heads wearily to the inner office. He does not turn the lights on and crosses the carpeted room silently. He sinks into the large, leather swivel chair and switches on the desk lamp, which bathes the desk area in a pale bluish-white light. And he waits.

He dozes off and is startled awake by the sound of the door in the outer room banging closed. There is a sharp rap on his own door, and it opens seconds later, his visitor not bothering to wait to be asked to come in.

"Good evening, Ben."

"Sir. I have some papers for you to sign." Attorney Benjamin Arcinas holds the papers aloft as he crosses the room. It's been a long day, and his hair—often artfully arranged in large curls and dyed a shade of red that does not occur naturally on this earth—is limp and greasy.

The director imagines that the air in the room has been rendered immediately noxious by Arcinas's barely masked hostility. "Yes. You can leave them on my desk. But please, have a seat."

Arcinas ignores the request and instead taps the sheaf of papers with one forefinger. "I need them by tomorrow morning."

"And you will have them by tomorrow morning," the

director says. After more than a year of working with him, he's no longer surprised at being ignored by Arcinas. So he adds, more firmly this time, "But please. Have a seat. I need to discuss something with you."

The other man takes a step forward, then stops. "Discuss? Or have you already decided?" When the director doesn't respond at once, he arrives at his own conclusions. "You have. And you just called me in to tell me."

"We have to do what is necessary."

Arcinas arches an eyebrow. "Well. Of course, if you *think* it's necessary . . ."

The attorney has been with the NBI for most of his working life. He is ambitious and self-serving and does not trust outsiders. When Director Lastimosa was new to the bureau, he quickly sized up who was allied with whom within the organizational hierarchy. Arcinas was, and is, a fiercely loyal ally of Assistant Director Philip Mapa, the man who had been tipped to head the bureau before Director Lastimosa's surprise appointment was announced. Had Mapa been chosen, Arcinas would likely have been his deputy. To the director, it's clear that this thwarted ambition is the key reason Arcinas has been so antagonistic toward him since he took the helm of the bureau. That antagonism has only been amplified by this plan to consult with another outsider—Saenz, a man with whom Arcinas has locked horns before and whom he clearly considers a threat to his reputation and standing in the law enforcement community.

"Ben, I need you to cooperate with me on this. We need all the help we can get. You're swamped with work as it is. Everyone else has too much on their plate already, and we can hardly keep up."

"Oh, of course I understand the rationale, sir," he says, unable—unwilling—to rein in his sarcasm. "I just hope you've considered the impact of this move on the morale of your people."

"I have. And I am quite certain that our people want to get to the bottom of this." The director stands and looks directly at him. "You most of all, Ben. Am I right?"

There's nothing else Arcinas can do, for now. He puts the papers on the desk and walks out.

4

THE FOLLOWING WEEK, Saenz begins work on the case. The boy was about thirteen. His facial skin was completely peeled off and his internal organs neatly carved out of his body.

Saenz has been consulted because of his expertise as a forensic anthropologist, one of only three in the country who have trained under the famous American expert Clyde Snow. He earned his doctorate from a French university in the late seventies, specializing in physical and medical anthropology.

As a rule, forensic anthropologists are primarily consulted on problems with the identification of skeletal remains. However, Saenz's skills extend considerably into other aspects of forensic science, including advanced training in forensic pathology, which enables him to perform autopsies on persons who have died of unnatural causes.

Through consulting with various branches of the police and other law enforcement agencies, Saenz has gained an intimate knowledge of their investigative methods and techniques, as well as their frustrating inadequacy. Over the past few years he has formed a theory about murder in the Philippines that would prove highly controversial if he ever went public with it.

Unlike police in the United States or Europe, Philippine police and law enforcement authorities do not compile statistics on missing persons on a nationwide basis. Most people with a missing relative are advised to turn to a local radio or television station to issue a *panawagan*—an appeal to the public for help or information to locate the person. Often, that's as far as things go; little police effort, if any, is expended toward following up on the cases after that—unless, of course, the victims are wealthy or influential.

The police do not bother to systematically record how many of these persons do turn up later, whether dead or alive—or how many people remain missing and for how long. Indeed, the recording of all crime is largely inadequate and sloppy. Little attention is paid to determining patterns: a missing person's physical type or age, the geographic area in which he or she disappeared or reappeared, the condition in which he or she has been found.

Saenz surmises that the country's hidden murder rate is probably far above the numbers reported as part of Philippine National Police's annual murder statistics.

Taking this logic one step further, he also concludes that serial killing is not as impossible a phenomenon in the country as popular perception and opinion seem to suggest, but one that local law enforcement has barely any capability or inclination to detect. This is because little, if any, comparison is ever made between the particulars of murders committed at different times or places. Here, again, the poor recording of crime information comes into play, as well as the ineffectual communication and coordination between agencies and even units within the same agencies.

Whenever he finds himself at a social occasion that brings him into contact with law enforcement officials, Saenz tentatively trots out his theory. It is quickly withdrawn when some police general smiles patronizingly and says, "You've been watching too many foreign movies, Father Saenz; there are no serial killers in the Philippines." The reasons offered simultaneously amuse and anger Saenz. "Our neighborhoods are too congested, our neighbors too nosy, our families too tightly knit for secrets to be kept and allowed to fester. We have too many ways to blow off steam—the nightclub, the karaoke bar, the after-work drinking binges with our fun-loving *barkada*. We're too Catholic, too God-fearing, too fearful of scandal."

Saenz wants to tell these men, *No, sir, it is you who have been watching too many foreign movies. Such killers can be found all over the world, not just in the West—in China, India, Indonesia, Pakistan, South Korea, Hong Kong. Japan has a fairly long list of them, as does South Africa. What makes you think the Philippines is so blessed by God that we would be exempt from this kind of evil? It isn't. It simply hasn't developed the necessary frameworks, the physical infrastructure and human skill sets, required to recognize and track down such killers.*

Saenz knows only too well that if he wants to change the collective mind of local law enforcement, he has to present data. The police are quite happy to argue theory with a priest, but they are intimidated by statistics, by hard facts, by numbers. Saenz feels that effective policing and law enforcement requires the proper collection, storage and processing of information.

These particular murders are another opportunity to begin compiling that data.

WHEN SAENZ ARRIVES at the bureau, he is escorted to a drab, windowless office where one of Director Lastimosa's deputy directors, Jake Valdes, is waiting.

Valdes is in his midforties but looks easily ten years younger—like a graduate student, with his straight, black hair, wire-rim glasses and plaid shirt.

"Good morning, Father," he says, extending his hand to shake Saenz's.

"Director Valdes," Saenz replies.

"We're just waiting for Director Lastimosa and Attorney Ben Arcinas."

"Ah, yes. Ben." Saenz has encountered Arcinas in two cases before, and he is well aware that he is not the good attorney's favorite person.

Valdes's gaze settles upon the priest. "Director Lastimosa is aware—"

The door opens. Benjamin Arcinas saunters in, and the atmosphere fairly crackles with the force of his antipathy. He throws a folded newspaper down on the table in the center of the room, drags a chair out and sits facing Valdes, pointedly ignoring Saenz.

"Can't stay long," he says, tilting his head toward the newspaper. Saenz knows the front-page headline is about a brazen bank robbery that took place in broad daylight three days before; a security guard and a passing cigarette vendor ended up dead. "Have my hands full with Agribank today."

Of course you do, Saenz thinks to himself. *It's a high-profile case that everyone's watching, and the chairman of the bank is a known golf buddy of your* padrino, Mapa.

Saenz doesn't say a word, though, merely watches with growing interest the dynamic between the two other men. Valdes, he notices, has gone from friendly to distant, not even sparing Arcinas's newspaper a glance.

"Regardless of what you have on your plate today, you'll have to wait for Director Lastimosa."

"He knows I have no patience for these long meetings," Arcinas retorts sourly.

"I guess you'll just have to find some," Valdes answers, his face unsettling in its blankness. They hear footsteps outside the open door, and then the director looks into the room.

"Good. You're all here." The director walks in and closes the door behind him. Saenz and Valdes both give him respectful nods of acknowledgment, but Arcinas fishes the lifestyle section out of the newspaper and leans back in his chair, pretending to read.

Director Lastimosa pulls up another chair and sits down. "Anything good in the cinemas, Ben?" he inquires. It's a gentle, veiled rebuke, but unmistakable nevertheless. Saenz notes the barely there smile that plays on Arcinas's lips as he folds up the newspaper again, satisfied that he managed to get a mild rise out of Director Lastimosa. He slides the newspaper back toward the center of the table, then stretches his short legs out in front of him, the feigned casualness calibrated to indicate disdain for the meeting's other participants.

Director Lastimosa draws his lips together in a tight line

but says nothing. Valdes pulls up two chairs, one for Saenz and one for himself. "Thank you," Saenz murmurs as he takes his seat.

"Shouldn't Director Mapa be at this meeting?" Arcinas asks.

Valdes takes off his glasses, wipes the lenses with a handkerchief. "Emergency leave." Without the glasses, his eyes seem very small.

Arcinas looks from him to Director Lastimosa and back again. "Really?" When he receives no answer, his eyes dart from person to person once more, settling finally on Saenz. "How convenient."

"He was told about the meeting, and he said he would come. He changed his plans at the last minute." Valdes puts his glasses back on, and his eyes appear sharper somehow. "Golf," he adds, and he makes the word sound like an obscenity.

"All right, let's get down to it," Director Lastimosa says. There's a hint of impatience in his voice, and all three of them involuntarily straighten up in their seats—even Arcinas. "Ben, you know Father Saenz, of course." Arcinas merely grunts in reply. "We've asked him to take a second look at what we have on the two Payatas murders. Jake?"

At the mention of his name, Valdes nods, stands and walks to a small filing cabinet in one corner of the room. He opens the top drawer and takes out a set of pink folders, then returns to the table and hands the folders to Saenz.

Saenz lays them down on the table in front of him, then quickly leafs through the contents. He ignores Arcinas's heavy sigh of boredom. After a few moments, he looks up at the director. "There's not much in here."

Arcinas bristles. "The second body was found just last week. These things take time, as you very well know."

"It's an observation, Ben, not a judgment," Director Lastimosa says, then turns to Saenz. "But yes. There isn't much beyond what the local police have given us. Those are mostly their notes and reports."

Saenz is dismayed, but he's seen this too many times before to be surprised. "I'll look through these again more thoroughly. I suppose you've considered revisiting the site where the second boy was found?"

"Thought you might want us to do that," Jake says. He glances at the director. "Shall I put Rustia on it?"

"As soon as possible, please. Today if he can manage it."

Arcinas has removed a pen from his pocket and is twiddling it through his fingers idly. "It's probably just some drunken or drug-crazed pervert who got angry when he couldn't get his way. We see it all the time, especially in slums like Payatas." When there's no reaction, he forges on. "I'm not saying that we shouldn't investigate this, but I don't get the extreme focus on it. We've got bigger, more pressing things to take care of."

Valdes opens his mouth to say something, but decides against it. Saenz can think of many things he'd like to say, but he knows it's not his place to say them, so he waits for the director to speak.

"I know you're not that naïve, Ben, so there must be another reason why you refuse to see how important these cases are. Is it because you think the victims themselves are unimportant?" The director leans forward, glaring at Arcinas. "Or is it because you have a problem with me?"

Arcinas breaks eye contact, his defiance giving way to an almost childish sullenness. He slumps back in his chair and stares at the wall opposite him. Saenz catches Valdes and Director Lastimosa exchanging glances. The room is quiet for a while.

The director clears his throat. "Father?"

Saenz turns a page to study a photograph of the second boy's body. "I can't say with finality from just looking at pictures, but . . . these injuries do not look like the work of someone who was drunk or drugged or otherwise not in control of his faculties. And the fact that they are so similar to injuries inflicted on another victim . . ."

Valdes folds his arms on top of the table. "So you're confident it's the same person?"

"I can't be completely sure at this point; I've just started. But from what I can see here, in these reports, they look too similar for us not to consider the possibility of a single perpetrator."

Arcinas snickers but says nothing.

Valdes looks at him. "It's not unthinkable. In the past we've had bodies popping up all over the city that look like serial vigilante killings. Heads wrapped in shirts, hands tied behind their backs. Cardboard signs on the bodies that identify the victim as a drug pusher or a rapist or a carnapper. Similar injuries, similar methods of disposal, similar staging."

"Any luck finding the killers?" Saenz asks.

Valdes shakes his head.

Saenz heaves a sigh of resignation. "With this one . . . as you yourself told me earlier, sir, if you have two bodies now, there may be more. You just haven't found them yet. And there may be even more of them down the road."

"Now that's just scaremongering," Arcinas begins to protest, but the director holds up a hand to shush him.

Saenz continues. "We may have to look at other deaths in the area—compare the injuries and the circumstances, see if there are parallels."

Valdes shifts uneasily in his seat. "That could take a while. And how far back do you want to go? We don't have infinite resources."

"How far back *can* we go, given your current resources?" Saenz asks.

Valdes turns to Director Lastimosa. The director considers the question a few moments. "Realistically, I'd say six months to a year. That's manageable, Jake?"

"Should be. We'd need to realign some staff temporarily."

Saenz doesn't want to have to say this, but he has no choice. "I'm afraid we may need to dig all the way down to blotter level, sir."

It's an unpleasant prospect, but Valdes and the director know as soon as Saenz says it that it's necessary. Crime statistics are chronically underreported or misreported across the country, as law enforcement officials at every level try to massage the numbers to create the illusion of better performance. Discrepancies have been estimated in as many as 60 percent of crime incidents, with some station commanders seemingly more interested in staying in office or snagging promotions than in presenting a true picture of criminal activity in their areas of responsibility. Discrepancies also arise when authorities at the level of the *barangay*—the country's smallest administrative unit— neglect to submit incident reports, or submit selective or whitewashed reports. So Saenz doesn't trust the completeness of police reports at the station level.

Arcinas stands. "I don't know about you, but I don't have the time to dig through blotters."

"Sit down, Ben."

"What he's asking us to do is—"

"*Sit down.*" Director Lastimosa is not usually one to bark at his subordinates, but it's obvious to Saenz that Arcinas is working on his last nerve here. "We won't take shortcuts here. These children are just as important as your celebrities and politicians and bankers. This case falls within your purview, so I expect you to do what needs to be done."

Arcinas slides back into his chair, sulking. "You can't even be sure you'll get the police or *barangay* to cooperate."

"We'll find a way." Valdes turns to Saenz. "I've had those files photocopied for you. I'll arrange for Rustia to come and see you before you leave this morning. And we'll let you know soon how we're progressing on the blotters."

"Thank you."

Arcinas looks around at everyone. "So we're done here? I can go?"

Director Lastimosa waves his hand to dismiss Arcinas. The director seems very tired now; Saenz notes the lines of strain on his forehead, around his eyes and mouth, the ashen tinge of his skin. Arcinas forcefully pushes his chair out from underneath him, its legs scraping loudly on the cement floor. He leaves the room, allowing the door to bang shut behind him.

Valdes studies the director's face closely, plainly worried. "Are you all right, sir? You don't look well."

The director waves again. "I'm fine. Being in the same room as Ben saps me." He gives them both a tight, forced smile. "Don't tell me you don't feel the same way." He stands. "Father? You're good with this so far?"

"Yes, sir." Saenz's brow is creased with concern. "Director Valdes is right. You don't look well."

"Nothing that a cup of coffee and some peace and quiet in my office won't cure." He walks to the door. "I'll see you later in the week then, Father?"

"Yes, sir."

His footsteps recede down the hall. "Is he going to be okay?" Saenz asks.

"He's had a tough week. He'll be fine." But even Valdes doesn't look convinced by the words coming out of his own mouth.

THAT NIGHT, SAENZ writes an email to Jerome, now in Chicago for his conference. He gives him the broad outlines of the two murders and asks if he might be able to help, as he has done with several prior cases. He sends off the email and then reads other emails for about a quarter of an hour.

He is about to log off and get ready for bed when he hears the familiar ping of the chat program running in the background of his computer. He clicks on the window.

JLucero: Knock knock.

JLucero: Anybody home?

Saenz1911: Hey. When did you get in?

JLucero: Yesterday morning.

JLucero: Got your email. Sounds urgent.

Saenz1911: It is.

JLucero: This why Lastimosa came by to see you last week?

JLucero: You didn't say anything that evening. Didn't want to pry.

Saenz1911: I had a lot on my mind.

Saenz1911: So when are you back? I've forgotten.

JLucero: In about two weeks. Conference is on all week, then still have two lectures to deliver.

Saenz1911: Can't be helped then. Ok to bug you with this when you get here? Might be tough going.

JLucero: When have I ever said no? :-)

JLucero: But you okay on your own for a while?

Saenz1911: Thanks.

Saenz1911: Yes, yes. Could take a while to get the paperwork moving anyway.

JLucero: Heh. Not surprised. Keep me posted?

Saenz1911: Of course.

JLucero: Okay. Gotta run. Keynote starts in about an hour. Bus coming to pick us up.

Saenz1911: Go, go. Knock 'em dead.

JLucero: I will if I don't take a shower first.

Saenz1911: You know, I really didn't have to know that.

JLucero: :-)

JLucero: It's for your edification.

JLucero: Go to sleep. Talk soon!

Saenz logs off.

5

THE REST OF the week comes and goes, and it's Monday when Saenz gets the call from Valdes. When he arrives, he's escorted once more to the drab, stuffy room where they last met. This time, the table at the center of the room is stacked with folders. Valdes is waiting for him, looking glum. Behind him are two young men, perhaps in their mid-to-late twenties.

"Borja and Estrella helped sort through these, Father."

The two give him small bows of respect, whisper "Father" in greeting. He smiles at them, asks for their first names.

"I'm Ed," says the taller of the two. "This is Norman."

Saenz shakes their hands, then picks up one of the folders. The papers inside are photocopies; he guesses that the precincts did not want to relinquish the originals. He asks Valdes, "Did you have a hard time getting your hands on these?"

"Hard enough," Valdes says. "They thought it was an audit."

"Which it kind of is."

"Well, we couldn't tell them that or else we'd never get anywhere. The last official audit got three station commanders sacked."

Same old story, Saenz thinks to himself. "Find anything?"

The three other men look at one another and hesitate, and Saenz knows immediately from their body language, from the small, strangled sounds that they make in their throats, that it can't be good.

Valdes nods in the direction of two folders lying on the table, separate from the rest of the stacks. "Two other bodies with similar mutilations. Both found in the dumpsite." He watches as Saenz reaches for the folders, flips rapidly through their contents. "One found in March, the other found in April."

"Where are they now?"

"You might want to sit down for this. The police and the

barangay couldn't get any leads on either the identities or the possible killers. When nobody turned up to identify and claim the bodies, they were carted off to the nearest paupers' cemetery."

Saenz tries to study the papers again, but he's so angry that he can't concentrate. "That's it? Just like that?" He feels a throbbing behind his left eye that radiates out to his temple.

"Are you surprised?"

"Maybe not surprised. But certainly disgusted."

"We see this all the time," says Ed. "When local police hit a dead end, the remains are simply taken and buried somewhere. Not enough space to hold them for very long."

Saenz says to Valdes, "We have to find those bodies."

"I'm already on it."

"And Ading Rustia? Did he find anything new at the site where the second boy was found?"

"That's the one piece of good news we've got for you, Father." Norman steps forward with another folder. "He said he found a tattered shirt of a fabric similar to fibers found on the body." He hands the folder to Saenz.

Saenz takes it and opens it to skim the first page. "It's not much, but it's something."

Valdes's cell phone goes off, and he tugs it free from the holder attached to his belt. He checks the screen. "Sorry, Father, I've got to run. You all right here?"

"I'll be studying these for a while, thank you."

"Okay. Ed's coming with me, but if you need anything, Norman here will help."

Valdes leaves with Ed, and Norman pulls up a chair to sit beside Saenz.

"You think those other two were killed by the same person?"

Saenz sighs. "Can't be sure until I've had a chance to examine the remains. But if these reports have recorded the injuries correctly"—he taps the folders on the desk in front of him—"the similarities are impossible to ignore."

———

ABOUT AN HOUR later, Norman offers to get coffee for both of them. A few minutes later, somebody knocks on the door and opens it a crack.

"Father."

Saenz smiles when he recognizes the face and the voice. "Ading."

The door opens fully, and Fernando Rustia walks in. They shake hands. He's a tiny man, the merest fraction of an inch over five feet, in his midforties, extremely neat, with round, sad, deep-set eyes and large ears that stick out of the sides of his small head.

Rustia surveys the room with some distaste. "I see they chose the best possible room available for you."

Saenz chuckles. "All the other rooms were taken."

"Heh," Rustia replies, and that's about as much as he's going to say. He reminds Saenz of a tarsier, particularly in the way he swings his head swiftly to look at his interlocutor during a conversation, always seeming to miss his mark by an inch or two. Some people find it uncomfortable to speak with him since he seems constantly to be looking at them from out of the corner of his eye. And because almost everyone at the bureau is taller than he is, the situation is aggravated by the upward tilt of his head—it's rather like being assessed by a furtive hobbit.

Saenz, whose mind observes and collects people's odd mannerisms, finds this quite endearing. His association with Rustia goes back several years, and he knows him to be the finest crime scene investigator in the bureau—perhaps in the whole country.

"Excellent work on the site where the second boy's body was found," Saenz says.

"Thanks. You've seen my report?"

Saenz nods. "Yes, I was just reading it. You were fast."

Rustia shrugs. "Would have been faster if I weren't swamped with work. But the director said this was a priority, so . . ."

"Thanks, Ading. I appreciate this."

"Been getting a lot of work since he came on board. Good on one hand, but too much work and I could make mistakes."

"Have you told him?"

"You don't want to be the complainer, you know?"

Saenz shakes his head. "You should tell him. I think he'll listen."

Rustia gives him the weary look of the perpetually disappointed. "Every director listens, Father. I've yet to meet one that's actually done something to change things here."

The door opens again. It's Norman, bearing a paper cup of scalding hot vending machine coffee in each hand. When he sees Rustia, he gives him a quick nod of greeting.

"'Ding. Coffee?" he offers, carefully setting both cups down on the table within Saenz's reach.

"No, thanks. Had too much coffee for one day. Thanks for giving Father Saenz here my report."

"No problem."

Saenz takes a sip of coffee and finds it exceedingly bad—completely lacking in richness and aroma and dominated by a flavor akin to burnt tobacco. He sets it aside, careful not to allow his face to register displeasure, but Norman notices anyway. "We've got sugar, Father. You want some sugar?"

Not all the sugar in the archipelago can improve this coffee, my boy, Saenz thinks. "No, it's fine. I'll just wait for it to cool a bit." He turns back to Rustia's report. "Think we can use this information to get an ID on the boy?" he asks both men. "Maybe someone's looking for their son. Maybe they'll recognize the shirt fabric."

Rustia doesn't look too hopeful. "There aren't many missing persons reports from the area, Father. It's a transient population. People come and go all the time, and kids or teenagers who disappear from their families are often presumed to have run away."

Norman, however, is a little more upbeat. "We'll be contacting those who've come forward to ask for help. Who knows? We might get a hit."

Saenz1911: *Ding dong.*

Saenz1911: *Anybody home?*

Saenz1911: *There are two more bodies. NBI's trying to get them exhumed.*

Saenz1911: *Anyway. Hope first lecture went well.*

Saenz1911: *Try to catch you tomorrow.*

Saenz1911: *Night.*

JLucero: *Wait wait.*

JLucero: *Am here. Two more?*

JLucero: *You still there?*

Saenz1911: *Sorry, brushed teeth.*

Saenz1911: *Yes, two more, similar injuries.*

JLucero: *And nobody raised a stink about them?*

Saenz1911: *There was a cursory investigation, but no results. So the barangay authorities decided to get the bodies buried quickly.*

JLucero: *They went on the blotters, surely?*

JLucero: *Otherwise how would you have first known about the injuries?*

Saenz1911: *Blottered, yes. But not transmitted to higher levels.*

JLucero: *???!!*

Saenz1911: *Was that the sound of your jaw dropping?*

JLucero: *I really shouldn't take the Lord's name in vain.*

JLucero: *But I sure feel like it.*

Saenz1911: *After you take it in vain please lend it to me*

Saenz1911: *I promise to give it back to Him when I'm done*

JLucero: *But why? I don't understand.*

Saenz1911: *Apparently the excuse was that there was no room at the nearest morgues to hold them.*

> *Saenz1911: If you ask me, it was sheer laziness and*
> *expediency.*
> *JLucero: Shameful.*
> *Saenz1911: Hang on. Phone.*

Saenz picks up the ringing phone on his desk. "Saenz."

"Not asleep yet, are you?" It's Rustia; he's never been one for niceties.

"No, working. What's up?"

"Sorry to disturb you at this hour, but I think you might want to come over."

Saenz glances at his wristwatch. "Now?"

"Now. I think we've got an identification on the second boy."

"The one with the tattered shirt?"

"That's him."

"Be there as soon as I can."

When Rustia hangs up, Saenz returns to the chat with Jerome.

> *Saenz1911: Have to run.*
> *Saenz1911: Ading thinks the second boy can be identi-*
> *fied.*
> *JLucero: Go, go! Keep me posted.*
> *Saenz1911: Will do.*

SAENZ FINDS RUSTIA leaning against a doorframe, his arms crossed over his chest. He is watching Jake Valdes trying to console a visibly agitated couple. They are standing some distance away in the middle of the corridor, and the woman is distraught, almost hysterical. Saenz stands beside Rustia, taps him lightly on the shoulder.

Rustia looks up. "Father."

"Ading." Saenz glances at the couple. "Are those the parents?" he whispers.

Rustia nods. "Boy's name was John David Mendoza."

"Absolutely sure?"

"They identified the shirt material. And from photographs, they found a birthmark on his left arm, just inside the crook of the elbow. Mother hasn't been able to sit still since."

The father stamps his foot in anguish and frustration. Valdes is trying to placate him. But then the mother begins to wail, and the father loses it completely; he's shouting at Valdes now, demanding to know why they haven't put the boy's killer behind bars yet. His voice bounces off the hard walls, rings in their ears.

Instead of meeting the man's anger head-on, Valdes maintains a respectful silence. Saenz recognizes in the deputy director's face and body language—the way his features relax into calm concern, the way he holds his body straight yet loose—a kind of mental distancing, allowing him to absorb the man's rage without taking it personally or feeling compelled to respond in kind.

Saenz turns to Rustia. "Probably doesn't feel like it right now, but good work, Ading."

He shrugs. "We were lucky with the shirt and the birthmark. Next time, maybe not so lucky."

Saenz pauses, then asks, "What about DNA? The bureau has new equipment, right?"

Rustia smirks. "We got it last year. But you remember what they kept telling you then? 'We can't carry out DNA testing just yet because we're still building our database.' Plus, with no guidelines on collection and storage of samples at local police and health units—well, you get the picture, no?"

Yes, I get the picture. The priest sighs. "Hey. You think Director Valdes will let me talk to the parents?"

"No harm in asking him." Rustia stops to listen to the father's continuing tirade. "But—maybe not tonight."

6

AFTER HIS CLASSES the next day, Saenz heads back to the NBI. Jake Valdes has arranged for him to sit down and talk with John David's parents.

He waits for them in a small office with dingy cream walls and fluorescent lighting. The chairs have rusty metal legs, and their fatigue-green upholstery is cracked and flaking off in places, exposing the yellow rubber foam underneath it to dust and grime. There are two desks in the room, their cheap wood veneer peeling back in the humidity like shavings of cheese. Saenz has been in countless rooms like this before, all of them ravaged by decades of bureaucratic neglect and systemic inefficiency. They are depressing to be in for any length of time; but somehow, they also harden his resolve.

Someone knocks on the door; it's Ed Borja. "Father . . ." he begins, and as he opens the door wider, Saenz sees the Mendozas, small and hesitant in the corridor. Their eyes are puffy, no doubt from crying. No amount of washing can hide the fact that their clothes are old. They are both wearing worn rubber slippers, and Saenz surmises that they are much younger than they actually look, their faces and bodies worn down by hard, unrewarding work, exposure to the elements, constant deprivation.

Saenz stands as Ed leads the couple into the room. He's careful with them, as if they're fragile. They stand together in the middle of the room, leaning toward each other. The man's left shoulder touches the woman's right one, but the corresponding hips don't touch, as though they're used to leaving room there for a child. The sight of that empty space, the knowledge of what is no longer there, tugs at something inside Saenz.

"This is Father Gus," Ed explains to them. "He wants to ask you a few questions about your son."

The father looks at Saenz. "But we don't know very much," he says, a plaintive note in his voice. "We only found out yesterday."

Saenz quickly moves to position two chairs in front of them, then wordlessly invites them to sit down. "I am here to help. I am hoping to understand how this might have happened to your boy," he tells them when they've settled uneasily into the chairs. "But to do that, I have to ask you a few questions." He fishes out a small notebook and a pen from his back pocket.

The father and mother exchange wary glances, then look to Ed, who's now sitting at one of the desks, for cues. With a nod, he prompts them to proceed.

At this, the father speaks again. "What do you want to know?"

"First, when was the last time you saw John David?"

"Jon-jon," the mother volunteers.

"Jon-jon," Saenz repeats. "The last time—before he disappeared?"

The couple look at each other again. "It was a Saturday morning," the man says slowly. "He didn't finish his breakfast. He said he was going to meet some of his friends in Payatas."

Saenz considers this a moment. "You mean, you don't live in Payatas?"

"We live in Manggahan, with my brother and his family." Manggahan is one of the nearby *barangays*.

"And Jon-jon's friends—they're from Payatas?"

"We don't know. Maybe. Jon-jon used to go there almost every day."

"To visit his friends?"

The man shakes his head. "No. To dig through the dump."

He says it matter-of-factly, but the reality of it stings Saenz: the boy was a scavenger.

"He worked in the dumpsite."

The man nods. "He collected bottles, scrap metal, anything that he could sell."

Saenz must choose his words carefully. "Did he go to school?"

"Only up to grade four." The man touches his wife's hand. "We couldn't afford any more schooling. A few years ago my wife had to stop working because she has a lung condition. I can't hold a regular job because I'm an ex-convict. Nobody wants to hire someone like you. So I do odd jobs here and there—some basic carpentry or plumbing or electrical jobs. But they don't pay very well."

"I see. So Jon-jon helped with the family expenses?"

"Yes. We depended on his earnings to get by. Often, he would bring food from the dump."

Saenz's eyes widen. "From the dump?"

"If he couldn't find metal or wood or paper to sell, he would look for food—anything thrown away that could still be used. If it was too spoiled or rotten, he would mix it together for pig slop and sell it. If there were scraps that could still be eaten, he would bring them home. Vegetables, fruit. Moldy bread. Pig fat, animal skin. Bones to make soup."

Saenz says nothing for a few moments, trying to take this in, and the man tries to fill the awkward silence. "It's still food, you know. We just put it all in a pot and boiled it so that we wouldn't get sick. Most of the time, that's all the food we had."

Saenz isn't naïve; he's always known that this is the sort of existence that the country's poorest live from day to day. But to hear about it firsthand, told with such apathy and resignation, is a different thing altogether.

"Do you have any other children?"

"Five. Jon-jon was the oldest. He just turned thirteen in January. The rest are too young to work."

Depended on his earnings. All the food we had. Too young to work. Saenz does not want to be angry, but he is: not at the hapless parents, who probably could not have done any more for their children under the circumstances, but at everything else.

"Jon-jon's friends—do you know any of them? Can you give me some names?"

Again the father and mother look at each other, trying to remember. But they come up with nothing. "Jon-jon didn't talk about them much. We never met any of them."

Saenz nods. "Did he get into any fights that you know of? Did he have any problems with anyone?"

"No. He never told us anything. He was always very tired when he came home, you know? Rain or shine, he would go to the dump after breakfast. He only kept away if he was sick or if there was a typhoon."

"If he didn't go, we didn't eat." It's the woman talking now, her voice soft and sad. It is as simple and as complicated as that: this family lives hand-to-mouth. *Isang kahig, isang tuka,* one scratch, one peck: a day's work for a day's food.

Saenz has to force himself to put his anger aside, to focus on getting more information. "Did Jon-jon say where exactly he was meeting his friends?"

"No. But he used to go to the parish church there once in a while. He said they gave out free food on Saturdays."

Ed raises his hand like a schoolboy to catch Saenz's attention. "We can ask around the parish, see if they knew Jon-jon."

"Yes, Ed. Please do. That would be most helpful." Saenz glances back at the couple. "Where did Jon-jon sell his goods?"

They pause to think about this, and the mother says, "He and the other waste pickers just went to any of the nearby collection stations along Commonwealth." Saenz has seen those—filthy, decrepit structures with mounds of scrap metal, and wood, and cardboard, and bins full of discarded bottles.

"Did he have any trouble with anyone there?"

"No. No trouble." The mother bites her lower lip, thoughtful. She continues: "But he didn't tell us much. He just worked and worked. He didn't complain, but he was always very quiet anyway. He didn't like his cousins, but he couldn't avoid them—we live in a small place, just a shanty, and there are fifteen of us. So he just went to work. It gave him a reason to be out the whole day."

Saenz leans forward. "He didn't get along with his cousins, then?"

"Just the usual stuff between boys."

"How old are they?"

The mother seems surprised. "About his age, or younger."

The father adds, "The oldest is Sonny. He's thirteen."

Too young, Saenz thinks, *statistically unlikely to have been involved.*

Saenz asks a few more questions about Jon-jon's routine and activities, but the parents can't give him much. Overall, they give him the impression of a family fragmented by poverty, drifting numbly through days and nights of hunger and deprivation. There is love there—he doesn't doubt it; it's in their eyes when they talk about their dead son—but there isn't the full engagement in, or awareness of, the boy's life that might give Saenz the information he needs.

He concludes the interview and rises to his feet. Ed stands too and opens the door, ready to usher the couple out of the room.

"Thank you for coming to talk to me," Saenz says.

They nod, mumble their thanks and begin to walk to the door. But the mother turns back to face Saenz.

"You're a priest. How can you possibly help us?"

Saenz is momentarily stumped by the question. It would be useless to tell them that he's done this before, that he's been trained to assist in cases like their son's.

It's a humbling question, and one he doesn't have a suitable answer for. "I don't know yet," he says at last, and it's the truth.

She doesn't look satisfied, but his honesty is enough for now. She nods and follows her husband out to the corridor. Ed smiles at Saenz sympathetically; he knows what it's like to be asked that question and to not know the right thing to say.

When he leaves the room, Saenz notices Ben Arcinas waiting outside the door, a paper cup in his hand.

"Nice answer, Father," he says, his tone mocking. Then he ambles off down the corridor, seemingly without a care in the world.

———

> Saenz1911: *You're probably out.*
> Saenz1911: *But the boy's been identified.*
> Saenz1911: *Spoke with the parents today.*
> Saenz1911: *He worked the dump, picking waste.*
> Saenz1911: *He was pretty much the breadwinner of the family. At thirteen.*
> Saenz1911: *Something not very not right in that alone.*
> Saenz1911: *Anyway.*
> Saenz1911: *Will email details.*
> Saenz1911: *Night.*

Saenz leans back in his chair and tilts his head up toward the ceiling, hoping to relieve the strain in his neck and shoulder muscles. He slips his feet out of his shoes and then starts to remove his socks using his toes.

He sits in the dark for a minute or so, then decides to get ready for bed and get some sleep. He stands, yawns, stretches his arms and bends from side to side.

Then the chat program pings him.

> JLucero: *You still there?*
> JLucero: *When I was thirteen, I was in school.*
> JLucero: *I wasn't very happy, but I was in school.*
> JLucero: *Well, you know that.*

Jerome had been a high school freshman at thirteen and Saenz a young priest. Their paths crossed first when Saenz had signed up to teach a biology class at Jerome's school while wrapping up his MA at the university. Ferdinand Marcos's martial law had been in place for nearly a year, and Saenz was quietly active in the opposition against him.

> Saenz1911: Hey. You're there.
> Saenz1911: You had your own cross to bear.

Jerome was one of the quietest boys in Saenz's class. And yet, as his tests and papers would eventually show, he was also one of the brightest. He sat by the windows, and Saenz would often see him staring out at the trees. At other times, he would fall asleep at his desk. He did not have many friends; his parents hardly ever turned up at parent-teacher conferences. Moving about on campus, he tended to keep his head down, avoiding eye contact. He walked with a limp; some days it would be more manifest, and the boy would be, by turns, listless, distracted or easily startled. Saenz knew almost immediately that he came from a troubled home, that he bore the brunt of the trouble in it, and that the limp was not from any congenital condition but had been acquired.

> JLucero: Did the parents give you any leads?
> Saenz1911: Not much that was useful.
> Saenz1911: At least, not useful yet.
> Saenz1911: Maybe some of it will make sense down the line.
> JLucero: I suspect none of it will make sense however far down the line we go.

Saenz knows this to be true. Even though he's done this many times before—tried to understand the complex interactions between power, poverty and crime in this country—in the end, none of it makes any sense.

Take Jon-jon, for example. He was young and small, just

the perfect weight for foraging in the unstable mounds of rub-
bish. He would have been light on his feet and fast, able to
pick through a load of freshly dumped garbage quickly, in
constant competition with other trash pickers for the most
valuable finds. His life and health would have been in per-
petual jeopardy: from rival scavengers, from disease, from
infection by medical waste or poisoning by industrial waste,
from the toxins produced by the ceaseless ferment of the landfill.

In a different kind of society—a better kind—he would
have been in school, would have had a chance to play,
would have had better food to eat and cleaner air to
breathe. And if he still died the way he eventually did,
society's guardians, its authorities and lawmen, would have
left no stone unturned to find out who was responsible.

> Saenz1911: *But we'll keep going anyway?*
> Saenz1911: *In spite of that?*
> JLucero: *You lead. I'll follow.*

Nearly twenty-five years earlier, Saenz had tried to befriend
the young Jerome, tried to understand what had been going
on in his life and his home. But while the boy responded in
small ways—he became more active and attentive in Saenz's
classes—he never fully opened up to his teacher, nor gave a
complete picture of the troubles in his family. The school year
ended, and Saenz was soon caught up in other things, eventually leaving the country to begin doctoral studies in France.

When he returned to Manila to research and to teaching
several years later, Saenz was pleasantly surprised to encounter
Jerome—now a young man—in his theology class at the university. He was even more pleased to learn that he was now a
Jesuit novice.

Saenz could tell that Jerome was still working through
many issues from his past and did not trust people easily. They

built their friendship slowly—at first, mostly through study and work. As mentor and student, they found common ground in their intellectual curiosity and their thirst for social justice. By the time of his ordination, Jerome had already chosen clinical psychology as his field of study. When Saenz began to do volunteer work to help identify the murdered victims of the dictatorship, Jerome was drawn in as well, providing free counseling for the families left behind. From there, their individual work took deeper turns into the study of violent crime. Jerome is now a clinical psychologist and at thirty-seven has already written a number of landmark papers on sexuality, violence and crime in the Philippines.

The friendship between the two has deepened significantly; they have developed an extraordinary rapport more closely resembling the tie between father and son. Although no two men could be more different in character and temperament, they find themselves on either end of a baffling mutual affinity. It is so strong that sometimes they startle themselves by finishing each other's sentences and thinking similar thoughts almost simultaneously. In the last two decades, they have become each other's consciences and sounding boards.

Jerome shares Saenz's views that serial killing is not a solely Western phenomenon and that the inadequacy and sloppiness of local police methods and intelligence techniques stand in the way of its detection.

Saenz1911: *Thanks.*
Saenz1911: *These boys—it's almost as though they don't matter.*
Saenz1911: *Nobody is watching.*
JLucero: *"Could you not watch with me one hour?"*
Saenz1911: *Matthew 26:40?*
JLucero: *I'll watch with you.*

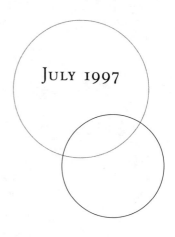

JULY 1997

THE SKY IS overcast, and the puddles on the streets reflect thick piles of clouds, rolling slowly where the winds take them.

Green is the only color that rain intensifies; the grass and the trees look as though they have been retouched with a giant brush by some great, invisible hand. Natural smells are heightened: the scent of flowers, of turf, of moist, peaty soil.

After the rain, life—earth, foliage, frogs—momentarily reclaims human attention from those things which are not life. Everything else—the cars, the buildings, the dingy shop signs and crumbling waiting sheds, the garlands of electrical wiring that line the streets, the rusting metal and concrete and plastic that jut out singly or in masses to stab the city air—everything else recedes into a damp and quiet dullness.

The dead things know their place.

In the laboratory, a watery daylight weaves through the vertical blinds. It settles on the floor and the furniture in an uneven wash of gray.

Gus Saenz slides a computer chair forward on its casters and motions for Jerome to sit down.

"Let's go over it again, Jerome." The older priest now begins taking notes on a fresh pad of ruled yellow paper.

"Okay." Jerome takes the chair, straddles it and leans forward so that its back cushions his chest. He tilts his head down and closes his eyes, beginning the latest in a series of nightmare journeys through the Payatas of his mind.

"Statistically, the odds are that it's a man. And it's a safe bet, given that he's apparently not afraid to go into the landfill, that he knows the area well and probably lives or works in or around it. Since he doesn't seem to have aroused any suspicion after all this time, it's also likely that he's a familiar figure in the community."

"Or has made himself one," Saenz fills in. "He's no longer a stranger to anyone; he's become part of the everyday pattern."

Jerome nods.

"Go on."

"He waits for victims of opportunity. The watching and the waiting are as important to him as the act itself."

"What about the time of the attacks?"

"Given what we now know of the days and the dates, he strikes on the weekends—most likely Saturday evenings. Most of the men are drunk on Saturday evenings—those paid their wages at the end of the week still have money to burn."

Saenz shifts in his seat and taps his pen against the pad. "Victims?"

"All boys, eleven to thirteen years old. Small for their age; he likes them small. He stuns them first, just one heavy blow on top of the head, most likely with a rock. Maybe he's not very strong. Maybe he needs to immobilize his victim first, and quickly; if the boy were able to call for help or fight back, he might panic and run."

Saenz turns to look at a sheet of paper taped up on the upper right hand corner of the huge whiteboard; it's a photocopy of a partial impression of a shoe. It was found and correctly processed by a particularly sharp SOCO officer in the mud near the site where the sixth victim's body was discovered. Saenz had made certain the man's superior knew he had done well.

"Men's size six," he says, nodding. "Ordinary rubber rain boots."

"Very cheap, very common."

"And very washable." Saenz rolls his chair over to a nearby desk and rummages through a pile of papers, photocopies of police reports for the Payatas area in the last seven months. "No reports of any unconsummated attacks on boys in our age group. He's been really lucky so far."

"Not so much lucky as skillful. His timing is excellent, and so is his choice of victim and circumstance." Jerome opens his eyes but does not look up, and then rubs his chin with his thumb—something he does when deep in thought. "He probably doesn't find them in the dump, and he doesn't kill them in the dump, that's almost certain; it's too open, too accessible. Wherever he catches up with his quarry, he immobilizes him and then takes him away, somewhere he's certain he won't be disturbed."

"And the injuries?"

Jerome pauses. "He stabs the victim. Once or twice; that's all he needs to finish him off. The evisceration, the mutilations—are all postmortem. He's not torturing them. He works neatly around the heart, the other organs, the genitals. We haven't found any of these at the scene; it seems likely that he's keeping them as trophies and probably has a container or two ready to hold them."

He rolls his chair over to Saenz's desk and, without standing, reaches for the pile of case folders they've compiled on the killings. He opens them one by one, each time focusing on one of the photographs in them. He swivels the chair around so that he can see Saenz. "Six killings so far. Given what we've seen of the last three, and if we're to believe the case reports on the first three, the bodies bear no physical evidence that the killer obtained some sort of sexual gratification from them."

"But with the removal of the genitals, Jerome—there must nevertheless be some sexual dimension to the killings."

"I'm not discounting the possibility of that, no. I'm just stating the fact that there is no trace evidence that indicates that he violated the boys before or after death." Jerome taps the folders against the edge of Saenz's desk. "In accounts of serial killings throughout the world, the removal of hearts and other organs isn't new."

"But neither is the excision of genitals or the mutilation of faces."

"No. But in these cases we're looking at, the mutilation of the faces is very specific. He slits the throat just under the chin, from ear to ear. He slips his fingers into the slit and peels the skin back over the bones, with the aid of a knife and some other instrument." Jerome shakes his head. "The flaying of the face is not a random act. It's significant to him; he's done it consistently over time, with six different victims. In most killings similar to ours, this is an act of depersonalization."

"So you think that's what he's doing?"

"Yes." Jerome bites his lower lip, his forehead creased in concentration. "But is he depersonalizing his victim? Or is he, in some way, projecting himself onto the victim? Is he depersonalizing himself *through* the victim?"

Saenz stops to consider this, and then turns to the board and writes it down: *DEPERSONALIZING VICTIM? OR SELF?*

Jerome waits for Saenz to finish scribbling, then slumps forward more heavily, like someone coming out of a trance exhausted. He puts his hands over his face. His eyeballs are throbbing, blotches of dull red pulsing through the black behind his closed eyelids.

"Tell me again, Gus, why do we do this?" he asks aloud, not really expecting an answer, palms cold against his warm forehead.

Saenz caps his pen and tosses it, along with the yellow pad, on top of the papers on his desk. He leans back in his seat and folds his long-fingered hands together. "Boredom?"

The younger priest spins himself around slowly in his chair. "I have an interesting life."

"You think you have an interesting life. And for the most part, you do. You teach, you say Mass, you conduct research, see patients. Travel. Lecture. You do everything you're supposed to do the way it's supposed to be done. Once in a while, there's a chance to do more. And you take it."

Jerome snickers. "Right. I get it. My life can't just be

interesting. It has to be *meaningful*." He feigns a kind of wounded solemnity, as though he were baring his soul to a sympathetic talk show host, and Saenz cannot help but chuckle.

"Something like that, yes."

Jerome stops his slow spinning and looks at Saenz, at the planes and angles of his face, the grey advancing against the once-blue-blackness of his hair. Odd how this familiar face can calm him, even now that he is no longer a schoolboy.

"I'm no crusader, Gus," Jerome mumbles, then presses the heels of his palms against his aching eyeballs to relieve the strain.

Saenz shakes his head. "No, my boy," he says, so quietly that the other man does not hear him. "You're just an ordinary man."

8

THE DIRECTOR ARRIVES at the television network with little fanfare—so little that his vehicle is held up at the gate while security checks take place. He waits patiently in the back seat, but his driver is bristling.

"They shouldn't make you wait like this," he grumbles.

"Relax, Peping. I'm sure it won't take long."

Peping used to drive the director's predecessor around; he's used to having an armed escort, to gates and doors opening without question—to basking in reflected glory. What's that old saying? *Ang langaw na nakatuntong sa kalabaw*, the fly standing on the water buffalo's back.

"Maybe, sir, you should consider reinstating your escort. After all, you're an important official, doing a dangerous job. Bad things have happened to people less important than you. It's like tempting fate."

This is not the first time Peping has made this most helpful recommendation; the day the director told him he would be doing away with the escort and using his own personal vehicle, Peping looked as though the sky had caved in on his head. Over the last few months, the driver has continued to put forward his view, gently at first, then with increasing zeal.

"It's just a suggestion, of course. I mean, who am I to tell you what you should and shouldn't do? I'm just a driver. You're the one who knows best. You—"

"Tell me, Peping, has Human Resources given you a date for your transfer?" The director has known for several weeks that Peping has applied for a transfer to the staff of one of his deputies, a holdover from the previous administration. That deputy has an armed escort and a nice, sleek, government-issue vehicle—much more Peping's speed.

The trouble is, the director isn't supposed to know about the transfer application. The idea was that a new driver would simply turn up at his home before work one day. Peping goes pale, then beet red.

"Sir, I—well, they haven't . . . I hope you—"

At this moment, a woman in a wildly flowered blouse and black leggings rushes over to the gate and begins to berate the security guard on duty. The director recognizes her—Lally or Lilly—as one of the producers of the talk show he will be appearing on in about half an hour's time. She waves frantically to Peping, then ducks her head to peer through a window and into the back seat. When she sees the director, her face brightens in recognition, and she waves even more frantically, then turns back to the security guard. He scurries to draw the gates open for the director's vehicle to pass.

When they draw up level to the woman, she motions for Peping to roll down the window on his side, and she peers into the car.

"*Naku*, sir, I'm so sorry!" she says, breathless with exertion. "I already sent a visitor advisory to security, but this guard is new; he's not familiar with procedure."

"That's all right," the director replies calmly.

She turns to Peping. "Boss, you can park in the visitors' parking area behind Studio Two. You remember where that is, right?"

Peping nods.

"Okay, sir, I'll see you inside!" she sings out as the car begins to move away. "Sorry that you had to wait!"

"It's not a problem."

They drive to the back of the studio in silence. When the director steps out of the car, Peping is quick to offer assistance with his briefcase.

"By the way, sir—about my transfer . . ." he starts.

The director wordlessly declines the offer of help and

begins to walk away. "Don't worry, Peping. I won't stop you. You should work with people who understand you."

Peping watches as the director disappears into the studio. Then the driver whips out his cell phone and dials a number.

"Old man's in the studio now."

EVEN THOUGH THIS isn't his first time, he's still a bit intimidated by the lights, the equipment, the flurry of activity in a television studio just minutes before the start of a live program.

"Director Lastimosa?"

He glances up. "Your Eminence."

Cardinal Rafael Meneses clasps the director's hand with both of his own. "I was very pleased to hear that they'd invited you tonight as well. How are you?"

"I am good, thank you."

"Awfully busy, I suppose?"

"As I imagine you are."

Cardinal Meneses is a small, rotund man in his late sixties. As a prominent religious leader, he is powerful, charismatic, well loved. His public persona is benevolent and jovial, and he is always ready with a smile, a joke, a pat on the back. But the director knows that beneath the affable exterior is a cunning mind and a steel backbone. Along with other cardinals and members of the Church hierarchy, he has stood up to a dictator and witnessed his downfall. As one of the Church's most influential voices, he denounced the regime's excesses from the pulpit in carefully crafted sermons and pastoral letters.

But as an old-school cleric with extremely conservative views, he has also smilingly held off advocates of church reform and reproductive health. And, if gossip and speculation are to be believed, he has spearheaded the Church's damage control efforts in the wake of allegations of sexual abuse and misconduct by several of its priests all over the country.

The cardinal comes closer to Director Lastimosa now,

gently tugging on his arm and leaning in so that he can speak without being heard by anyone else.

"I understand that one of our brothers is assisting you with a case."

Ah, there it is. He had wondered if it was going to come up in conversation, and now it has. "Yes, indeed."

That smile now—kind, but with a hint of displeasure at the edges of the mouth. "Gus Saenz is one of our best minds. You couldn't have chosen a better man."

The director nods. "So I've gathered. He has quite a solid reputation, here and overseas."

"Hmmm, yes. We're very proud of him."

The director blinks once, slowly, as though he's putting the Cardinal into sharper focus. "I suspect that certain events of the last few months have given him cause to doubt that."

"Events of the last . . . I'm sorry?" The smile fades from Cardinal Meneses's face. "I'm afraid I don't understand."

The director looks down at him sadly. "Neither do I, Your Eminence. Neither do I."

But before the cleric can say another word, Lally rushes toward them, a panting ball of relentless energy. She turns first to the director, then to the cardinal. "Sir, Your Holiness, makeup first and then places on the set!"

The cardinal tears his gaze away from the director and puts on his usual kindly smile for Lally's benefit. "You've promoted me," he jokes. "I'm not the Pope."

"Not yet," the director says under his breath as he walks away, heading to the makeup room.

THE TALK SHOW is *Harap-harapan,* and tonight's discussion revolves around the case of a German priest who had been arrested for the sexual abuse of several children in Palawan several months before. By the second segment, the discussion has turned to how the Catholic Church disciplines errant priests.

"Well, you have to understand that there are well-defined

processes and procedures for reporting cases of misconduct by our priests to the Vatican," the cardinal says.

The host, veteran anchor Vergel "Gil" Salceda, seems unconvinced. "But Cardinal, how do you address concerns that such incidents are ignored by Church authorities, or possibly even covered up?"

Director Lastimosa has come to expect it: the way the smile stays plastered on Cardinal Meneses's face but leaches out of his eyes when he's forced to talk about something he finds disagreeable. "Well, Gil, I admit that it may seem that way because most investigations conducted within the Church are confidential. But I want to assure you and your viewers that the Church authorities—the superiors of the priests involved, our bishops, our cardinals—we are all obliged to report such incidents to Rome."

Other guests chime in—one, a lawyer, expressing agreement with the need for confidentiality in such cases; the other, a representative from a women's advocacy group, demanding that the German be denied extradition and tried in the country.

Gil then turns to the director and asks for his opinion. He considers the question a moment and then says, "You know, I've always believed that the Church—well, any church, not just the Roman Catholic Church—is entitled to discipline members of its hierarchy or its flock for misconduct in a manner consistent with the principles of the faith."

He sees, out of the corner of his eye, a broad smile spreading over the Cardinal's face. "However, I think there is a clear difference between mere misconduct and crime." Within the span of a single sentence, the smile turns sour: a not-smile. "I think as soon as a priest crosses the line into molestation and sexual abuse, it becomes a civil matter, a law enforcement matter, and a matter for the country's courts. That's the best way, I think, to put an end to these accusations, these concerns of any cover-up."

The cardinal clasps his hands together on top of his belly. "Oh, come now, Director Lastimosa. You think putting such cases through the mill of the justice system will allay such fears? If anything, it will make them worse." His eyes narrow, even as the not-smile remains fixed on his face. "The Church enjoys the trust and confidence of many Filipinos. It has its defects, its failings—no institution is without them—but it has credibility. Certainly more, I think you will agree, than our courts or our law enforcers, no?"

The director crosses his long, thin legs and clasps his hands together in a perfect though unintended imitation of the Cardinal's pose, no doubt angering him even more. "But Your Eminence, is it a credibility built on what people don't know, rather than what they do know? If it is, that isn't really credibility at all, is it? When you quietly move a priest from a diocese where he has victimized two or three young parishioners to a new diocese where he is at liberty to do the same thing again, you're not building up your credibility; you're just postponing the day when you lose it."

"Well, Director Lastimosa, if you're speaking of any specific cases, I would be happy to discuss them with you after this program and demonstrate to you that we are doing our best to address any transgressions that are brought to our attention."

It's a veiled challenge.

Director Lastimosa looks down at his clasped hands. "Forgive me, Your Eminence. I was speaking in generalities. But I think, and I'm sure you will agree, that some things are better dealt with in the cleansing light of transparency and openness rather than in the darkness of secrecy. What's true of the government is also true of the Church, yes?"

The cardinal shifts restlessly in his seat. "What you call secrecy, Director, we call confidentiality, and it is aimed at protecting the innocent. And the innocent can either be the victims or the wrongly accused."

At this point, Gil calls the last commercial break, and

the smile disappears completely from the cardinal's face. Without looking up, he pretends to fiddle with the cord of his lapel mic as the other guests exchange banal pleasantries with Gil.

It's during the end of the commercial break that the director notices the studio has grown unbearably cold—which is strange because he finds that he is sweating. He fishes out a handkerchief from his trouser pocket and wipes away the tiny beads of sweat that have formed on his brow. By the time the program is in its last few minutes, his mouth is dry, and he is short of breath. Gil is asking questions of the panel, and they answer one by one, beginning with the cardinal. The director can barely comprehend what they're saying; the studio lights seem terribly intense, and he is now feeling a sharp pain, similar to indigestion.

Gil turns to him last, and he manages to crank out a suitable response without stalling or stammering. But he knows that he is in serious trouble when he begins to feel pain shooting down his left arm. He grips the armrests of his chair and struggles to hold on until Gil wraps up the show. The theme music comes on, and the credits roll.

He's vaguely aware of Gil and the other guests rising to their feet and shaking one another's hands. The cardinal turns to him and holds out his hand.

"Director, always a pleasure." His tone of voice indicates that the past hour was anything but a pleasure for him.

The director rises unsteadily to his feet, fingertips still touching the armrests. For a split second, he allows himself to think that it is going to be all right, that he remains fully in control of his aging body. He lifts his right arm to take the cardinal's hand, but the studio lights begin to dim, until they dwindle into little pinpricks of light, until they fade into the darkest of nothing.

9

SAENZ GETS JEROME'S call at around half past midnight.

"Seen the late night news?"

Saenz sits up in bed. "No, why?"

"Director Lastimosa. Keeled over after appearing on *Harap-harapan*. Looks like a heart attack."

Saenz swings his long legs over the side of the bed and feels around the floor with his feet for his slippers. "Just what we need," he sighs. "Which hospital?"

"St. Luke's."

"Ready in half an hour."

"Got it," Jerome says. "Hey, could you have some coffee ready for me when I get there? I get the feeling this is going to be a long night."

"I HAVE NOTHING against hospitals," Jerome is saying as they walk down the hall.

"Nonsense," Saenz replies, waving a hand in the air. "You hate hospitals. The only way you would be caught dead in a hospital is if you were actually dead."

"Not true. I was in a hospital just last year, and, as I recall, I was very much alive."

"Yes. With acute dyspepsia. Which developed into acute dyspepsia because you refused to go to a hospital while it was just plain, old, non-acute dyspepsia."

Jerome smirks at him. "Yes. I should listen to a cranky old man who won't come within a five-kilometer radius of a dentist's office."

Saenz opens his mouth to protest, then closes it again without saying another word. At that moment, Jerome puts a hand on his arm to stop him and nods toward the end of the hall.

Immediately, Saenz's face darkens. It's Cardinal Meneses,

speaking in hushed tones with a small clutch of people outside the hospital's intensive care unit.

"What's he doing here, of all places?" Saenz whispers.

"He was a guest on the show too." Jerome studies Saenz's grim face. "Look, we could come back later in the morning. We probably won't be able to see the director anyway, at least not until visiting hours start."

"I'll not be scared away from doing what I came all the way here to do."

He begins to move, but Jerome's hand tightens around his arm. "Think carefully about what you're going to do next, Gus. Sound advice that you're always giving me. Now I get to give it back to you."

Saenz says nothing for a while, and then makes up his mind. "You're right, of course. Absolutely right." He pats Jerome's shoulder gently. "Okay, let's get out of here."

The two priests are about to leave when they hear a voice call out.

"Father Saenz?"

They stop, and Jerome casts a warning glance at Saenz. Saenz nods, *I understand*, then steels himself to face the owner of that voice.

"Your Eminence."

The cardinal approaches Saenz with both arms outstretched, ready to embrace him. But Saenz makes no move to do the same; he waits until the other man lowers his arms and instead offers his hand. Saenz takes it in both of his large hands and bends his head to kiss the cardinal's episcopal ring. When he lifts his head, their eyes meet, and the looks they exchange are glacial.

"Director Lastimosa is in a stable condition," the cardinal says. "But he's very, very weak. The doctors say the next forty-eight hours will be crucial."

"Will he need surgery?"

"Eventually. But not until he's much stronger."

Saenz nods. "Where's the family?"

"His wife and two eldest children were here earlier. Now it's just the eldest keeping watch. I presume the others will return during visiting hours."

"As will we. Good night, Your Eminence. Or rather—good morning." Saenz is already walking away when the cardinal draws his attention once more.

"By the way, Father Saenz—I think it's admirable how you've decided to help the director with his case."

"You just had to say something, didn't you?" Jerome mutters under his breath, too softly for either man to hear.

Saenz's eyes narrow. "I do what I can."

"Yes, of course. I am . . . familiar with your zeal to do what you can, wherever you can."

Saenz goes completely still. It's as though a hood has dropped over his head, and his face becomes unreadable, a porcelain mask. When he speaks, his voice is calm and low.

"There are many different ways to give witness to faith, Your Eminence."

The cardinal smiles. "Some, no doubt, more pleasing to the Lord than others. But there are times when our hands are tied and we can only do so much."

"Or so little."

Jerome clears his throat, moves closer to Saenz. "Father," he says quietly, but loudly enough for Cardinal Meneses to hear, "we should all get some rest if we're to see Director Lastimosa later in the morning."

Neither of the two seem to have heard him, or if they have, they have both simply chosen to ignore him.

"Come, come, Father Saenz," the cardinal says, his tone falsely soothing. "The Holy Mother Church has ways of keeping her house in order."

"Sweeping dirt under the rug is not one of them," Saenz

says coldly. "Shunting the dirt around quietly in different places so that one is no longer quite certain where to look is not one of them. Not in the Holy Mother Church that I know. Not in the Holy Mother Church that fed me and raised me and nurtured me to become one of its own."

The smile on the cardinal's face remains there by sheer force of will. "I see that you remain upset about Monsignor Ramirez. I can assure you—and you have access to all the documentation—that the inquiry into the matters you raised in 1983 and 1985 was conducted according to canon law, and with integrity and transparency."

"Indeed. An inquiry that the Church should have left in the hands of the police. An inquiry that, given the circumstances, given the individuals involved, could only have resulted in one outcome."

"You and I will always hold differing views on the nature of that inquiry, Father Saenz. But at the end of the day, what matters is that we acted in the best interests of the Church."

"The Church's interests are not more important than the interests of the children Father Ramirez has victimized," Saenz says, his voice a quietly menacing rumble. For what seems to Jerome like minutes, Saenz stares down at the cardinal, who stares back defiantly.

It is Saenz who breaks the staring contest off. "But whatever allows you to sleep soundly at night, Your Eminence." He turns his back on Cardinal Meneses and starts walking away. "Come, Father Lucero. We have another long day ahead of us."

IT'S PAST 6 A.M. when it finally occurs to Peping to telephone Attorney Arcinas. If the man is annoyed at being roused from sleep, his mood quickly slides into livid after being told why.

"Eleven o'clock. He collapsed at eleven o'clock last night, and you're only telling me now?"

"I called Director Mapa and Director Valdes first. Then I called Mrs. Lastimosa."

Mapa and Valdes are Assistant Director and Deputy Director for Administration, respectively; they would logically be the first in the organization's call tree to be informed and mobilized in situations like this. Still, it galls Arcinas that a man he has instructed specifically to keep an eye on the director should be so lax.

"Where is he?"

"He's at St. Luke's, Attorney."

"And where are you? Why aren't you with him?" he demands.

"I'm at home, sir," Peping stammers.

"Since when?"

"I . . . I got here maybe ten, fifteen minutes ago."

"Well, why did you leave him there?"

"I . . . uh, there was nothing else for me to do. His family was with him, and they told me to go home and rest."

"Moron," he says in a low voice, barely able to restrain himself. Then, more audibly, "You should have waited to see who would come to visit him."

"I . . . uh . . . I could go back," Peping offers weakly.

"It's too late now," Arcinas answers coldly. "I'll go myself."

"I'll meet you there, sir!"

"No. You go to Mrs. Lastimosa and see if she needs the car. You put yourself at her disposal all day today and tomorrow too, if she needs it. Don't make me tell you twice."

He hangs up on the driver, then falls back upon his pillows and stares at the ceiling.

"Do I have to do everything myself?" he asks aloud, of no one in particular.

10

NEWS OF THE director's heart attack is splashed all over the morning papers, fodder for drive-time talk radio and talk TV. Most of the commentators focus on his age; they say that he has taken on such a demanding job—one that should be handled by a much younger man—at an age when most people are already enjoying their retirement or, at the very least, getting ready for it. Some are talking about replacement candidates, as though he is already dead and his post left vacant.

Jerome folds up his newspaper and slams it down on the table in disgust. The tender yolks of two sunny-side-up eggs on a plate laid out for him wobble in terror.

"Three names. Three names, and every single one of them an unmitigated idiot."

"Or, you could sit down and just enjoy your eggs," Saenz says, peering at him over the rims of his glasses.

"Unbelievable," he continues, fuming. "You have to wonder what goes on in people's heads."

"No, I don't," Saenz says, pouring Jerome a cup of coffee. "And I'm a much happier man for it. Come, sit, sit. No use complaining about the world's freest press—we fought for it, we got it, now we have to live with the nonsense that it spews out."

Jerome sullenly takes his place at the breakfast table. He picks up a fork and pokes at the crusty brown edges of the egg whites.

"Besides, we have more important things to worry about."

"Oh? Like what?"

"Got a phone call from Director Mapa this morning."

Jerome drops the fork on the plate with a clatter and leans back in his chair. "That can't have been good."

Saenz shakes his head, and Jerome notes that he is putting an excessive amount of sugar into the cup of coffee he's just poured for him. When Saenz notices his alarm, he says, "You're going to thank me for this third teaspoon when you hear what he had to say."

"Let me guess. They're removing us from the Payatas investigation."

"No, but they're thinking about it."

"Already?"

"Apparently our dear friend the task force chief has appealed to the good assistant director to rethink their approach, now that Director Lastimosa is indisposed."

"Arcinas," Jerome says. "He certainly moves fast."

"He saw an opening, and he took advantage of it. I can't say that I wouldn't have done the same thing in his position."

"No, you wouldn't have."

Saenz chuckles. "Go on, those eggs aren't going to eat themselves. We'll head over to the hospital when you're finished."

"I think I've lost my appetite."

THE DIRECTOR IS fully conscious but weak. When Saenz sticks his head through the open door, the old man lifts a heavy hand off the bed and motions for him to come in.

The curtains have been drawn, and the lighting in the room is dim. Saenz walks quietly and carefully toward the hospital bed.

"I won't take long, sir," he says in a low voice. "Just wanted to see how you were doing."

The director nods. "My children are convinced that I should travel to the US for surgery. I'm not so sure."

"What do your doctors say?"

He swallows with some difficulty and then points to the pitcher of water on the side table. Saenz takes the glass beside the pitcher and fills it with water. He waits while the director adjusts the incline of the bed with the controls at his fingertips. When he's in a semi-upright position, Saenz carefully brings the glass to his mouth, and he takes a few sips, then lies back on the pillows. "They're of two minds. Traveling could put a strain on me while I'm still very weak, but the longer we put off surgery . . ."

"Do you think you can make the trip?"

The director closes his eyes and is silent for quite some time; for a while Saenz thinks he has drifted off to sleep, but then he begins to speak again.

"Do you know why the president appointed me to this post?"

It's an unexpected question. "Because you were the best man for it?"

He shakes his head weakly. "I'm just warming the seat for someone else, Father. A protégé of one of his major political allies. He's much younger and still a bit green. But he's hungry, he looks the part, and he'll take this job when he's good and ready."

"I don't understand. An outsider? Or someone who's already in the bureau?"

The director nods, his eyes still closed. "Waiting in the wings."

"Philip Mapa."

"He and Ben Arcinas go way back. Arcinas is ambitious, but he's never going to be up for the top job. Not . . . *magisterial* enough. But Mapa is, and so he's happy to hitch his wagon to Mapa's star. They're both just waiting for me to make a mistake." The forefinger on his right hand begins tapping at his stomach, and Saenz cannot tell if it is intentional or involuntary. "I'm in my seventies, Father, and not a young seventies either. This heart is going to give way sooner or later. I wouldn't mind handing it all over to them first thing tomorrow, if I didn't have this unfinished business . . ." His voice trails off again, but to Saenz, the meaning is clear.

"Then you'll have to do it. Get the surgery."

He opens his eyes. "The minute I'm out of the country, some of my people will try to make things difficult for you."

In his mind, Saenz says, *They've already begun*, but he holds his tongue. He's afraid that the man is too weak to handle it.

"We'll manage."

"Jake Valdes," he says, and then his face contorts in a twinge of pain. Saenz waits until it passes before speaking.

"Your deputy."

"He's been with the bureau a while too, as you're aware. But I trust him." The tubing of the IV drip lodged in his left hand trembles as he gestures weakly toward the small table beside his bed. Saenz quickly realizes that he is asking for a pen and a small notepad, and he hands it to him. Laboriously, the director writes down one series of numbers, then another, and then hands both pen and pad back to Saenz. "If you have any problems, you speak to him. I can't promise that he will be able to override Director Mapa's decisions, but at least he can run interference and give you access to resources and information you might otherwise not have."

As Saenz folds up the piece of paper and puts it into his pocket, the director lays a hand on his arm.

"Father. The work you are doing for us . . ."

Saenz pats the director's hand gently. "You don't have to tell me, sir. I'll do what I can."

The sun's come out today. I have to go to work.

Sometimes I wonder if the people I work so hard for appreciate me enough. They come to me suffering, in pain. I do what I do and make it better. Then they go away and never give me a second thought. They pass by me in the streets, and the most that some of them can do is nod. Almost all of them fail to recognize me.

When I think about it, though, I guess that's okay. I don't want them to recognize me. It's really better that they don't.

11

THE VOICE ASSAILS Director Lastimosa as he drifts back into consciousness. Its owner is issuing instructions over a cell phone in a tone simultaneously languid and imperious. Ben Arcinas does not bother to take down his volume a notch even though the director is resting. A slight lift of one eyebrow is all that he can muster to acknowledge that the director is awake. He rattles off a laundry list of things for the person on the other end of the line to do.

When he's finally done, he turns to the director. "*Oh,*" he begins, "you're still not looking so well. When are you going to be released?" As always, his aftershave is overpowering, a wall of scent so dense that one could bounce a coin off it.

Who let you in here? the director asks, but only in his mind. "Thanks for coming, Ben," he says instead. "Looks like your day is packed." His smile is wan.

If Arcinas notices that his question has gone unanswered, he doesn't let on. He moves a bit closer to the bed. "It always is. Oh, by the way. I came here to tell you that Director Mapa has given me the green light to proceed in a parallel direction with the Payatas case." It's delivered with an obvious relish that borders on delight.

"I see." Underneath his blanket, the director clenches his fists. "He hasn't cleared this with me."

"I think he'll tell you when he drops by tomorrow," Arcinas says airily. "Maybe he was afraid you were too sick. Anyway, he's officer in charge while you're away, so he—"

"Being OIC does not give him blanket authority over critical matters such as this. He knows this. *You* know this."

Arcinas shrugs. "I just do what I'm told."

"What you're told? Or what you tell Director Mapa you want to do?"

Arcinas barrels on. "You'll be pleased to know that we'll be questioning suspects soon. And before you have another heart attack, I can assure you that it's all being done very methodically. Father Saenz himself couldn't possibly do better."

"Ben," the director says, tension surging through his chest, bubbling up his throat like bile, "is this really more important to you? The recognition, the credit? Would you really put it above finding whoever is responsible for these killings?"

"I don't know if it's your medication or your sickness that keeps you from seeing this, but that's exactly what I'm trying to do. Except that you have more faith in your priest than you do in your own people."

"If you move with as much"—he pauses to find a suitable word, but fails—"fanfare as I fear you will, we might lose him."

Arcinas steps back. He seems genuinely hurt by this, his face wearing a look that the director has seen on dogs that have just been kicked. *"Fanfare,"* he repeats softly.

"You know what I mean, Ben."

"You must think we're all clowns," he says, still in that same small, quiet voice. "Why did you even accept the directorship, I wonder? You're too good for this bureau, or any of us."

"Ben," Director Lastimosa says, as gently as he can. "You're an intelligent man. You know that certain things need to change. That the things that used to work for us before won't always work anymore—that in fact, they're already working less and less. You know that we can do so much better."

"I know it was better before you came along." His face is shuttered now, the eyes cold. "But we've survived worse crises, and we'll survive you. You're a political appointee. If you don't die before the next presidential election, you'll be replaced."

"You'd better stop talking, Ben, before you say anything you'll truly regret later."

"I've said all that I'm going to say. Enjoy your stay here, sir." He turns and leaves.

The room is still and silent now, but the director's insides are churning. He lies back on his pillows and tries to relax, closing his eyes and taking deep breaths. But he knows it's coming; he can feel it, that same sense that all control is slipping rapidly, inexorably away.

He reaches for the call button and presses it while he still can.

12

THE MONDAY AFTER the director is rushed to the US for treatment, Saenz is poring over his expense records for the month with some concern. The laboratory is funded largely by grants and donations; although Saenz runs it as efficiently and frugally as possible, there are times when it overshoots its monthly budget and he has to dip into his own pocket to bridge the gap. Over the last few years, as the number of consultations has increased and the level of external funding has fluctuated, those gaps have grown larger and emerged more frequently.

He is checking the balance in his bank account and calculating how much he will need to draw from it to pay Tato and the utilities bills when Jerome sticks his head in the door. A quick glance at Saenz's desk and his face brightens.

"*Otap!*" he cries in delight. He makes a beeline for a small pack of the flaky, sugary cookies, which are buried under a pile of newspapers.

Saenz looks incensed. "You mean you came here just for that? And how did you even know that I had them on my desk?" he demands.

It's Tuesday—Jerome's busiest teaching day—so Saenz knows he has not had lunch in between classes. This explains why he is already reaching for two or three more cookies even before he has had a chance to finish the one in his mouth.

"You always have *otap* on your desk," Jerome says, a few flakes of the cookie falling from his mouth onto his shirt. "Or *barquillos*. Or *paciencia*. Or *lenguas de gato*." It's true: Saenz's wilderness of a desk is a treasure trove of snacks for the person who knows where to look. And Jerome—who, barring inclement weather, emergency meetings and other acts of God, always turns up on Tuesday afternoons at four thirty sharp, half-starved and ravenous—knows exactly where to look.

"You could go to the cafeteria for a change, you know. They have real food there. Things you can eat with a spoon and a fork. Things you actually have to pay for."

Jerome pauses in mid-chew, looking perplexed. "But why on earth would I deny myself the pleasure of eating at your expense?"

Saenz sighs. "And here I thought you enjoyed my company."

"Oh, but I do!" Jerome replies earnestly. "Because your company always involves free food."

They share a laugh at this private, long-running joke, and then Saenz turns serious. He waves a sheaf of papers at Jerome. "Look at this. We're short again this month."

"Eh?" Jerome licks the cookie sugar and grease from his fingers, wipes them on his jeans and then takes the papers and studies them. "I thought you were going to get the third tranche of funding from that Japanese foundation last week."

"So did I. That would have kept us going for at least another six months. But I called Mrs. Iwasaki on Friday, and she said the release was delayed."

"Any idea when it's going to happen?"

Saenz shakes his head. "Worse still, it could be an indication that future tranches are being reassessed."

"What?" Jerome's eyes widen. "Can they do that? Aren't those already committed under some kind of memorandum of understanding between the foundation and the university?"

"Well, there's any number of ways out of an MOU."

"Hmmm. Any expense items you can shuffle around in the meantime?"

"I've done all the shuffling around I can do this month. But Tato needs to get paid, and so do the power and water bills. I also need to give Susan her allowance from the lab for helping out with administrative duties here and there."

"Will Tato take a promissory note?"

"On principle, I would rather not do that. I never have, and I'm not about to start now."

Jerome leans forward. "I hate to float this idea, but . . . what about the diocese?"

Saenz draws his lips into a thin, tight line. "After what happened with Cardinal Meneses? I don't think the diocese would give me a strand of used dental floss if I asked for it."

They sit in glum silence for a while; then Saenz forces himself to smile cheerfully. "Ah, well. It's not as though I have a wife and four children to feed." He snatches the pack of *otap* from Jerome's hand, feigning annoyance. "Certainly I'll have to rethink this whole free food policy over the long term."

Jerome looks at the cookies—now beyond his reach—dejectedly. "You do realize that austerity measures imposed without consultation are often met with protest?"

The phone rings, and Saenz picks up.

"Good morning, Father."

"Good morning, sir." At this, Jerome looks up. *Director Valdes*, Saenz mouths silently. Jerome immediately stands and moves closer. "What can I do for you?"

"Listen, I've got my hands full with the Miss Teen Philippines scandal today. Seems like everyone is baying for blood."

Saenz chuckles. Two nights ago, one young woman was crowned the winner in a beauty pageant; the next day, one of the judges was crying foul, saying that the name announced on coronation night was the wrong one. He accused the other judges of conspiring with the host to falsely bestow the crown on the wrong contestant. It's yet another ridiculous scenario playing out on the country's evening news programs and the front pages of newspapers.

"I'll be tied up all day trying to organize this new task force the mayor has convened to investigate the incident. But I think you need to see Attorney Arcinas as soon as possible. Today, if you can make it."

"Why? What's going on?"

"He's tried to keep me out of the loop, but someone has told me that he's moving on the Payatas case independently.

Apparently he's pulled up a list of previous sex offenders in the area, and he's begun rounding up possible suspects for questioning. Normally, that's exactly what we'd do, but in this particular case . . . well, I don't need to tell you what that means."

It means that he's drawing unwanted and unnecessary attention in the community. Saenz sighs. "I still have another class to teach and counseling at night. How about tomorrow?"

"The sooner the better, Father." Saenz hears the fatigue in Director Valdes's voice. "And when you do see him, I'd appreciate it if you kept my name out of it. The man has Director Mapa's ear, and with Director Lastimosa indisposed, my position here is vulnerable. Besides, I think I can continue to be more useful to you if I appear to be impartial."

"I understand, sir. I'll make an appointment to see him tomorrow morning."

"If you ask me, I wouldn't bother making an appointment— I'm quite sure he'll refuse. I'm also sure that he'll be at the office all morning. He won't miss a chance to chair the morning media conference. I suggest you simply turn up at his door unannounced. He wouldn't dare make a scene in front of the reporters and draw attention to your presence." A beat. "Although, if you ask me, Father, you would draw attention just by walking through the door."

The deputy director ends the call, and Saenz puts the phone back in the cradle.

"Problem?"

"What's your schedule looking like tomorrow morning?"

"Nothing on it that I can't clear. Why?"

"It looks like we need to pay a certain task force chief a visit."

13

ATTORNEY BENJAMIN ARCINAS has always reminded Jerome of a rattlesnake, small brained and venomous. He has a heavy-lidded, reptilian look about him. His face has a layer of expertly applied foundation, and his well-manicured nails are covered in a coat of sheer polish.

It's been less than a week since the director's health problems first came to light, but already Arcinas has grown ever more audacious. Whereas initially he had intended to divert resources and manpower from the Payatas investigation to other cases from which he could gain media exposure—a Binondo businessman's kidnapping, the arrest of an army lieutenant for alleged drug trafficking—he has now apparently seen the value in milking the Payatas killings for media mileage.

"Hmmm . . . this is very interesting, Father Saenz . . . all very interesting . . ."

The stubby fingers with their ridiculously polished nails keep flipping, flipping through the pages of a report that the two priests had prepared for Director Lastimosa prior to his departure for the US, and Jerome is certain that the blank snake eyes are not really taking anything in. He shifts impatiently in his seat twice, fidgets with the wooden crucifix hanging from a cord around his neck, sighs audibly in exasperation until Saenz puts out a hand to gesture for him to calm down.

"We believe the killings take place during the first weekend of every month. Statistically, the odds are that the suspect is male. From the blows to the head and the wound slicing patterns on the body, it's likely that he's right-handed—"

"Oh, well. That eliminates the ten to twelve percent of the population that's left-handed and makes things so much easier for us, Father."

The older priest ignores the lawyer's sarcasm and chooses a gentler, more patient tone.

"I urge you to take a look at the other details of the report, Ben. We've tried to create as accurate a profile of this killer as possible, using physical evidence from the bodies as well as what we know from the community. I can understand your reluctance to undertake this kind of psychological profiling of criminals—even in the developed world, it's still an evolving science. But it's produced a significant number of arrests and convictions. Most of your people have a solid legal background, and that's all very good. But I'm sure you recognize that this situation demands far more of you and the bureau than just legal expertise."

"You forget, Father, that this institution has been around since 1947." Arcinas opens a drawer in his desk, then sits back in his chair and puts both feet up on the drawer, his body language calculated to convey the appearance of relaxed authority. "Even further back to 1936, if you count the creation of the Division of Investigation under the Justice Department. We've accomplished a great deal all these years by doing things the same way we've always done them."

"Of course you have." Saenz leans forward in his seat, putting his arms on the edge of Arcinas's desk and threading his fingers together. "Listen, Ben, I'm not trashing your efforts here. But I don't need to tell you of the successes that have been attained with these techniques. You're far more up-to-date on developments in the international law enforcement community than I am."

There is a momentary gleam in the lawyer's snake eyes. Saenz catches it, identifies it as the pleasure a bureaucrat takes when he knows he has authority over someone else. When he knows that someone is trying to obtain his cooperation.

"Work with us here, Ben," the priest continues in as persuasive a tone as he can muster. "As far as we can tell, the mutilations are significant. They are not random or gratuitous. This man is erasing his victims' faces. He is carving out their organs, their hearts. If we believe that every act is symbolic, he appears to be removing everything that makes them human. We are dealing with a man—"

"Yes, yes. I know. A serial killer." The lawyer says the word slowly, with a mocking gravity: *seeer-yal*. A corner of his mouth curls up in an expression of mildly amused sarcasm.

It is all too much for Jerome. The younger priest rises so forcefully from his seat that it is almost knocked over backward onto the dingy, mustard-yellow carpet.

"Come on, Gus. We're wasting time. This man clearly has no grasp of how serious this case is, or worse still, he doesn't care. All he cares about is getting his face on television."

Arcinas gets up as well, hands bunched into fists and wedged against either side of his potbelly. A vein in his left temple bulges like a fat, green worm.

"No, no, this isn't the way—" Saenz begins, but Jerome is not about to be stopped.

"Look at the profile, Arcinas. Your killer is a man at most about five feet five inches tall—not stocky, someone who doesn't trust himself with a conscious victim. Someone the kids in the area would know, or even trust, someone whose presence in the community wouldn't arouse suspicion."

"Really, Father Lucero, my men are one step ahead of you. We may actually nab our suspect within days."

The two priests are momentarily stunned into silence

It's Saenz who finds his voice first. "What did you say?"

Arcinas gives them a self-satisfied smile, the lashes feathering over his eyes almost coquettishly. "You've both been very helpful, but I think we can take it from here."

Saenz brushes aside the implied dismissal. "You have a suspect. Is he in custody now? How? Where?"

The lawyer is now busy shuffling papers on his desk, and his tone is brisk, almost cheerily official. "Now, Father, you know I can't tell you that."

"Why not?"

"Procedural restrictions. Yes, yes. Certain technicalities.

But we're very grateful for your assistance. Very grateful, really. We'll make sure you're given due recognition when we're done."

"We were asked to assist in this case by the director himself," Saenz says quietly.

"It's too bad the director is overseas, but if he were here, I'm sure he would agree with me that the bureau can handle the situation on its own from this point on. Of course, you will both be paid for your services."

Saenz starts to walk to the door. But midway he stops and turns back. This time the tone of persuasive rationality is gone, and in its place pure menace.

"For your sake, Attorney Arcinas, I hope you do get the right man."

14

JEROME IS GRADING papers on a Saturday morning. He's comfortable in an old T-shirt and even older striped pajamas, sitting at his desk, mug of steaming hot coffee within reach and sunlight streaming in through the windows. The monsoons have taken the day off, and the first unequivocal sunshine in two weeks is spreading over the metropolis.

When he hears the knock on the door, he doesn't answer it immediately; perhaps whoever it is will go away. The papers need to be graded by Monday, and there are other things to prepare for next week's classes. But when he doesn't respond, the person knocks again, and this time it is with the rhythmic pattern that Jerome associates with only one person. With a sigh, he leaves his comfortable seat and his hot coffee and his papers and opens the door.

"It's the weekend," he grumbles.

"Happy weekend!" Saenz chirps.

"I have papers to grade."

"So do I." The older priest breezes in through the open doorway.

"Yet here you are. No, wait, don't. I just made that coffee—" But it's too late; Saenz has already taken possession of the mug and proceeded to drink down the contents.

"And very good coffee it was," he says.

"Don't you have any other friends?"

"None who will come with me to Payatas on a Saturday morning."

At the mention of the dumpsite, Jerome turns serious. "Payatas? Why? What's up?"

Saenz leans against Jerome's desk. "We determined it was likely that the murders were committed on the first Saturday of every month since February. Something's been nagging at me all this time, but there's been so much happening these last few days that I kept getting distracted. I knew there was something about the first Saturday of the month that rang a bell, but I couldn't pin it down." He thrusts his hand into one of the pockets of his jeans and fishes out a small notebook, opens the cover and flips through the pages. When he finds what he's looking for, he hands it to Jerome. "My notes. From when I spoke to Jon-jon Mendoza's parents."

Jerome takes the notebook and studies the open page. *Saturday—parish—free food.* He looks up at Saenz. "Payatas it is, then."

JEROME AND SAENZ arrive at the parish church in time to see Father Emil bent over a huge, bubbling pot of *arroz caldo*. A look of surprise crosses his face, but it's quickly replaced by cheerfulness. He raises the ladle in welcome, spraying his shirt as well as a few kids with drops of the thick, yellow porridge.

"Hello! What brings you two here today?" he greets them, while dispensing bowl after bowl and keeping the more aggressive children in line. "Here you are; don't spill it— Wait! You'll get your share; don't push."

Saenz laughs, then deeply inhales the aroma of gingery broth and toasted garlic layered with the scent of freshly cut spring onions. "This is exactly how I pictured you, Emil. Knee-deep in *arroz caldo* and children."

"Sorry, Father Gus." The parish priest hands over rationing duties to a pair of nuns hovering close by. "Saturday is always a busy day in the parish."

"Nothing to apologize for," Saenz says. "We just thought we'd have a look around."

For a moment, Emil seems worried. "It's about the case, isn't it?" He looks at Jerome, then back at Saenz. "But you've been here before."

"Not on a Saturday."

"A Saturday." Emil is even more concerned now. "What does it have to do with Saturdays?"

"We don't know yet." Jerome looks around the church grounds.

Saenz puts an arm around the parish priest's shoulders and leads him away from the hubbub of children gathered around the massive pot. Jerome follows close behind.

"The parents of one of the boys we've identified say that the last time they saw their son, he'd said he was coming here," Saenz says in a low voice. "To the parish. On a Saturday."

Emil is taken aback. "Wait. Wait a minute. Do you think—"

Saenz holds both hands up to placate him. "We don't think anything yet, Emil. Honestly. It's a lead to follow up, that's all. That's why we came here. We wanted to see what happens at the parish on weekends."

Jerome steps forward. "If you could give us some idea of what goes on here, especially on Saturdays, we might be able to pick up something."

Emil's brow is furrowed with worry lines. "Everything that goes on here on the weekends is above board, and highly visible to everyone who comes here. I've never had any problems or any reason to . . . You mean, you think . . ."

"We don't think anything," Jerome repeats, kindly but firmly. "Why don't you take us through the Saturday activities? There may be no link to the case after all."

Emil again looks at both of them, one after the other, and pauses to think. "Well . . ." Then he squares his shoulders, clearly having come to a decision to cooperate as best as he can. "The parish has all kinds of initiatives. Aside from catechism on Sundays, we have livelihood training, parenthood seminars, a feeding program. Look over there," he says, pointing to a tentlike structure where about a dozen women are seated on plastic chairs, listening to a woman speaking in front of a blackboard. "That's a class on basic household accounting, and the woman is a volunteer sent by city hall."

"Is that new?" Jerome asks.

"New? The classes you mean? No, goodness. We've been

doing them for about six years now. We know all the volunteers; they've been with us on and off for as long as the classes have been in place."

Saenz looks at the tent. "Maybe you could give us a list anyway. Would that be a problem?"

"No, not at all. I'll send it to you Monday."

Jerome walks on ahead of the other two. "What about that?" he asks, pointing to a large vehicle that looks like a converted bus parked in one corner of the church grounds. Painted on the side, in large blue letters, a reminder to local voters: MOBILE MEDICAL AND DENTAL MISSION: A PUBLIC SERVICE PROJECT OF COUNCILLOR CESAR MARIANO. There is a line of mothers waiting patiently in the shade nearby, seated on or standing near makeshift wooden benches as their children run in circles around them.

"Free clinic," Emil says, standing beside Jerome. "That's been around since even before I became parish priest here. The vehicle may have changed once or twice, and so has the name of the politician." He chuckles, acknowledging the common practice of local politicians having their names emblazoned on waiting sheds, mobile clinics, ambulances and fire trucks. It's a way to ingratiate themselves to local voters, using the very facilities, equipment and services that the voters themselves have financed with their taxes. "The doctor who runs it is a longtime community health officer for the district, Dr. Alice Panganiban."

"And how often does the free clinic come here?" Saenz asks.

"They're here every Saturday. Dr. Alice, two female nurses, a dentist." At that moment, the door to the mobile clinic opens and a slim, white-clad woman in her early thirties steps out, her hair tied neatly in a ponytail. "That's our dentist, Dr. Jeannie Santa Romana."

"And all of them have been coming here for years?"

"Oh yes."

Jerome shrugs. "Oh well. Can we have all the names anyway? Just as a precaution."

"Sure, sure."

When Jerome turns to Saenz, he finds him gazing off in the direction of the nuns and the cooking pot. At that same moment, a child runs up to Emil and eagerly shows him a page out of her coloring book; the priest gets down on one knee to engage her in animated conversation. Jerome takes the opportunity to move closer to Saenz.

"What is it?"

"Feeding program." Saenz is looking intently at the seemingly endless line of children inching their way to the pot, laughing and joking. The children range in age from about two or three years old to as old as perhaps thirteen or fourteen. Saenz turns back to Emil, waits for the child to finish and run off before speaking. "Tell me about the feeding program."

Emil rises to his feet. "The feeding program? We've been doing that for years too. Only difference is nowadays we get help from some of the councillors in the district."

"Since when?" Jerome asks.

"Let's see . . . maybe nine, ten months? Less than a year, that's for sure."

"And how does that work?"

"Usually the councillors' people provide the ingredients, and we do the cooking, as we did today. But sometimes they send packed meals."

"Oh? How often is that?"

"About once a month. Every first Saturday."

Saenz is careful not to register surprise or excitement at hearing this, but Jerome has noticed the minute shift in his tone. "And those meals—where do they come from?"

"Oh, I'm not sure," Emil says, oblivious. "I guess they've got caterers they use for their political events."

"Hmmm. Same people every time?"

"I suppose so. I think Sister Fe and Sister Lucia would have a better idea." At this point, another child runs up to Emil, and the parish priest gives Saenz and Jerome an apologetic look before attending to the little girl.

Quietly, Saenz says to Jerome: "I think I'd like to have a quick chat with the good sisters."

IN JEROME'S CAR on the way back to the university, Saenz is unusually quiet. Jerome knows not to interrupt his thoughts; he doesn't even play music on the car stereo as he drives.

As they turn into the main road heading to the campus, Saenz finally speaks.

"In many ways, the community is a closed system. The elements within that system interact in ways that are fairly predictable over time. Those interactions also change in fairly predictable ways. But what happens if you introduce a new element? How does that element behave within the system? What changes does it bring about?"

"You're talking about the food deliveries."

Saenz nods. "Both Emil and Sister Fe say they started less than a year ago. The packed meals are unmarked, so they're not from any of the better-known fast-food chains. The same people make the deliveries every time. The meals arrive hot, so wherever they're prepared, it can't be too far from the church grounds."

Jerome's car swings through the university's gates. "So the next logical step is to speak with the councillors who fund the meals."

"We may have to wait till next week, though. I don't think anybody will agree to see us on a weekend."

"And we're more than midway through the month. Which means the first Saturday of next month isn't that far off."

15

THE FOLLOWING MONDAY morning, after his only class of the day, Jerome stops by Saenz's office. He opens the door without knocking. "Any luck?" he asks, and then he realizes that Saenz is on the phone.

Saenz claps a hand over the mouthpiece. "You're just in time," he says in a quiet voice. "Talking to an aide of Councillor Cesar Mariano."

"The councillor directly involved with the parish feeding program."

Saenz nods. "I'm this close to getting an appointment," he says, holding thumb and forefinger together to indicate how close. "But I need you to give me a good excuse."

Jerome rolls his eyes. "Why is it me who always has to come up with the dodgy plans?"

"Because you have a gift for it. Quick!"

Jerome plops down in a chair in front of Saenz's desk. "Tell him . . . Tell him that Emil sent you. To talk about a community development project that we hope he can spearhead. Imply that there'll be lots of votes in it for him."

Saenz grins at him. "You see? A gift." Just then the person on the other end of the line returns with some news, and Saenz picks up the thread of the conversation.

Jerome listens as Saenz makes an appointment for that same evening. When the conversation ends, he says with some admiration, "That was fast."

"Much faster than we'd anticipated, eh? Turns out he's tied up all week, and this is his only free slot."

Jerome pauses, and then asks, "So why don't we just tell him the real reason we want to see him?"

Saenz speaks slowly, as though he himself is still working out the rationale for this initial subterfuge in his mind. "We don't know anything about this person yet. We don't know if the meal deliveries are connected in any way with the killings. And as he's directly involved in the feeding program, we need to be careful."

Jerome looks down at his shoes as he considers this. "Right. I see your point."

Saenz stands, pats him gently on the shoulder. "Let's just get a foot in the door, okay? And we improvise from there."

THAT SAME EVENING, they find themselves sitting in the living room of Councillor Cesar Mariano. When he comes out to greet them, his handshake is firm and quick, his manner brisk and businesslike. He settles into a cushioned chair with wooden armrests, relaxed but not slouching.

Mariano is a small man, an architect by profession, fairly well-to-do. His short, coarse hair stands up stiffly like the bristles of a toothbrush, and his round, deeply cupped ears seem to billow out at the sides of his head like tiny sails. He reminds Jerome of those troll dolls with their wildly colored hair sticking up and out; children are supposed to rub the hair for good luck. Jerome imagines that the councillor would object to having the same done to him. He also notes that the councillor is not a man much given to smiling, which makes him wonder how the man managed to get elected in a country where skilled glad-handing is a prerequisite for election to public office. He seems a serious, no-nonsense sort, the type people can count on to get a job done without too much of a fuss. However, he is a bit puzzled at their interest in the food deliveries.

"We have a list of caterers who handle these things for us. Big meetings, community events, political rallies, that sort of thing."

"I understand from Sister Fe Boncayao that you've been using the same caterer for all of the parish meal deliveries from the start."

Mariano thinks about this for a moment. "You know, I can't be sure. My office helps to fund and source the meals and supplies, but my staff handles the details for me, you see." Another pause. "What's the matter? Did somebody get food poisoning or something?"

Saenz shakes his head. "No, no. We are looking for a caterer—someone who can offer reasonable prices and is already familiar with the parish. You see, we're organizing a fundraiser for the parish. Father Emil is thinking of building an activity center for the children. Keep them busy; keep them away from drugs."

"Oh." A beat, and then: "So why isn't he with you?"

"Busy meeting with potential donors," Jerome steps in. "I expect he'll come to see you about this in a few weeks too."

"Hmmm."

"We're hoping to at least break ground on the project before Christmas," Saenz says, choosing his words with care. "But as you can imagine, we . . . don't have a lot of time or money to put this fundraiser together. If you could refer us to your regular caterer, it would save us a great deal of both."

Mariano taps his fingers on the armrests of his chair. "I don't have the contact numbers, but I can get my assistant to give them to you. How soon do you need the information?"

"The sooner the better," Jerome says, trying not to sound too eager.

The councillor walks over to a desk on one side of the room, takes a pen and begins to scribble a note on a piece of paper. Then he shuffles back and hands the paper to Jerome. "That's her number at the office. Give her a call; she'll be in all day tomorrow."

"Thank you," Jerome says, folding it up and putting it in his pocket.

Mariano looks at both of them. "Still not sure why you told my assistant this was urgent, though," he says quietly.

Saenz meets his gaze without flinching.

"For you and me, Councillor, it isn't. For those children, it is."

It's depressing to read the papers or watch the news. Everyday something bad happens—a bank gets robbed, a war breaks out, a child gets raped—and nobody can do anything about it. Not the police, not the press. Not the mothers and fathers, not the lawyers or the priests.

We are all powerless in the face of evil.

No, no, that's not true. We are powerless when we wait for other people to act on our behalf.

Yes, that's it. The truly powerful man is the man who stands alone.

16

THOUSANDS OF MILES away in Boston, Massachusetts, Director Lastimosa is lying in bed in his son's home, recovering from surgery. It has been a peaceful morning; he is reading a newspaper and eating some oatmeal. His prognosis is excellent, and the doctors have advised him to taper off the pain medication as soon as he can, to break the pain cycle. His chest still hurts, but a little less each day, and he takes it without complaint. He has already begun a program of light exercise, including slow stretching and brief walks.

There is a knock on the bedroom door, and then his son, David, opens it cautiously.

"Pa?"

"Dave."

"You feeling okay?" There is an undercurrent of anxiety in David's voice that makes him fold up the newspaper, push away the bed tray and sit up straighter in bed.

"I'm fine. What's wrong?"

"Umm . . ."

The director impatiently whacks the bedspread with the folded-up paper. "I'm not dying just yet, Son, so tell me."

David is taken aback by this uncharacteristic display, but quickly realizes that his father must be bored after several weeks of relative quiet. "Jake Valdes called."

"Jake? What did he say?"

"He wanted to know if you were well enough to talk to him. He said he had some news on a case you've been watching closely."

The director reaches out to remove the blanket covering his legs, but his son rushes to the bed. "Is he still on the line?"

"Pa, he's—Wait. Wait a minute."

"Let me talk to him," the director says, struggling to get out

of bed and completely ignoring David's frantic gestures of placa-
tion.

"Pa!"

"What? I need to talk to him, and your phone's downstairs."

"Pa, please," David says, practically begging. "Look, you've
got an extension here. Right there on the desk by the window.
See?"

The director looks at the desk. "I didn't hear it ring."

"We turned off the ringer after you arrived from the hospital. So you could sleep."

"All right," he answers crossly. "So let me talk to him."

"I told him to call back, Pa."

"Call back? But why did you—"

"Because I needed to see if you felt well enough to take the
call." David runs a hand through his thinning hair in agitation. "Mama would kill me if you had another episode on my
watch. Look, he said he'd call back in half an hour, okay? I'll
bring the phone closer to you and turn the ringer back on, but
you have to stay in bed. Okay? Can you do that for me,
please?"

"Treating me like a child," the director grumbles, as David
leaves the room.

Jake Valdes calls less than half an hour later.

"It's Arcinas," he says glumly. "He's detained a suspect in
the Payatas case."

"And?"

A pause. "I don't know what to tell you, sir. He seems to
have followed standard procedure and all, but . . ."

"It doesn't feel right," he says, completing Valdes's sentence
for him.

"No, sir. I just feel . . . No."

The director picks at one corner of the blanket while he
considers his next move. "Tell Director Mapa to call me
within the hour. Tell him I want to be briefed on how Arcinas
found his suspect."

"Okay," Valdes says. "Not sure how happy he'll be to take my call at this time of the night."

"It's only half past nine on your side of the planet, Jake. He'll live."

ASSISTANT DIRECTOR MAPA is all warmth and concern when the director answers the phone. "How are you feeling? Is there anything at all that we can do for you from here?"

Director Lastimosa tries to keep his tone of voice cool and even. "I hear Ben has already detained someone in the Payatas case."

"Oh, yes. Yes, he has." Mapa is enthusiastic. "We're getting ready to announce it at a press conference tomorrow."

"Are you sure you want to do that, Philip?"

"Uhh—yes. Yes, it's a good . . ." But the enthusiasm has drained away, leaving Mapa guarded. "Why, what's the problem?"

"I need you to tell me how he found this suspect."

"How he—well, the usual ways," Mapa answers, unable to mask his irritation. "He talked to residents, he looked through prior complaints, he—"

"So this suspect—he's been in trouble before?"

"Oh yes. Public indecency. Acts of lasciviousness."

"Convictions? Or mere complaints?"

Mapa groans. "He's had complaints filed against him, sir. We know this for certain."

"And that's it?"

"What do you mean, that's it? Ben did everything by the book, just the way you would have wanted it done if you were here."

"What kind of complaints? How many? Have they been verified? And most important of all—what do you have that ties him directly with the killings?"

"He's confessed!" Mapa is highly agitated now. "What more do you want?"

"And how was that confession extracted from him?" Director Lastimosa presses him. "Philip, we can't afford to take short cuts here. Once you hold that news conference and confirm that these killings have taken place, once you present that suspect, you'll have very little room to maneuver."

"What for?"

"What do you mean—" and then Director Lastimosa realizes he's talking to a brick wall. "Look, Philip, if you don't understand what for, I don't have the time to explain it to you. But while I'm still director, I hope my advice counts for something. And my advice is: I wouldn't hold that press conference if I were you."

The director puts the receiver down. He pushes the entire instrument away from him, settles back on the pillows and pulls his blanket up to his waist. Then, he closes his eyes. He is exhausted but resolute.

David has seen that look on his father's face too many times not to know what it means. It's clear that he's come to a decision. The realization fills David with dread.

"Pa," he begs. "Please. You're going to kill yourself."

The director doesn't open his eyes. "They'll hold that press conference, against all good judgment. I just know it. It will alert the real killer, and he'll find even better ways of evading us. Or he might simply go elsewhere and slip out of our grasp."

"Pa. You need more time to rest. You were supposed to recuperate for six to eight weeks, and it's been barely two. Your doctors here won't give you clearance, we'll have to sign a waiver, there'll be all sorts of complications—"

"A week from now, and no later," he says, and David knows there's no arguing when he uses that tone. "If you would be so kind as to buy the ticket today."

17

IT IS JEROME'S turn to say the six o'clock Mass at the university church, but this evening he keeps the homily brief. Saenz has invited him to dinner at his family's home, and Jerome has hardly ever passed up such an invitation.

The drive to Makati is murder as usual. There are patches of EDSA, the metropolis's main highway, where all vehicles are at a complete standstill, and there is little for him to do but gaze at the fading orange-and-lavender light of the setting sun reflected in the dingy glass windows of the buildings that line the avenue. And then in certain stretches the bottleneck clears, and the vehicles spill forward like beans from a jar, accelerating with a mad, pent-up energy, racing to claim every available space. He has lost count of how many times he has almost been sideswiped by other vehicles trying to squeeze past him. The completed flyovers are absolutely no help in easing the traffic situation, and neither, as far as he can tell, is the Metro Rail Transit. He pounds on the horn with the heel of his palm, like many other irate motorists on the highway, and then shakes his head: *conduct unbecoming a man of the cloth.*

When Saenz is driving, he is not given to pounding on the horn, Jerome reflects; instead, he seems to grow calmer the worse the traffic gets. In a situation like this, Saenz will usually slide one of his beloved cassette tapes into the car stereo, if there isn't one playing already, and analyze the finer points of the music, the performance, even the instruments used. Jerome envies him his ready access to peace, the core of quiet he seems to possess.

Jerome is quite the opposite. Blunt to the point of occasional abrasiveness, he has few friends, although those he does have—brothers in the order, colleagues and students from the university—will go the last mile for him. Jerome is restless, dogged and questioning—the type, Saenz says, "who does not suffer fools gladly." A contradiction of a man: on one hand an intense, volatile temperament, on the other a surprisingly gentle, compassionate nature.

"All that tai chi really pays off, eh?" Jerome kids his mentor on occasion, and all he gets in reply is, "In time, Grasshopper, you too will know these things."

Saenz's family lives in a small, gated community in Makati. The parents own valuable urban real estate, while the children have expanded the family's assets to include a small chain of computer stores and a start-up firm that makes financial and retail software for large corporations.

Jerome has known Saenz's siblings since he was a teenager. They are all small and fair and fine boned, taking after their mother. Only Gus stands out, with his sharp features, tawny skin and unusual height. Jerome has long taken it for granted—but has never actually sought confirmation—that Saenz was adopted as a child.

It was not in their physical features but in their collective character as a family that Jerome first noted the qualities they shared with Saenz. He recognized in each of them the same genuine warmth and graciousness, the same keen intelligence that he saw in his mentor.

Jerome had entered their home for the first time as a reserved, awkward teenager. His ears buzzed with their multiple conversations, their easy, often raucous laughter. After years of living in his own very quiet home, where his parents rarely spoke to each other and even more rarely to him, Jerome had felt himself become almost giddy with an inexplicable happiness, wonderful and bewildering at the same time. Felt his breathing go quick and shallow, as though he were discovering something new, something he had only heard or read about in books. *Of course happy families exist. Of course.*

It is nearly half past eight when Jerome finally drives up to the house. Ranulfo, a driver for one of the Saenz siblings, pauses in the middle of cleaning the windshield of a car and waves at him, and he waves back. Ranulfo drops the rag into a bucket and scurries toward Jerome's car, directing him to an empty parking space along the curb, not far from the gate of the house.

"Parallel parking," he grumbles. Hands gripping the steering wheel, he eases into the space, then he switches off the ignition and pulls up the hand brake.

"Evening, sir." Ranulfo holds the car door open for him.

"Hi, Ranulfo. Has Father Gus arrived?"

"Yes, Father. He is waiting for you inside."

"Thanks."

He walks up the marble steps to the huge front doors and rings the bell, then waits a few minutes until one of the maids opens the door.

"Hi, Father," she says brightly.

"Hello, *Manang* Delia."

"They're in the living room. Adrian and Cecille just got back from their honeymoon."

"Really?" Jerome officiated at the wedding of Father Saenz's youngest brother, Adrian, some two months before. "It will be good to see them."

She bustles off down the long corridor. He follows his nose, which has caught the scent of stir-fried vegetables and barbecued spareribs and steamed seafood. The family has an excellent cook, and at these family gatherings Saenz himself will always have cooked at least one of the dishes.

The console table in the dining room is laden with chafing dishes full of food, and Jerome happily picks up a few morsels here and there to pop into his mouth: a broccoli floret, a butterflied prawn, a bit of tender pork sparerib stewed in black bean sauce—a signature Saenz dish.

He realizes how hungry he is; he has not eaten since an early lunch at around 11 A.M., and that had been an unremarkable tuna sandwich and a cup of sugary black coffee.

"All this food and nobody to keep it company." He shakes his head. "This isn't right."

He goes off to look for Saenz and the rest of the family.

In contrast to the usual laughter and talk, the family is gathered silently around the entertainment center in the living room: twenty-eight-year-old Adrian and his young wife, Cecille; tiny Marian, who is several years younger than Gus and oversees the computer store chain, as well as her husband. The twins, Tommy and Tony, who are both MIT graduates, both computer engineers, and married to a pair of sisters who are also twins. Cholo, who oversees the family's properties. Vicky, who handles investor relations for a Top 100 corporation. Quirky, funny, startlingly intelligent Vicky, with whom Jerome was infatuated many years ago while still in his teens.

Saenz stands in the middle, a head taller than his six brothers and sisters. They are all watching an hourly newscast on one of the top networks.

Jerome moves into the circle, and the siblings turn, smile and pat him on the back. They know only too well that he needs to hear the news, however, and step aside to let him through until he is standing beside Saenz.

On the screen, a perfectly made-up female newscaster is saying: *"The suspect is believed to be behind the killing of a young boy in the Payatas area. NBI Task Force officials say the boy, whose body was badly mutilated, was found last month. Authorities also say they purposely did not release details of the murder to avoid a panic in the community."*

Arcinas appears, all hooded eyes and unnatural swirls of reddish hair. "Yes, we had outside help, but to the credit of the bureau's personnel, this case was solved with in-house expertise."

The newscaster comes back on the air to say the full story will be broadcast during the late evening news. But neither of the priests is listening anymore.

"You think he's the one?" Jerome whispers to Saenz.

"I hope so," Saenz says. "Dear God, I hope so."

18

IN THE HUGE, open-concept newsroom of a major television network, Joanna Bonifacio glances up every now and then to watch the late night news on one of a dozen television monitors set on stainless-steel brackets on the wall she faces. She is simultaneously making short work of a newspaper crossword puzzle and chewing a large wad of bubble gum.

The room, divided only by chest-high partitions of heavy industrial plastic and grey mohair, is almost deserted. An old dot matrix network printer can be heard tapping out news scripts and reports from the international wire services.

The arctic atmosphere, necessary for the maintenance of broadcast equipment, is air-conditioner sterile aside from occasional stray smells of brewed coffee and toner for photocopiers.

Joanna straightens up in her seat when she sees the NBI's Benjamin Arcinas, smug and smiling, on-screen.

"Look, Wally," she calls out to her boss, the executive producer for *First Person*, the weekly current affairs program for which she writes. Wally Soler is half dozing at the desk behind hers, feet propped up on the edge. She turns around, notes that his socks are mismatched again tonight, then grabs an ankle and gives it a good shake. "Arcinas changed his hair color. Again."

Wally wakes, stands, stretches himself out with a yawn: a tall, chunky man with salt-and-pepper hair, a square face lined in all directions, small, shrewd eyes. He tilts his head back and puts his face up close to the television set, peering shortsightedly at the screen.

"Hey, it's redder now."

"Yeah, kind of strawberry." She blows a large bubble from the wad of gum in her mouth. "Geez. He sort of looks like Nancy Drew."

Notwithstanding Arcinas's paranoia about the press, Joanna Bonifacio really does have it in for him. She has dedicated a large measure of her efforts as a crime reporter to pointing out the most awful errors—and there are many of them—in his handling of criminal cases. And she has done so in precise detail on one of the highest-rated programs on the country's largest broadcast network.

She is not on his Christmas gift list.

"What's he talking about?"

Joanna frowns, waves her hands. "Quick, Wally Wonka, turn it up." She is given to calling her boss strange names.

Wally turns up the volume just as the newscaster is saying, *"The suspect is believed to be behind the killing of a young boy in the Payatas area. NBI Task Force officials say the boy, whose body was badly mutilated, was found last month. Authorities also say they purposely did not release details of the murder to avoid a panic in the community."*

Joanna snorts. "Who covered the NBI today?"

"Claire," Wally says as the broadcast cuts to the junior reporter interviewing Arcinas. Claire Manalo is one of several young and pretty news trainees whom the network predictably favors—with better pay, better opportunities, better support— over older, less telegenic but often more capable journalists and producers.

"I take one sick day—one sick day in *three years*, mind you—and NBI coverage goes to hell," Joanna grumbles. "Look at that. She didn't press Arcinas. She swallowed everything he tossed out without questioning a single thing. What is it with these kids? Easy on the eyes but short on the brain cells." She pokes Wally's belly with a forefinger. "When am I going to get that liposuction budget? Huh? *Huh?*"

Wally chuckles; as a veteran of many newsrooms, he knows all too well the resentment of seeing plum assignments going to better-looking, or better-connected, or more self-promoting upstarts.

"You're not fat, Joe. You're Simone Signoret. You're ample. Curvy. *Zaftig.*"

She raises her eyes heavenward. "Do you even know what that word means?"

He clips her across the top of her head in response.

"Ow," she protests.

She blows a noteworthy pink bubble, which bursts and flattens over her chin. Absently, expertly, she lifts it off with her tongue as she turns her attention to the corkboard on the partition in front of her desk. Something makes her lean closer, and seconds later she is practically tearing off the papers and photographs pinned to the cork as she searches for something underneath.

Wally watches all this, puzzled. "What is it? What's wrong?"

"The dead boy's injuries," she says. "The mutilations they mentioned."

"What about them?"

"So familiar," she says, thinking aloud now, scanning the few documents left on the corkboard. "Something I've already . . ." and she reaches for a small sheet of lined paper, torn from a spiral steno notebook and covered in her own thin, spidery handwriting. She reads it, and a moment later slams the palm of her hand on the top of her desk, then thrusts the sheet of paper under Wally's nose.

"See? I was right. They're familiar. The injuries. The way they were described. Look at this. In February, they found a boy at the landfill site. Dead, naked, similar injuries. A few media outlets picked it up, but nobody was interested for very long."

"Except you," Wally says, studying her notes.

"Long enough to find out that they managed to identify the boy. Ryan Molina. But nothing came of the investigation, and there were no other leads. Or, more likely, nobody bothered to look for any more leads." She takes the paper back from Wally. "I held on to this because . . ." She shrugs. "I thought the kid deserved better. I thought I might want to go back to it when I had the time."

"But you didn't have time," Wally says, and he's right; often the daily grind of the newsroom makes it impossible to revisit past stories whose trails have grown cold.

Joanna looks up at him sharply. "I do now. Don't I?"

Wally clears his throat. "Why do I feel a headache coming on?"

Joanna lifts an eyebrow the merest fraction of an inch, and by that fraction Wally is subtly but effectively reminded of many things. That she has a graduate degree in anthropology from a French university. That she speaks four languages aside from English and Tagalog. That she worked three years in Osaka for the United Nations Asia and Far East Institute for the Prevention of Crime and the Treatment of Offenders. That she has paid her dues working the police beat for two major dailies.

"Come on, Wally. You know me. I'd never give you a headache without a corresponding reward."

Conceited old cow, Wally thinks, then permits himself a private laugh. *She's just like her father, God rest his soul.*

"Don't tell me about it. Just get to work. You want Manny to come along?"

Manny is a cameraman, Wally's photographer-sidekick from the old days when they were both still working for one of the big-name broadsheets in the Port Area. When Wally moved into broadcasting, Manny thought he would learn how to operate a video camera. This was well over a decade ago, and Joanna is not sure that he has quite learned how.

"Not time for the camera just yet. And Manny—you know, the last time you assigned him to me, most of my footage was out of focus. And he smokes like a chimney." Joanna is allergic to cigarette smoke.

"He's big and he can look out for you."

Wally sees Joanna as the daughter he never had. What he did have, though, was four or five failed relationships in the last two decades, all collapsing under the strain of late hours, low pay, dangerous assignments, hard drinking. Serial infidelities on both sides. Didn't seem to be much point in having children.

Joanna's father was Wally's best friend from those early days when reporters still used carbon paper and typewriters, and Wally was godfather to Joanna and her sisters. He'd always been especially fond of Joanna: she was old for her age, observant, quiet but persistent in her *whats* and *hows* and *whys*. She grew up big and gentle like her father, with her mother's drive and neuroses and a sharp, probing intelligence all her own.

"Big, nothing. He's slow and—"

"Yeah, yeah, I know. He smells bad."

Joanna has already begun gathering up her things.

On her way out, she presses her palm against the man's forehead affectionately, then removes her hand and scurries away, as fast as a woman of her height and size can scurry.

Wally puts a hand to his forehead. He peels something off it, then looks down at the bit of paper.

It is a tiny Bazooka Joe comic strip.

GUS SAENZ IS a light sleeper. At any time in the night, he can tell if any of the other priests on the same floor is awake or has left his quarters. He remembers sounds in the night, voices, doors opening or closing, the flushing of a toilet down the hall. He remembers if the room grew warmer or colder in the course of his slumber. He has, on occasion, been known to answer questions or join in the conversations of other people in the same room—often coherently—while asleep.

Tonight, sleep, or what passes for sleep, eludes Saenz. In his quarters, he lies in bed in the semidarkness and stares at his long, pale feet propped up on a pillow at the end of the bed.

Tonight, the moon is full. The lacy shadow of the curtain unfurling in the wind passes over the skin of his feet at almost regular intervals, and he holds his breath until the shadow comes again.

Skin.

He has a scar on his left foot, long and wide, its surface paler than the skin that surrounds it. He got it when he was a young boy, thanks to the particularly nasty slip of a new, clumsily held pocketknife, a Christmas gift from his father.

He flexes his foot so that the scar catches the full light from the moon before the curtain's shadow passes over it.

At a certain angle, the foot appears perfectly smooth and unblemished.

He and Jerome have agreed to meet at the NBI in the morning. Jake Valdes says he will try to convince Arcinas to allow them to speak to his suspect. Saenz is deeply grateful for this intervention, because he knows Arcinas would never agree to it if he himself made the request.

Saenz recognizes that this is a crucial moment, and with all humility, he hopes and prays that Arcinas has found the right man. And yet, he wonders if anyone can—if it is possible to detect the scars that lie under the surface, to get at the diseases that take root not in blood or muscle, not in bone or pulsing organ, but in the mind, which can cunningly hide its ills beyond the reach of X-rays and electronic probes and surgical needles.

He wonders if he knows enough to recognize the scars when he sees them, just beneath the skin of some, deceptively normal man.

He flexes his foot again, and the scar reappears. It is a while before he closes his eyes, and when he does, there is one question in his mind.

In what kind of light will I see your scars?

19

"ALL RIGHT, I'LL let you talk to him. But only for a few minutes." Arcinas closes the folder on his desk ceremoniously, as though closing the book on their involvement in the case. "Though there's really no point. He's confessed to everything."

Jerome's face is grim, his teeth tightly clenched. He is holding his anger back in a supreme effort of will. *Humble pie time, Jerome*, he reminds himself; the need to get at the truth is more important than his own professional pride.

"Still," he says, and the words come out clipped, "I think the director would want us to question him."

Arcinas's snakelike eyes narrow. "The director has given me full operational control over this case from here on, and now that we've brought it to such a successful conclusion, I'm sure he would agree with me that your—uh, assistance—is no longer necessary."

Okay, that's it, Jerome thinks. "Which direc—," he begins, but this time Saenz is ready. His arm shoots out to restrain the younger priest, and he turns to Arcinas.

"Precisely because you have concluded this case so well, you must be anxious to ensure the correctness of this arrest."

A trace of apprehension touches Arcinas's face, but it is quickly replaced by a look of undisguised antipathy. "All right. Ten minutes."

On their way downstairs with the officer Arcinas has assigned to assist them, Saenz and Jerome see a tall woman with a serious face taking the steps two at a time. A small man, about five feet two inches tall, lugging video camera and kit, struggles to keep pace with her.

She stops short when she sees them.

"Father Saenz," she says, holding out her hand to the older priest, and Jerome is startled at both the easy familiarity with which she greets Saenz and at her deep, throaty voice—a cross, he decides, between Lauren Bacall and Bela Lugosi. "*Voici!*"

Saenz's face registers surprise, and then he smiles broadly in recognition. "Joanna—*salut!*"

The woman takes the older priest's hand and shakes it vigorously, then begins to speak to him in rapid French. "I'm not surprised to see you here. How's the weather up there?" she asks, tilting her head in the direction of Arcinas's office.

"Very sunny. Arcinas is quite pleased with himself."

"Ah, Arcinas. The nutcase," she snorts in contempt. Then she scrutinizes Saenz's face. "But you suspect it's all a scam, right?"

Saenz shrugs. "I have no idea, Joanna." He pauses as Jerome clears his throat, then switches to English. "My manners. Joanna, may I introduce my friend Father Jerome Lucero?" He turns to the younger priest. "Jerome, this is Joanna Bonifacio. She was one of my students at the *Institut de Paléontologie Humaine.*"

"That explains the French," Jerome says with a grin. He holds out his hand, and she takes it; her grip is like a construction worker's.

Her eyes search you, he thinks. *For uncertainty. For dishonesty. For fear.*

The woman gestures toward the cameraman, who has put down his equipment and is now wiping sweat off his brow with a checkered handkerchief that has seen better days. "Leo, my colleague," she says, and the compact, dark brown–skinned man flashes them a brilliant but gap-toothed smile.

"Joanna is a producer for that crime show. *First Person.*"

Ah, Jerome thinks. *First Person.* Loud, sensational, top-rated, five years running. Often intelligent. Occasionally brilliant.

"Unusual career choice," Jerome says. He meets her gaze and holds it without flinching.

"Why?" she asks, a quiet challenge in that single word. For a few seconds he imagines that she is considering decking him, but unexpectedly, she gives him a conspiratorial wink: *you're all right.* "It's my apostolate, eh, Father Lucero?" She shifts her focus to Saenz once more. "So, come on, Father. I've been hanging around here since last night, but nobody will tell me anything."

"Operationally, that was probably very wise of them." He chuckles.

She ignores the good-natured jibe. "There was another one. In February. It made the news but was quickly overshadowed by bigger stories. So I have lots of questions. How many others have there been? Why didn't he talk about them in his little press conference yesterday? And why haven't they come out into the open and warned the public until now?"

"I'm sorry, Joanna. I wish I had answers for you. You'd better go and talk to Ben. I'm sure he'll see you."

"Yeah, right." Another snort; she rubs the tip of her nose with the back of her hand, a mannerism Saenz knows well from her student days in France. "I gave him hell with that bank robbery a couple of months ago, remember? He'll be jumping for joy to see me."

Saenz shakes his head; Joanna is a good friend and an excellent pupil, smart as a whip—and just as pleasant. Which is to say, not at all.

"*Je suis désolé*, Joanna. You know I can't give you any information until this whole matter is settled."

"*D'accord.*" She shrugs, then pulls a thin silver case out of her back pocket. It is an oddly elegant thing, something Jerome would not immediately have associated with this gruff giant of a woman. He notices that it is engraved with the initials ACB.

As she takes out a calling card, she catches him studying the monogram and snaps the case shut. "My dad's," she says dismissively as she shoves it back into her jeans pocket and out of sight. "Old-fashioned frippery, if you ask me, but useful on occasion."

Jerome detects a note of profound sadness underlying her self-possession.

Joanna turns to Saenz again. *"Voici ma carte,"* she says, handing the card to the older priest. "If you need to talk to anyone, Father, I don't have to tell you I'm your best bet."

"Better yet, you don't have to tell me you'll be hounding me from now on, *n'est-ce pas?*"

She winks at Jerome again, then practically leaps past them and up the stairs toward Arcinas's office. Leo the cameraman gives them the same gap-toothed smile before taking up his equipment and following her.

"Interesting woman," Jerome says.

"A first-rate mind, Joanna," Saenz says, as they proceed down the corridor with the slack-faced officer who has been waiting at the foot of the stairs all this time. "And a genuine pest."

Before they enter the room, Saenz takes Jerome by the arm and pulls him to one side. "What will we be looking for?"

Jerome glances at the officer to see if he is listening, but the man is fiddling with a set of about a dozen unlabeled keys hanging from a key ring made of bent wire.

"Not sure. If he is who Arcinas says he is, he wouldn't have confessed so easily. The care with which the murders are committed, the absence of witnesses, the uniformity of the mutilations—they all point to a highly organized mind."

"Sir?" The officer has finally found the right key and is now holding the door open for them.

"You do the talking, Jerome. I'll sit in and observe."

20

THE ROOM IS windowless, with walls painted a drab institutional grey. There are two fluorescent rods in the ceiling, but only one of them is working, and it emits only the faintest glow. There is a small wooden table in the middle of the room, with two wooden chairs on opposite ends of it. Two other chairs, side by side near the door, are the only other furniture in the room.

"Looks promising," Jerome says, his lips set in a grim line. "What did they say his name was?"

"Ricardo Navato. Carding for short."

Saenz takes his place quietly in a corner of the darkened room.

The door opens again and two officers escort a young man in handcuffs into the room. Jerome waits until he has been seated at the table and the two other men leave. Then he takes the second chair.

The suspect is young—*perhaps too young*, Saenz thinks to himself—in his late teens or early twenties. He is thin, with spindly legs and arms, narrow shoulders, curly, close-cropped hair. Both eyes are almost swollen shut, and his upper lip is split in two places. Evidently he found himself on the receiving end of that brand of tender loving care for which several quarters of the Quezon City police are known before he was transferred to NBI custody.

"Hello, Carding," Jerome begins cautiously. "How are you?"

The young man doesn't say anything. He shifts in his seat, his expression difficult to read because of the injuries to his face.

"My name is Father Jerome. Father Emil sent me to see you. You know him, right?"

Carding shrugs, then slides lower in his seat.

"How are they treating you here?" Jerome asks.

"Just fine." He is cold, still, suspicious. In the dullness of the young man's eyes, Jerome can imagine the cramped space in which he lives; the tacky, plastic matting laid over a dirt floor; the empty containers of PX cheese balls and chocolate gathering dust on wooden shelves. The octopus wires that hook up electric fan and lights and battered old refrigerator to an illegal connection. Outside, there would be well-worn clothes—yellowed whites and fading colors—hanging dripping from wire clotheslines or collapsible space-saver hangers made of cheap plastic.

Jerome knows the mingled smells of infrequently washed bodies and stale food and bar soap and old cooking oil that hang over Carding's days and nights like frayed mosquito netting. He knows there is a store not far away where the young man can buy cigarettes and chewing gum and single-serve packs of three-in-one coffee. He sits there at night drinking cheap gin and beer with other jobless dead enders, in what passes for a social life, muttering about their lack of money and the better-looking girls in the neighborhood in the same numb monotone he speaks in now.

"Do you know why you're here?"

Another shrug, another refusal to meet his gaze. Jerome folds his hands together on top of the table and leans forward. Then, a curious thing happens: the young man looks down at the priest's hands, at the ring on his right middle finger, a heavy but beautifully wrought gold band surmounted by a small disc of onyx, the onyx inlaid with a golden Greek cross. His eyes stay on the ring; it is something Jerome picks up quickly. The priest adjusts his hand ever so slightly, and the other man's eyes follow, glued to the ring.

Beautiful thing, isn't it?

"They tell us that you killed all those children."

"I did," he says dispassionately.

"How many?" Jerome moves the fingers of his left hand and covers the ring, casually, a test; when he looks up, he sees that it has also disappeared from the other man's consciousness and that his attention is now focused on the priest.

"I can't remember."

"Five or six?" Jerome prompts.

Fidgeting in his seat now, wary of a trap. "Six."

The priest raises an eyebrow. "You must have been very angry."

No response.

"Have you lived in Payatas a long time?"

"All my life."

"So you knew those children. You'd seen them around." Jerome glances at Saenz and is mildly puzzled to find him staring intently at Carding's feet. "Maybe you can tell me why you chose them."

Carding shifts again, masking his growing unease with impatience. "Why are you asking me? You just answered your own question. I knew them; I'd seen them around."

Jerome waits. "Father Emil says he knows you. He says you're a good kid and that he knows your mother."

At the mention of his mother, the young man's shoulders droop slightly. Jerome feels a shift from defensiveness and suspicion to anxiety and fear.

"Did you ever talk to him about the things you did?" he asks gently.

"No, I couldn't tell anyone."

Jerome lowers his voice. "Why did you kill them?"

"I was angry."

"About what?"

Jerome feels that the younger man is on the verge of crying, but the tears do not come; he holds them in check with fierce self-control. He may be frightened, but he is also tough, a veteran of dump and slum: he will not cry in front of a man, even if that man is a priest. "Look, you'd be angry too, you know? Living like I do. No job, no money. My mother is sick. The doctor told me that I have to take her to live somewhere else, that being near the dump is not good for her. Where will I take her? We have nowhere to go. We have to live on what I make from the dump. There are no steady jobs for people like me."

"So how do you get by?"

A small, bitter laugh escapes him. "Don't you know, Father? People are so generous here. Politicians, rich people, the Church. Everyone is so eager to help people like me."

Jerome says nothing, only waits until Carding grows uncomfortable with his silence.

"I do odd jobs occasionally. Carry this, lift that. Every once in a while I help to load and distribute food and groceries from the local government."

Without looking, Jerome knows Saenz has leaned forward to listen closely. "Distribute food—you mean like the free meals for the parish church on Saturdays?"

"I help load; I help unload. In, out. Sometimes I get twenty pesos. Sometimes all I get is one of the meal packets. Hey, better than nothing, right, Father?"

Saenz stays in the shadows, listening.

"When you killed the children—what did you use?"

"A knife."

The lack of detail is telling, so Jerome presses him. "What kind of knife?"

"A small one." When Jerome says nothing, the young man tries once more to fill in the gap of silence. "I would offer them something—a soft drink, a cigarette, a snack. When they came with me, I would do it."

"What exactly did you do?"

"I would . . ." He hesitates, and Jerome notes that sweat is beading on his forehead, above his upper lip, along his neck. "I would take off their faces."

"How?"

There is a soft, hesitant rapping on the door. He glances up in time to see Saenz open it a bit, a slice of light coming through the crack. There are whispered questions and answers. The door closes again.

Jerome turns back to Carding. "How did you take off their faces?"

"I would cut them off."

"Using what?" Jerome is pushing harder now, trying to imagine pounding heart, warm, quivering organs, the smell of blood, comparing what his mind conjures up with the reality of this neighborhood tough, with his flat voice and his dispassionate, too-ready answers.

"The knife. I sliced off their faces. I took their hearts; I cut off the boys' . . . things."

"The *boys'* things," Jerome repeats thoughtfully.

But they were all boys.

"And the girls? What did you do with the girls?"

Suddenly Carding sits up straight. He clears his throat and tilts his head to one side, as though measuring Jerome. "But they were *all* boys, Father."

It's as if he'd momentarily forgotten what he was told to say or how to say it and has just now remembered.

Another interruption, but this time there is someone else outside the door: Arcinas, banging angrily on the wood with his fist. "All right, that's enough." The lawyer's voice is muffled, but there is no mistaking the anger in it.

Jerome nods, then stands up. "Okay, Carding. Thank you for talking to me. I'm sorry I took up so much of your time."

"It's okay, Father."

Jerome moves away from the table, then seems to remember something and turns back to the young man.

"Do you realize how serious this situation is, Carding? How much trouble you're in?"

The swollen eyes blink once, twice. Arcinas bangs on the door again.

"I mean . . . You know you could get the death penalty for this, don't you?" There is urgency now in Jerome's voice. "Regardless of what they promised you—you know that it could happen, right?"

The young man swallows, lowers his eyes, stares at the tabletop. "Yes, Father."

Jerome turns around, and although he cannot fully see Saenz's expression in the shadows, they have exchanged the same look of unease. Seconds later, the door is unlocked from the outside, and Arcinas pushes his way in, his face livid.

"What took you so long?" he demands of the priests, as two other men following close behind him take Carding and hustle him out through the other door.

Jerome bites one side of his lower lip, gives Arcinas a look filled with all the scorn and disgust he can muster. With one final glance at Saenz, he brushes past the lawyer and into the hallway without saying a word.

Saenz looks dispassionately at the lawyer.

"The truth, Ben. Sometimes it takes a while."

Then he eases out of the room and leaves Arcinas alone, fuming in the semidarkness.

JEROME SHOVES A cassette into the tape deck of the car as they drive out of the NBI grounds. Saenz grits his teeth and braces himself for some extremely reckless driving. The powerful *presto* movement of the Summer concerto from Vivaldi's *The Four Seasons* blasts through the car's interior.

"You want to tell me where we're going now?" Saenz says, trying to make himself heard above the music.

"We're paying Councillor Mariano's caterer a visit."

AT THE NBI'S parking lot, Joanna Bonifacio has been sitting in the car, waiting for the two priests to leave the building. She watches as they come out the side entrance and proceed to their car, grim faced.

"How come we didn't ambush him?" Leo asks.

A network grunt for over a decade now, having moved up from driver to light man, assistant cameraman to cameraman, Leo is a veteran at shoving microphone and camera lens in the faces of unwilling newsmakers. Murder suspects, government officials involved in various scams, pregnant starlets who only months before were professing their virginity—Leo has hounded these and then some, all in the line of duty. And Saenz is just famous enough to warrant an ambush interview.

But after almost a year of working with Joanna, he knows the ambush is not her style. She finds her own way and usually ends up with footage of raids being conducted, arrests being made, hostages being rescued or released.

"It's not the right time," she says. Joanna can be infinitely patient.

21

THE CATERING COMPANY operates out of the home of Mrs. Erlinda Salustiano. With large sections of roof tile missing and its white paint now a dingy grey in places, the blue-and-white bungalow has seen better days. It's in the Fairview area, straight down Commonwealth Avenue and not too far from Payatas. There's a makeshift *carinderia* set up in front of the gate. It's shielded from the elements by a canvas awning; beneath it, a glass-fronted wooden counter displaying trays of tired-looking pastries. Four sticky, grease-stained plastic tables and their diners take up most of the sidewalk, forcing pedestrians to step down from the curb to get past.

When Saenz and Jerome get there, they find Mrs. Salustiano herself manning the chafing dishes. She's a thin, middle-aged woman with a hard face and greying hair cut in a severe pageboy bob. When they introduce themselves, she looks at them warily but continues to serve customers. Jerome notices she takes an inordinately long time to dole out portions, counting every chunk of meat, every cube of carrot and potato, every chickpea and raisin, every last teaspoonful of gravy, until she is satisfied that she has maximized the cost-profit margin of each serving. Only then will she grudgingly hand it over to the customer. Jerome glances at Saenz to see if he's noted this as well, but Saenz is already grinning at him mischievously. The older priest presses his lips tightly together to keep himself from laughing, because they're here for a serious reason.

It's not a very large operation, she tells them—for sit-down events, they can only handle around one hundred fifty guests. But providing meal packages is much simpler, requiring fewer materials and less manpower.

She's a cousin of Councillor Mariano's assistant, so she

often gets first dibs on any informal catering jobs the councillor's office needs to outsource. The provision of free meals at
the parish church on weekends is one of those jobs.

"Why are you asking all these questions? Was there a problem with any of the meals we prepared?" she asks guardedly,
looking from one priest to the other and back again.

"No, no," Jerome says reassuringly. "Not at all. But we do
need your help with something." He draws a folded piece of
paper from one of his shirt pockets, unfolds and then refolds it
in a different way so that she can see. It's a copy of the charge
sheet against Carding, with a picture of his face on one side,
and Jerome is careful to show her only the picture. "Have you
ever hired this man to help with your deliveries?"

She sets down the ladle she is holding and squints at the
photograph. After a few seconds, she shrugs and says, "I don't
know. I don't go with the van when it makes the deliveries;
I'm far too busy. But my son does." She turns and yells in the
direction of the glass-fronted counter. "Oy! Rommel! Come
here."

From behind the counter rises a head, then the shoulders
and, finally, the torso of an enormous man—just around five
feet eight inches tall, but easily three hundred pounds if he's
an ounce. He looks to be in his late twenties; his eyes, tiny and
black, are set in a pale, doughy face; his body is nearly as wide
as the counter, and he has no neck to speak of.

He looks at his mother in irritation. "What do you want?"
he whines.

"I said, come here," she says, more shrilly this time. "Lazy
clod," she complains to the priests as Rommel lays a handheld video game down on the counter and ambles over to
them. "Nothing but video games all day, all night. Never
helps with either the cooking or the customers." She turns
to face the jiggling mountain of pale flesh that is her son and
waves the piece of paper in front of his face. "Look at this.
You seen him before? At the church?"

He studies the photograph, then looks at her and then back at the photograph, his mouth open and lower lip slack. "Who's he?"

"How should I know?" she asks, her voice rising even higher. "They want to know if he's ever helped you with the deliveries."

Rommel turns to look blankly at the priests. "Why do you want to know?" He reaches out for the paper with sausage-like fingers, but Saenz takes it from Mrs. Salustiano's hand before he can unfold it and study it more closely.

"We just need to talk to him, that's all. We're checking if his family is eligible for the church's Christmas gift-giving program just a few months from now."

It seems to take a moment or two for this to register in Rommel's mind, and while they wait, they are treated to the sound of his loud breathing, his lungs straining to expand against the pressure of his excess weight.

"That looks like Carding," he says. "First few deliveries, he was always hanging around the church gates. So me and Mang Omy, we told him to help unload the boxes from the back of the minicab."

"Who's Mang Omy?" Saenz asks.

"Our driver," Mrs. Salustiano says.

"And Carding—he's been helping you with the deliveries ever since?"

"Yeah."

"Do you pay him?" his mother asks in dismay, pinching his fleshy arm hard. "Out of our profits?"

"He gets a free meal or some pocket change every now and then, Ma," Rommel wails in protest, even as his mother continues to poke and pinch his arm. "Stop that. *Stop.*"

"You lazy—you stay in the minicab, don't you? You let Omy and whoever it is you yank off the street do all the work while you stay in the minicab and play with that stupid thing. You're just like your good-for-nothing father, leaving me to do all the work while you—"

"*Maaa,*" he bleats woefully, and he turns to Saenz and Jerome with a look of supplication. "See what you've done? We were just having a quiet day. Please go away."

"We just want to—"

"We already told you what you want to know, so you'd better leave," Mrs. Salustiano screeches. "We're running a business here." She turns on her son again. "Something which you don't seem to understand. You pick up some layabout hanging around the church and you . . ."

Saenz looks at Jerome; there's nothing more to learn here. They thank Mrs. Salustiano and excuse themselves, but she doesn't pause even once in her rant.

JEROME REMAINS SILENT throughout the drive back to the university, knuckles white as he grips the steering wheel, the car weaving in and out of traffic in near-suicidal bursts of speed. Saenz tries to relax in the passenger seat; from the corner of his eye, he can see the concentration in the other priest's face, knowing only too well that it is devoted to matters other than driving.

When they pull into the parking lot outside the building that houses the laboratory, Saenz gets out of the passenger side, but the younger priest remains in the car, thinking.

Saenz moves to Jerome's side and motions for him to roll down the window.

"You think Arcinas took the path of least resistance."

"He's not a complete idiot. They would have chosen Carding well. They haven't told us much about him other than that he's confessed to the killings. But I'm sure if we checked into his background, we would probably find a repeat offender, someone with a string of sex-related crimes. Molestations, maybe. Flashing."

"We can't ignore the facts. We now have confirmation that he's connected to the meal deliveries."

"But you said it yourself—the community is a closed

system. Carding has lived there all his life. Why is he killing now? What has triggered it that wasn't there before?"

"We don't know everything about him, Jerome. His history, the pressures he's under. It could be anything."

Jerome looks up at him sharply. "You mean, you actually think he's our man?"

"I'm not saying that." Saenz leans against the hood of the car, near Jerome's window. "I'm saying, let's look at everything that we have and don't have. He fits our physical profile of the killer, the height, the build—he even has about a size-six foot, as far as I could tell. Remember the imprint of the rain boot? And then let's consider the things he knows about the killings. He knew what kind of weapon was used. He knew about the faces. He knew about the genitalia."

"But think about it, Gus. They wouldn't even have had to coach him, really. All they had to do was ask stupid questions that gave the details away, coupled with some expertly administered police brutality." Jerome stares down at the steering wheel, trying to organize his thoughts. "But even without that, it's the grey areas that make me wonder."

He pauses, long enough that Saenz has to prompt him to continue. "Grey areas?"

"He kept looking at my ring. That tells me he wants things, material things, a shot at something better in life. He said he killed those kids because he was angry. But his anger was about general things: poverty, his mother being sick, not having a regular job. You don't kill kids because life is hard. You might steal; you might attack a cop. But you don't kill the way our kids were killed: in a highly specific, organized way."

"So what you're saying is . . ."

"I'm saying our man is focused. There's nothing random about his choice of victim. He remembers how many times he's killed. He does it the way he does it for a reason. He sees himself as a victim, sees the killings as some kind of redress.

And he's smart too. You said it yourself—the way the weapon was handled, the way he left little that could be traced back to him, the way the faces were removed—there's a precision, a symmetry to his work." Jerome looks up at Saenz again. "Gus. Do you honestly think Carding is capable of all that?"

Saenz shakes his head sadly. "You already know the answer to that."

At this, Jerome throws his hands up in the air. "Then what do we do?" He looks out beyond the almost-empty parking lot, beyond the street and the buildings, beyond the chicken-wire fences and the traffic on the road outside. "And you know what? We're just days away from the first Saturday of August."

And Saenz finds himself staring off in the same direction, thinking the same thought.

If Carding is the wrong man, another victim is going to turn up soon.

22

SAENZ IS IN the middle of a working lunch in his office at the Anthropology Department when Jerome calls.

"Lunch?" Jerome asks.

"Can't," Saenz says, his mouth full.

"But you're eating already," Jerome protests.

"Susan gave me a peanut butter sandwich."

"You hate peanut butter."

"You're not helping, you know." He takes another bite then keeps talking. "Anyway, can't stop for a proper lunch. Rushing a paper."

"Which one is this?"

"School of Science and Engineering."

"You mean the science and spirituality thing? That's tomorrow morning, isn't it?"

Saenz groans. "I'm supposed to talk for ten minutes."

"Well, how far along are you?"

"I've written about a minute and a half."

Jerome shakes his head. "You definitely don't have time for lunch."

"What, you're giving up that easily? I'm open to persuasion."

"You're less than twenty-four hours away from a ten-minute presentation, and you've only got a minute and a half down. Only thing I'm persuading you to do is to keep working."

Saenz sighs in mock despair. "Some friend you are. Where are you off to? Katipunan?"

"I'm not telling you, because as soon as I say where, you'll be bolting out of your office. Stay put and work on your paper. I'll bring you a doggie bag from wherever I have lunch."

"It had better not be a peanut butter sandwich," Saenz says glumly. Just then, there's a knock on his door. "I've got to go. Someone at the door. I'm serious—no peanut butter or I won't speak to you for a week." He hangs up, then calls out: "Come in!"

The door swings open, and Rommel Salustiano's massive body appears on the other side. He is wearing baggy khaki trousers and a polo shirt that used to be black but has now faded to grey. There are sweat stains on his armpits, collar and chest. He looks dully at Saenz with his tiny, black eyes, his mouth hanging open. Even from this distance, Saenz can see the saliva glistening on his lower lip.

"Mr. Salustiano?" Saenz asks, trying not to sound too surprised.

Rommel spends about half a minute breathing noisily before shuffling through the open door. "Hi, Father." He stops just inside the threshold and doesn't close the door behind him.

"Hello." Saenz rises to his feet slowly, feeling a vague sense of unease. "What brings you here?"

He points with a large finger to a chair in front of Saenz's desk. "Can I sit?"

"Yes, certainly. Come."

The chair is a spindly thing with a wooden back and seat and thin iron legs. It creaks when Rommel sinks into it. This close, Saenz can smell the musty scent of clothing carelessly washed and dried, mixed with the heavily pungent tang of persistent body odor.

"What can I do for you?"

Instead of answering, Rommel reaches out for a plastic canister that holds Saenz's pens and pencils, reading aloud what's printed on the outside: "La Salle-Ateneo Golf Classic." He stares at the letters for some time, still breathing heavily, then puts the canister back on the desk. "You play golf?"

"No, I just like freebies." Saenz waits for Rommel to react, but the man just stares blankly at the mess on his desk. "Rommel, is there anything I can do for you?"

Rommel looks at him, and then the tiny eyes narrow. "You didn't come about the gift-giving program."

Saenz straightens up in his chair, the unease much deeper now. "Excuse me?"

"The other day. When you came by asking about Carding."

He leans back in the chair, and it groans under his weight. "I hadn't seen the news yet when you and the other priest were at the house. I only saw it that same night."

Saenz laces his fingers together on top of the desk. "What news?"

Rommel giggles, a small, high-pitched sound. "Oh, you know what I mean." He half rises from his chair and leans forward, his chest pressing against the edge of Saenz's desk. "You're famous, you know. I didn't recognize you at first. But as soon as I did, I put two and two together." He smiles, his eyes narrowing further even as his entire demeanor grows more animated, more enthusiastic. "I'm sharp that way," he says slyly. "My mother doesn't think so, but I am."

Saenz remains still in his chair, alert to possible danger. Rommel's physique may not fit their profile of the Payatas killer, but Saenz knows only too well that a profile is little more than a series of probabilities, and therefore no profile is completely accurate. "Why exactly did you come here, Rommel?"

Rommel snickers. "The police and the NBI say Carding killed those kids." When Saenz doesn't say anything, he snickers again and then bestows a bright smile upon the priest. "But you don't think so, do you?"

The unease in the pit of Saenz's stomach has turned into fear. If Rommel were to try to harm him, he could probably fight him off, but Rommel has youth and bulk and unpredictability on his side. "Rommel, I've really got nothing to do with—"

"Because he's not smart. Right? You don't think he's smart enough to have done all that." Without warning, he reaches out and touches Saenz's computer monitor, turning the screen a few degrees toward him. But Saenz quickly stands and moves the monitor back to its original position.

"Look, I'm really busy right now," he begins, but Rommel cuts him off again.

"Who do you think did it? I mean, you must have some

idea. They say you're one of the best; that's why the police keep calling on you."

At that moment, Saenz sees Jerome framed in the open doorway. "I thought I'd go for pasta—Oh." He stops short at the sight of Rommel.

"Jerome," Saenz says, and there is more than a slight note of relief in his tone. "You remember Mrs. Salustiano's son."

Jerome looks at Saenz, then back at Rommel. "Yes, I remember. What's up?"

When Saenz looks at Rommel again, he is back to staring blankly at the things on the desk. "Hi, Father." He stands and lumbers toward the door, briefly giving Jerome an unpleasant whiff of his body. "Gotta run. Maybe I'll see you both at the church sometime." And he's gone, his broad shadow gliding along the walls of the corridor.

Jerome turns to Saenz, confused. "What was that all about?"

"I have no clue," Saenz says, frowning. "But it's certainly the most surreal visit I've had in this office in a long time."

Jerome steps back out into the corridor briefly, checking to see if Rommel has indeed left. Then he reenters the office and closes the door, locking it. "Did he threaten you?"

"Not really. But he was behaving quite oddly." Saenz sits down. Rommel's visit has left him more than a bit shaken. Jerome scans the desk, finds a glass of water beside a small dish holding a half-eaten peanut butter sandwich and hands Saenz the glass. The older priest takes a few sips and sets it back down on the desk.

"You think he might know something about the killings?" Jerome asks.

"Even if I did, we don't have anything on him but the fact that he's involved in the meal deliveries. And with the NBI satisfied that they have the right man—"

"Not the entire NBI. Just Arcinas and his allies."

Saenz nods. "Right. Still, I don't think we'll be able to do much at the moment but keep Rommel in mind for future questioning."

23

DODONG HAS HAD a tooth out earlier today, and now the empty space in his gum is throbbing.

Maybe I should get some ice, he thinks; at one peso per plastic bag, it is Payatas's pain reliever of choice. The boy fishes in his pockets for some loose change and counts out his money as he walks down the empty street, to the only *sari-sari* store he knows will still be open at this time of the night.

He is small for fourteen, but his legs are starting to gain some muscle. They carry him quickly now over the dust and the pebbles and the puddles of oily water to Aling Pepang's.

He stops suddenly and turns around. "Sssst," he hisses, "who's there?" No answer but the barking of the neighborhood's mangy strays. The shanties, with their rusty corrugated-metal roofs and their walls of cheap plyboard and scrap wood, are some twenty meters away. The narrow, unpaved path that passes for a street is deserted. The ooze and stench of the landfill seeps through the ground, weaves through the air, a constant phantom presence.

Dodong stands completely still for a moment, listening, waiting. There's been talk of boys disappearing, hushed whispers about someone, man or monster, who steals them away from the streets and the storefronts and the safety of their homes and discards what is left of them in the dump.

Dodong doesn't want to believe any of it, the idle talk of the old ladies with their mouths full of pins, of the young women sitting on the steps of their houses picking lice out of each other's hair, of the men steeped in their gin and spouting nonsense.

Now, thinking about the talk and the friends who have gone missing and the dark empty street before him, something—some cold foreboding—sweeps over the crests and ridges of his brain, and he shivers.

He keeps walking, but as he walks, he again notices the dull pain of something no longer there in his mouth, and the tip of his tongue flicking again and again, curious and unaccustomed, to that pulpy emptiness.

A few moments later, Aling Pepang's store is in plain sight. But it is closed; none of the men had money for the usual beer revels tonight.

The fear sweeps over him again like wings, coming quickly, gliding away, swooping back down.

He turns back hurriedly and stuffs his coins down the right pocket of his shorts. But there is a hole at the bottom of the pocket, and the coins slide out. He stoops with a muttered curse to pick them up one by one from the dirt and the pebbles.

He looks up too late. He sees the rock, descending as if from the night sky, but not the hand that holds it.

WAKING UP BREATHLESS and in terror as if from a bad dream.

He does not know where he is. His left eye feels very strange, the lid thick and heavy, even though his right eye seems to be open.

He tries to touch it but he cannot move his hands.

Something in his mouth. He whimpers. A rag of some kind, smelling foully of gasoline and old blood.

Where is he? Lying on his back on the floor of a dark room?

He tries to calm down, tries to orient himself with his surroundings, with his own body, which feels curiously heavy and unresponsive. Yellow light, then blackness. Yellow light, then blackness. The pain in his left eye, intensifying as he becomes more aware.

Yellow light, then blackness.

Is the room moving?

He tries to sit up, but the pain in his left eye, in the whole left side of his head, is unbearable. He starts to panic. No, no, no.

Yellow light, then blackness.

Then blackness.

Okay, it's okay, sssshhhhh. Yes, I know it's dark. Isn't it better? It's always better when it's dark because nobody can see you, nobody can watch you. No, don't cry. It's your fault. See, all I wanted was to be left alone, but you kept looking at me, following me with your eyes, watching me.

See, I wouldn't have to do this if you had just ignored me.

You were there too, anyway. So what made you different? What made you better than me? What gave you the right to look at me and talk about me and laugh at me?

Anyway, it's too late now. Ssshh, this won't hurt. Well, maybe a little, but not for long.

24

Joanna gets the call at three thirty in the morning. Her contact at the Quezon City Police Department was about to come off his shift when the discovery was radioed in.

A few minutes later she is on the line with Leo, who has been roused from sleep by his young wife. Whispered instructions, where to meet, what equipment to bring. Then Joanna replaces the receiver in its cradle.

The man lying beside her stirs, then turns to her in the semidarkness.

"Again?" he asks sleepily. She kisses him on the forehead, strokes the soft, light-brown hair cut close to the scalp and caresses the broad barrel chest by way of an apology.

In his line of work, nobody ever calls in the dead of night. Still he forgives her for her sudden departures.

His large, powerful body is always invincibly warm in this freezing room; he likes to turn up the air conditioning and have her burrow into his warmth. For a few moments she considers staying here, her cheek against his chest, letting his heartbeat lull her back into warm, safe sleep. Then, very reluctantly, she sits up.

She watches the outline of his body under the covers, and out of habit she reaches out and runs the soft, fleshy pad of her right thumb across the long, brown lashes of his left eye. The eye shuts tighter as the other one opens. Green flecked with gold, catching what little light there is in the room.

"Give me one good reason."

She cannot think of anything to say.

"Thought not."

The huge hands with their thick fingers come up behind her head and pull it against his chest. She breathes him in, the smell of soap and warm skin and cigarette smoke. She loves the smell of him, even if she is allergic to secondhand smoke. He cannot, will not stop smoking, and she has to take antihistamines before she sees him. Small sacrifices, like not being able to go out with him in broad daylight, the slight twinge of envy she feels seeing lovers walk through malls and parks with their arms locked around each other. His daylight hours do not belong to her, and neither do these nights; she steals them like a common thief from a wife and children whose faces and names she does not want to know.

Someday soon these sacrifices will not seem so small, and these nights will not be enough. She cannot bear the thought of that day coming, and yet somehow she cannot wait for it to come.

His arms tighten around her so quickly and so intensely that she has to suppress a gasp. Then he relaxes his hold and pats her bare bottom. *All right*, he is saying. *Get going if you must.*

She lingers a few seconds more, then unwillingly leaves the bed, heads for the bathroom and steps into the shower. She stands under the hot spray for a long time, wondering how she came to be here, why all her choices have led to this exact circumstance, leaving the married man in her bed in the middle of the night to rush to where a child lies dead.

She closes her eyes and musters all her will not to think this particular thought anymore.

Still a bit groggy after her shower, she returns to the bedroom. She gropes in the dark for her jeans, pulls them on, snaps on her bra. Throws on a shirt and finds her shoes.

"It'll be wet and miserable out there, buddy," he mumbles reproachfully.

Sometimes he talks to her like she is a man. It does not matter. He does not touch her like she is one.

"I know," she answers so quietly he cannot have heard.

She closes the bedroom door behind her. Her wallet and

keys are on the side table in the hall, and she sweeps them up with one hand. She yanks her raincoat off the hook on the front door and leaves the apartment.

THE POLICE HAVE already arrived by the time she and Leo get there. A small crowd of about fifteen, twenty people from the neighborhood has formed not far from the line of police cars. After a few questions, Joanna learns that the body has not been recovered yet, that the crime scene has not even been cordoned off. The policemen themselves are in a tight huddle around their vehicles, drinking coffee, talking to the trash picker who found the body. Clearly, they are waiting for something—crime scene personnel, most likely.

She turns to Leo. "You think we can get up there?"

"Dangerous in the dark," Leo answers, but he's already hoisting his heavy camera up onto his shoulder.

"We might not get another chance."

"Then let's do it."

They quickly discover how difficult it is to get up the mound of trash. Every foothold is precarious, every step a struggle for balance atop the shifting garbage and sliding mud. And yet they're only at the fringes of the landfill. At the very center, the mass will, in theory, be even more unstable: loose garbage on the surface, layers and layers of compacted, rotting garbage in the middle and, at the bottom, a pool of filthy leachate. Now Joanna understands why the most effective trash pickers are children and small teenagers: the lightness of their bodies allows them to tread nimbly over this treacherous landscape.

After what feels like hours, she is standing bareheaded in the drizzle, looking down at what is left of a young boy of about twelve or thirteen years old after two or three nights out in the dump.

Leo is stepping carefully around the body according to her

instructions. Nothing must be disturbed. The porta-light shines dull yellow on the ruin of the boy.

The rats have gotten to the body.

There is neither face nor heart, the latter removed through a gaping hole in the chest. She bends forward to examine the body more closely, hands thrust deep in the pockets of her jeans, taking care not to pitch forward.

Same technique, same timing.

So many wounds, but so little blood. Was he killed here, in the dump? Was he hunted, running in the dark, through the garbage?

The moment of falling. She remembers a Jacopo Pontormo drawing in black chalk, the strokes so faint that the figure is hardly visible. What was it called? *Il giocatore che inciampa,* "Player Tripping Up": the terrible dismay in the wide eyes, in the open mouth. The helplessness in the outstretched arm. *Is that how you looked when he finally caught up with you?* she asks the dead boy, then straightens up.

Suddenly it seems very cold.

A large black rat is caught in the beam of the porta-light. Leo says, "Shoo!"

The rat stands on its hind legs and raises itself up higher, sniffing the air. Studying the light with bright, black, curious eyes, unafraid.

Suddenly, a voice booms out at them. "Hey, you're not supposed to be here." It's a burly plainclothes policeman, panting from the exertion of getting up the mound. He lumbers toward her, grabs her by the arm.

The rat scurries off, squealing, squealing.

Joanna yanks her arm away, and the policeman grabs it again. Leo keeps the camera rolling.

"Stop it," she snarls. "Stop touching me."

The cop glowers at her in return. "You're not supposed to be here," he repeats, louder this time, as though he thinks she is either deaf or stupid, or both.

"I got you the first time," she mutters, then turns to Leo. "It's okay. Let's get out of here."

They start down the muddy slope strewn with garbage, and Leo keeps the porta-light turned on so they can pick their way through the darkness. She struggles to maintain her balance, her natural revulsion for dirt forcing her to concentrate intensely on her path.

When she gets to the pavement, near the line of police cars, she picks up her pace.

"Ah, Ben," she says aloud once the police are out of earshot. "You've really stepped in it now."

25

BEN ARCINAS ARRIVES at headquarters, out of breath, disheveled, his hair and jacket wet with rain. He was so preoccupied on the drive over, so distracted as he parked and emerged from his car, that he has failed to notice that he is in fact holding an umbrella in one hand, his briefcase in the other. He is only reminded of it when he gets to the glass doors, where he fumbles with the door handle and drops the umbrella.

"*Leche,*" he swears under his breath. He picks up the umbrella, fumbles with the door again, and is surprised when someone holds it open for him. He looks up into the stony face of Jake Valdes.

"Good morning, Ben," Valdes says. "Glad you could make it."

"Of course I could make it," he snaps. "It's my goddamned case, isn't it?"

Valdes wisely refrains from meeting his crossness head-on. Instead, he turns around and says, "Come upstairs with me."

"I don't have time to chitchat with you. I've got work to do. I have to—"

"You have to come upstairs with me." Valdes says it firmly; there's no room for argument.

Still, Arcinas is defiant. "Why?"

"Because the director wants to see you."

He brushes past Valdes, knocking against the deputy director's left shoulder in his haste. "I just spoke with him on the phone on the way here. He knows where to find me."

"I'm not talking about Director Mapa, Attorney Arcinas."

It registers dimly in Arcinas's mind that Valdes has addressed him by a formal title and not his first name. When Valdes walks down the corridor, Arcinas remains rooted where he stands, the knuckles on both his hands pale from gripping the umbrella.

Valdes turns around, his face impassive. "You'd better hurry. You have a lot of explaining to do."

ALL HIS LIFE, Benjamin Arcinas has fought against his circumstances. The youngest son in a brood of nine, he was not going to be like his brothers and sisters, who accepted who they were and did little to better themselves. Not for Ben Arcinas the prospect of a dead-end life in a hovel in Tondo similar to the one where he was born to poor parents. Not for him the eking out of a living selling *balut* and garlic-fried peanuts like his mother and father.

From early childhood, Ben Arcinas showed an unusual fastidiousness in the care of his person and his surroundings. Meticulously sweeping their tiny shack and the even tinier yard outside. Chiding his older brothers and sisters if they left dirty dishes in the sink or came in from work or school smelling less than pleasant.

He scraped up enough money from odd jobs for his first manicure at thirteen. The pleasure of having money and of being attended to as though he were someone important—ah, even after many years he can still remember what that first time was like.

In school Ben Arcinas envied the more well-off students who would come to class in cars driven by their office-worker parents. He wanted to have his own car someday. Perhaps even his own driver.

Young Arcinas knew school was the only weapon at his disposal in a tough world, and he worked hard and long at it. Not brilliant, but with a plodding intelligence that was sufficient to get him through high school with honors and eventually into a third-rate law school. Passed the bar after three tries. Took his family to Ma Mon Luk in Cubao for an obligatory *comida China* celebration from which he excused himself a tad too early.

He went off afterward to his own private celebration with

himself and a bottle of imported, ridiculously overpriced beer in the lobby of a swank hotel. He nursed that beer for hours, ignoring repeated attempts by waitresses to interest him in another one, gazing up at the trompe l'oeil ceilings, watching well-heeled patrons and observing their manners. It was the first of many such celebrations.

Entering the civil service, Ben Arcinas had a way about him that made government employees of lesser aptitude think they were in the presence of someone who was too good for grunt work.

In a politely unbending manner, he would decline to do general tasks like photocopying and filling out forms, assigning them regally to the nearest female, even though certain such females may have outranked him in the *plantilla*. He perfected a smile that was both tolerant and condescending, as he had seen on so many of his bosses, believing that if he acted the part, he would eventually get the part. He devoted his energies to attaching himself to team leaders and supervisors who could further his career, and often they did.

Early in his career, he made a conscious decision to get involved in any capacity in prominent cases that drew the attention of media and of more powerful officials. He learned, quickly and well, how to project and promote himself, how to make each small achievement seem much bigger than it really was, how to grab credit and deflect blame.

In the few government offices where he has worked, he has always managed to vault over his former superiors, always taken great pleasure in referring to them years later as his "men."

The government has supplied him with a good car, and a driver.

Benjamin Arcinas recognizes brains and breeding when he sees them and always, always seeks to subvert them, even in ways of which he is unconscious. This is particularly true in his current position, were he has attained a measure of status and celebrity. He has paid his dues, has earned the right to have people jump when he snaps his fingers.

These two priests—well-spoken, well-mannered, intelligent beyond any measure he could ever hope to attain—annoy and intimidate him at the same time.

The smile, he recognized early on, would not work on them.

He's seated across from Director Lastimosa now, with Valdes standing at the director's right hand, arms folded over his chest, his expression neutral, as always. Philip Mapa is seated in another chair, and the unfolding scene is a revelation to Arcinas. Mapa has spent most of the last half hour washing his hands of Arcinas and laying the blame for the latest killing squarely at his feet.

"You know, when you told me not to proceed with that news conference, I knew you were right. But Ben here was so insistent that he had the right man." Mapa—his matinee-idol face dark with false concern and anger—points a finger at Arcinas. "You've misled me. You've made fools of all of us, and you've embarrassed the bureau. I'm recommending a suspension pending disciplinary proceedings."

Had Arcinas not seen this sort of thing happen so many times before—often with himself in Mapa's shoes, selling a colleague or a subordinate down the river—he might have been surprised to hear these words coming from the mouth of the man he has served so loyally for so long. But this is how the bureaucracy works, and in its own strange, warped way, it's democratic. The wheel of fortune always turns: today you're stabbing someone in the back; tomorrow the knife is lodged deep between your shoulder blades. Arcinas always had disdain for the people who pleaded for their jobs when their fortunes changed. *You should have some dignity. You should shut your mouth and let a lawyer do the talking for you. If you can afford a lawyer, that is.* He stares down at his nails, trying to stem the rising flood of panic he is feeling at the imminent loss of his job and his stature, trying to calculate whether or not he can even afford his own lawyer.

You should have some dignity. You should shut your mouth.

"Ben?" Director Lastimosa's voice slices cleanly through Arcinas's muddled thoughts.

"Sir. I—"

"You knew your man wasn't the killer. Yes or no?"

Arcinas hesitates. Had he known? Had he really been that desperate? Or did he think that doing things the usual way would produce the required results? "I . . . I thought there was a good chance that he was."

"Based on what evidence?"

"Based on . . ."

"Prior complaints, this says," the director says, leafing through Ricardo Navato's file.

"Yes, sir, and . . ."

"Circumstantial evidence." Lastimosa closes the file, then pushes it away from him. "In other words—nothing."

"That's right," Mapa says, slapping the director's desk for emphasis, then turning to him. "Sir, we should file an administrative case against him immediately—"

"Shut up, Philip."

"Excuse me, sir?"

"You heard me. Shut up."

Mapa is dense enough to feel offended. "But I—"

"Whatever negligence and stupidity Ben here got up to, he got up to under your watch. It's command responsibility, Philip. You might have heard of the concept; if not, I suggest you look it up. It means that if any administrative cases are going to be filed, your name will be right on top of the list."

"My name?" Mapa's voice rises several decibels. "I've got nothing to do with his actions." Then, just as quickly as he lost his temper, he is back to being his unctuously pleasant self. "And don't forget—there are people outside this organization who will be very displeased if I'm dragged into this."

Director Lastimosa glances up at Valdes, and as if on cue, Valdes moves the telephone on the desk closer to him. "You really want to play that card with me, Philip? Fine." He picks up the handset and starts punching out a series of numbers on the dial pad. "I'll call him right now. Let's see if he'll still back you for my position when he finds out what your bright boy here has done."

"Wait," Mapa says. "Who are you calling?"

"Why, our mutual friend in the Palace, of course. Did you honestly think I would allow you to blackmail me with your connections forever?" He presses a button to activate the speaker, and the sound of a ringing phone fills the room. "Shall I tell him that everything Ben here did was not just with your approval but under *your* instructions?"

There's a click, and then a voice at the other end of the line says, "Hello?"

Mapa springs out of his chair and slams his hand down on the hook switch, disconnecting the call. "Look, you old bastard," he says, abandoning all pretense of courtesy or deference, "I won't be bullied by a dinosaur like you. You wouldn't even have this job if I hadn't agreed to wait a few years. I'm what this bureau needs; that's a fact, and the Palace knows it. You belong in a nursing home, if not in a coffin. That's my seat you're occupying, so don't you forget it."

Arcinas is taken aback by this display, so naked in its ambition and bile that even he finds himself revolted. But Director Lastimosa merely sits back and looks at Mapa dispassionately.

"You may go now, Philip."

"I'm not finished—"

"Yes, you are. Jake, would you ask our boys to escort Philip outside? I think we've heard enough from him for one day."

Valdes picks up the telephone handset, but before he can make the call, Mapa strides toward the door, his rage pulsing through the room like a shock wave. He doesn't look back as he opens the door and slams it shut behind him, the force of the act shaking the walls and rattling the picture frames hanging on them.

There is a momentary silence, and then Director Lastimosa turns to Arcinas again.

"You see, Ben? That's what happens when we forget why we're all here. When the little political games we play become more important than the job we're entrusted to do. You used to know the difference. I know; somebody's told me. I would have sacked you on the spot today if that person hadn't interceded on your behalf."

Arcinas's eyes widen. *Who in this whole godforsaken agency would stick up for me, especially now? Nobody has ever really liked me here, and I've stepped on so many toes.*

"You're not sacking me?" he asks, incredulous.

"If you don't cooperate with me, I will. You have a second chance here, Ben, but if you waste it, I'll have no qualms—not just about sacking you, but about throwing the book at you. And don't think you're off the hook with that stunt you pulled either. Another child is dead because you didn't do your job right, and we can't sweep that under the rug. But for now, I'm asking you: are you going to help us—and I mean, *really* help, not just try to advance your own interests?"

Arcinas rises to his feet unsteadily. "Sir, I—I'll do whatever you tell me to."

"Does that include providing the necessary assistance to Father Saenz and Father Lucero?"

He's surprised by how quickly, how easily he is able to say it. "Absolutely, sir."

Director Lastimosa nods. "All right, then. I expect you'll make the calls as soon as you leave my office."

"I will, sir." He stands there another moment, unsure of what to do next.

"Well, what are you waiting for?"

Arcinas nearly trips over his own feet in his hurry to leave. But then he stops and glances back at the director.

"Sir—may I know who vouched for me? I mean—in spite of . . ." He's not quite sure how to finish the question, so he leaves it hanging while he waits for the answer.

The director exchanges a look with Valdes and then sighs. "Perhaps I'll tell you someday, Ben. When you've earned the right to know."

26

SAENZ IS IN the shower, and his CD player is turned way up, Carlo Bergonzi singing Rossini's rousing "La Danza." He sings along with the Italian tenor, his own powerful, resonant voice bouncing off the bathroom walls, *"Già la luna è in mezzo al mare / mama mia, si salterà! / L'ora è bella per danzare / chi è in amore non marcherà!"* while the water beats on the shower curtain.

Suddenly the volume is turned way down. Saenz stops, turns off the shower taps quickly and listens. There is no other sound coming from the bedroom.

The priest draws the curtain aside, reaches for a towel, and wraps it around his waist. He cracks open the door and sees Jerome sitting at the foot of his bed, reading a newspaper.

The younger priest looks up.

"Most stereo component systems come with a control knob that can reduce the volume of even the loudest aria."

Saenz pads out of the bathroom on wet feet. "But I can't hear it from inside the shower," he protests.

"No, but a bunch of very old and very grumpy Jesuits can hear you very well from downstairs." Jerome folds the newspaper. "Heard the news on the radio?"

Saenz nods, then shuffles toward his closet to look for something to wear. "Arcinas called early this morning. Apparently the director came back over the weekend. Severely jet-lagged, still in pain from the surgery and crabby as hell."

Jerome's eyes widen in concern. "What? He's barely three weeks out of surgery. How did he—Nevermind."

Saenz nods. "Here's the rub. He found out even before Arcinas did."

"Oh boy. There's one pair of shoes I wouldn't want to be in."

"Uh-hmmm. I doubt he enjoys being in them himself. What's your schedule look like?"

"I won't be seeing patients until late this afternoon."

"Good. Have you taken a bath?"

Jerome stands and heads for the receiving room. "What, it can't be that time of year already."

MALOU KNOWS HER boss is in trouble—big trouble. He was called to the office at the crack of dawn, and had spent the better part of three hours in meetings upstairs. When he came down, he looked like he had been bullwhipped.

Ill or not, the director is a terrible man to cross.

Now Attorny Arcinas is not taking any calls, certainly not from the media, who have been ringing the office nonstop since after 4 A.M., when news broke that another boy's body had been found, and are now camped in the lobby, waiting for him to make an appearance. He refuses to talk to anyone. He has given strict instructions that the only people to be allowed in to see him are the two Jesuit priests and that they are to be ushered in immediately.

Malou brought him a cup of coffee about an hour ago, but he waved it away; she will try to convince him to snack on a cheese pimiento sandwich and a Zesto orange drink from the canteen in about fifteen minutes. She thinks, with an innocent loyalty and concern that would have touched him—if he were the type of person to notice or to care—that maybe a snack will cheer him up.

She glances up at the wall clock every five minutes or so to check the time. When she decides it's time, she puts the sandwich and the drink on a plate and knocks on his door. He doesn't answer. She hesitates a moment and then lets herself in.

Arcinas is sunk in his big leather swivel chair with the blinds on the windows drawn. The chair is bobbing gently up and down with its back to the door.

"Sir, please. Eat something," she says, setting the plate down on his desk and sliding it closer to him. When he doesn't respond, she moves closer, steeling herself for his anger. "Attorney?"

The anger doesn't come; in its place is a numb dullness, as though all his sharp edges have been blunted by whatever it was that took place in the director's office.

"Sir?" she says, tapping him gently on the shoulder and then gesturing toward the plate.

He stares blankly, first at her, then at the plate and its contents.

"I don't . . ." he begins, and then his voice trails off.

Malou takes the sandwich, still wrapped in plastic wrap, and puts it in his hands. "Have a sandwich. You'll feel better." She waits a few seconds, and when he doesn't toss the sandwich away, she takes the drink pack, pulls off the attached straw and punches it through the hole on top.

"I've done something wrong," he says.

She nods. "You wouldn't be the first," she says, handing him the drink.

"You don't understand." He refuses the drink and sets the sandwich back down on the plate.

"Yes, I do," she says. "I'm retiring next year, Attorney. I've seen all sorts of people come through this agency. People who are happy to sit around and just wait for the next paycheck, and people like you who want something more."

When she sees that he's listening to her—really listening, for the first time perhaps in the eight years she's worked under him—she's emboldened to speak her mind. "You think you're the only one here who's done stupid things, even bad things, to get ahead? You can't spit in this building and not hit someone who's done the same, or worse." Malou smiles, half-bitter, half-resigned. "You think anyone's going to remember any of this a year from now? No. Only the small folks like me remember, and nobody pays any attention to us anyway. The people on top—people like you—you'll all have bigger things to worry about soon enough. That's the way it goes. The wheel never stops turning." She takes the sandwich and shoves it back in his hands. "Now eat something, before those priests get here."

⌣

IN THE CORRIDOR on the way to their meeting with Arcinas, Saenz puts his hand on Jerome's arm and they stop. "He'll probably ask us back."

"Not that he could ever have fired us."

"This is true. If he does ask, will you be nice?"

Jerome sniggers. "Goodness, no."

Saenz sighs. "I had to ask. Diplomatic at least?"

"Can I gloat for a few minutes?"

"Jerome. A child died to prove us right."

It's a sobering fact, and Jerome reluctantly puts away his feeling of vindication.

They find the secretary absent from her usual place in the anteroom. Saenz peers through the open blinds on a glass window cut into the front wall of Arcinas's office. Today the attorney looks different. Saenz notes that the languid, reptilian look has been replaced by a kind of troubled alertness. Even his very hair seems distressed, sagging instead of curling up and around his head in the usual manner. The manicured nails tap nervously on the glass-topped desk.

Saenz raps on the window to catch Arcinas's attention. When he sees them, he practically jumps out of his seat and throws the door open.

"Gentlemen . . . Father Saenz . . ."

Jerome flops down into one of the chairs without being asked, props his left foot up on his right knee, his fingers drumming a quick rhythm on the tattered leather armrests. "It looks like you have a situation here, Attorney."

Arcinas clears his throat. "I . . . we . . ."

"Apologize?" Jerome asks.

"We appear to have . . ."

"Found another victim?" Jerome offers helpfully. "Arrested the wrong man?"

Arcinas wipes sweat from his brow with his bare hand. His

foundation, applied hastily with unsteady fingers as he tried to calm himself down earlier this morning, is now caked with perspiration and oil.

"The boy—we were lucky that he was found so soon. His parents were able to identify him at once." He holds a thin folder out to the older priest, and Jerome notices that the hand is shaking a little. "His name is Conrado Sacobia. Went by the name Dodong. He lived in Manggahan."

"We would be happy to extend any assistance to you, Attorney. Give us a little time to study this, and we'll be in touch soon." Saenz stands, takes the folder and shakes Arcinas's hand firmly. "All right, Father Lucero, let's get back to work." And he hustles Jerome out of Arcinas's office.

In the parking lot, Saenz says, "You're awfully quiet."

Jerome unlocks the car door, his face glum. "Still think you should have let me gloat a little."

I feel so much better today. So light and unencumbered. I think I can actually get through the day, through the rest of the week.

I am filled with an astounding sense of peace.

I wish it could be like this everyday.

27

AT THE NETWORK, Joanna has decided to skip lunch in favor of previewing Leo's tapes from the crime scene. Bleary-eyed from lack of sleep, she nurses a large mug of industrial-strength coffee, flouting company regulations against bringing food and drinks into the preview or editing suites.

Leo comes in, claps her on the back. "Hey, Boss. How is it?"

"It's too damn dark."

The cameraman peers at one of the two preview screens. "Hmmm," he says, feigning grave concern. "Must be because we shot it at four o'clock in the morning."

"Shut up."

The camera moves slowly up the length of the child's body, from the feet up to the ruined face.

"We've got to mosaic that," she says, taking down the time code on the tape.

"Black and white," Leo suggests. The network has an unwritten rule that gory news footage should be altered so as not to offend the sensibilities of viewers.

"If we take it to black and white, you can still see—" Joanna begins. Then off-camera they hear the policeman's voice.

"Hey, you're not supposed to be here."

The camera lens, which had moved from the child's head over to the area around the body, sweeps up in a sudden, jagged movement to Joanna and the approaching policeman.

"Wait, wait," she says, reaching out to stop and rewind the tape.

"Why?" Leo asks.

She watches again as the scene is replayed. "There, look," she says, tapping the screen with a forefinger. "Did you see that?"

"What?"

She stops, rewinds, taps the screen again. "There. That thing. Just before the camera moves to me."

Leo knits his brows, still not seeing anything. "Try a slo-mo?"

She slows down the tape speed so they can view it frame by frame. Moving from the child's head to the ground around the body. A rat comes into view. The rat rears up on its hind legs, snout in the air, whiskers twitching, beady, black eyes registering red.

Garbage, mud. The policeman's voice, garbled to a low snarl by the much slower playback speed.

Then the glimmer of something in the mud. Less than twenty frames, then the camera whips to Joanna.

Joanna fiddles with the preview knob again.

There it is. Something thin and metallic, not too long, protruding from what looks like a black tube.

"What is it?" the cameraman asks.

"I don't know. Could be just scrap. Seems pretty out of place there, though." She sits back, frowning. Takes a sip of coffee. "Leo, can you dub a copy of that for me? I need to go and take a shower; then I'll swing by and pick it up."

"Sure. What are you going to do with it?"

She stands and heads for the door. "Go to confession, I think."

JEROME IS IN the middle of routine paperwork for the university when Joanna stops by. She knocks on the door of his faculty office, then opens it without waiting to be acknowledged.

"Hey, Father Lucero," she says.

He looks up. "Miss Bonifacio."

"How's it hanging?"

"Vertically, last time I checked. What can I do for you?"

She chuckles, pleased that the priest can give as good as he gets. She comes into the room, pulls up a chair and makes herself comfortable.

"Father Gus isn't in his office, and he's not at the lab. So I thought I'd come and see you instead. We were up at the dumpsite. Leo and I. When they found the body."

"Ah."

She unzips a capacious black backpack, retrieves a VHS tape from its depths and slides it on the desk toward him.

"We managed to get about four minutes of footage before the police kicked us off the dump. Leo picked something up on tape that I thought just didn't belong there. Looks like some kind of pick or probe. Thought you and Father Gus might want to take a look."

Jerome leans forward and picks up the tape. "Thanks. Can we keep this for a while?"

"It's all yours. We have the original in the office." She stands. "Tell Father Gus if the both of you figure out what it is, I'm buying lunch."

Jerome stands up as well. "Thank you, Joanna. We'll get on this right away."

With a wink, she is gone.

HALF AN HOUR later, Saenz swings by Jerome's office from a faculty meeting.

"Starving," he announces in a booming voice.

Jerome picks up Joanna's VHS tape and waves it in the air. "From Joanna," he says, and Saenz scowls.

"I can't eat that."

"She stopped by. Wants you to look at this. It's from the crime scene this morning."

Saenz's expression changes to keen interest. "So she was there. Where she wasn't supposed to be."

Jerome nods. "Said their camera caught something in the dumpsite that didn't look like it belonged there."

"Have you looked at it?"

"Thought I'd better wait till you got back." He takes the tape, wheels his office chair toward the television and VHS player set up on one side of the room and slides the tape into the player.

The footage is raw, unedited, unaltered in any way, so when the camera first pans to the boy's body, both Saenz and Jerome are jolted, even though they have been bracing themselves for the sight. They exchange quick glances, then continue watching. The camera moves slowly and smoothly at first, but then the motion becomes abrupt and jerky each time the camera-man moves to a different position around the body.

"Wait, what's that?" Saenz asks, pointing at the screen.

Jerome looks. "What's what?"

"After the rat. Can you rewind it?"

Jerome rewinds the tape, but the footage moves too fast for him to see what Saenz is pointing at. "What is it?" He rewinds again, cross with himself that he can't make anything out. On third viewing, he catches a glint from the camera's portable light bouncing off something half-buried in the mud. "Wait, was that it? What *is* that?"

Saenz is already halfway to the door. "Bring the tape. We're heading to the NBI."

ABOUT THREE HOURS later, they're sitting across a wooden table from Ading Rustia; he's just viewed the tape several times, and the look on his face is bleak. "None of my boys worked the scene last night. I mean, this morning. It was handled by Quezon City police," Rustia says. He sniffs. "Not very good for you."

Saenz nods. "I've already asked if they took photos or found anything at the site. No to both."

Rustia snickers, a curious clicking noise. "Huh."

"Can we do another search?" Jerome asks.

"We could try. But it would have to be done quietly. The QC boys get very annoyed when anyone steps on their turf."

"Would you work it for us?"

Rustia's hand glides over the desk, then pulls a clipboard

over to him. "The earliest I could do it is early tomorrow morning. I think I had better do it alone, though. I trust my boys, but any leak could make life difficult for me."

Saenz stands up and holds out his hand. "Thanks, Ading. I really appreciate it. Will you let the director know yourself?"

Rustia's tiny hand is completely engulfed in the priest's large one. "Yes. Maybe I'll get a promotion. What do you think?"

28

AT THE LABORATORY the next day, the telephone rings as Saenz is examining the remains of a man believed to have been "salvaged"—summarily executed—by government troops some twenty years before. The man was a twenty-three-year-old community organizer and activist in the province of Nueva Ecija. Suspected of ties with the Communist New People's Army, he disappeared after a lightning rally of farmers and students in Manila in the early 1970s and had not been heard from since. His family believed he had been rounded up by the Metrocom, along with a few other activists and students who had taken part in the rally. He was one of the thousands—fifteen hundred by one count, more than three thousand by another—who fell victim to salvaging. It was a term perverted by the regime's goons to refer to the extrajudicial killings that had become a dirty open secret of the dictatorship.

Saenz had been involved in the mapping and exhumation of the man's burial site in the hills to the east of Nueva Ecija a few months earlier. After several procedural and logistical delays, the remains finally arrived in Manila last week.

Saenz has spent most of the morning sorting, cleaning and laying out the bones into the framework of a human skeleton. He has arranged most of them in the same position in which they were found, cross-referencing his work with a series of photographs taken of the remains during the exhumation process. But there are still a few loose bones that he has yet to put where they belong.

At the sound of the telephone, he sighs, carefully laying a carpal bone to one side. "Great timing," he grumbles. Seated on a tall stool with casters, he pushes himself away from the table where the man's remains are laid out and strips off one rubber glove to take the call.

"Saenz," he answers gruffly.

"Before you yell at me, you should know that I have food," Jerome says.

"Do you intend to bring it over?"

"Not if you yell at me."

"You have my solemn word that there will be no yelling if food is brought over."

"Ten minutes."

Saenz hangs up. He puts the glove back on and returns to the table. At the time of the exhumation, it had seemed to Saenz that the man had been shot in the back of the head while his arms were tied behind his back. Looking at the skull now, it appears that the man had been kneeling; it's an initial observation that Saenz will seek to verify when he examines the bullet trajectory later. There are green stains on the skull, mainly concentrated around the bullet hole itself—the patina of copper sulfate from the corrosion of a copper bullet. He reaches for one of the photographs to check the exact position of several strands of rotted rope that had been found with the remains. From what he can gather, the strands would have lain against the small of the man's back, where his wrists had been tied together.

But before he can position the strands, someone knocks on the door.

"*Ayayay*," he mutters in exasperation, then strips off his gloves and pushes himself away from the table again. He gets up and walks to the door.

"I thought you said ten minutes?" he says as he opens it. Immediately his nostrils are assaulted by the unwashed smell of Rommel Salustiano.

"Hello, Father."

Saenz tries to conceal his surprise. "Rommel. Hello." He's immediately on his guard, apprehensive. "What brings you here?"

"Can I come in?"

Saenz casts a quick glance over his shoulder at the table where the skeleton is laid out. "Listen, I'm afraid that I—" he begins, but Rommel is already walking through the door.

"So this is where you work," he says, running his fingers along the edge of a desk, then ambling over to one end of the room to stare at one of the da Vinci studies on the wall.

Saenz stands behind him, feeling a mounting sense of unease. "Sometimes, yes. Is there anything I can do for you, Rommel?"

The young man shifts his attention from the wall to focus fully on Saenz. "I was right, wasn't I?"

"Right about what?"

"Carding." He breathes heavily for a moment, then comes closer to the priest. "I asked you if you really thought he killed those boys." He tilts his head, studying Saenz's face with a smile. "But you never believed it, right? I didn't think you did. And then, so soon after the NBI boasts about his arrest, another victim turns up." By now the smile is gleeful. "Told you he wasn't smart enough to have done all that."

Saenz steps back, careful not to make hasty movements. "Rommel, I'm afraid I'm not at liberty to discuss any of these issues with you."

Moving surprisingly quickly for his size, Rommel steps into Saenz's personal space, his flabby face mere inches away from his own. "Just tell me, okay? Just admit you didn't think he did it. You knew it was someone smarter, right? Someone who could plan and calculate."

Seconds tick by as Rommel breathes onto Saenz's face. His tiny eyes are alight with an unnerving intensity.

And then Rommel turns away and heads straight for the table where Saenz is working. Before Saenz can stop him, he picks up a bone—the dead man's left femur—then points it straight at the priest. "Because if you didn't know—if you believed that it was Carding—well, you're not very good at what you do after all, are you?"

"Put the bone down, Rommel," Saenz says calmly.

"What?"

"The bone. Put it down." More firmly this time.

Rommel looks down at the femur in his hand as though he's perplexed at how it got there. Then, he takes a few steps closer to Saenz with the bone outstretched. Saenz steels himself to parry a possible blow when he hears Jerome's voice at the door.

"*Pancit canton* and—" he announces ceremoniously, holding his arms up with plastic bags of takeout in his hands. But at the sight of Rommel holding the bone to Saenz's face, his expression changes, and he raises his voice sternly. "What the hell is going on here?"

Rommel's face goes blank at once, as though a lightbulb has been switched off inside his head. Instead of hitting Saenz as he appeared ready to do mere seconds ago, he hands him the femur slowly.

"I was just returning this bone to Father Saenz."

Saenz takes the bone and moves carefully away from the sweaty giant, eyeing him distrustfully.

"I think it's time you left, Rommel," he says.

Rommel nods, then lumbers toward the door, Jerome stepping aside to let him pass.

He's already outside the door when he turns around to grin at both priests.

"I was right," he warbles. "You know I was right." And then he's gone.

Jerome closes the door and locks it, then sets the food down on a desk and rushes to Saenz's side. "Are you all right?"

Saenz nods, putting the femur carefully back in its place. "I'm fine. But two unexplained visits from Rommel Salustiano—"

"—is two unexplained visits too many," Jerome says. "That was definitely a threat. Right?"

"I'm not sure if that was a threat, to be honest." He heads to the desk and picks up the phone. "But after this second visit, I am sure of one thing: I'd be an idiot if I didn't tell Arcinas to check on his background and his whereabouts last Saturday."

A frown creases the space between Jerome's brows. "He doesn't fit our killer's profile—at least, not physically."

"No, he doesn't." Saenz shakes his head. "But that behavior just now? That wasn't normal." He begins punching out numbers on the phone. "And you know what? I would hate to be so attached to the profile that we won't consider any other possibilities."

29

SUSAN IS RUSHING back to the department to get some papers photocopied when she bumps into Saenz; he's emerged from his office in search of coffee.

"What are you doing?" she demands, eyes wide with alarm. "Why are you still here?"

Saenz looks down at her, equally alarmed by her expression. "Why? Where am I supposed to be?"

She lets out a tiny squeal of frustration and hustles him back through the door of his office, a woman barely five feet tall shooing a six-foot-something chicken back into its coop. Once inside, she begins to shuffle through the chaos on top of his desk.

"*The Magic Flute!*"

"The magic what?"

She finally finds what she's looking for and fishes out an envelope from beneath a pile of correspondence. She spends another few seconds locating a letter opener, leaving Saenz momentarily concerned that she plans to bury it in his chest. Instead, she uses it to rip the envelope open. "You're supposed to be at the CCP tonight! *The Magic Flute!*" She waves the envelope at him. "See? You've got tickets!"

"I do?"

"*Hay, naku.* Look," she says, gesturing at a suit bag hanging from a hook on the whiteboard behind him. "Remember? I made you bring that extra shirt two weeks ago because I knew you'd forget to bring one today."

"Was that supposed to be tonight?"

She rolls her eyes. "No, I'm just trying to annoy you for no good reason. Yes, it's tonight! And don't pretend you don't know."

"But I don't even like opera," he protests weakly. By this time, he's already remembered that he was supposed to go and already figured that he can't possibly bamboozle Susan.

She sticks her hand into the mess on his desk once more and yanks out from within it a CD of Strauss's *Der Rosenkavalier*. "Yes, you do," she says, thrusting it under his nose as proof.

"I don't like Mozart," he moans, even more weakly this time.

She wags a finger at him as she might do with a spoiled child. "Mrs. Iwasaki from JapanConnect sent you those tickets, and she expects you to be there. I don't need to tell you how much we need their sponsorship right now. Which reminds me, where's Father Lucero?" When all she gets from Saenz is a blank look, she throws her hands up in the air and then picks up the phone on his desk. "Between the two of you, I'm going to have a heart attack," she grouses. "Father Lucero? Where are you? Do you know that you're supposed to be on your way to the CCP with Father Gus?" A pause. "What do you mean, '*when*'? Right now! It's the gala premiere of *The Magic Flute*!"

Saenz scowls. "I have no clothes for a gala of any sort," he mumbles, but loudly enough for her to hear. "And neither does he."

She scowls right back. "A clean, well-pressed shirt will do," she tells him firmly. "And as for you, Father Lucero," she says into the phone, "you're to bring the car around in ten minutes. Or else." She puts the receiver down and circles around the desk to shoo Saenz out of his chair. "You have no time to just sit around, Father! You've got to change your shirt!" She yanks the suit bag off the hook and shoves it into his hands. "Now! Go!"

When he scurries off to the men's room to change, Susan collapses into a chair, exhausted. "I swear, it's like supervising toddlers," she complains to God in His heaven.

TWO HOURS LATER, Saenz and Jerome are standing behind the banister of one of the sweeping staircases at the main lobby of the Cultural Center of the Philippines. The invitation says 6:30 P.M., but it's past seven, and there's no sign that the performance is about to start. Instead, they're treated to a garish display of Manila's wealthy and powerful—aging socialites and their offspring, politicians, members of the country's business elite and movie stars, all powdered and perfumed, sequined and beaded and embroidered to within an inch of their lives.

"I should have brought a pair of sunglasses," Jerome says.

"You don't own a pair of sunglasses."

"Keep dragging me to these things, and I'll have to invest in one. Heads up. Mrs. Iwasaki's spotted you."

Saenz turns to be greeted by a middle-aged woman in a tailored grey suit. Mrs. Atsuko Iwasaki is a sparrow in the sea of preening peacocks and flamingos around them. Her fine, straight, greying hair is tied back in a neat chignon, and she is wearing the bare minimum of makeup. She bows before Saenz, who bows even lower before her.

"Mrs. Iwasaki, good evening."

"Father Saenz," she says, her voice as gentle and restrained as her demeanor. "Thank you for coming tonight."

"I'm very happy to be here. How have you been?"

"Very well, thank you. We have been busy"—and she looks askance at all the glamorous mayhem around them—"preparing for this."

"I'm sure you've had your hands full."

Mrs. Iwasaki smiles at him, but the smile is tinged with anxiety. "Father, I am happy to tell you that the third tranche of funding for your laboratory will be released very soon. Next week, in fact."

"Thank you." But Saenz detects hesitation in the way she's said it. "But—"

"I am sorry to report that we have had to reevaluate our commitments to various organizations this year." The outside corner of her right eyelid begins to twitch—a tiny, almost invisible flutter of muscle beneath her thin skin. "And the board has decided to reallocate part of your funding to other uses."

Saenz takes a deep breath, lets it out slowly. "I see. How large a part, then?"

"This and subsequent tranches will be reduced by forty percent."

Behind Mrs. Iwasaki, Jerome opens his mouth and starts to say, incredulously, "Forty per—" but Saenz silences him with a sharp look.

"I see. That's quite a substantial amount. Did they say why?"

"I'm afraid I am not informed of all the reasons behind such reallocations at my level, other than that they believe there are more pressing needs." Her language is formal, but her regret and embarrassment are real, almost palpable.

Saenz shakes his head and smiles gently at her. "I understand, Mrs. Iwasaki. Is there any way we can appeal the decision?" But her silence and apologetic smile are answer enough. "Ah, well. These things happen. We'll just have to manage without that forty percent."

"I am truly sorry, Father Saenz. We will communicate this formally next week when we issue the check for the third tranche. I just thought—well, I felt that I . . ."

Saenz realizes that she is deeply saddened by the situation, and he reaches out to pat her arm. "I understand, Mrs. Iwasaki, really. Thank you for letting me know, and I look forward to speaking with you next week. But now let's enjoy the rest of the evening, shall we?" And he flashes her one of those signature Saenz smiles, warm, genuine, devastating. He bows again, and she reciprocates.

"Ah," she says, catching a glimpse of someone in the crowd behind them. "Mrs. Urrutia. She is one of our honorary board members. If you will excuse me, I must assist her."

Saenz and Jerome crane their necks in the direction she indicates. They see the prominent society matron Veronica Urrutia, dressed in a gown of heavily embroidered, magenta silk shantung with elaborate swirls of seed pearls and crystal beads on the neckline, cuffs and hem. The high neck and long cuffs hide a scrawny neck and wrists. Her hair, dyed a glossy copper, is twisted into a vertiginous bun at the top of her head. Once famously dubbed the Philippines' Doris Duke by a fawning lifestyle columnist, the seventy-two-year-old woman is the heiress to a vast retail empire and the mother of an incumbent senator. She fancies herself a philanthropist and gets frequent mention in society columns for one high-profile charity project or another.

To the two priests' dismay, Mrs. Urrutia is slowly walking the red carpet arm in arm with Cardinal Rafael Meneses. Saenz turns away quickly, but Mrs. Iwasaki has called out Mrs. Urrutia's name. Before the two priests can make their escape, they find themselves in a huddle with the socialite and the cardinal.

"Thank you for coming, Mrs. Urrutia." Mrs. Iwasaki also bows to the cardinal. "Cardinal Meneses, so good of you to come too."

"I'm so glad Mrs. Urrutia invited me," he says, beaming, first at Mrs. Urrutia, then at Mrs. Iwasaki. His expression changes only ever so slightly when he turns to Saenz. "Father Saenz. I didn't know you had an ear for opera."

"It depends on the opera. Enjoy your evening, Your Eminence," Saenz says, and steps aside to allow them to pass.

"Oh, is that the famous Father Augusto Saenz?" Mrs. Urrutia trills. "Come, let's have a look at you."

Saenz bristles at her patronizing tone but keeps his tongue in check. "Mrs. Urrutia," he says, bowing slightly to her. "Pleased to meet you."

A bony finger tipped with a coral-painted nail jabs at him. "So you're the one who's been giving Monsignor Ramirez so much trouble."

Saenz's eyes widen, and even Cardinal Meneses appears taken aback.

"Excuse me?" Saenz asks.

"Come, Mrs. Urrutia. I believe seating has started," the cardinal says, trying to usher her toward the middle of the lobby, away from the small group. But she balks at being steered away.

"I'm the chairman of the board of *Kanlungan ni Kristo*."

"I'm aware of that, ma'am," Saenz says.

"I keep hearing of the problems you've been causing us. Especially Monsignor Ramirez."

Saenz straightens up to his full height and looks down at Mrs. Urrutia dispassionately. "Is that so? I wonder then if you've also heard of the problems Father Ramirez has been causing the very children your charity purports to help."

The diamonds dangling from Mrs. Urrutia's ears tremble as she shakes her head vigorously. "No, no, no. All lies. All conjecture. You've not been able to prove a single thing. Now if you could do even a fraction of the good that Monsignor Ramirez has been doing all these years, you might—"

Mrs. Iwasaki emits a small peep of distress and confusion at this rapid and unexpected spiral into unpleasantness. At this, the cardinal tries once more to appease Mrs. Urrutia and guide her back toward the rest of the crowd, which has already begun to stream into the theater's entrances.

"Mrs. Urrutia, it's time that we—"

"Let me tell you this, Father Saenz," she says, refusing to be placated. "A man of God doesn't try to drag his brothers down when they're doing so much to help others."

Out of the corner of his eye, Saenz sees Jerome, so angry that the color of his face is moving rapidly from red to purple. When he opens his mouth to speak—undoubtedly to say something scathing to Mrs. Urrutia—Saenz puts a hand on his arm to restrain him and then looks at Mrs. Urrutia.

"Mrs. Urrutia, a man of God does not help himself while pretending to help others. Good evening." He pivots away from the woman and motions for Jerome to follow him.

But Mrs. Urrutia isn't finished yet. "What goes around comes around, Father. And sometimes it comes around in ways you can't foresee. For example, in the flow of funds that you need to run that amateur laboratory of yours."

A gasp of dismay from Mrs. Iwasaki, and Jerome sees tears spring to her eyes.

Saenz stands very still. The cardinal finally manages to escort Mrs. Urrutia away, and the priest hears Mrs. Iwasaki whisper remorsefully, "I'm sorry. I'm so sorry, Father," before she leaves to attend to other people.

"Gus?" Jerome asks, his forehead creased with concern. "Gus, are you all right?"

"He will be, soon enough."

It's Director Lastimosa in a wheelchair, one of his sons standing behind him. The director has unhooked the loop of his medical face mask from one ear and is doing the same with the other one.

"How—what are you doing here, sir?" Saenz asks in astonishment. "Shouldn't you be at home, resting?"

"And miss this low-key display of good taste, social responsibility and fiscal prudence?" The director's eyes twinkle as he hands the mask over to his son and clasps his hands together over a fine grey *barong*. "I wouldn't even think it."

"Personally, I don't have the stomach for Mozart tonight," Saenz says. He turns to Jerome. "If you want to stay for the performance, go ahead. I think I'll catch a ride back."

"Gus."

"I'm good. I'll see you in the morning." Saenz bows to the director and begins to take his leave. "Director Lastimosa—"

The director reaches out to grasp his hand firmly. "Father Saenz. You surprise me."

Saenz frowns. "I'm not sure I understand."

"Surely you're no stranger to these high-society matrons, with their pet priests and pet cardinals? They underwrite their projects, they fund their charities, they bask in the reflected glory when the priests are elevated to the higher echelons of the Church."

"You mean—you heard all that?"

"Jonathan and I were right behind you. And Mrs. Urrutia is not exactly a quiet woman." The director grasps Saenz's hand and shakes it vigorously, as though by doing so, he will be able to jolt him out of his black mood. "Come now, Father Saenz. The old bat may have won this round. But people like you and me—we win simply by surviving yet another day."

He motions to his son, indicating that he wishes to be pushed toward the theater entrance. "Come, gentlemen. The Queen of the Night awaits."

30

A TROPICAL STORM has brought heavy rains to Metro Manila and other parts of Luzon. Quezon City is a commuter's nightmare, with floods hitting waist-high levels in certain areas, and creeks have overflowed all over the city. Many streets are impassable, and traffic is snarled nearly everywhere. The road outside the university is packed with vehicles.

Saenz and Jerome have decided to wait at the laboratory for the traffic to ease before heading off on personal errands. Saenz is scribbling notes on his examination of the salvage victim's remains. Jerome is curled up on the lab's hideous but comfortable brown velour couch, reading for Monday's classes. They go about their respective tasks in companionable silence.

The peace is disturbed by a knock on the door. They exchange glances, and then Jerome unfolds himself and rises from the couch. He walks to the door, opens it a crack at first and then wider, framing a damp and disheveled Ben Arcinas in the doorway. He is carrying a folded, dripping umbrella in one hand and a blue plastic bag in the other.

"Father," he says to Jerome. Then he looks over at Saenz. "Father."

"Ben!" Saenz says in surprise, getting up to greet him.

Arcinas hands him the bag. Saenz looks inside and finds about a dozen small *monay*, chewy bread rolls with a pale brown crust and soft white insides. Saenz is touched by the gesture and waves Arcinas inside. "Come in, come in." He waits a moment while Arcinas opens up his umbrella and sets it down near the door to dry. "Thank you for these. What brings you here in this weather?"

Saenz hands Jerome the bag, but Jerome eyes it with mild suspicion and sets it down on the couch beside him. Since the murder that came after Carding Navato's arrest, Arcinas has been unusually subdued and cooperative. For Jerome, who

deeply dislikes the lawyer, it has been like dealing with a completely different person.

"You asked me to get my people to check Rommel Salustiano's background and to question him about his whereabouts
on the night of the last killing."

"Yes."

Arcinas takes the seat that Jerome offers him, then looks
around the laboratory for a moment.

"It's a lot . . . smaller than I thought it would be." He says
it softly, with neither rancor nor condescension.

Saenz chuckles. "We've a lot less money than you might
think."

"But don't you—I mean . . ."

"We're good at begging for funds, if that helps," Jerome
offers.

The lawyer is silent for a while, as though weighing what to
say next and how to say it.

"We don't think Rommel is involved in the killings, Father.
Aside from the fact that he doesn't fit your profile—"

"Which we've conceded from the outset."

". . . and that his feet are too big for the imprint we found
at the scene of the sixth murder, he has an alibi for that night.
And pretty much every night one of our kids was killed."

"And that is?"

"His mother. Apparently, they're busiest on weekends, and
they'll take any job they can get. Guy wants to go and have a
life, hang out with friends, maybe meet a girl. But he's pressed
into service all day, Friday, Saturday and Sunday, driving,
helping load and unload, helping set up and dismantle for
catering jobs. The night of the last murder, he was helping at
a wedding."

Jerome leans back on the couch, folding his arms over his
chest. "That's not just the mother covering for her son, is it?"

"We don't think so," Arcinas says. "My boys talked to several people at the wedding—guests, members of the family,

even some of the waiters hired by the Salustianos. He was seen manning the food warmers the whole night. And I mean the whole night—there was dancing and karaoke up until the wee hours."

Saenz frowns. "Just because he was seen doesn't mean he was there the whole night. He could have left, killed the boy and then come back just in time for karaoke."

"The event was in Santa Rosa, Laguna. On a rainy Saturday night. And you know what a little rain does to the traffic on the South Super Highway."

Both priests sigh. "From Santa Rosa to Quezon City and back? In slow-moving traffic, with a murder in between?" Jerome calculates. "Easily three, four hours." He turns to Arcinas. "What else did you find out about him?"

"He's got a university degree but hasn't held a paying job in the last four years. So he helps out with the mother's business instead. Last relationship was more than six years ago. He has a few friends, and they all like to hang out and play video games." Arcinas slides a hand in the pocket of his jeans and draws out a small notebook. He leafs through it until he finds what he's looking for. "He's an only child. The family used to be pretty well off, but the father left them to start a family with another woman when Rommel was in the sixth grade. So the mother had to work to make ends meet. From all accounts, she's been very bitter about things for years."

Jerome looks at Saenz. "I guess that explains the whole 'good-for-nothing father of yours' bit."

"It also explains how a house that big could end up looking so run-down and dilapidated."

Arcinas nods. "Rommel and the business are all she has. And she's got her fingers closed really tight around both of them."

"Did he say why he came here? Twice? And threatened Father Saenz the last time?"

"He says he was curious, and that he wasn't intending to

threaten him. He said he got excited that you came by to ask about Carding. And then he got even more excited when . . ." Here Arcinas pauses, clearly trying to phrase the next part correctly. "When the last boy turned up just after we'd announced Carding's arrest."

Jerome looks skeptical. "That's it? He was curious? Excited?"

Arcinas lifts his hands in a gesture of helplessness: *that's all I have for you.* "To be honest, the way he talked—it seemed like you were the coolest thing to happen to him in years."

Saenz nods. "Okay. I guess that's as far as we can go in that direction."

"You sure?" Jerome asks.

"Until we find something more solid to connect him to the murders, there's nothing to justify pursuing this any further." Saenz extends his hand to Arcinas. "Thank you, Ben. I really appreciate your looking into this for us, and your coming all the way out here to tell us what you found out."

Arcinas stands, shakes the priest's hand. "Thank you for seeing me." He reaches out to shake Jerome's hand as well. Jerome sees him to the door, but Arcinas pauses.

"Look, I don't want you to think that I . . ." It's not quite right, so he begins again. "I honestly thought that I . . ."

Saenz knows what he is trying to say. "Ben, I understand. Look, it's a tough situation all around, and I know you and your boys all have so much to do—"

"No, Father," Arcinas says, shaking his head. "When I found out about the last boy, I just . . . It's not . . . acceptable. And I didn't want you to think that it didn't matter to me." He looks at Jerome. "Both of you." He picks up his umbrella and quickly folds it up. "Well, good night."

Jerome closes the door behind him.

"Well, what do you think?" Saenz tosses Jerome the frayed, green tennis ball he regularly uses as a stress ball, and Jerome catches it deftly with one hand.

"I guess that's a dead end, then? And we're back to square

one?" Jerome sits down on one of the couch's armrests and begins bouncing the ball off the big whiteboard opposite him, with its table of facts about the murders. "What I still can't figure out is, why one victim every month? Why not every week, every two weeks?"

Saenz slides his glasses lower along the bridge of his nose. "We've hypothesized that some circumstance, some aspect of his monthly routine, brings him in contact with his prospective victims during the first week of every month."

Jerome shakes his head. "But he could go back anytime if he wanted to."

Saenz stands and draws closer to the whiteboard, removing his glasses altogether. Absentmindedly, he cleans the lenses with the edge of his shirt. "Or maybe it's some kind of inaugural ritual. You know. Something to start the month off right." He folds up the glasses and slips them into his shirt pocket. "After all, you've already posited the idea that he's able to function normally in society. Maybe he needs to get it done so he can—well, maintain that normalcy for the rest of the month."

Jerome thinks about this and decides that it is plausible. For a few minutes, the *donk-donk-donk* of the tennis ball on the whiteboard is the only other sound in the room, save for the rain.

Saenz moves to the couch and flops down on it with a heavy sigh. Then he sees the bag of *monay* that Arcinas brought with him. He fishes two of the rolls out of the bag, motioning to Jerome to take one and biting into the other. That first bite sends a shock of pain through his right lower jaw as the hard crust presses down on his weak tooth, and he moans, abandoning the roll and rubbing his jaw where the pain is worst.

Jerome shakes his head in exasperation. "What did I tell you about that tooth?"

The older man is rubbing his cheek in a circular motion

with the heel of his left hand. "Nothing I didn't already know."

"How bad is it?"

"Bad enough. I hate hospitals and dental clinics. They give me—" He pauses and then stands. "Wait a minute."

Jerome is concerned. "What's wrong? Is it very bad?"

Saenz hushes him with a wave of the hand. "No, I'm all right. Listen. The police, the NBI have assumed all along that there was nothing by which to identify the other victims, right?"

"No clothing, no parents coming forward, no dental records."

"Yes, but consider this: when Tato and I made casts of the boys' teeth, we found they weren't completely wanting in dental care. Some had rather old fillings; some had undergone proper tooth extractions."

"Right. You told the police and the NBI." Jerome pauses. "But they never followed up because . . ."

Saenz's shoulders sag, and he doesn't need to explain further: it's because these boys were throwaway victims, and the police weren't going to expend more than the barest minimum of effort to find out their identities or who was responsible for their deaths. As for the NBI, Arcinas had frittered away already limited resources on his own ill-conceived investigation.

Saenz continues. "But when we last saw Emil—do you remember? They had one of those community mobile clinics on the church grounds. A clinic that he said had been operating even before he'd been assigned to the parish."

"So you're saying . . . ?"

Saenz is almost vibrating. "I'm saying there's a chance they may have treated our boys"—he takes a whiteboard marker and begins ticking off squares on the matrix—"two, three, five and six."

Jerome stands beside him, concentrating hard on the

whiteboard. "Community clinics, free services. Free services, poor clients. Poor clients . . ." He looks at Saenz, his eyes wide as he comes to the end of his free-associating. "The boys might have dental records after all."

"A service to the living, an unintended service to the dead." The other man has already begun bustling around the room. "I'll get the casts. You bring the car around front."

Jerome is halfway through the door, but then he stops. "Wait a minute. Who are we going to talk to at this time of night?"

Saenz pauses from the task of piling the plaster casts of the victims' teeth into a black leather bag and smiles. "Our friendly neighborhood city councillor."

Jerome grimaces. "He's not going to buy the fundraiser story anymore."

"Then we'll just have to tell him the truth."

JOANNA WATCHES AS Jerome Lucero strides purposefully to his car, climbs in and swings it deftly out of its parking space. *Ah, finally.* She grins to herself. She sits up straight and shakes her head to clear the drowsiness.

Jerome pulls up toward the building entrance and waits, the engine idling. Joanna sees him looking out the car window, surveying the parking area. She is far enough away that he cannot see her.

Now Saenz is coming out of the building with a large black bag. He gets into the passenger seat; the door slams shut, and the car roars away.

Not yet time for Leo, she decides. But she starts up her engine, the blood racing through her brain. The rush is better than any drug.

31

THEY ARRIVE AT Councillor Mariano's home just as he is winding down from a day of relief operations for residents in several flooded areas of the district. He is tired, hungry and irritable.

"First you ask me about the food deliveries. Now it's the medical van." He slides down in his armchair until he is at a comfortable slouch, but the look he gives them is anything but comfortable. "I was wondering why Father Emil wasn't with you the last time you were here, but I let it go because, hey, you're priests. But there isn't going to be any fundraiser, is there? It was just a story."

Saenz leans forward. "I'm sorry, Councillor. It just seemed the best thing to do at the time. I'm sure you've heard by now of the—"

"The Payatas killings, yes. When you called again this evening, I thought I had better get some answers fast. Father Emil told me you were both involved in the investigation. And that you might have been following a lead when you came to ask me about the food deliveries."

Jerome nods. "We wanted to know if there was a link between the food suppliers and the suspect the NBI arrested."

"That Navato guy? The one they had to release anyway?" Mariano snorts. "Did you have something to do with that arrest?"

"No."

Mariano's wife, a pleasant, matronly woman in her mid-forties, comes into the living room, asks him if he wants her to prepare anything for the guests. He asks for coffee despite the priests' protests, and she bustles off into the kitchen.

He waits till he's certain she's out of earshot.

"I understand why you didn't tell me the truth the first time. You didn't know me; you still don't. But one thing you should know about me: I don't appreciate being lied to. Even by priests. Even by priests on important business. From now on, if you need anything from me, you tell me straight. We clear on that?"

Saenz nods. "Very."

Mariano stares angrily at both of them. Then, just when they expect him to send them away empty-handed, his face relaxes a little bit. "Tell me what you need."

Saenz and Jerome look at each other, and then Saenz turns back to Mariano. "We need access to the clinic's dental records."

Mariano sits up straight, lets out a low whistle and begins scratching the back of his head. "You realize those are confidential, right?"

"We need to identify the dead boys. I don't see any other alternative at the moment."

The itch at the back of Mariano's head appears to be growing worse—Saenz and Jerome can actually hear the rasp of his fingernails against his scalp. "You could apply to the courts. It should be no problem for the NBI. I presume you're working with them, right?"

Jerome can hear the words—they're practically a refusal—but something in the councillor's manner and tone of voice, something he can't quite put his finger on, gives him the courage to say what's on his mind. "That could take weeks, sir, and we just don't have that much time." He looks Mariano in the eye. "If we can identify those four boys, we might be able to find out what they had in common. And if we do that, we might be able to prevent another death."

Mariano's eyes look about ready to pop out of his skull. "Four?" he asks incredulously. "Plus the one who . . . Just how many are we looking at, exactly?"

"Seven."

The councillor sinks back slowly into his armchair, stunned and dismayed. "And this is happening in *my* district?" He balls a hand into a fist. "And what have the police, the *barangay* officials been doing all this time?"

Saenz and Jerome say nothing, and that's enough for Mariano, he already knows the answer. He rises to his feet, his small frame stiff with anger, and excuses himself to use a phone on the other side of the room, while his wife brings in a tray of coffee and *lenguas de gato*. The conversation—at least, what they can hear of it—is brief, brisk, efficient.

"Where does she live? Oh, UP Village? Mahusay Street . . . Do you have her phone number? Nine-two-four . . . All right. Can you swing by in about half an hour? Okay. See you then."

He dials another number.

"*Doctora* Panganiban? Yes, ma'am, it's Cesar. How are you? We missed you at the job fair. Well, you know the mayor. He made me promise to bring you next time. Yes, well, I'm sorry it's so late, and on a Friday night, too, but I really need your help. Can you tell me if more than one mobile clinic services the Payatas area? Oh, only that one. That's what I thought. Well, I'm going to have to ask your permission to access the clinic's dental records."

He stops, then glances at Saenz, telegraphing with one look the misgivings of the woman at the other end of the line. "Yes, ma'am, I know they're confidential . . . but you see, some people from the NBI are here. They're conducting an investigation. Yes, ma'am, that problem with the young boy . . . Yes, on television, just the other night."

Mariano turns away from them completely, lowering his voice so that the priests can't make out more than a word here and there. Twice the councillor runs his hand through his Bermuda-grass hair, seemingly frustrated, and the set of his shoulders appears tense. He paces the length of the wall, back and forth, back and forth, as he speaks with the doctor.

Jerome casts a sidelong glance at Saenz. "It's not looking good."

Saenz says nothing, merely waits.

Mariano hangs up. When he looks around and sees the two priests' expectant faces, he holds his hand up: *you'll have to wait; I don't have anything for you just yet.* He resumes his pacing for about a minute or so, and then the phone rings again.

"Well, as soon as possible. Tonight, actually." He begins to nod vigorously. He looks at Saenz again, but this time, to Saenz's relief, his face is less tense. "You can? You will? Of course we can pick you up. In about half an hour? Yes, ma'am. Thank you very much. We'll see you soon."

He replaces the instrument in its cradle and turns to them. "All right, gentlemen. Dr. Panganiban says she has no objections, but it's not solely up to her. The dentist, Dr. Jeannie Santa Romana, has to agree to give you access."

"So what do you suggest?"

"Dr. Panganiban is willing to help us convince Dr. Santa Romana. She's asked her to come to the district health center, where all the records are kept. They're quite close. After I shower and change, we can swing by Dr. Panganiban's house and pick her up. Just wait for me, and we'll all leave together. Excuse me."

As he disappears upstairs, Jerome leans forward to whisper to Saenz.

"Come the next elections, he's got my vote."

32

THEY ARRIVE AT the district health center at midnight in a convoy of two vans and Jerome's car. When Saenz, Jerome, Mariano and Dr. Alice Panganiban, the district health officer, enter, Jeannie Santa Romana is waiting in the center's tiny lobby.

"Jeannie," Alice says, reaching out to hug her. Jeannie allows herself to be hugged, but it's clear from how her hands remain firmly in the pockets of her jacket and the way she tilts only her head toward Alice that there's some resistance to what she's been called here for.

Alice seems to understand this at once. She puts her arm around the younger, smaller woman's shoulders and ushers her toward Mariano, Saenz and Jerome. "You know Councillor Mariano, of course?"

Jeannie gives him a very small smile, a tiny bow of respect, and then extends her hand, and Mariano grasps it in both of his. "Thank you so much for agreeing to meet us here at this hour, Dr. Santa Romana."

She looks at Saenz and Jerome, her eyes wary. "I'm not really sure I understand what's going on."

Mariano takes a step back. "This is Father Gus Saenz. And this is Father Jerome Lucero." He waits for them to shake hands with Jeannie, then continues. "They're helping with the NBI investigation into the killing of that boy in Payatas."

"Alice told me. But . . . I'm not sure I should just give them access to the dental records without a warrant." She turns to Alice with a worried face, seeking her backing.

Alice shoots her a sympathetic look. "*Hija*, I am concerned about that too. But the Councillor says . . ."

The way Alice leaves the sentence hanging, the way everyone around her seems to be burdened by some grave worry, alarms Jeannie. "What does he say?" She searches each face for answers. "What is it? What's going on?"

"It's not just that boy," Mariano says.

"What do you mean? Were there others?" She gleans the truth from their collective silence. "How many?"

"Seven," Saenz says.

Jeannie's eyes blink rapidly. "*Seven?*"

"So far. And there will be more if we don't identify the other dead boys, and find out what they might have had in common."

The young dentist stares at the chipped, scratched blue linoleum tiles on the floor.

Mariano stands beside her, puts a hand on her shoulder. "If you have any doubts, Dr. Santa Romana, I assure you that I will take responsibility for this." He looks at all four of them. "I don't think anyone will question this, but if someone does, I will face them. This needs to be done." He squeezes her shoulder gently. "Look, Doctor. People break the rules every day in public service. Might as well do it for something worthwhile, no?"

"And you're okay with this?"

He nods.

Jeannie stares at him for a moment and then finally appears to have made up her mind. She digs into the pocket of her jacket for a set of keys. "This way."

There is little else for the rest of the party to do once Saenz begins working. The councillor leaves two of his people and one of the vehicles with the priests, then offers to take Alice home. Jeannie insists on staying to help.

In the tiny records section of the community health center, Saenz, Jerome and Jeannie spend long hours studying the dental charts of dozens of patients in the victims' age group, pulling out those whose treatment histories were similar to the information they had on the four unidentified victims' teeth: the shape and material of all restorations, caries, discoloration, malformations, or diseases. They compare these records with the priests' dental X-rays, intra- and extra-oral photographs, master casts.

The work proceeds through the night. At around 6 A.M., Mrs. Mariano arrives in the other van, bringing coffee; thick, hot *champorado*; salted fish; fried eggs. The coffee goes quickly, but the food is left to grow cold. Some of the health center staff—two nurses and a medical intern—arrive to attend to a handful of patients outside, but Jeannie manages to steer them clear of the records room. The center closes early, and they're able to continue working without being disturbed.

By early morning of Sunday, the three are tired and utterly dejected. None of the records on file match the information that they have. When Mariano and Alice drop by, Saenz, Jerome and Jeannie are slumped over tables or draped over hard plastic chairs, worn from lack of sleep.

"What happened?" Alice asks, as Mariano carries in a box of food and sets it down on a desk.

The three stir slowly back to life. Jerome groans, his neck and shoulders stiff, and Jeannie shakes her head sadly. "No luck," she says.

Alice sinks heavily into one of the empty chairs. "Oh my."

Mariano looks at Saenz. "So what now?"

Saenz rubs his eyes with one hand. "I honestly don't know."

Jerome lifts both hands up in defeat. "I'm out of ideas."

Alice gestures toward the box. "Have something to eat, then. Maybe something will come to you." She pushes the box closer to Jeannie. "There are sandwiches there, and juice."

Jeannie opens the box and begins distributing food, and Saenz and Jerome accept gratefully, only just beginning to realize how hungry they are. They unwrap their sandwiches— ham and cheese on buttered white bread—and eat, silent, weary, glum.

Alice rises from her chair with a sigh. "I'd better start putting some of these files away," she says to no one in particular. She takes a small stack of records from a desk piled with them, checks the initials of the surnames, then heads to one of two green metal file cabinets to refile them in the proper drawers. She returns to the desk and picks up another stack. "Some of these are really old. Hope you didn't have to go through all of them."

Jeannie shakes her head. "No. Just the newer ones, where the patients were in the same age range as the victims."

Alice nods. As she refiles the second stack of records, she says, absently, "Wonder if Alex's records are here as well. They probably are, but you know how he is."

"Yeah. They probably are," Jeannie says, preoccupied. "I know he files them there when he remembers."

But Saenz is immediately alert. "Alex? Who's Alex?"

Jeannie glances at him. "Dr. Alex Carlos. He's my alternate. He comes in on days when I can't be here or at the mobile clinic, because I need to see patients at my private clinic in Old Balara." She sees that he's very interested. "Why?"

"Is there a chance that there are some records that are in his keeping, and not here?" Saenz asks.

Alice shuts a drawer. "There is, actually," she says. "He's a good dentist, but so absentminded when it comes to paperwork. Jeannie, he might still have some records in the mobile clinic that he's forgotten to file here."

Jeannie rolls her eyes. "I keep reminding him to do that. Okay, let me call him." She leaves the group and goes to the outer room to make the call.

When she's out of earshot, Mariano faces Saenz and Jerome. "And what if that's a dead end as well?" Their gloomy faces are all the answer he's going to get for the moment, and he doesn't force the question, because he doesn't have any answers either. They wait in silence, the only sound and movement in the room that of Alice's refiling of records. She's made three trips between the desk and the file cabinet before Jeannie returns.

"Alex says he still has a whole pile of unfiled records at the mobile clinic. He's dropping by with them in about an hour."

"What did you tell him?" Saenz asks.

"Just that I was going through the files and looking for the records of some of my patients, so I asked him to bring whatever he still had there."

Saenz says to Alice, "Maybe it's better if you and Jeannie dealt with him by yourselves. I'm not sure anyone else should see us here."

She nods. "Come, Jeannie. Let's just wait for Alex in the lobby."

IT'S NEARLY NOON when Dr. Alex Carlos finally arrives at the health center. Jeannie watches him park his car, get out and open the trunk. He takes out a large cardboard box and heads to the entrance, where Jeannie holds the door open for him.

"Thanks for coming by on a Sunday to bring these in for me, Alex," she says.

"No problem. Records?" he asks, cocking his head in the direction of the records room.

"It's fine. You can just leave them here," Alice says, tapping the surface of the reception desk.

"They're heavy," Alex warns. "And there's another box in the trunk."

Jeannie tries to hide her annoyance, but she's not able to do a very good job. "These should have been filed centrally."

"And then what?" he snaps at her. "You'd have to come back and dig them out all over again if the patients return to the mobile clinic."

Alice and Jeannie have both grown familiar with Alex's flashes of temper—surprising because he's usually such a quiet, placid fellow—so Alice moves quickly to defuse the tension. "It's okay, it's okay. We'll work out a system eventually. Just let Jeannie look for some of her patient records in here today. Alex, go and bring the other box in. There's a good man."

Alex stares at Jeannie a moment, then turns his back on

her and walks out the door to fetch the second box. Jeannie begins to say something, but Alice puts a hand on her shoulder to restrain her, nodding toward Alex, who's visible through the glass window. Jeannie takes a deep breath, then busies herself with opening the first box.

The door swings open, and Alex walks in with a smaller box. He doesn't set it down on the desk beside the other one. Instead, apparently having regained his good humor, he helpfully offers again: "They're heavy. Why don't I just bring them into the records room for you? That way Jeannie doesn't have to sort through them out here in the lobby."

"It's fine," Jeannie says without looking at him. "I'll just have one of the interns move them tomorrow."

Alex looks to Alice for a cue, and she smiles at him.

"Thank you, Alex; it's fine. Just put them down on the desk. There you go. Did we interrupt your Sunday plans? No? Well, thanks so much for bringing these in." She keeps up a constant stream of patter until he's out the door, then waves at him as he gets back into his car and drives away.

She locks the door just as Mariano steps out of the records room. "All there?" he asks.

"All here."

By noon of Monday, all but one of the four remaining victims have been identified. Saenz telephones Arcinas at the NBI with the results; he requires a second verification by a forensic odontologist at the bureau. He suggests, once this is completed, that Emil accompany his men in the unpleasant task of informing the families.

Jeannie and the two priests have caught only snatches of sleep in the last forty-eight hours; even if Jerome knows little about the procedure for identifying individuals through dental records, he has not left the health center, except to buy food and coffee.

Worn out from lack of sleep, they neither complain nor

stop to rest longer than an hour. They know only too well that there are families waiting for news, wondering if the police are doing anything other than shuffling their missing persons reports around in their filing cabinets. There are empty places at dinner tables, empty spaces in shared beds. There are others lying awake at night with their eyes wide open, despairing in the hard, unyielding dark.

The work of the last two days and nights will end this waiting; not happily, but mercifully. Their minds are not clear enough at this point to process the full significance of three victims having been identified from the batch of records from the mobile clinic, other than the obvious: that they were all patients there. Any deeper analysis will have to wait until they've managed to get a few hours' rest.

Alice arrives for work while Saenz is on the phone. A stout, efficient woman, she helps Jerome clear away the stacks of files and records the three have waded through since Saturday night.

They hear voices in the outer room. "It's the health center staff," Alice says. She's about to go outside to talk to her people when Jerome stops her.

"I wouldn't tell them what we've been doing here these past two nights," he reminds her. She pauses, nods in understanding, then goes outside, Jeannie tagging along behind her.

Jerome tucks dental casts, X-rays, and photographs, along with the dental records of the three identified victims, into the black leather bag, just as Saenz wraps up his conversation with Arcinas.

"To NBI?" Saenz asks.

"To a proper meal and a hot bath first." Jerome picks up the bag.

When they leave the records room, the lobby is empty, save for a young, slim man, possibly in his late twenties, dressed in khakis and a white, short-sleeved, collared shirt. He's sitting in one of the chairs in front of the reception desk, reading a newspaper. He doesn't look up when Saenz and Jerome make their way to the door and leave.

They know. The tall man knows. They're watching me now.

No. He doesn't know. How could he? Don't be silly. You'll be all right. You feel good. You felt good last night, felt good this morning. Don't let a little thing like that shake you.

But what if they do know? Why did they come here? Jesus, mercy, Mary, help. So near, so near. They must know something.

He looked right at you. He's probably watching you now.

Stop sniveling. That's what they want you to do. Stop it stop it stop it.

Be a man.

33

SAENZ COMES IN to work early the next morning to prepare for a 9 A.M. faculty meeting. On the way to his department office, umbrella tucked under one arm, he stops by his pigeonhole to check for mail. He finds two scholarly journals, several faculty and university notices and one letter envelope made out of heavy, cream-colored linen paper.

He slides the journals and notices back into the cubbyhole but takes the envelope and studies it on the way to his office. There's no postmark, no return address, just his name and office address written in a small, precise hand.

"Morning, Father Gus," says one of the department secretaries as she passes him along the corridor.

"Morning, Maila," he says. The envelope is curiously light and thin. He stops by a window and holds it to the pale light.

It's empty.

Saenz turns the envelope over to open it and finds that it has been sealed with tape instead of with the adhesive strip on the flap. He stares at this for a moment, then turns around.

"Maila," he calls out, and begins walking back the way he came.

She's some distance down the corridor, but she stops when she hears his voice.

"Yes, Father?"

"I don't think I can come to the meeting today. Could you tell Dr. Achacoso that I'll explain later?"

"Oh, okay," she says. "You won't be in your office, then?"

"Probably not. But I'll call her later."

"All right, Father." She waves goodbye and disappears into the department office.

Saenz steps out into a light drizzle. He opens the umbrella and heads for the laboratory, a ten-minute walk away.

JEROME SWINGS BY a fast-food joint on Katipunan Avenue for a cup of coffee and a breakfast sandwich. He begins eating the sandwich in the car as he drives into the campus. The lawns are a vivid green after the rain, the streets slick.

He parks in the usual place, opens the door. He picks up a small stack of books and papers with one hand, his coffee in the other, and holds the half-eaten sandwich between his teeth and lips as he gets out of the car. He puts the coffee on the hood, shuts and locks the door with his free hand, retrieves his coffee and makes his way carefully toward the laboratory building.

He is almost at the steps when the glass doors swing open and Saenz rushes out. He takes quick strides toward Jerome, removes the sandwich from his mouth, bites into it and says, mouth full, "We have fan mail."

"Eh?"

Saenz holds the glass doors open for him. "When I got to the department this morning, I found an envelope in my pigeonhole. No postmark, no return address."

"Addressed to?"

"Father Augusto Saenz, S.J. Then my office number at the department."

Saenz takes the coffee from Jerome as they enter the outer office. He takes a few sips and motions for the younger priest to follow him into the laboratory.

"Hey. That's *my* breakfast, you know."

"I know," Saenz says, still chewing. "Always tastes better when someone else pays for it. You of all people should understand."

Before Jerome can retort, a young, slim man in tight, black jeans bounces toward them, whistling a tune, backpack slung over one shoulder. He breaks out into a sunny grin with big, blindingly white teeth when he sees Jerome.

"Tato. What are you doing here so early?"

"Just got paid, Father J," the young man answers.

Tato's English speech is a linguistic anomaly—a little bit surfer dude, a little bit Bronx; it's completely put-on, picked up from endless hours of watching MTV. However, since he has been using it for as long as Jerome has known him, it is impossible to imagine him speaking any other way.

"Don't spend it all in one place."

Tato stops bouncing. "Awww, man, I got a line on a vintage Strat: Brazilian rosewood fingerboard, one-piece maple neck, clay dots. Pretty banged up after being passed from hand to hand since the sixties, but I think with some TLC . . ." His spindly fingers fly in the air as his face contorts itself into a rock-and-roll sneer. Both priests are stupefied.

"Yeah, but can you play it?" Jerome asks.

Tato starts bouncing again. "Hey, Father J, for about twenty grand, I'd better learn how, huh?"

Saenz shakes his head and waves him away. "Go away, Tato. I'm an old man. I can't take you this early in the morning."

The young man laughs and saunters off while the priests head toward the laboratory.

"I presume he was talking about an electric guitar," Saenz says as he walks through the door.

"Or a chainsaw. Hey, since when do you pay your assistant twenty thousand for one autopsy?" Jerome demands. "And could you use another one?"

The older priest snickers. "Tato makes money from far odder jobs than being my assistant. Besides, you can't stand the sight of blood."

"Sure I can. It's the touching things I can't stand."

"Uh-hmmm." Saenz proceeds to the drafting table and flips on the switch to illuminate the plastic plate.

The cream linen envelope is on the table. Jerome moves closer to examine it as Saenz goes to his desk to look for his glasses. "Nice."

Saenz looks up. "Isn't it? What's he telling us?"

"He's a man of taste?"

"Close enough." Saenz finishes off Jerome's sandwich. "Observations?"

Without touching the envelope, Jerome studies the address, written with a fine-tipped sign pen in small block letters, evenly spaced, the address lines straight. "Neat handwriting."

"*Very* neat," Saenz says. "What else? Notice anything unusual about the envelope?"

Jerome reaches for a box of disposable plastic gloves lying on the table, and yanks out a pair, and pulls them on before handling the envelope. "Well, for one thing—there's nothing in it." He shoots Saenz a questioning look. "Otherwise we'd be looking at the contents first, right?"

"Yes. Go on."

Jerome turns the envelope over. "Sealed with tape and nothing inside it. Why seal it with tape when it can be sealed with the adhesive strip?"

"Good. Any ideas?"

Jerome frowns. "To protect the adhesive?"

"Right. Because?"

"Because . . . if you used the adhesive strip to seal the envelope, opening up the envelope would . . . tear up the adhesive strip. Right?"

"Good. And why wouldn't you want to tear the adhesive strip?"

Jerome feels a tingle of excitement. "If there was something on it that you wanted to preserve."

Saenz claps him on the shoulder. "Well done. Take a look." Saenz spreads the flap open and holds a magnifying glass over the adhesive strip.

Jerome bends to look through the lens. At first he can't see anything, but then he realizes that there are random lines on the strip, as though a pointed instrument like a pin had been used to scratch the adhesive. The scratches are the same cream color as the envelope itself, faintly visible against the pale yellow adhesive. "Hmmm."

Saenz slides a strip of photographic negative onto the plate. "You can see the lines better on this." It's the flap of the envelope in greyscale: the lines a darker charcoal against the paler grey field of the adhesive strip.

"Now look at these." Saenz slides three photographic negatives closer to the envelope. Jerome has seen these before: they are photographs of the instrument marks on the chinbones of three of the victims. The grooves, Jerome notes, are markedly similar to the lines on the adhesive of the envelope.

"I've measured the width of these marks against those on the victims," Saenz says. "It could very well be the same instrument."

Jerome taps the plastic plate with the magnifying glass. "This is probably a stupid question, but can you lift a print off paper?"

"Not stupid at all. Modern techniques allow the lifting of prints from almost any surface." Saenz pauses to think, then shrugs. "I suppose I could do it here. Iodine fuming, or ninhydrin, the standard chemical workup. Maybe enhance it with zinc chloride if the image isn't very good." He lifts an eyebrow and turns to Jerome. "By the way, I'm no expert in fingerprinting techniques. Anthropology is my main area of expertise."

"If anyone can do it, you can," Jerome says with a chuckle, but his amusement is short-lived. "But you would have thought of it by now. Unless . . ."

The older priest nods. "Number one, if he's smart enough to know what we're doing, he's smart enough not to leave a print. Number two, a print will probably help the police build a case against our man after he's caught. But it won't help us with trying to identify him." He shakes his head, clearly frustrated. "At the moment, nearly all existing fingerprint records in the country, criminal or otherwise, are in manual storage-and-retrieval systems. So, fingerprints are not the way to go."

Neither of them speaks for a while, and then Saenz slaps his thigh with the palm of his hand. "Ading. He was supposed to have gone back to the site where the seventh body was found."

"You haven't heard from him yet?"

"No," Saenz says, annoyed with himself for having let this slip his mind. He rushes to the outer room to ring Rustia. He picks up the phone and dials Rustia's number at the NBI.

"Rustia."

"Ading, it's Saenz."

"Father." The relief in Rustia's voice is plain to hear. "I've been trying to reach you since Friday night."

Saenz thumps his forehead with the heel of his palm. *Silly, silly, silly.* "I'm sorry, Ading, I was tied up all weekend. What can you tell me?"

A deep sigh on the other end of the line. "Well, for one thing, I thought I could go to the crime scene the day after we last talked, but I didn't get to go until late the day after that. We were down two technicians last week due to illness and we were already stretched like you wouldn't believe before then. Didn't even have time to stop and try to get a hold of you till Friday night." Rustia clicks his tongue, exasperated with the situation. "Really sorry about that, Father."

"It couldn't be helped, Ading. Seems like that's always going to be a problem for you."

"Here's another problem, Father. Seems like the local police didn't do a very good job sealing off the area. When I got there, there were—shall we say—tourists. Couple of people, kids and adults, gawking at the place where the boy was found. Asked them to leave, but I think we were too late. Whatever that thing on the tape is, it's gone. Could your reporter have taken it herself?"

"I don't think so." Saenz considers the possibility for a moment and then shakes his head. "No, Joanna is aggressive, but she won't go as far as obstruction of justice."

"Well, maybe the scavengers got it. I'm sorry, Father."

"It's okay, Ading. Thanks for trying."

Saenz returns to the laboratory, and Jerome knows the news is not good.

"Who was that?"

"Ading Rustia." The older priest sighs. "He got to the crime scene a day late. Found that the site wasn't properly processed, or protected afterward."

Jerome bends forward to take another look at the grooves through the magnifying glass. "He's smart, all right. He's aware of the possibility that you may have found the instrument marks already. He wants to know if you can find his little postal clue: it's been sent in contempt. He's letting you know he knows who and what you are, and that he's not impressed. He's also told you that he's watching you."

Saenz nods, switching off the light under the plate. "Up until today, he hasn't attempted to make contact. Maybe he didn't even know we were involved in the case." He frowns. "So why now?"

Jerome rests his elbows on the table. "Well, Arcinas hinted at private assistance in his television interviews. And you've been consulted by the police before, in some very public cases. How about that Bonifacio woman? Maybe she's put the network news team on to us. We haven't been monitoring all the news about the killings. It doesn't take a big leap of the imagination."

"Hmm. Or maybe . . ." Saenz takes a seat, then begins drumming his long fingers on the desktop. "Maybe we struck a nerve somewhere."

"Maybe." Jerome takes the photographic negative of the marks on the envelope and holds it up between thumb and forefinger to the dim grey light of a window. "The question is, which one?"

"Well, we'd better find out soon," Saenz says, crumpling the empty cup and tossing it into the trash bin before glancing at a calendar on his desk. "First week of September will be upon us in the blink of an eye."

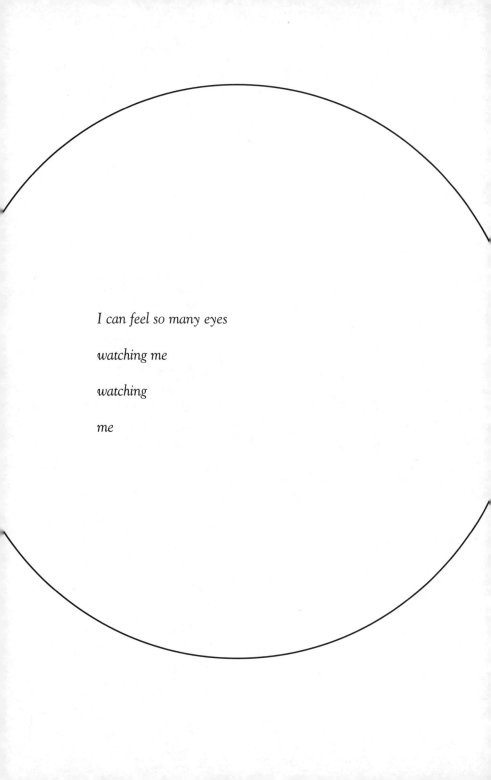

I can feel so many eyes

watching me

watching

me

"But Mary kept all these things, and pondered them in her heart."

Luke 2:19

34

EDITH SOLIS HAD given birth to Noel under difficult circumstances, to say the least.

She had been fifteen, working on weekdays at a tiny *carinderia* in Krus na Ligas. The father had been a newspaper delivery boy, all of sixteen years old. He would come to the food stall on a beat-up red bike, a wad of folded bills hooked around the middle finger of his right hand.

Edith was pretty then, small and brown and neat, with large eyes and straight, black hair. The newspaper boy was tall for his age, lean, all long legs and fingers. He had a ready smile, liked to flirt with the *carinderia* girls.

"Next time I come, I'll buy all your leftover food," he would say. "That way you can close early and we can all see a movie." And while the other girls would titter and laugh, Edith would look away, conscious that the young boy's eyes were on her.

Joel. Edith remembers his name, even though it has been thirteen years since those hot and sweaty nights in his cramped shanty home, rushing breathless through sex before his mother or brothers came back from wherever it was they had gone to in the morning. Fast and furious through something she thought was love.

Her mother had smacked her hard across the cheek when she told her she was pregnant. Edith never went back. Nothing really to go back home to, no younger brothers or sisters for whom she might have stayed, just a mother either needling her constantly for her wages or passed out drunk on a tiny cot that served for a bed.

Edith stayed with a succession of friends, finding odd jobs to earn a meager living: tending a fish stall at the wet market, cleaning the yard at a local day-care center, washing clothes for a UP professor's family.

She worked until she got too big with Joel's baby, and then

in her eighth month, when she was down to her last two hundred pesos, a surge of blood and water alerted her that the child was coming as she walked bareheaded in the hot sun along Don Mariano Marcos Avenue.

Someone could have made a movie out of it, she would joke much later, after the long, excruciating labor at a community hospital where she lost so much blood, where the baby came out and did not breathe for several minutes. They put him in her arms and gently told her to say goodbye, but she refused. She held him and talked to him, all but willed him to come back to life.

She didn't want to name him after the father who disappeared even before she knew she was pregnant. When she first saw her son, she cried, in anguish that he could be dead, in joy that he was so well formed and perfect for such a tiny, tiny thing.

From me, she whispered to herself in awe at that moment. *He came from me*.

After a few years, all these things became just a memory, something interesting to tell Noel when he was big enough to understand. The first years were difficult ones. One infection after another, first the ears, then the throat, then the lungs. She queued up—in burning sun and pouring rain—for the largesse of politicians, for the mercy of the Church, for handouts from private charities and public agencies. She charmed her way back into the odd jobs she used to do, and when the charm failed, she begged in the streets for food, for loose change. No sacrifice was too big, no obstacle too great, because she was determined to feed, clothe, obtain medical attention for him.

He didn't crawl until he was over a year old, didn't talk till he was almost three. Thin arms and legs, the head just a little too big for the body, large, serious eyes like her own. She thought he would die before he was five. Nights awake, praying, weeping, hoping the neighbors wouldn't complain about his constant wailing.

And then somehow it all became right in his sixth year. He filled out, grew taller. He began to play like normal children, to run and shout and get into scrapes like the rest of the neighborhood boys.

Edith found work as a seamstress, realized soon afterward that it was something she could do well.

The boy was not smart and did not do very well in school. But he was observant, learned practical skills quickly. It pleased her that when she came home at night tired and hungry, she could ask him to perform simple chores. Wash the dishes. Cook rice. Fetch water. He was a good boy.

He came from me.

And then he was gone.

Today she is hanging the clothes out to dry on a line already sagging with other people's washing. No matter. She has known her neighbors for years, and they know what belongs to whom.

It has been several months since he disappeared, but she still washes the boy's clothes. The whites need special attention, underwear and school uniforms. She washes them and soaks them in bleach every once in a while, so they don't develop yellow spots in the box where she keeps them.

She does not hear the two men coming until they are right behind her. When they say her name, she almost jumps.

She is about to ask them what they want, but something in their faces stops her cold.

The laundry basin, still half-full of wet clothes, slips from her grasp.

No. Don't tell me. Don't tell me.

THE MEN CAME to tell Binang today, after more than five months.

Since they left over an hour ago she has been sitting in the half-light, staring down into a small oval mirror perched on what passes for a windowsill.

She is looking at the face in the mirror. She sees an old woman. Lined face. Thin, dry lips. Tight, iron-grey curls.

Binang gave birth to her sixth child late in life, when she was forty-two. She had not thought she would ever have another one; the first five came in rapid succession, beginning when she was eighteen. It was a hard life, made more difficult by a husband who worked as a plumber only when he was sober. Which was rarely.

Binang looks in the mirror, absentmindedly twirling a strand of hair around a finger, and wonders where her young self went. Fifty-four. How many times in the last two decades had she doubted that she would make it this far? So many possibilities. An accident while crossing the highway after years of dodging murderous passenger jeepneys. A fire sweeping through the neighborhood, densely packed with wooden shanties.

Or just plain wearing away and giving up, the likeliest possibility of the lot.

When she learned that she was pregnant with Lino, she was filled with a kind of fury she thought she would never feel again. *Why, why, why? I'm too old. I'm too tired.*

Damn Edong. Coming home drunk that New Year's Eve twelve years ago, putting his arms around her and grinning with his grey lips and stained teeth. How she hated him when he came near her like that, reeking of beer and gin, cigarettes and old sweat.

She had tried to push him away, and that always made him angry. The first few times she said no, he merely laughed and persisted in his playful advances. One too many times, though, and he changed. Binang saw his whole aspect transformed, as though he was becoming someone else right in front of her eyes.

He drew himself up to his full height, a good five inches taller than her. His shoulders rose, and he stood with his feet planted firmly apart. The smile disappeared; the eyes grew cold. And when he came for her, there was no saying no.

Her friends used to tell her it wasn't rape if the man was your husband. She didn't say anything, but inside she seethed; she wanted to take a knife to their faces.

When Lino was born, Binang sent him off almost immediately to be raised by her eldest daughter, who was married and had a child of her own.

"It's your turn, all of you," she said, cold and resentful. "I've served you many years. It's time you started taking care of each other."

Edong up and died not long after, bad gin taking its toll on his liver.

The boy grew up not far from his mother's home, seeing her as a sullen, hostile old woman who for as long as he could remember seemed to have an especial dislike for him.

She never hit or scolded him. Whenever she saw him, however, a look of intense displeasure would spread over her face, as though she had just had a mouthful of bitter medicine. If he happened to be eating a meal at her home, she would set the old tin plate that held his food in front of him with a clatter. She spoke to him only when ordering him to be quiet, to behave or to run an errand.

When he was about six, he came to see Binang with his sister Susing and her two children—his nephews, although they were about his age. He saw, as he had seen many times before, how Binang doted on the two other boys. How she smiled and cooed to them in a way she never did with him.

When Binang went behind the frayed curtain into the shanty's kitchen to prepare a snack for them, Lino blurted out to his sister: "*Lola* doesn't like me."

Susing glared at him. "Be quiet."

"It's true. *Lola* doesn't like me."

Alone in the dark, tiny kitchen, Binang began to cry.

That was six years ago.

Where did all that time go, and what did she do with it? Today, it dawns on Binang that her youngest son died not

knowing who his real mother was. Nobody had ever bothered
to tell him.

ON AFTERNOONS WHEN she has no washing to do,
Lolita Bansuy sells *maruya* and *turon* to help make ends meet.
They sell very well; Lolit is a good cook. Her snacks are usually gone just two or three hours after she sets out to sell them.
During rainy weather she sells *ginataang mais*, kernels of corn
boiled in sweetened coconut milk, or *goto*, rice porridge made
with the stock of beef and tripe and spiced with garlic and
ginger, prepacked in single-serve plastic bags.

Almost everyone in the cluster of shanties behind the
school knows Lolit. She is a short, chubby, jovial woman who
has a constant smile on her face. And although she is widely
acknowledged to be a busybody, few people can resist her
good-natured jibes and infectious laugh.

Poor, homely, working as an itinerant laundrywoman, living from hand to mouth, Lolit has an extraordinary talent for
happiness.

The only thorn in her side was her boy. Thirteen-year-old
Vicente—Enteng for short—went around with a rough, glue-
sniffing crowd of mostly older boys; he often acted as their
lookout during burglaries, in exchange for a meager cut of the
takings.

He had grown, in the space of a few years, from a quiet and
well-behaved child to a tough, sour-faced, belligerent ruffian.
Money in his pocket, speech peppered with obscenities. Swaggering through the neighborhood like a big tough man,
sneering at adults who warned him to stay away from their
own children.

Lolit had tried to talk to him, cajoled, scolded; the boy
would merely stare out the window, then hurry out of the
shack when she was done, ready for whatever thievery or mis-
chief his mates would propose that day.

She would be left alone then, wondering if the change in her son was because he missed his father. Jun died when Enteng was nine, a good man defeated by a weak constitution and a bout with pneumonia following weeks of back-breaking work in the new wet market along the highway. The construction crew, most of them paid less than the minimum daily wage, had to rush to finish the structure; the mayor wanted it completed before the elections. Enteng had loved his father, clung to his hand when he picked him up from school, hung on his every word.

The boy had watched Jun suffer, long nights when the man would alternately shiver from chills and sweat from fever. Not enough money to get him to a hospital or give him all the medication he needed, even though Lolit took in even more washing, nearly running her own health into the ground.

Enteng watched his father die while Lolit was doing some other family's laundry in a subdivision further down the highway. Saw the light go out of his eyes, the gentle face go slack.

The boy knew better than to telephone her employer's house. They would need whatever money they could scrape together for his father's funeral.

Unafraid, he crept into the cot beside the dead man. Held his father's limp hand in his own small one. Waited patiently for several hours in this position. Finally fell asleep, as he had so often done before, resting his head against his father's arm. That was how his mother found them.

Afterward Lolit would see Enteng's eyes following other boys his age, walking with their fathers to familiar places: the waiting shed near the overpass, where Jun used to buy his cigarettes. The tricycle stand near the school, where he would wait for his son after class. The Jollibee in Fairview, where he would bring his small family once every few months for a Sunday burger-and-fries treat.

She had tried to keep that going, but of course it was never the same. There would always be someone missing, someone who might have been sitting across the table from them, eating a regular Yumburger, if things had been different.

Such sadness and longing in the boy's eyes, but he never said a word.

Then, a year later, a purse snatching, his first run-in with the police. Witnesses said he didn't do it; the older boy who did had passed the purse on to him and dissolved into the noontime crowd at the junction of Tandang Sora and the highway.

Enteng, the budding juvenile delinquent, not quite as fleet of foot or swift of reflex. Running straight in the direction of a few traffic cops who had parked their patrol vehicles on the side of the highway.

And afterward the first of several visits from the police.

Lolit's boy disappeared several months ago. Some of her neighbors were relieved, both for her and for themselves. She knows this, but keeps it to herself. She tries to stay cheerful, hoping that he will come home soon. Or someday.

Today two men she has never seen before come toward her, wallets ready. She asks them what they want, and they both point to the *maruya*.

"Five pesos," she says, and one of them, the taller one, hands her a ten-peso bill. "You're not from here, are you?"

"No, just passing through," he says between bites of banana fritter. "Looking for someone."

"Eh, who?" she asks, curious.

"Maybe you know her," the other one says. "We need to talk to her about her son."

He fishes a crumpled piece of paper from the back pocket of his trousers, unfolds it and reads.

"Mrs. Lolita Bansuy. Son's name is Vicente."

35

SEVEN VICTIMS, SIX names. Laid out on a whiteboard like this, with the photographs, the dates, the details written in Ben Arcinas's slanty handwriting inside neat squares, it's almost like any other chart or table, dry and cold and dull. Except they all know what each of these squares represents; they've all seen it—or what's left of it—with their own eyes.

They're sitting in a conference room at the NBI: Saenz and Jerome, Arcinas, Jake Valdes and Director Lastimosa, and Cesar Mariano. They're transfixed by the grid on the whiteboard, the room silent save for the drone of an old air conditioner.

Director Lastimosa is the first to speak. "Well, we've identified most of them. What do we know about them?"

Valdes takes his glasses off and begins cleaning them with a handkerchief. "They all lived in the vicinity of Payatas: two from Payatas proper, two from Manggahan, one from Litex, one from Riverside. All poor. Two trash pickers. The rest is on that grid."

"I presume you've sent people to interview the families?"

"Yes, sir," Arcinas says. "So far we haven't come up with anything useful yet."

Lastimosa shifts in his seat. "Make sure you give Father Saenz and Father Lucero a copy of everything you've got, Ben. Their view of what's useful might be different from yours."

"Of course, sir."

Lastimosa turns to look at Mariano. "Councillor, you were saying something about community surveillance?"

Mariano nods. "The other day I convened the *barangay* officials in my district—most of them come from the four communities Director Valdes mentioned. I strongly reprimanded them about the handling of the killings and told them they would face severe sanctions." He pauses. "But then

I realized they might be able to help you in your investigation. They may be lazy, they may be complacent, but they know these neighborhoods. We could rope them in to keep a close watch on comings and goings, to conduct night patrols—basically to tighten security in the communities."

Valdes puts his glasses back on and turns to Mariano. "Right. And they would be familiar to residents, so their presence in the neighborhoods wouldn't be unusual. How many warm bodies are we looking at, Councillor?"

"Officials and *barangay* security officers combined—something like thirty, forty men."

Saenz glances at Jerome. "If we had more eyes and ears on the ground, we might be able to detect something out of the ordinary. But someone has to coordinate. And they need to be communicating with NBI and the police constantly, so if anything happens, response will be as quick as possible."

"Jake and Ben will take care of that," the director says. "Councillor, they'll sit down with you after this meeting to map out plans and logistics. I imagine the highest deployment would be in the evenings and the closer we get to the end of the month, yes?"

"Yes, sir," Mariano says.

The director looks at all the worried faces around the conference table. "All right, gentlemen. Let's keep our wits about us. We don't have a lot of time left before we add another name to that grid."

ON THE WAY back to the campus, Saenz is extraordinarily quiet.

"Something's bothering you," Jerome says.

"Uh-hmmm."

"Don't you have a dental appointment soon?"

"Not today. Tomorrow."

"So. Not the dental appointment. Share?"

"I wish I could, but I don't know exactly what it is."

Jerome gets to a traffic light just as it turns red, and he stops, so it's safe to take his eyes off the road for a moment. "What do you mean?"

"It's been nagging at me since Tuesday, when we received the envelope. I keep trying to grasp whatever it is, to hold it still and examine it, but it keeps dancing away from me, just out of reach."

"What could it be? Something about the envelope, then?"

"Maybe. Or the envelope and the weekend we spent at the district health center." Saenz shakes his head briskly, as if to waggle the tenuous thought loose. The light turns green, and they're moving forward again. "It's maddening, like an itch you can't scratch."

"Maybe it'll come to you after a good night's rest."

Saenz looks out at the passing scenery: at the people in the buses and jeepneys, at the dirty buildings, at the garlands of black power cables that line the streets of the metropolis. "Maybe," he whispers unhappily, and Jerome doesn't even hear him.

36

THE POUNDING AT Jerome's door will not stop. He sits up, fumbles for the clock on the bedside table and groans when he sees the time, dragging himself out of bed and into the receiving area of his small quarters. The hair on the back of his head sticks straight up, and he pats it down carelessly, without much success.

He peers through the peephole in the door.

"This had better be important," he says, unlocking the door and stepping out of the way just as Saenz swings it open, waving a small Kraft envelope at him.

"I've made a terrible mistake, Jerome."

Jerome scratches his scalp and yawns. "And a good morning to you too."

"I failed to see the forest for the trees."

Jerome shuffles toward one corner of his Spartan private quarters, where a small kitchen table holds an electric kettle and several mugs. Saenz follows close behind him. "Only God can see the forest at three in the morning," the younger priest mumbles. "We ordinary mortals can barely keep our eyes open." He turns on the stove, looks through the drawers for sachets of instant coffee

Saenz ignores Jerome's crabbiness. "Listen. I was so excited about identifying the bodies that I missed the obvious."

"Are you talking funny?"

"What?"

The younger priest scowls. "Your speech. It sounds funny. Like you have a bit of a lisp."

"Oh." Saenz scowls back. "I'm getting to that. Where was I? Oh yes. I missed the obvious."

"Which is?"

"That our killer could be working in the mobile clinic himself."

Jerome stops, the open flame of the gas stove forgotten for a moment before he sets the kettle over it and turns to Saenz.

"Possible. But—"

"Our mystery envelope came a day after we were seen at the district health center. My guess is, the staff at the center is the same, or almost the same staff that works the mobile clinic."

"But Emil said the mobile clinic has been around for years. If we follow the same logic we pursued when we were considering the meal deliveries, why didn't the killings begin much earlier?"

"I'm not sure yet, but what if there were personnel changes? Workers move and get replaced all the time." Saenz pauses to think. "What if someone came to the clinic from somewhere else. Maybe he's done this before; maybe he hasn't. Maybe he's under some kind of strain, or something about the community and its residents triggers that strain? What if the killings are, indeed, some kind of—"

"Weird inaugural ritual to start the month right," Jerome breaks in. "So he takes advantage of his job in the mobile clinic—"

"To select his victims," Saenz finishes for him. "Emil said the clinic comes to Payatas every Saturday. So he has time to choose, time to observe without drawing attention to himself. As you've said: there's nothing random about his targets."

Jerome is putting instant coffee into two mugs. "Of course. The precise bladework would indicate some medical training; the obvious intelligence behind the selection and the . . . But who?"

The older priest opens the envelope and takes out a set of negatives. "I'll need your medicine cabinet."

He has been in Jerome's bathroom before and knows that the medicine cabinet has a small fluorescent rod perched above the mirror.

The two now squeeze into the tiny bathroom, and Saenz

tapes a rectangular piece of acetate, backed with a sheet of onionskin, to the fluorescent rod, creating a makeshift viewing panel. Next, he tapes the ends of four strips of photographic negatives to the acetate.

"What do you see?"

Jerome puts a hand to his chin and rubs it for a moment. "Instrument marks on the chinbones." He studies them closely, then taps the fourth strip. "Except for this one." His eyes widen, and he turns to Saenz. "That's the flap. The flap of the envelope you found in your pigeonhole."

Saenz nods.

"But the marks themselves look so similar."

Saenz smiles broadly.

"Complete dental restorative system."

"Sorry, what?"

"There's a packer for packing fillings into cavities, a dental explorer for probing into the nooks and crannies of a tooth . . . and this." The older priest reaches into his envelope and takes out a metallic object with a rubber handle, about seven and a half inches long, with the metallic end curving into a slight, blunt hook. "An elevator. Used to pry up the roots of the tooth until they can be extracted with forceps."

"Where did you get that? No, wait." Jerome laughs, grabbing the dental instrument from Saenz. "I remember now. That's why your speech sounds funny. I'm impressed."

"She wasn't. I was a wreck of a man when she was done with me."

The younger priest raises an eyebrow. "Please, spare me the details." He looks back at the instrument in his hand. "But wait—how can you be sure this is it?"

"I can't. There are probably a few other things that can make these kinds of marks. But we have to start somewhere. I told you I'd measured the instrument marks. These things are made in several sizes, but this one seems to best match the marks, in the width—these have five-millimeter blades—and in the character of the grooves. And these rubber handles give you a good grip even if there's a lot of blood. And then there's this." Saenz opens the envelope again. "That footage of the last crime scene from Joanna. I took the clip and fed it into the computer. That thing in the mud? Have a closer look."

He hands Jerome a high-resolution printout of the strange black-and-metal object half-buried in the mud, caught by Leo's camera lens.

Jerome lays the elevator against the printout. He compares the two for a few seconds. "But why on the chinbone?"

Saenz strips the acetate off the fluorescent light and leads Jerome out of the bathroom, back toward the kitchen table. The kettle has been boiling for minutes. Jerome switches it off, takes a quilted potholder from a hook on the wall and removes the kettle from its base. He pours hot water into the two mugs and begins to stir the coffee.

"We know from the clean incision at the neck that he would slit the skin under the chin first, from ear to ear. I think he needed help to peel the skin back from the chin, so he would hook this under the skin and flesh, using it much like you would use a chisel, and start to pull the skin upward. But it couldn't have been easy. For an instrument so thin, these things are pretty tough, made from surgical steel or chromium; the skin and flesh would tear in places. So he'd hook in again and again, and in the process of pulling the skin over the chinbone, he would leave these marks."

They both stare at the instrument, glinting cold against the dark wood of the tabletop. For Jerome, the nightmare journey seems clearer than before. In his mind, the scent of blood is stronger, the slippery viscosity of it, the tender resistance of flesh peeling back from bone.

"Gus. You realize what this could mean?"

Saenz nods. "We need to have a talk with Jeannie."

I can feel them. Scurrying in circles around me, smaller and smaller circles like rats around a crust of bread or a piece of cheese. Waiting, waiting, waiting for the right moment. The moment when I slip up, when I make a mistake, when I get careless.

I can hear their feet. Some of them pass by the gate, on the sidewalk; they think I can't see them. Some of them are brave enough to rattle the gate; they bring my mail, my bills; they ask for donations. Some of them get into the house while I'm sleeping, and I wake up, and I hear their feet on the stairs, yes I do.

I can hear their thoughts.

The priest knows. He's coming for me.

Let him come, then. Let him come soon. And then all this will be over.

37

"I DON'T UNDERSTAND. Are you telling me I'm a sus-pect?" Jeannie asks Saenz incredulously.

She had agreed to meet with Saenz and Jerome at the health center after hours on Monday, along with Councillor Mariano and Dr. Alice Panganiban. Now, her small face is pale with worry.

"We don't have a suspect yet, Jeannie," Saenz says, as gen-tly as he can, because he can sense her rising panic. "We just want to understand how things work at the mobile clinic. How often it goes to the parish. How often you're there."

"The clinic is there every Saturday," she says, looking to Alice for reassurance. "Alice and two nurses, plus a dentist and a dental assistant."

"How long have you been working there?" It's Mariano asking.

"Five years—isn't that right, Alice?"

"Six here at the district health center, almost five at the mobile clinic," Alice confirms.

Jeannie turns back to Saenz. "But now you're asking how often I'm here. That must mean you think I'm involved."

"We're not saying that," Jerome says. "But perhaps you can tell us—do you remember treating any of the victims?"

"No! I honestly can't. I would have told you already, the day we identified those three, if I did."

Saenz is quiet, and everyone looks to him for direction.

He turns to Jeannie again. "You said, that day, that you had an alternate. The one who always forgets to file records here."

Jeannie nods. "Alex. Alex Carlos."

"Is he regular staff here?"

Alice shakes her head. "No, he's got his own practice, but he comes here Mondays and Fridays."

"And he goes to the mobile clinic too?"

"Yes. Every first and third Saturday of the month."

Jerome recognizes at once that familiar light in Saenz's eyes. "Since when?"

"Well . . . almost since he started with us. Right, Alice?" When Alice agrees, Jeannie continues. "He's been with us—what? Less than a year?"

"So he's the newest on staff?"

"Relatively new," Alice says. "He joined us . . . let me see. December last year. No, November."

"Anyone else new?"

"There's Joji, our dental assistant. She's only been with us three months."

Saenz picks up a pen and begins tapping Alice's desk with the capped end. Then he springs out of his chair. "Jerome. My briefcase. In your car."

"Sure. What is it?"

"I need the envelope."

Jerome nods, runs out of the room. Saenz turns to Jeannie and Alice. "The records of the three boys we identified last Sunday: Vicente Bansuy, Noel Solis, Lino Alcaraz. We had them photocopied for the NBI, but we left the originals here. Please get them for me."

The two women scamper to the records room, and Saenz is left alone in Alice's office, feeling the vaporous threads of an elusive thought becoming more distinct, more concrete.

Jerome gets back first. "Here," he says, slamming Saenz's briefcase down on Alice's desk. Saenz quickly unlocks it and fishes out the envelope, now encased in a resealable plastic bag. He lays the envelope, address side up on the concrete.

Jeannie bursts through the door, brandishing three sets of records, and Alice comes up right behind her. "Here," Jeannie says, thrusting the papers into Saenz's hands.

He pushes some of Alice's papers and gewgaws away and then spreads the records out on the space he's just cleared. All four of them stare at the papers for a moment or two. Alice and Jeannie have no idea what they're supposed to be seeing, but Jerome picks up on it almost immediately.

"That's it," he says. "That's what's been nagging at you since you got the envelope."

Saenz nods. "Jeannie." He points to the dental records of the three boys. "Is that your handwriting?"

Jeannie glances at the records again. "No. No it isn't."

"Whose is it?"

"It's Alex's."

ALICE AND JEANNIE tell the priests that Alejandro Benitez-Carlos Jr. is thirty-four, a good worker, single and living alone in an apartment in Quezon City. He has a small private practice, although they don't quite know where it is. On the days he's on duty at either the health center or the mobile clinic, he comes to work early, lunches alone, and is always the last to leave at the end of the day.

They say he's professional, reserved: a quiet man who keeps mostly to himself. He's unremarkable, except perhaps for rare flashes of temper; not loud or explosive, but, as Jeannie describes it, unsettling. "He scares me sometimes, to be honest," she says.

When Saenz asks what he looks like, Alice produces a small photograph from his personnel file. Saenz recognizes him immediately: the man who was seated at the reception desk when they finished the identification work on Monday.

The priests leave the health center with strict instructions for Alice and Jeannie to act normally around him. "We're not law enforcers, Alice," Saenz reminds her. "This all has to go through legal channels first."

In the car on the way back to the university, Jerome asks: "So, what now? Do we advise Valdes and Arcinas to arrest him? Or do we ask them to conduct a background check on Alex Carlos first?"

Saenz doesn't answer at once. His fingers drum a rapid beat

on his thigh, and he's restless in his seat. "I'm wondering if there isn't another way. A possibly faster one."

"What do you mean?"

"Our friend the news producer, and her army of contacts."

38

By Quezon City Hall, Toyang Bailon, Clerk II at Human Resources, waits at the fried squid ball and fish ball stand of the *tiangge*, an open-air market with various stalls selling clothes, shoes, toys, processed food, rice and produce.

It is four o'clock in the afternoon, and people have started leaving their offices, dropping by the *tiangge* for any last minute cooking needs before making the journey home.

It is sweltering hot even in the shade, and strands of her hair are sticking to the nape of her neck. She buys a plastic cup of *sago't gulaman* with ice and a stick of doughy squid balls at a snack stall. The vendor motions to a jar of sweet-and-hot sauce, and Toyang dips the stick into the jar, careful to tuck the file folder she is carrying under her arm so the sauce doesn't drip on it.

She has just taken her first hot mouthful when someone taps her on the shoulder.

"Eating again, Toyang?" the tall woman says.

"Eh, *Ate*, how are you?" Toyang chews hurriedly, sets down her drink at the stall's tiny counter, then dabs at her lips with some napkins from a plastic cup on one side of the counter.

"I'm okay. How about you? How are the kids?" the other woman asks.

"They're doing well. Pinky is learning how to walk. How about you? When are you going to start having your own?"

"I don't know. Maybe someday, Toyang. Listen, did you find what I need?"

Toyang wants to pursue the subject of kids a little more—she can't help but be curious about this strange woman. But as usual, the other woman wants to push the topic out of the way and get on to business. It wouldn't be the first time; talk of marriage and kids and family always seems to make her nervous.

The government employee takes the folder and hands it over.

"That's his service record and some of the pre-employment requirements he submitted for his application. He hasn't been in any trouble, no administrative cases or disciplinary action. Good boy," she adds unhelpfully.

The other woman opens the folder and begins leafing through the papers inside, saying nothing. After a few minutes of reading, she looks up. "This is really good, Toyang. I appreciate your help." The woman reaches deep into the pocket of her jeans and pulls out a five hundred–peso bill. "Hey, this is for Pinky."

Toyang steps back, waving her hands, squid ball stick in one. "No, no, *Ate*. It was nothing. Really, it was no trouble at all."

"No, Toyang, I insist. You always pull through for me."

Toyang blushes a deep red. "*Ate naman*, you don't need to pay me."

The other woman takes her hand and presses the bill into it. "Buy her a pretty dress. Tell her it's from *Ninang*."

Toyangs nods, whispers her thanks. Watches the woman walk down the line of stalls and disappear into the crowd.

CIONY IS TAKING a break from the morning's work, sitting in a quiet corner of the University of the Philippines' registrar's office with a soft drink and two *suman*. A phone rings in another part of the large office, and she hears the slap-slap of someone's slipper-shod feet as they approach her.

"*Manang* Cion, you've got a phone call."

Ciony is surprised. "Eh? Who could that be?"

"Don't know; she wouldn't say."

Ciony leaves her snack on the table and ambles over to the phone on her desk. "Hello?"

The voice at the other end of the line is familiar to her. "*Manang* Cion. How are you doing today?"

"Oh, it's you. I haven't seen you in a while. How are you?"

"I'm fine, *Manang*. How is *Manong* Jess? Has he retired already?"

"No, next year. He says he wants to go back to Pangasinan. I keep telling him his friends are all here and he'll be bored silly over there."

A chuckle at the other end. "Ah, let him try it and see if he likes it. I know him. Pretty soon he'll want to be where the action is." Ciony's husband, Jess, works for the university police force. He never went to college, but is nevertheless an intelligent man, sensible, decent.

"I hope you're right. Besides, his doctor is here. Anyway. What can I do for you?"

Ciony listens for a minute, takes a pen from the holder on her desk and scribbles some notes on a pad. She says "yes" several times, then "Okay, I'll see what I can do," before launching into a detailed account of her most recent bout of rheumatism and her granddaughter's recovery from chicken pox.

THE FOLLOWING MONDAY, the phone rings in Saenz's faculty office. "That should be Ben's boys," Saenz says.

Jerome nods and answers the call. "Yes?"

"Hey, Father Lucero. Is the joint jumping?"

"Ah." It occurs to him that the reporter's voice sounds very like a drag queen's. Perhaps she smokes a lot. "Joanna." He glances up at Saenz, and the other priest immediately comes close. "How are you?"

"I'm okay."

"You sure? You sound like you have a sore throat. Do you smoke a lot?"

A chuckle at the other end, as though she has heard this question many times before. "Haven't touched the stuff in years, Father. Guess that makes me a drag queen, eh?"

Jerome almost drops the receiver. "Gus is here; hang on a second," he says hurriedly and hands the instrument over to the older priest as though it carries an electrical charge.

Saenz takes the phone from him with a puzzled smile. "Joanna, *comment vas-tu? Ah, vraiment?*" Jerome rolls his eyes in exasperation. "Listen, Joanna. Jerome is here, and his French is very bad. Shall I put you on speakerphone? I would like him to hear this."

Saenz presses a button on the phone and replaces the handset. Immediately the sound of the woman's deep, gravelly voice fills the room.

"I'm faxing you some information I dug up on Alex Carlos."

The two priests look at each other. *Already?* Jerome mouths silently to Saenz.

"Relax, Father," she drawls, as though she has heard him. "You do your job, and I'll do mine. The long and short of it is, you have one fairly smart suspect on your hands. Comes from a poor family, but he's been granted scholarships almost throughout his entire academic life, culminating in a dentistry degree from the University of the Philippines. He has no immediate family in Manila; his parents moved to Bulacan soon after his graduation from college—apparently they have relatives there. Their address is on the documents I'm faxing you."

Jerome is shaking his head. "How did you get all this?"

"Contacts, Father Lucero," the woman says, in a tone of good-natured jest. "Do you realize the civil service is a huge untapped information resource? And it doesn't respond very well to NBI agents throwing their weight around either."

Saenz takes a deep breath, a tad peeved yet hugely grateful at the same time. "Joanna, you are a gem."

"That's your diplomatic way of telling me I can scratch the hardest surfaces, eh, Father?" She laughs softly. "You know there's no such thing as a free lunch, right?"

Saenz chuckles. "Of course. When this whole matter is settled."

The woman hangs up.

In a few minutes, the papers begin coming through: birth and baptismal certificates, school records, newspaper clippings. Saenz takes the documents off the machine, one by one, and hands them over to Jerome.

Jerome shakes his head, half in admiration and half in amazement. "A one-woman NBI," he says as he pores over the faxes. After a few minutes, he waves a piece of paper at Saenz. "Guess where he finished secondary school."

Saenz looks above the upper rims of his glasses. "Payatas High?"

Jerome nods. "Favorite son." He pauses to think. "Bulacan. That's not far. Could be worth a day trip. What do you think?"

"I don't know. Maybe Ben can get the local NBI office to interview them."

Jerome's nose crinkles, as though there's a foul smell in the room. "I'm not sure how much help that would be, to be honest."

"I see what you mean." Saenz knows Jerome doesn't have a very high regard for the interviewing skills of most NBI agents. "Can you spare the time?"

"I think I can move things around and free up most of tomorrow."

"All right, then. But you'll need a good story. Something that won't alarm them."

Jerome smiles. "I thought you said I had a gift for this sort of thing."

39

JEROME DROPS BY the laboratory very early the next morning, before his drive to Bulacan. Saenz meets him outside.

"All set?"

"Pretty much. If I'm able to find and speak with the parents, I should be back this afternoon."

"And your story?"

"I'm Alex's spiritual advisor, and I've been concerned because I haven't heard from him in a while."

"That's a good one. You don't have to hide who you are, and you don't have to fabricate too much."

Without another word, Jerome gets into his car. The window on his side is rolled down, and Saenz pats him on the shoulder, giving voice to the anxiety they're both feeling. "Get back as soon as you can."

THE LABORATORY IS quiet when Saenz returns. He is feeling a bit bleak at the moment; he spent three or four hours tossing and turning last night, unable to sleep. He eventually gave up, got out of bed and began going over his notes on the killings.

It is almost 9 A.M., and the sun is high in the sky outdoors. Saenz does not turn on the lights and draws the blinds. Now the lab and its adjoining rooms—the reception area, the office, the photo lab—are as cool and dark and quiet as he likes for thinking.

He settles into the swivel chair behind his desk, stretching out his long legs to put his feet up on the desk, and picks up the remote for the CD player. The faint strains of the *andante* from Bach's Partita in C Minor—*let's see, this is Sergey Schepkin on the piano here*—fill the room.

Saenz imagines the notes to be tiny birds, no bigger than

the tip of his little finger, spreading their miniscule wings, gliding from this room to the others, flying up toward the high laboratory ceiling or seeking out the dim, quiet spaces.

Quiet spaces.

The thought comes to him, clear and whole.

He needs a quiet space.

He swings his legs from the desk, reaches for the phone, dials a number, and then waits.

"Hello, Alice. Gus Saenz here. Yes, thank you. Listen, Alice, I need to know something. You said the driver of the mobile clinic has complete access to it at any time. But could anyone else get the keys and take the vehicle out without anyone else finding out? Or is there a duplicate set of keys?"

He waits a few seconds for the answer, and when it comes, he takes a deep breath. "That's what I thought. Thanks a lot, Alice." He hangs up and then dials another number.

"Director Valdes? Father Saenz here. Yes, thank you."

On Saenz's desk, dwarfed by pen caddy, tape dispenser, and diskette storage box, is a plaster figurine of St. Ignatius of Loyola, no more than three inches tall. The saint is depicted wearing armor—a coat of mail and breastplate—and carrying a sword. Saenz has had it for so long that the faux gilding on the armor has almost completely faded. He's brought it with him every place he's ever worked, every country he's ever lived in for longer than a week. Absently, instinctively, he reaches out to touch it and then cradles it in the palm of his hand.

"I have a name for you."

When the brief conversation is over, he replaces the receiver in its cradle, leans back in the seat, stretches out his very long legs and closes his eyes, St. Ignatius still nestled within his hand.

H E   W A K E S   U P with a start and immediately senses that he is not alone in the darkened room.

"How long have you been sitting there?" he asks in Tagalog.

"Not long," the woman says, hands clasped together. She has been watching him sleep, unsure if she should wake him; he looks awfully tired. She stands and approaches his desk hesitantly, then stops. "I didn't mean to disturb you."

Saenz rubs his eyes, then shakes his head. "It's okay. Did Susan send you here?"

"Susan?"

"My secretary."

"No, Father, I just asked around."

He notices that he's still holding on to the figurine of St. Ignatius and sets it back in its old place beside the pen caddy. He stands up, bends his torso from side to side, easing out the kinks in his back from falling asleep in his chair. Then he walks slowly toward the door to turn on the lights. He blinks hard when they come on, and so does she.

Short and round-faced, she is dressed in black stirrup leggings and a blue printed shirt. Cheap, flat canvas kung-fu shoes, caked with mud. Dry, brown skin on feet and hands, years of ironing and washing and cooking.

Saenz doesn't know who she is, but he knows why she is here. Several such women—someone's wife or mother or sister—have come to see him in the past, in this same room, for more or less the same reasons.

Powerless and angry at this moment, he feels a strong urge to break something.

"Which one was he?"

"Vicente," she answers quietly. "Enteng."

He nods in understanding.

"He got into a bit of trouble the last two years. You know how boys can be. Fell in with the wrong crowd. Hardly said a word to me the last few months before—before . . ." She chokes up, falls quiet. Then, briskly, "I shouldn't have come. I'm sorry."

Turning away now, in a hurry all of a sudden, words tumbling out of her mouth: "I know you must have a lot of things to do. You're famous. Sometimes I see you on the news when I watch TV at my neighbor Gloria's house. Usually we just watch telenovelas."

She picks up her things from the floor; a black shoulder bag with the mock leather cracked and peeling in places, a brown canvas carryall with a bank's logo, dingy from years of use. A package rolled up in a red-and-white-striped plastic bag.

"I'll tell Gloria I met you. She won't believe it. She thinks you look like an *artista*." Talking a mile a minute, then abruptly thrusting the package out toward him. "There. That's what I came here for. I cooked them only about an hour ago. I rode a jeep and the traffic was bad, but they're still warm." Waving it almost in his face, though not meaning to be rude.

"I know what you did for my boy." Her voice cracks, but she recovers fast. "Take it; it's good. I make it everyday, sold out by five o'clock. People who've had it say it's the best they've ever tasted. Go on, take it."

The priest reaches out to take the package, which is warm in his hands. He opens it up. The smells of caramelized sugar and ripe, sweet jackfruit. When he looks at her again, her face is wet. He moves toward her, but too late. She is rushing to the door on her short legs, bags tucked under her arm, mud-caked soles slapping on the floor.

"Well, I'll let you get on with your work now," she says, words flung quickly, carelessly over her shoulder. "It will be a busy day for me too. I made those, but I have to make another batch for selling when I get home."

"Mrs. Bansuy," is all he can say.

Halfway out the door now, talking, talking still. "I'm going now. You eat that while it's still warm, you hear? Best you'll ever taste. I have to go. It looks like it's going to rain, and I forgot my umbrella." She leaves the door ajar.

Alone again in the room, Saenz sinks into his chair slowly. He bends his head and stares into his bag of *turon* for what seems to him like a very long time.

They're coming to get me. Coming on their big, quiet feet they're coming.

I want my mother. I want my father.

40

"I'M VERY SORRY, but I'm afraid I can't help you much. We haven't heard from Alex in over a year." Flora Carlos is looking at a photograph of a thin, small, wide-eyed boy, hair neatly combed and parted in the middle. "You probably know more about what's going on in his life right now than we do."

Jerome pinches his forearm to reassure himself he isn't dreaming. The boy in the photograph has the same thin, small-boned frame as the killer's victims.

"How old was Alex when that picture was taken?"

"Oh, about thirteen, fourteen. He was small for his age. We didn't have very much then. Not that we do now."

Mrs. Carlos is a small woman, with thin wrists and arms and a neck lined with pale green veins; they web delicately from her jawline down to her protruding collarbones. She is seated on a discolored, threadbare sofa, wearing a lavender cotton housedress with purple flowers. The dress has been washed so many times that the flowers are only a shade or two darker than their background, mended so many times that the fabric is fraying beneath the stitches.

When Jerome introduced himself at the door, the first thing he noticed about Mrs. Carlos was how guarded she was. But as he speaks to her, he's struck by how talking about her son seems to be a strain on her; she halts every once in a while, as though afraid somebody else is listening.

"He didn't tell me very much about his childhood," Jerome says. "Was he ever in trouble when he was a child? Any disciplinary problems in school?"

"No. He was a good boy, very smart." She cranes her neck slightly and points to a series of frames on the wall behind her. "Look at those. Those are all his awards."

Jerome stands and steps carefully over his backpack, which he set down on the floor earlier. The walls are a curious shade of yellow in this tiny, two-bedroom house; the windows are small squares cut high in the walls, close to the ceiling. Inside the house, it is hot and muggy; the air is still, lying thick and warm and sticky on his skin.

Thirst, heat, claustrophobia—Jerome is feeling all three in equal measure. He wipes his brow and moves toward the wall to get a closer look.

There are awards for good conduct, first or second honors, loyalty awards from the Payatas High School. It is the same school some of the victims had attended.

There are interschool Quiz Bee awards, "Best in English and Science" awards, certificates for annual scholarships from the city mayor's office all the way to second year high school.

Here was Alex, overwhelmed by a *barong Tagalog* at least two sizes too big for him, shaking the mayor's hand. Alex in his white school uniform speaking in front of a live television audience; on the wall behind him, the words NATIONAL QUIZ BEE FINALS spelled out in large styrofoam letters covered in gold foil. Alex with a broad smile on his face, waving his grade six diploma in the air.

An exceptional young boy.

Jerome wonders if he was ever athletic; the absence of PE or athletic awards, or any picture of Alex in high school citizens' army training, puzzles him.

He remembers his own CAT experiences. At fifteen or sixteen, most kids want nothing more than to be popular, to belong. And CAT is one of several ways a teenager can gain recognition in his or her peer group. Most teenagers he knows—students of his or the sons or daughters of friends—have a treasured bunch of CAT pictures; they may have hated the course, but they love the trappings: the uniforms, the polished shoes, the gleaming belt buckles and shiny swords, the heavy Garands, the black berets, the symbols of rank and the authority over others.

"Did Alex like PE? Sports?"

From the corner of his eye, he sees Mrs. Carlos turn slowly to look at him. Something in her posture changes, an almost undetectable stiffness creeping up from the tiny waist to the back and shoulders, to the neck and arms and the hands that hold her son's photograph.

"No." Jerome thinks her voice sounds odd, far away and alert at the same time.

"How about CAT?"

"He was a medic."

A *medic*. Jerome himself had been a medic in high school; because of his limp, he had been advised by doctors against engaging in too-strenuous physical activity.

A medic. The dead end of CAT. They wouldn't have let you march for fear of heat exhaustion. They wouldn't have given you shiny spangles on your uniform; they wouldn't have drilled you for Parade and Review. The most they would have let you do was to hand out water and ammonia-laced cotton balls.

No wonder you don't have CAT pictures.

When he turns to her, she is looking at him with her head tilted to one side, as though she is seeing him for the first time. There is something in her eyes, a watchfulness that makes him uncomfortable, and he turns back to the frames on the wall. *Okay, where was I?*

Scholarships from the city mayor all the way to—all the way to his second year of high school? What happened in the last two years?

"Was he a scholar all throughout high school?"

Mrs. Carlos looks absently down at the framed photograph, then turns it over and over in her hands, the way a child does when trying to figure out how a new toy works.

"If you truly knew my son, wouldn't you already know most of these things?" she asks quietly. "Why are you really asking me all these questions? Is he in some kind of trouble in Manila?"

Jerome hesitates a moment. "That's what I'm trying to find out, ma'am. He's been coming to see me regularly for the past year or so, but the last few months he seemed under a great deal of stress. And then, he simply stopped coming. I tried to contact him, but he never responded."

She lays the photograph on her lap and then looks at Jerome squarely.

"You're very concerned about Alex, even for a . . . spiritual adviser. I don't know anyone who would leave Manila and come here just to check on him." She's challenging him now. "If I picked up the phone and called my son right at this moment, would he want to speak with you? Would he even know you?"

"Mrs. Carlos, you just told me you hadn't heard from Alex in more than a year," he says, challenging her as well. "I'm guessing that doesn't mean simply that he hasn't called you; it also means you've not been able to reach him. Or at least that he hasn't been answering your calls or letters."

Her shoulders slump at this. "Who are you, then? Are you a doctor? Or a policeman? Has something happened to him—is that why you're here?"

Jerome uses the most sympathetic tone he can muster. "As we speak, Mrs. Carlos, the NBI are seeking your son's help in investigating a series of murders of young boys in Quezon City. All of the victims"—he indicates the photograph in her hands—"looked like Alex in that picture. Same build, almost the same age."

"What are you saying, then?" She shifts her position, stares at Jerome. Seconds tick by. A fly, round and fat, its thorax gleaming green in the light, lands on Jerome's hand and crawls slowly, jerkily up his wrist. "They think he killed them," she says finally. "*You* think he killed them."

The fly darts away when she rises to her feet and sets Alex's photograph down on the coffee table. "You must be thirsty. I'll get you some water." She disappears into the small kitchen. Jerome can hear the creak of a freezer door, the clink of ice against glass, the sound of water from a tap.

She emerges from the kitchen carrying a glass of iced water with wet hands. She offers it to him. When he accepts, she absentmindedly wipes her hands on her housedress, the imprint of her palms and fingers clearly visible on the material, and returns to her place on the sofa.

She waits for Jerome to take a sip of water before she speaks again. "I don't suppose you . . . well, of course not; you're a priest. You *are* a priest, aren't you? That's what you said, anyway. You probably don't know what it's like to have a child."

Jerome doesn't say anything; if she's in the mood to talk, he knows better than to interrupt her.

"Alex was such a good boy. So good, I couldn't believe how lucky we were. And such a beautiful child, with those big eyes, that fine nose. Never gave us trouble a single day in his life. Oh, he'd cry a little when we couldn't afford to buy him those plastic toys he'd see in the market. Or sometimes he'd run so fast and fall and scrape his knees, and he'd come home to us bawling. But otherwise . . ."

She reaches for her son's photograph again and gazes down at it sorrowfully. "You're given a good child, and you try to raise him well, even though you have next to nothing. And then sometimes . . . something happens. And he isn't your child anymore."

Jerome waits for her to say more, but she slips into silence now, lost in her thoughts. "I don't understand, Mrs. Carlos," he says gently. "Help me to understand."

The front door opens, and a man walks in. He's a small man in his late fifties or early sixties, with thinning hair. He is slightly stooped and bowlegged, and Jerome wonders if he has ever worked at a job that required him to lift heavy weights. The man is not surprised to see Jerome—his car is parked out on the street, after all—but his expression is questioning.

"This is a friend of Alex's," Mrs. Carlos tells him.

Jerome stands, holds out his hand. "Mr. Carlos?" he asks.

The man looks at the offered hand and does not take it. "A

friend?" he asks. Not unpleasant but not friendly either. "What do you want? Alex isn't here." His gaze shifts warily from Jerome to his wife and back again.

"He was asking if we'd seen Alex lately."

"Why?" He asks it of both Jerome and Mrs. Carlos.

"He says the NBI are looking for him."

"What for?" The man eyes Jerome up and down. "You don't look like you're from the NBI. Or the police."

"I'm not—"

"He's a priest," Mrs. Carlos says. "He was asking whether or not Alex liked PE. Weren't you, Father . . . ? I forget your name."

"Lucero. Jerome Lucero."

Mrs. Carlos nods. "Father Lucero here was asking if Alex liked PE."

At this, Mr. Carlos's face darkens in anger. "Get out. Get out of here, and don't you dare come back."

Jerome is bewildered. "I'm sorry, Mr. Carlos. I'm just trying to help. Please, just give me a moment, and listen to what I have to say."

He doesn't listen, only glares at Jerome. "How dare you come to our home, sticking your nose into things that don't concern you? I don't care if you're a priest. You're not welcome here. Get out!"

"You should just tell him." Mrs. Carlos is strangely calm. She's not looking at either of them. Her attention is fixed on the young boy in the photograph.

Mr. Carlos moves toward his wife and tries to take the picture away from her, but she clings tightly to it. "Stop it," she pleads. "Stop it. You know why they're looking for him. We both know."

"Be quiet, Flora. You're talking nonsense. Here, give that to me." He succeeds in yanking the frame from her grasp, then spins around to face Jerome. "Out. Now. And stay away!"

Jerome looks helplessly at Mrs. Carlos but realizes he

doesn't have a choice. He excuses himself and heads out the door.

The heat hits him like a blast from a furnace, but he's glad to finally be breathing fresh air. Flecks of ground glass in the concrete shimmer in the noonday sun as he makes his way to the car. His shadow on the ground is distinct, its edges sharply defined. When he touches the handle of the car door, it's burning hot, so he reaches for the towel he keeps in his backpack. That is when he realizes that it's still inside the house.

When he turns back to get it, he bumps into Mrs. Carlos and sees her clutching it.

She thrusts it almost violently into his hands. It's an angry gesture, but her face tells a different story.

"San Francisco de Asis," she whispers. "Wait for me. Please. I won't be long."

Jerome notices that Mr. Carlos is standing in the doorway of the house, waiting for his wife, his brown, lined face stern.

Jerome nods. "Thank you," he says.

He can feel their eyes on him as he gets into his car and drives away.

41

ABOUT AN HOUR later, Jerome is still waiting inside one of the alcoves at the church of St. Francis of Assisi. It's oppressively hot, and no one has turned on the electric fans to keep the warm, sticky air moving inside the church. Why bother when the church is practically empty? There are only three or four other people scattered among the pews.

Sweat trickles down Jerome's nape, down his back. His undershirt is soon soaked, matted to his skin. He is thirsty again.

He sees a shadow fall across the pews in the nave nearest him and, seconds later, the slight figure of Mrs. Carlos. She must have dressed in a hurry, because she's still in her *tsinelas*, the worn red flip-flops she was wearing at the house.

"Mrs. Carlos," he calls out, careful not to disturb the others. She turns and sees him. She's nervous; that much is plain. Her eyes dart everywhere, making certain she hasn't been followed, before she enters the alcove.

"I can't stay long," she says, her voice barely above a whisper. "I want to know: are you really trying to help him?"

"Ma'am, even if you went and checked with my order right now, or with my university, you would know that I'm telling you the truth. I can give you the telephone numbers—"

But she waves the suggestion away. "There's no time for any of that anymore." She looks at him ruefully. "You have a kind face. Do you teach? Young people? Boys?"

"I used to, yes."

"Alex, he . . . Did I tell you he was a good boy?"

"Yes, you did."

"You asked me whether or not he liked PE, or sports. He didn't. He liked to play when he was a child, but he was never really good at anything—basketball, badminton, none of that." Now she's wringing her fingers together in her lap.

"Something changed. Something changed him, when he was in his second year of high school."

"What was it? What happened?"

She waits a moment: one final hesitation before the truth. "Sometime last year, he told us he'd seen his old PE teacher from high school. Mr. Gorospe. Isabelo Gorospe." There's anger, old and deep, in her voice. "Tell me, Father, do you believe in evil? You must believe in evil—you're a priest, after all."

Jerome has a hollow feeling in the pit of his stomach, a sense that he already knows what she's going to tell him next. "I do."

"A few days—maybe a week—after that meeting, he said he wouldn't be able to see us for a while." Her large, dark eyes, so like Alex's, are brimming with tears.

"Why? What happened between him and Mr. Gorospe?" Jerome asks.

"Flora!"

Jerome and Mrs. Carlos are both startled as Mr. Carlos rushes toward them. "What are you doing?" he demands, his voice echoing in the dome of the alcove. He turns to Jerome, as the other people in the nave glance over their shoulders at the commotion. "You again! Didn't I tell you to stay away from us?"

"Alex is in trouble. If Father Lucero can help him . . ."

Mr. Carlos takes her by the wrist and tries to drag her away, but she struggles. "Stop it! Stop it, Papa!" She wrenches free of his grasp, then runs to the back of the alcove, putting distance and a series of pews between herself and her husband.

"We didn't do anything," she sobs to Jerome. "We didn't ask questions."

"That's enough, Flora."

"Mr. Carlos—"

"We sent Alex to a public school in Quezon City," she continues, cutting Jerome short. "We couldn't afford anything better. When it all began—when he started changing—we didn't know what to do, who to trust. We were too poor, too stupid. How could anyone expect us to know? Who would listen to us?"

Mr. Carlos sinks down into a pew, cradles his head in his hands. "Mama, please."

"Papa, don't you want to help him?" Mrs. Carlos asks her husband. He looks up and holds her gaze a long moment, their faces creased with deep-rooted anguish, pale with fresh fear. As Jerome watches, they seem to reach a wordless understanding, and then Mr. Carlos turns to him.

"He became rebellious," he says. "Withdrawn. We thought he'd begun taking drugs, but physically he was the same—small but healthy. He came home late all the time, and we never saw him with friends."

Mrs. Carlos sobs quietly, a leitmotif of misery to the numb drone of her husband's voice.

"Of course we started fighting. His mother and I would scream a lot, but we tried, we tried so hard to reach him. One day—" He chokes, and his eyes fill with tears. "One day I woke him up early for school, and I saw him. There was blood on the sheets, on his shorts. Not much, just spots here and there. But I panicked. Started shouting. He tried to get away, but I held him by the shoulders. I couldn't make him understand that I was trying to help him. I thought he was sick."

Jerome puts out a hand, touches the man's shoulder gently.

"He begged me not to hurt him. He said he would be good; he would do what I wanted. Then he wriggled free and ran to the bathroom. He locked the door, but I pounded and pounded until it flew open. I made him show me."

Jerome is stunned. He imagines that the scenario Mr. Carlos just described might have only served to exacerbate the young boy's trauma. But he cannot judge them—cannot be perceived to be judging them. "What did you see?"

"He was bleeding. He was sitting on the toilet seat, trying

not to cry, but he was trying even harder to keep himself from flying at me. From *killing* me."

Even after all these years, Mr. Carlos still seems shaken by the memory of that day. He keeps running a hand through his sparse hair, plastering what's left of it down onto his sweaty scalp.

"What did you do?" Jerome asks. "Did you tell anyone? Did you try to get help?"

A harsh little laugh. "Help? From whom?"

"You didn't tell anyone?" Jerome looks at the husband, then at the wife, then back again, trying to tamp down his disbelief. "Did you not understand how seriously your son was being hurt?"

Mrs. Carlos comes closer, her voice now eerily calm. "We were afraid. Nobody talked about such things back then."

Jerome doesn't quite know what to say. "You pulled him out of school, at least?" They shake their heads. "So you let him stay there?" he asks, and he restrains himself in the nick of time from asking, *You allowed it to go on?*

"He was on scholarship at Payatas High. If we pulled him out, we would not have had enough money to send him to school."

"But the scholarships stopped anyway, right?"

They both hesitate. "His PE teacher arranged for him to continue," Mr. Carlos says. "To this day, we're not sure how."

A well-dressed woman—one of the few other people in the church—gets up from her pew and walks toward the exit, the clicking of her heels bouncing sharply off the walls and ceiling of the nave. Jerome waits until the sound has faded away.

"But the person who did this to Alex—it was the same teacher, yes? Mr. Gorospe?"

"Yes." Flora Carlos reaches out blindly for her husband's hand, and he takes hers. "At the time, after Alex's grades started dropping and nobody would sponsor his studies any more, Gorospe came and talked to us. He said he'd take care of Alex, that he was just going through a normal phase that all young boys go through. Told us not to give up on our son."

Mr. Carlos puts an arm around his wife's shoulders. "We were so grateful. It wasn't until years later that Alex told us it was Gorospe who—" and he stops; the words are just too horrific to say aloud, in a church, to a stranger.

Jerome leans back in the pew, taking stock of what he's learned. It's shattering: when the scholarships dried up, Alex's abuser had manipulated the situation, used the family's poverty and need to keep him in school so he would have ready access to him.

"You told me you haven't seen Alex in more than a year. That was around the time he'd seen Gorospe after so many years. Right? When was it? If you last saw him more than a year ago—that would have been around the middle of last year? May, June?"

"May," she whispers.

"He told you that it didn't end well. And you . . ." Jerome pauses to consider what he'll say next. "You decided—again—not to tell anyone or seek help."

They remain silent, but their faces say everything. Jerome understands, on an intellectual level, what they are feeling: love and concern for their son, shame at their inability to prevent or seek redress for his suffering, guilt at keeping their son's secret. But on an emotional level, he's surprised to find that he's angry with them somehow.

"That's why he said he wouldn't be able to see you again for a while. That's why you weren't surprised when I told you the police were looking for Alex." He realizes now the implications of what he's learned. "If I went back to look for Gorospe—would I be able to find him?"

Mrs. Carlos shakes her head.

Jerome stands slowly. "Is there anything else you think I should know before I leave?"

Mr. Carlos also rises to his feet. "We did not want any of this to happen."

Mrs. Carlos reaches out to touch his arm. "Father, if there's any way you can bring him home to us . . . We are not bad people. And whatever he has done, Alex is not a bad person."

"You should talk to his friends. The ones who knew. The ones who . . ." and here Mr. Carlos's voice falters, and he takes a moment or two to regain control over it. "Alex wasn't the only one."

Jerome nods. "I understand."

He excuses himself, but the Carloses say not another word to him. They turn instead toward each other, lost in their private torment.

As soon as he can get a decent signal on his cell phone, Jerome calls Saenz's faculty office. When he doesn't get an answer, he tries the phone in the laboratory.

"Saenz," says the voice on the other end.

"I'm heading back now."

"Anything useful?"

"A lot. Can you ask Arcinas to dig up whatever he can on someone named Isabelo Gorospe? He used to be Alex Carlos's PE teacher at Payatas High School."

"Who's he?"

"If what Mr. and Mrs. Carlos told me is true, he might have been Alex's first victim."

There is a moment's silence at the other end of the line.

"Tell me what you know."

I and the public know
What all schoolchildren learn,
Those to whom evil is done
Do evil in return.

W. H. Auden,
"September 1, 1939"

42

BACK AT THEIR home, Flora Carlos is sitting on the bed in Alex's room, wide eyed and unblinking in the dim, yellow light of the room's lone light bulb. She has her son's photograph lying in her lap.

"Mama," her husband says, stroking her back gently.

"Was it a mistake?" she asks him, anxious to the point of panic. "To talk to that priest? You think it was a mistake, don't you?"

"Mama, I don't know what to think any more." He sinks down beside her, then lies back, staring at the ceiling, his legs dangling over the edge of the bed. "You realize he's never stayed in this room? All these years we've had this house, he's never slept here. I don't even know why we kept this room for him."

"Because he's our son. Our only boy." She turns to him. "What if he never comes back to us? What if we lose him?"

"Mama, I think we lost him a long time ago."

She grimaces. "Don't be silly. That's not the same. If he is responsible for what happened to Gorospe—to those boys the priest was talking about—God knows what might happen to him."

Mr. Carlos doesn't answer, and so she smacks him hard on his thigh in frustration. "I'm serious. If they catch him, if he goes to jail . . . I suppose if I had to, I could live with that. But what if it's worse? What if—" and she shudders in horror, leaving unsaid the worst that she thinks can possibly happen.

He turns to his side, rests his head on his arm. "What do you want us to do, Mama? What *can* we do?"

When he looks at her face, it is hard, determined. "He needs us."

He sits up and then tries to put his arms around her, but she struggles.

"No. He has been through enough already. Do you want him to go to jail?"

"But Mama, it was you who—"

"No." She spits out the word fiercely, resolutely. "You call him. His number is by the phone. You go out there, and you call him now. You tell him they came looking for him."

"Mama, stop," he protests, when she starts pushing him off the bed, away from her.

"You give him a chance to get away," she says. "He did it; you and I both know he did it." When she hears herself say the words out loud, she is ashamed, and she claps a hand over her mouth, as though she has said an obscenity. Then she starts pushing him away again. "Go. Call him. You do this for him. You do this one thing for your son."

He stands, staggers through the door and heads toward the living room. He is wondering why his vision has suddenly become so blurred. When he puts his fingers to his eyes, they come away wet.

JEROME IS SO wrung out when he gets back to his quarters that he calls Saenz and asks to meet up the next day instead.

"Do you mind?"

"No, no. I understand. You've told me everything I need to know. Are you all right, though?"

"I will be. I think I just need to . . ." Jerome pauses, stabbing the surface of his wooden desk with the tip of a ballpoint pen.

"You're angry," Saenz says.

"I guess I am. It's all so . . . senseless. All this blood and suffering. The man should have been locked away decades ago," he fumes, and Saenz knows he's not talking about Alex. "If he had, who knows? Maybe none of this would have happened. I don't know. There are days when it's a struggle even to keep the faith."

"Go and rest, then."

"Thanks. See you in the morning?"

"You forget, we've both got big department meetings in the morning and I've got a make-up class after lunch. Can't wriggle out of any of them without getting into trouble."

"Afternoon then? Around three?"

"Good, off with you now. And remember that prayer from the Sarum Primer."

God be in my head, and in my understanding . . . God be in my heart, and in my thinking. Jerome hangs up, then takes a shower and goes to bed. He falls asleep almost as soon as his head hits the pillow.

He begins to dream.

In the dream, he is in a cold, dimly lit place—a garage or a warehouse, or maybe even a gym. When he looks up, he sees a number of small, shrouded figures hanging from a ceiling he cannot see, the figures swaying ever so slightly, wrapped up in heavy cotton gauze.

The faces are also wrapped. Thick bands of electrical tape cover the linen where the eyes and mouths should be.

When he turns around, he sees a small boy sitting on a toilet bowl. He is completely naked, his head resting on his knees. Blood is running in thin, dark, glossy streams down the sides of the bowl. Jerome feels himself walking in dream-slow time toward him.

The boy looks up, and Jerome sees his own thirteen-year-old face streaked with tears, a contorted mask of unnatural hate.

"I see you, Priest," the boy says coldly.

THE PHONE IN Alex Carlos's apartment rings six, seven times before he's able to pick up. Very few people know this number—Alex doesn't like phones or phone calls—so when it rings, he knows it cannot be good news.

It's his father.

He lets the man ramble on a bit without responding: something about coming home, something about being sorry for everything that happened to him. He can hear his mother's voice in the background, and she's weeping. He's tried to detach himself all these years, from his memories, from them, but he knows he can never get away completely, even though he's found a way to cope, however temporary.

His father says something about a priest coming to visit, about the police looking for him, and that's when he sits up and pays attention. "A priest? What did he look like? Tall, thin? No? No, that's the other one. Never mind. Where is he now? What did you tell him?

"Stupid. You stupid, stupid people."

He yanks the phone out of the jack and hurls the entire instrument against a wall. It breaks apart into about a dozen pieces, big and small. He moves closer to the wall, gets down on his knees to examine the broken casing, the fragments of metal and plastic.

He should have done this a long time ago.

43

JEROME HAS BARELY come through the door of the receiving area when Saenz bounds out of the laboratory.

"We're driving."

"You mean *I'm* driving. Where to?"

"Jake Valdes has found someone he'd like us to meet."

THEY MEET JAKE Valdes at a rundown, open-air vulcanizing shop along Don Mariano Marcos Avenue. Even in the late-afternoon heat radiating off the shop's rusting, galvanized-iron roof, he is cool and unruffled, his shirt crisp and dry at the collar and armpits.

"Thanks for coming," he says, offering his hand. Saenz and Jerome take turns shaking it. "You asked me to dig up anything we might have on Alex Carlos. The man who owns this shop was a high school classmate of his. He . . ."

A small man with a dour face emerges from a ramshackle shed behind the shop and comes toward them, a smoldering cigarette dangling from one corner of his mouth. He is a little wary of Valdes, but he eyes the two priests with ill humor.

"Guillermo Ricafrente," Valdes says. "Emong. He filed a police report last year involving Alex." He nods toward Emong, signaling him to speak.

He glances at all of them one by one, takes a puff and then removes the cigarette from his mouth.

"Hadn't seen him since high school, you see? So I thought it was strange, him coming here all of a sudden."

"What did he want from you?"

"I wasn't too sure. Kept talking about high school, how he hated it, if I knew where any of the other guys were."

"Other guys?"

He studies the three men through a haze of cigarette smoke.

"Our classmates. Wanted to know if I kept in touch with any of them."

"You were good friends?"

Emong shrugs. "We hung out together sometimes, along with a whole bunch of other boys. But he was kind of different—shy, quiet. We didn't talk much."

"What happened next?"

"He said he'd run into our old PE teacher, Gorospe. Thought it would be nice to pay him a visit. Surprise him, you know."

Jerome takes a step forward. "What did you say?"

"Told him to go by himself. I'm a busy man. Don't have any time to socialize."

"How did he take that?"

Emong tosses the spent cigarette onto the dirt floor and stubs it out under a dirty rubber slipper with tightly controlled fury. "Went crazy, you know? Started yelling at me, told me I was no friend. I told him, 'Look, *pare*, I barely know you. We weren't friends then, and we aren't friends now, you hear?'"

"And then?"

"He starts throwing things around here. My things, you understand? My tools, my materials. Nearly got hit in the eye with a monkey wrench. Then he took a jack and started hitting the hood of one of my clients' cars. That's when I lost it."

"Lost it?"

"I got mad. I told him, 'Look, *pare*, I don't want any trouble; you just leave us in peace now, or else we'll have you arrested.' When he wouldn't stop, I told my wife to call the police, the *barangay tanod*."

"Do you know what made him so angry?"

"How should I know?" Emong asks, his voice rising to a high-pitched whine. "Like I told you, I barely knew him anymore. He looked like he'd made it through life better than the rest of us, you understand? He's got decent clothes and a nice enough car, and then he comes here, out of the blue, and wants some kind of class reunion."

Valdes clears his throat and comes closer. "He tried to hurt you."

"Came after me with that jack, he was so angry. And the whole time we're yelling and he's chasing after me with that jack, the neighbors are hearing everything, you know? When people started coming out to see what was going on, he threw the jack at me, got into his car and drove off."

"And the police—the *tanod*—they didn't get here in time?"

"No," Emong says. He drags out a dingy plastic stool from one corner and sits down on it. "He was long gone by the time they arrived, the stupid bastards. I filed a police report and all, but nobody ever came back to talk to me about it. Guess they figured if I didn't die, it wasn't worth the trouble."

"When did this happen?"

"Round April—no, wait. May. It was May, last year."

Saenz and Jerome exchange glances, then turn to Valdes, who merely acknowledges their questioning looks with the slightest tilt of his head.

Jerome refocuses his attention on Emong. He's plainly angry. And while Jerome can understand that he would dislike Alex intensely after last year's confrontation, there's something else simmering beneath the anger. And he remembers Mr. Carlos's words in the church that afternoon: *Alex wasn't the only one.*

"Did you like Mr. Gorospe?"

Emong's face twists into a sour smile. "Like Gorospe?"

"You know. Was he a good teacher? Didn't you feel like paying him a visit?"

"Like I said, I didn't have time for all that nonsense. I wasn't Alex's friend, and he was stupid to ask me."

"But would you have gone—by yourself, if not with Alex?" Jerome is very still, and Saenz picks up on this stillness almost immediately. "To see your old teacher? If you knew where he lived?"

Emong blinks up at Jerome several times, as though he

can't quite grasp the question. He has not thought about high school since Alex's visit, and before that he had tried to put it out of his mind for the longest time. He had dropped out as soon as his father died; it was easy then to say he had to find work, to put food on the table and keep the family together. Mainly he had just wanted to forget. High school was one very long, very bad dream.

"I didn't like him all that much," he says, and he looks away from them as he says it. Jerome has seen it enough times to know what it is: dissembling.

"You didn't like him because he hurt you too. Isn't that right?" Jerome keeps his voice as steady, as even as he can.

Emong rises to his feet so quickly that the plastic stool topples over. "I don't know what you're talking about. *You* don't know what you're talking about."

"Yes, you do. That's why Alex came to see you. Out of the blue, just like that. Because he thought you, of all people, might understand."

Valdes studies Emong's face and then Jerome's. "What's going on, Father Lucero? What are you saying?"

But Jerome isn't paying attention to anyone but Emong. He sees it clearly now: the undersized frame, the thin limbs, the large eyes—Emong looks a lot like Alex, and in their teens, they would have looked exactly like the dead boys in the landfill, small for their age, small in the world, easy to frighten and take advantage of.

"He hurt you too," Jerome repeats.

He says it very softly, and perhaps that's what makes it all the more devastating. In a blur of movement, Emong shoots forward and lashes out with his fist, catching Jerome off guard. The fist connects, and Jerome falls backward on the dirt. Saenz rushes to help him, and Valdes tries to hold Emong back, but he's on the offensive now, trying unsuccessfully to stomp on Jerome's legs and thighs, kicking up clouds of dust and dirt. Valdes is barely able to overpower the smaller man, gripping his arms and lifting him bodily away from Jerome, avoiding the flailing, kicking legs.

Jerome staggers to his feet and puts a hand to his lower lip; it is split open and bleeding.

"All right, that's enough. Enough now." Valdes is still holding on to the wriggling Emong. "Calm down. Just calm down and let us explain."

"I don't need your explanations. Just get out of my shop."

"Please, just listen for a moment." Saenz waits until the man stops struggling, until his breathing slows. Over Emong's shoulder, Valdes shoots Saenz a look to reassure him that he has the mechanic under control. It's his cue to continue. "You've probably heard about the young boys found dead in the Payatas dump."

"Nothing to do with me," Emong answers dully.

Saenz lets this pass. "We think Alex may have been involved in these murders."

"So what?" Emong twists his head around to look at Valdes. "You said you wanted me to tell these people why I filed a police report against him. I already told them what happened; why are you all still here?"

Valdes's face is impassive, his tone firm without being harsh. "If there's anything more you can tell us—about him, about your time in school together—please don't withhold it."

Saenz looks down at Emong. "Please," he appeals to him. "We need to find out everything we can about him so we can understand why he's doing it."

"Well, why don't you just catch him?" He turns to Valdes again. "Why don't *you* catch him?"

Valdes releases him, and then adjusts his shirt, rumpled a bit in the scuffle. "We don't have any proof yet."

Jerome moves closer to Emong. "Look, anything you say will remain private. Nobody outside of this group will know. Will you help us? Will you tell us what you can remember about him?"

IT WAS SO long ago; what's the point of telling anyone? Nobody has to know.

But what about the boys? You've heard the talk in the neighborhood. All the rumors about the missing boys. Could it really have been Alex? How is that even possible?

What if he takes your boys next? Joseph is just about to finish sixth grade, not so bright but a good, hard-working boy. And Michael is so small.

And Alex knew where to find you.

What have you got to lose?

"THERE WERE SEVEN or eight of us," Emong begins. "We were small boys, about twelve to fifteen years old. We couldn't keep up with the rest of the class—all that running, all the contact sports and the calisthenics—so Mr. Gorospe used to make us stay after school, sometimes two or three at a time.

"He would take us to the gym, and he'd lock the doors. It would be dark by then—past six in the evening. He'd turn off the lights." He stops, wipes a grease-stained hand across his eyes as his face hardens in anger. "It wasn't enough that he would do things to us."

Jerome is appalled, and when he glances at Saenz, it's clear that he, too, realizes what Emong means. He would make you do things to each other, as well, Jerome thinks, filling in what Emong cannot seem to bring himself to say.

He's watching Emong carefully now, fearing that he might shut down if he's forced to examine his own past torments too closely. "Tell us about Alex," he says, shifting the focus away from Emong's own painful secrets.

"He liked Alex best. Alex was smart, clean, neat. He used to get us all together and tell us that Alex was his special boy, that he enjoyed everything Gorospe did to him. And we knew it wasn't true. We all felt sorry for Alex."

"The scholarships stopped in his second year."

Emong nods. "How could anybody expect him to go on? He

was a mess. After a while, it was just him, him all the time, and we all knew." He pauses, trying to remember more. "He couldn't stand it when we looked at him, and he used to pick fights whenever he caught any of us looking at him. He would sit all the way in the back of the classroom, and soon he was all alone; he wouldn't talk to anybody. When he had to, though, he would never look them in the face."

Jerome and Saenz exchange looks. "Didn't anybody complain about Gorospe?"

The mechanic sighs and shrugs, and they know what he would have said anyway: *Complain about what? To whom? We didn't want any trouble.*

"Thank you, Emong," Saenz says gently.

Valdes, who hasn't spoken for a while, asks: "Did you hear about what happened to Gorospe, then? After Alex came by?"

Emong shakes his head. "No. Why? What happened?"

"He was found murdered in his apartment."

44

AT THE LABORATORY the next evening, Valdes is holding the file on Isabelo Gorospe, dead at age forty-nine, former PE instructor at the Payatas District High School. "It says here the heart was cut out and the face removed."

"Any other details?"

"Well, no other injuries, but it was a messy job, blood all over the bed and the bedroom."

"Signs of forced entry?"

Saenz waits while Valdes scans the documents.

"No, the front door was unlocked, and there were bottles of beer on a table in the *sala*. His television set, his wallet, some money and other valuables were still in the apartment, so it couldn't have been a burglary. The investigators assumed Gorospe knew the killer, let him in, drank a couple of beers with him. They got drunk, had an argument; one of them ended up dead." He hands the file over to Saenz, who quickly flips through it.

"But they never found the killer?"

"No. There were no witnesses, and all the beer bottles had been wiped clean."

"Did they find the heart?" Jerome asks.

"No," Saenz says, still reading the file. "Whoever killed him must have taken it away."

He stands and moves to the whiteboard and its information grid. He takes a marker and draws a long, black line from top to bottom, to the left of the first column on the grid, creating a new column. At the top, he writes *Gorospe*, then *molester*, and ticks off the boxes for *heart* and *face* appearing in the leftmost column under the heading, *mutilations*.

"So he killed Gorospe, with two of the major characteristics of the seven recent murders." Saenz draws large circles around the two tick marks. "Which means the removal of the face and the heart is the central symbolic act. They antedate all the other mutilations—"

"Which are simply refinements of his technique. Or an elaboration of his rage." Jerome squints so that all he can see are the tick marks inside the circles. "Emong says Alex was Gorospe's favorite, his special little boy. But Alex didn't want to be special. He wanted to—"

"Erase himself." Saenz moves closer to the whiteboard, pushing his glasses lower on the bridge of his nose. "Become ordinary. If he couldn't help being a victim, he wanted at least to be like the ordinary victims, like Emong and the rest. And then of course, there's the fact that he didn't like being looked at by the others."

"So maybe that's why he's killing these boys. Killing Gorospe wasn't enough; the others were still alive."

Valdes stands beside Saenz in front of the whiteboard. "They still knew he was 'special.'"

Saenz nods. "But he couldn't kill them as adults. In his mind, the other boys stayed the same age, still too small for their early teens. In some perverse way, he blames them—"

"For being ordinary. For abetting Gorospe's special attentions toward him. For simply knowing." Jerome starts to pace back and forth. "You know what disturbs me about our conversation with Emong?"

Saenz nods. "There were seven or eight boys in the group."

"Exactly. He's at number seven. He could go for eight, but if he doesn't—"

"He could just drop out of sight? No, I don't think so. He's at a symbolic age—twenty years, give or take, past the trauma. He's escalating to a resolution, but I think at the end of it he'll realize that he still isn't satisfied."

"So he'll repeat the cycle?" Valdes asks.

"I'm more inclined to think he'll destroy the one thing that keeps reminding him of the trauma." Saenz draws a small stick figure thoughtfully on the whiteboard. "Himself."

"But surely not suicide?"

"No," Saenz says, "probably not. But he might place himself, consciously or unconsciously, in a position to end the violence one way or another—"

"By getting caught or getting killed." Jerome picks up another whiteboard marker and draws triangles under the arms of the stick figure; it is no longer a person but a set of balance scales. "And just as an authority figure started this whole mess, he's looking to an authority figure—the police, maybe even you—to bring it to an end. He knows he has to answer to society's justice, but only after he's exacted his own personal justice." Jerome caps the marker.

"So you're saying he's got nothing to lose." Valdes stands back, looking at the drawing, and then back at Saenz and Jerome. "That makes him a very dangerous man."

The telephone rings, and Saenz frowns. "Who on earth could that be at this hour?" Jerome tosses the marker onto the whiteboard's ledge and runs to answer the call.

"Hello." When there's no response, he asks, "Who is this?" Still no answer, so he hangs up.

"Who was that?" Saenz asks.

"I'm not—" Jerome begins, but the phone rings again. "Hello."

The person at the other end of the line doesn't speak, but Jerome can hear his breathing and the vague sound of human activity in the background. "Hello, I can't hear you very well," he says, and something in the way he says it alerts Saenz and Valdes. They come closer as he turns on the speaker. "You'll have to speak up, please."

Nothing, just the person's breathing and indeterminate background sounds. Saenz grabs the whiteboard marker, scribbles *pay phone?* on the whiteboard, makes a circular motion with his hand, a signal to Jerome to keep the other party talking. Jerome nods, then says, "Who is this? How can I help you?"

Then, the very faint sound of eight musical notes played in quick succession, the first four notes ascending, the last four descending, followed one or two seconds later by the muffled but unmistakable sound of a human voice echoing in a very large space. Saenz's brows knit together in fierce concentration; then his face brightens in recognition and he writes again—this time the word *mall*.

Again, he makes the circular motion, and Jerome says, "Look, it's difficult to know how to help you if you won't talk to me."

Valdes turns to Saenz. "Who do you think it is?" he whispers.

"Someone who doesn't want to be traced," Saenz whispers back. Then he writes *parents*, points to the word for Jerome's benefit.

Jerome nods again, understanding.

"If this is who I think it is," he says, "your parents are very worried about you."

They hear the person's breathing quickening, then the same eight notes again, and the muffled human voice—now recognizable as being female. It's the sequence of sounds when an announcement is made—usually by female sales staff—via the public address system at one of the country's more popular mall chains.

"You wouldn't be calling us if you didn't want to tell us something," Jerome says gently. "Your parents want nothing more than to have you back safely with them. Let us help you."

There's a loud crack, and then the line goes dead.

Leave them alone. Leave them alone or I'll kill you. I will. I'll kill all of you.

45

ALEX CARLOS IS dressed and ready to go to work. But
the minute he steps out of the gate of his apartment row, he
senses, as a mouse senses the presence of a cat, that he is
being watched.

He does not bother to look up, to scan the sidewalks and
hedges for an unfamiliar face or vehicle, or anything else out
of the ordinary.

Thinking quickly now. He rummages through his dental kit
and pretends that he has forgotten something, shoves a free
hand into his jeans pocket and fishes out his house keys.
Then, he heads back inside the gate, back to his apartment.

He closes the door behind him, locks and bolts it. He drops
the kit to the floor, runs his fingers repeatedly through his
hair, smoothing it, rumpling it, then smoothing it again. He
starts pacing, back and forth, bouncing on the balls of his feet,
thumbs drumming a nervous rhythm on either thigh.

The feeling below his belt, between his thighs is familiar,
all tense and loose at the same time.

Now the fear and the hate again, down deep in his stomach
where the blood and darkness live, and then a wet stain
spreading slowly from his crotch down the inside of the legs of
his jeans. He does not seem to notice; the bouncing becomes
increasingly agitated, up and down and back and forth, up and
down and back and forth.

Watching me again, always watching me, he says in his mind
to no one in particular. *Well, come and get it. Come and get it.*

He takes his kit and bounds up the stairs two steps at a
time; he is light on his feet and can go very fast when necessary. He enters his bedroom, heaves the kit onto the bed, and
throws open the closet doors.

No. I don't need anything. Not anymore.

He turns to the kit on the bed and opens it. The shiny

metallic things comfort him; he begins to hum, no particular song, just a little here and a little there, and then he stops and then begins again.

He takes out a dental instrument and a thin knife from the kit. The handle is made from black, heavy-duty rubber molded to fit either right hand or left, the six-inch blade of excellent stainless steel; the whole thing is perfectly balanced from blade to handle. Its cutting edge is straight and fine and razor-sharp; Alex whets and polishes it after every use. He shelled out a lot of money for this German-made beauty, and she has served him well, effortlessly negotiating the curves and angles of bone beneath yielding flesh.

He turns and rips a shirt from its hanger in the closet, wraps the instruments up in it. He stuffs the bundle down the small of his back, in the waistband of his jeans.

Okay. Come on now. Come to me.

His mind is so sharp, so focused. He can see the way before him so clearly.

Sometimes he fantasizes that he is a cat, because he is so light and quiet on his feet. He throws the bedroom window open and jumps out, onto the roof of an adjacent bungalow. He lands on his feet with a dull thud, crouched compactly with his knees to his chest. He looks around, satisfies himself that he is hidden from view by a taller building.

He walks easily, silently over the galvanized iron, toward the edge, then bends low for a moment before swinging soundlessly onto the front lawn. The sidewalk is only a few feet away.

He looks up and down the street. All clear; nobody watching on this side.

Not so smart after all, Priest.

SAENZ AND JEROME are among the last to arrive at Alex Carlos's apartment in the quiet, low-rise, lower-middle-class neighborhood of UP Village. It's on a pleasant-looking street, with shady trees on the sidewalk every ten to fifteen meters.

As Jerome parks the car, Saenz rummages through his utility kit, takes out two pairs of thin latex surgical gloves, shoves them into the pockets of his jeans.

From inside the car, Jerome is gratified to observe that Arcinas has had the place cordoned off according to Saenz's instructions. The media is in a small, irate huddle on the other side of the street, and curious onlookers are politely but firmly kept away. It is the most orderly crime or crime-related scene he has ever seen, and he takes a few moments to get used to it.

When the two men get out of the car, somebody shouts, and a gaggle of reporters and photographers surges against the human barricade of police officers. Jerome hears Saenz's name called out several times, followed by the usual string of uninformed questions. He smirks and privately thanks God that he is not as famous as his teacher; he knows he cannot muster the older priest's equanimity in the face of ignorance.

Then he spots Joanna Bonifacio on the fringes of the media crowd.

Unlike the rest of the reporters, photographers and cameramen, who are shouting and pushing and shoving against the police barricade for a better view, she is standing quietly with her hands deep in the pockets of her slacks, tall and solid and calm as a stone angel, a hint of amusement touching the corners of her mouth. She is watching their progress toward the apartment. Behind her, Leo is standing with his camera mounted on a tripod.

Their eyes meet, and Jerome acknowledges her presence with a barely noticeable movement of his hand. The tiny gesture is enough to catch her attention; she gives him the merest nod in response, then turns to give Leo instructions. Jerome quickens his pace to catch up with Saenz.

Arcinas meets the two priests at the door. His face is pale, eyes ringed with dark circles, as though he hasn't gotten enough sleep. There is none of the swaggering self-confidence of the last few months, and when Jerome glances down at the lawyer's fingers, he notices that the nails are ragged at the ends, as though from repeated gnawing.

"I haven't let anyone in yet." The tone is hopeful, seeking approval.

Saenz pats the lawyer's arm. "Good man." He turns to Jerome, hands him a pair of gloves, snaps his own over his hands. "Let's go."

Arcinas has an NBI photographer on standby—yet another of Saenz's instructions. The photographer follows the two priests into the apartment.

The living and dining area is small, uncluttered. Jerome and Saenz open cabinets and drawers. Nothing out of the ordinary: books, china, bric-a-brac. As if by some unspoken consensus, all three men go about their work wordlessly, quietly, except for the clicking of the photographer's camera.

Jerome feels a certain tension, as though the atmosphere inside the apartment were electrically charged, as though someone has just passed through the room and they can still sense his presence in the displaced air.

He glances over his shoulder at Saenz, finds him staring back.

Jerome spots a small writing desk in one corner. He walks over to it, opens the drawers. Bills for electricity and water, receipts from groceries and drugstores. Income tax returns.

He opens the last drawer and finds cream linen stationery and envelopes. He takes out a few envelopes.

"Gus," he calls out and waves them in the air for Saenz to see.

Saenz nods, a look of understànding passing between them. He heads for the kitchen, and Jerome follows. Then they both begin opening drawers and cabinets once more.

Plates, pots and pans, canned goods, a coffee maker.

A strange smell—like old meat, old blood—permeating the room.

In the cabinet under the sink, Jerome finds several pairs of black rubber rain boots. He calls out to Saenz, and he comes, bending forward to take a quick look over Jerome's shoulder.

"Let's have the SOCO boys bag those."

Saenz straightens up and then notices the avocado-green refrigerator. It is one of those American-made monsters, with two doors and a built-in ice dispenser. It is easily the most expensive thing in the apartment. *Must have bought it from a surplus supply store*, he thinks to himself. And then: *it's too big for a man living alone in such a small place.*

He opens the freezer door, finds nothing but a large bag of tube ice. Next, one of the refrigerator doors. The racks are empty, except for a few beers, a jar of peanut butter, and a small, black plastic tray filled with wilted lettuce and what looks to be watery Thousand Island dressing.

He takes a deep breath, says a brief, silent prayer, then opens the second door.

The two of them remain quiet as they survey the contents, then step back so the photographer can take pictures. The only sound in the kitchen is the whir of film through the mechanism of the camera as he clicks away.

After about a minute, the photographer stops. He brings the camera down to his chest and looks first at Saenz, then at Jerome. His face is pale, and he's clearly upset. He shakes his head.

Before they can stop him, he runs out of the apartment.

46

THIS IS NOT how he usually hunts. But tonight is different.

He waits in the shadows, behind huge stacks of water containers made from blue, industrial plastic. Running water is a rarity here, and people have to buy containers in which to store it when the communal taps grudgingly yield it. The owner of the stall has closed shop for the day. Alex saw the man heading home around seven o'clock. He has been waiting here ever since. Someone is bound to turn up.

The rock is wrapped with a rag, to keep it from slipping from his grasp at the crucial moment.

He hears footsteps. Crouching low behind the stacks, he catches a glimpse of a young boy.

He could be eight or nine or twelve. Alex does not care. He'll do.

DENNIS DOES NOT scream when he wakes up. He whimpers a little. The pain in his head is intense, throbbing. Something warm and wet trickles across his forehead, pulsing from his temple. He feels like throwing up.

He realizes he is being carried, slung over the shoulder of a man. They are headed in the direction of the dump.

Fighting panic, Dennis remembers all the talk about the monster that wanders the dumpsite and the dark streets of the shantytown. His meager dinner of rice and salted fish bubbles up from his gut in an acidic gruel, and he has to swallow it back.

He clenches his fists and begins to pummel the man's back as hard as he can.

The man only grunts.

Harder still Dennis pounds on his back, hoping he will be dropped on the ground and he can make his getaway. He feels now more than ever in his whole miserable life the need for a voice, for the ability to speak, scream, shout. A deformity of his palate and upper lips has made it impossible for him to do more than grunt or moan. His mouth, his wretched mouth.

He opens it and tries to bite the man, as hard as he can, through his shirt. But it is difficult to find a good spot on the flesh of his back. Finally Dennis arches his neck far enough to be able to sink his teeth into a portion of the man's arm, just above his elbow. He puts all his fear and terror and years of hunger and damp and deprivation into this bite. Maybe this time his mouth will serve him.

Still the man walks on, unflinching, toward the dump.

47

"I'm afraid I can't let you do this." Director Lastimosa is shaking his head, his lips set in a tight line. "We have people who can bring him in. Jake? Ben?"

"Of course you do," Saenz says. "But as far as we can tell, he's already tried to contact us twice. If there's a chance we can persuade him to come without a struggle, don't you think we should take it?"

It's Arcinas who is adamant. "We can't allow you to put yourselves in that kind of danger. Anyway, now that we know who he is, we can just pick him up."

"Ah, yes. And where will you start looking?"

"The dump, of course. And if he's not there, we'll organize a manhunt. We'll go national if we have to. We'll find him."

Saenz can already visualize the parade of guns and uniforms, the crackle of static from handheld radios, the flapping of feathers in a wild-goose chase. He shuts his eyes tight, the strain of the last few months beginning to take its toll now that the whole thing is almost over.

"We'll save you the trouble, Attorney. If you just work with us one last time."

"No," Arcinas says, folding his arms together and shaking his head. "Not this time, Father."

Without opening his eyes, Saenz asks quietly, "Director Lastimosa?"

"He won't agree, either," Arcinas says, but he casts a furtive glance at the director, unsure of where he really stands. "Father, be reasonable. You've no training in the apprehension of criminals. No field experience. If you—"

"It's not your decision to make, Ben," Saenz says, also looking at the director now.

An awkward silence follows, and for a minute or two, nobody feels compelled to break it. As they sit nursing coffee mugs in the director's office, Valdes turns up the volume on the television set. The Payatas killings are the top story on the early evening news. Saenz filters out the sensationalist babble of the anchor, focusing instead on the footage.

Onscreen, a clip of the exterior of Alex Carlos's apartment. Jerome's car pulling up to the curb, cutting to a shot of Saenz in his jeans, striding resolutely to the gate, his face grave and deeply shadowed in the late afternoon sun. In another shot of Saenz, Jerome is visible in the background, looking even grimmer than usual, his lips pressed together tightly.

The phone rings and Valdes picks up. He listens to the caller for a minute, then frowns and cups the mouthpiece.

"Missing boy. Mariano's *barangay tanods* just alerted our people. Someone saw a man who fits Alex's description dragging a boy of about twelve or thirteen away, toward the landfill. He apparently left a vehicle parked near the location of the sighting."

"A vehicle," Jerome repeats. "What kind of vehicle?"

"Small sedan, old model." Valdes returns to the person speaking on the phone and makes a few more inquiries. "Toyota. SBN253. That's Alex's license plate."

Director Lastimosa looks up at Valdes. "The boy—was he alive?"

"Looks like it, sir. Witness said he tried to fight back."

The director turns to Saenz. "We've got a boy alive. You still think you might be able to bring Alex back without a struggle? With adequate backup?"

"We can try, sir."

"But, Director," Arcinas begins to object.

"With adequate backup, Ben," Lastimosa says, silencing him. He fixes Saenz with a hard stare. "Just remember, my boys are authorized to take extraordinary measures if they see you or the boy are in grave danger."

Saenz rises to his feet. "Extraordinary measures, sir? How am I to interpret that?"

"Any way you please, Father, as long as you don't forget it." The director turns to Valdes and Arcinas. "Provide any assistance and support he needs. And bring that boy back alive."

WHERE ALEX CARLOS is, the air is alive with many voices, thick with unquiet memory. He is vaguely aware of how filthy he must be, but he can let that go for now or maybe for good—he can't be sure.

He can hear the boys whispering quietly among themselves, and they stand just far enough from him so that he cannot hear what they are saying very well. Once in a while one of them will look in his direction, and he fancies he can see a small smile on that boy's face.

The smile fills him with anger.

The boy is lying on the floor, his hands and feet bound with tape, a dirty rag stuffed in his mouth. He'd tried to fight, but Alex was stronger. He is scared but defiant. Every time Alex tries to come closer, he thrashes about like a fish caught on a hook, trying to kick him with his bound feet.

You think you're so brave, but you're not. You're no better than I am. Go ahead, shake your head. You think making fun of me will make things easier for you? It won't.

The past is alive and immediate in Alex's head. It meshes seamlessly with what's here and now, and this boy's face fits into the parade of faces that torment him in his nightmares: living faces and dead ones, from decades or months ago, each one smiling slyly or laughing openly at him.

I can take it. I don't care what you say or think about me. Go ahead, laugh. It's not like I'm the only one who gets it.

He could join the circle, but no, better to stay here, motionless in the dark, where maybe he won't be found. But he's always found anyway. And every time it hurts more and more, or is it less and less? And he is getting used to it so that it doesn't matter anymore.

The boy is trying to say something, mumbling and moaning through the rag.

What did you say? Come on, say it louder; say it so I can hear it, and I'll punch your faces and knock out your teeth. I will tear your flesh and rip out your guts and kill you, kill you all.

48

"AT LEAST WEAR the vest."

Jerome shoves the heavy, black bulletproof vest toward Saenz, but the older priest makes a face and waves it away. It still smells of all the bodies that have worn it before.

"No, no. It will only slow me down. I'll go as I am or not at all."

"Pity you can't be excommunicated for pigheadedness." Jerome uses his bare hand to wipe the sweat from his brow. He cannot understand why he should be perspiring so when the rain has been pouring for half an hour, the wind dipping low every now and then and whipping furiously around them.

They are in the covered porch of the parish church, and a few of the agents are gathered around them, preparing for the apprehension of Alex Carlos.

Jerome blows a puff of air out of his mouth, scratches his head and turns back to Saenz, searching the older man's face for reassurance. "Do you really think this is a good idea?"

"To begin with, I didn't think the priesthood was such a good idea, but here we are," Saenz quips. He reaches out and playfully rumples up Jerome's hair to annoy him, as he used to do when he was still his student.

Then, as Jerome smoothes his hair down, Saenz clutches the wooden crucifix hanging from its cord down to his chest, closes his eyes and says a brief prayer.

Arcinas walks toward them. "Okay, everybody's ready. We can go."

There are three unmarked cars waiting for them. Jake Valdes is standing by the first with three other agents; Arcinas and another set of agents are climbing into the last one. Saenz sees the familiar faces of agents Ed Borja and Norman Estrella through the windshield of the middle car.

Norman, who's at the wheel, waves at Saenz. "Over here, Father."

Saenz waves back. As he and Jerome enter the car, he sees two familiar figures in the rearview mirror, also entering another car parked some distance away—a woman and a man. He doesn't mention it to Jerome.

"It's too bad we haven't seen the interior of the gymnasium," Jerome says.

Saenz is looking straight ahead, at the rain lashing against the windshield.

"He won't be inside the gymnasium."

"Where, then?"

"You're the psychologist. Think about it. He wouldn't feel safe inside the gymnasium; it's the place where he was violated. No. He'll make his stand in the one place where he feels he's safe, in control."

"The mobile clinic."

"We know enough about the killings to know that he left very little blood at the sites where the bodies were found. Remember what we were saying? Someplace easy to clean. A garage. A bathroom. Possibly a vehicle."

"And a converted bus would be a logical place." Jerome pauses. "He tidies up afterward. The rubber boots. Everything can be washed."

Saenz nods. "If his safety zone is violated, he'll be forced to act."

"I don't like the sound of that."

The older priest sighs. "Get in line."

"Joanna, where the hell are you?" Wally Soler's voice booms over the cell phone.

"I'm following Arcinas and his boys. They've got Saenz tracking Alex Carlos." The woman has her hands full steering through the rain, keeping the phone balanced between her right ear and shoulder.

"Why didn't you bring Manny along?" The man's voice is a snarl. "You know you're not supposed to do these things alone."

She smiles. "Aw, Wally Bally FoFally, are you worried about me? No, really, that's okay; you can tell me. I'm touched."

"Shut up and give me your exact location, Bonifacio. I'm sending Manny to meet up with you."

She grimaces in the darkness. "Manny is old and slow. And smells bad. Anyway, I've got Leo with me."

At the mention of his name, Leo grins widely, his teeth the most visible part of him in the darkness of the vehicle.

"Leo is small and can't protect you."

"It's okay, Wally. Why you know, come to think of it, maybe my mission on earth is to protect Leo," she chortles, as Leo's grin turns into a pout.

She can see her boss now, standing by the phone with his sleeves rolled up, rubbing the bridge of his nose in weary resignation.

"Joanna, what am I going to do with you?"

In the past, sitting on the staircases and in the living rooms of houses she grew up in, Joanna has heard this same telephone conversation many times, with her dead father's voice in place of her own.

The voice at the other end of the line was always Wally Soler's.

"Worry about me, Wally," she says quietly. "Just like you did for Papa."

The man has nothing to say to this, and she knows that at this moment he is remembering his best friend, a big, tall, solemn man with a deceptively gentle face and manner. Many years ago, on a night very much like this one, Antonio Bonifacio went out on an assignment and did not come back alive.

Wally Soler will not lose the daughter the same way; no, sir, not if he can help it.

Ahead of her, the NBI cars slow to a stop.

"Have to go, Wallykins," she says with forced cheeriness. "Buy some doughnuts for when we get back."

When the line goes dead, Wally hangs on for a moment.

If anything happens to the stupid, mule-headed bitch, I'll skin her myself, dead or alive, God help her.

God, help her.

49

JUST MINUTES AFTER they leave the church, the agents' two-way radios crackle to life. It's Valdes. Ed responds, trying to keep his voice low, but it's clear something's wrong. He looks over his shoulder at Saenz.

"*Tanods* found the missing boy not far from here. Side of the landfill nearest the school."

"Alive?" Jerome asks, but from the looks Ed and Norman exchange with each other, the answer is obvious.

"So we're heading there." Saenz says it not as a question but as a matter of fact.

"It's just up the road."

It's not long before they see the flashing lights of police vehicles. A checkpoint has been set up, manned by *barangay tanods* and policemen, and the three NBI cars are waved through. They all come to a halt near the line of police and *barangay* cars.

Valdes steps out, motions for Ed and Norman to follow with Saenz and Jerome. They leave the car, walk bareheaded in rain that has dwindled to a drizzle. The smell of the garbage is overpowering. The ground is wet with rain, streaked with mud.

Valdes stops to talk to a uniformed policeman. After a few seconds, the policeman points toward the dump, and Valdes turns to make sure they're all following before heading in that direction.

It's less than two minutes before they see the body.

"It'll be at least half an hour before Rustia gets here," Valdes says.

Saenz nods. Tonight they cannot wait.

Somebody—Ed or Norman—hands him a large flashlight, and then everyone else steps back. Saenz switches the light on and then bends to examine the ground around the body.

Two black rats, their fur glistening with droplets of rain, turn toward the light but boldly stand their ground. Jerome hisses, a sharp and threatening sound, and the rats scurry away, startled.

Saenz moves the flashlight's beam so that it traces the outline of something in the mud: a footprint. "Men's size six?" he asks, seeking another opinion.

"Looks like it," Jerome answers. "Same garden-variety plastic rain boot."

Satisfied, Saenz steps carefully toward the body. He feels more than a bit ashamed of the way excitement and anticipation are warring with the sorrow and horror and revulsion within him. The shame feels like sand in his mouth, rough and gritty, and he wishes he could spit it out.

This is important; this is the closest they have ever come to him. They're separated from this young boy's death and the presence of his killer by a mere hour or two.

The body is lying facedown in the mud. Saenz holds up an open palm, and Jerome knows what he wants. He unzips a small plastic case and fishes out a pair of disposable gloves. He hands them to Saenz, who gives him the flashlight and quickly pulls the gloves on.

He lays a hand on the dead boy's back, between the shoulder blades.

"It's still warm." Saenz shakes his head, as though clearing away cobwebs in his brain. "I mean, *he's* still warm."

The two priests look at each other a few seconds in mutual understanding. How easy it is to see the dead person as a body, a thing, a piece of evidence.

Saenz holds the corpse by the shoulders, turns it over gently on its back.

The face is gone.

Jerome backs away; it is the first fresh corpse they have seen in this series of killings, and although he has seen dead bodies before, he is not fully prepared for the raw, bloody pulp above the child's neck. The yellow glow from the flashlight and the

headlights of the police vehicles enhances, rather than dimin-
ishes, the ghastliness of the sight.

"You all right?" Saenz glances up at him just as a beam from
one of the police cars' flashing lights catches Jerome's pallid face.
"Why don't you go back for a while? I can handle things here."

"No. I'm fine," Jerome says, more to convince himself than
Saenz.

Saenz turns his attention back to the body.

Domine, dirige nos.

With his gloved forefinger, he tilts the chin up and traces
the clean horizontal slash he had expected to find there.

The boy is still wearing shorts. He has been stabbed several
times in the chest. This time, aside from the flaying of the
face, the body bears none of the usual injuries—the evisceration, the removal of the heart and the genitals.

Saenz sees a tiny glint of metal in the mud. He reaches out
with a gloved hand, wiping away as much mud as he can to
expose the object but leaving it where it lies. It is a dental
elevator with a rubber grip. He moves aside a bit so that
Jerome can see it.

The sense of his presence is so strong, like the unsettled air
in his apartment when the two priests arrived there earlier.
Saenz remains absolutely still, listening as though he might
still catch his voice or footfall receding in the darkness.

The rats begin inching closer to the body again, watching
the men with eyes like small, shiny beads. One rears up on its
hind legs unsteadily, sniffing the air.

"Gus, look," Jerome says, gesturing toward the body with
the flashlight.

Saenz follows the path of the beam. On the inner side of
the upper arm, two thin, deep, blood-caked circles, a small
one on top of a slightly bigger one: the number 8.

The priests' eyes lock again, a terrible understanding passing
wordlessly between and through them, like a thin shaft of glass.

Saenz stands up, peeling his gloves off.

"What are you thinking?" Jerome asks.

Saenz shakes his head. "He falls outside of the normal pattern somewhat."

"Because of the absence of the other usual injuries."

"He's in a hurry, then. Dispensing with the rest of the ritual because he knows we're getting close." Saenz studies Jerome's face. "You all right?"

"I'm good," he replies, but Saenz can feel his profound disquiet when he asks, "We can stop here, right? And leave the rest to Valdes and Arcinas? There's nothing more we can do for the boy."

The rats begin squealing at each other, restless to have their turn at the body. For some reason, this makes Saenz unspeakably angry. "Not for this boy, no." He turns in the direction of the school. "But perhaps for the other one—"

"Gus. I really don't think—"

"Father Gus?" a voice calls out. A small man emerges from the tight huddle of NBI and police personnel and comes up to them. He is carrying a large, powerful flashlight in one hand and what looks like a heavy black toolbox in the other.

"Ading? That you?"

Rustia waves his flashlight in response, taking care not to shine the beam directly in their eyes. "Yes, Father." He moves forward with deliberate slowness, checking the mud around him as he goes. "We've got the tracks of a very large vehicle coming up this way. Something like a big bus."

"Good man. We saw a print or two near the body. Looked like rain boots."

"Hmmm. Okay. I'll deal with it. Anything else?"

"Dental elevator."

"Hmmm. Right. Did you handle anything much?"

"Used gloves and turned the boy over to see the injuries. Otherwise left as much as we could undisturbed."

Rustia pauses to consider the situation. "Not ideal, but okay. We'll be extra careful."

50

IT IS 11 P.M. on the first Saturday of September.

The cars pull up to the gates of the school: a drab, boxy three-story building with rows of darkened windows—all the same size and shape, all blankly looking out to the school yard like soulless eyes. There's a spindly flagpole right in front, surrounded by pots of dead or dying shrubbery. The gate has been busted open.

When Saez looks through the car windows at the people in the other NBI vehicles, they're all staring at the building, as if momentarily frozen. Even Ed and Norman are sitting stock-still, both peering warily through the windshield as though confronted by a colossus.

He finally decides to make the first move, popping the lock on the door with a loud click. "Wish me luck," he says to Jerome, swinging his long legs out of the car.

The drizzle getting stronger now, the wind picking up speed once more.

"Luck, nothing." Jerome says it sharply, his expression stern. "We'll be right behind you."

Saenz walks forward, his shoes squishing in the mud. As he approaches the gate, it becomes clear that a large vehicle has been rammed through it. The metal tubing, which frames rusty chicken wire, is crushed in places, and there are wide, deep tire tracks in the mud. He glances behind him, just as the other NBI personnel begin leaving their cars.

Valdes approaches Saenz, Jerome following close behind him. "You sure you want to do this?" Valdes asks, and Saenz can sense the concern beneath his usual detachment. "With the boy dead, there's no reason why we can't sweep in and make this arrest ourselves."

"I'm not making an arrest, Jake," Saenz says quietly. "Look, we have an opportunity here to understand what really happened. Why he killed those boys. What intervention might have prevented him from killing, and at what point. But that can only happen if we bring him out alive. Will you give me your word that you'll hold off doing anything drastic until there's no other option left?"

"That's a promise I can't make, Father. You know that."

"Jake. We've come this far."

Before Valdes can answer, they hear the wail of several sirens, and then several police cars, their lights flashing, come screeching up the road, encircling the three NBI cars.

"What's all this?" Jerome asks.

Confusion, understanding, and finally, anger, flicker across Valdes's face in rapid succession. "Police backup."

"Did you ask for that?"

Valdes makes a huffing, impatient sound, then smiles a cynical little nonsmile. "It just arrives sometimes, unasked for."

Saez understands at once: it's a turf thing. And right now, not his problem. He turns and begins walking away from them until he has crossed the schoolyard. He can no longer hear their voices. For a moment, he has to reassure himself that the fact that he cannot see Jerome and the others does not mean they are not there.

He glances upward without knowing why. The moon is three-quarters full in a murky sky, broad, grey scars across its sickly, yellow face.

The mobile clinic is parked just outside the gym, beside an old acacia with a gnarled trunk. One side of the converted bus is wedged against the trunk, the metal warped, the windows shattered. It's clear the vehicle was driven to this spot at high speed, so forcefully that it clipped some of the tree's lower branches. They lie in a tangled mess on the vehicle's roof, their wet leaves clinging to its sides and windows like seaweed. In the darkness, it seems to Saenz as though some massive, sinister creature has caught hold of the clinic, wrapping it in a grotesque, unbreakable embrace.

He walks over to the clinic slowly. The soft squish of his shoes in the mud seems too noisy.

The door creaks when he opens it. With a deep breath and a prayer, he takes his first step inside.

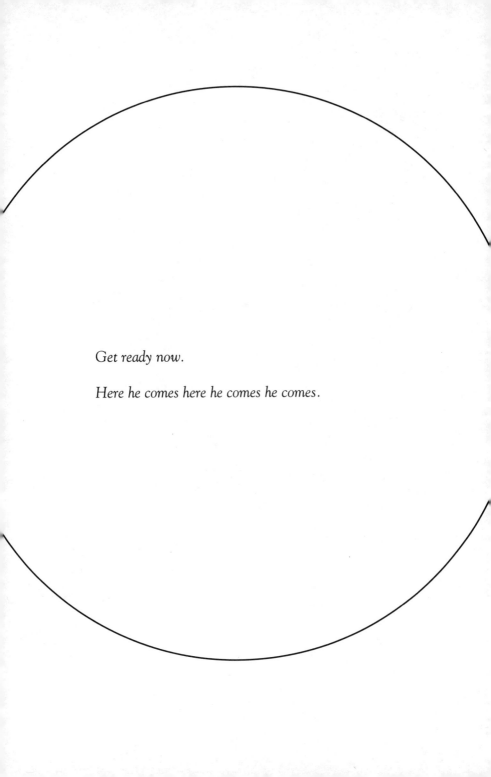

Get ready now.

Here he comes here he comes he comes.

51

ALL THE WORLD quiet—the kind of quiet one only hears underwater.

"Alex?" Saenz calls out, and the sound of his voice seems at once loud and muffled to his own ears.

He takes a moment to compose himself and becomes aware of the sound of heavy breathing with a slight asthmatic wheeze to it.

"Come on. I won't hurt you."

There is a smell in the mobile clinic—a fishy, rusty sort of smell, and Saenz quickly realizes that it is the smell of blood, and the blood is starting to go bad.

His right foot slides in front of him without his moving it, and he looks down. With his eyes becoming accustomed to the darkness, he can tell what the wetness on the vinyl mats is; they are awash with blood.

Pulsing along in time with his heartbeat, split-second snap-shots of memory flash strobe-like through Saenz's consciousness: a body on a gurney, scribblings like fat blue worms on the big whiteboard in the lab, organs in a freezer.

Sitting in the dentist's chair. Mrs. Bansuy's *turon*, warm and sweet. The raw wound in the place of a dead child's face.

All the little threads and paths leading to this night, this place.

AS SOON AS the camera is set on the tripod and the focus adjusted, Leo allows Joanna to look through the viewfinder. The thought comes to her the moment she sees Saenz's tall figure framed in the door of the vehicle.

Get the hell out of there, Gus.

AWARE OF SMALL lumps he can neither see nor identify squishing and oozing beneath the soles of his shoes, Saenz inches forward carefully. He's so tall that the top of his head grazes the ceiling of the vehicle, forcing him to stoop.

"Alex," he says again, his voice gentle as the brush of a butterfly's wing. He can make out the outlines of furniture and equipment in the clinic: a desk, a stool on ball casters, a dentist's chair, a filing cabinet. He searches for, but does not find, the irregular shape of someone crouching in the shadows.

At the far end of the mobile clinic is a pleated curtain hung on a series of rings. The curtain is drawn. The sound of breathing is coming from behind it.

Saenz sticks his left foot out and drags the stool toward him. He picks it up and holds it in front of his chest with the leg and wheels sticking out, using it as some kind of shield in case Alex springs out from behind the curtain to attack him.

"I know what happened," he continues. "What was done to you. I want to help."

The curtain moves, and Saenz ducks to avoid the object that's been hurled at him: a half-full bottle of ethyl alcohol. It moves again, and a plastic garbage pail lands at his feet. As far as Saenz can tell, it's filled with blood-soaked rags, but he doesn't look too closely. He's almost certain there's something else in there that he doesn't want to see.

"I think I know what he told you," he says. "That you were his special little boy. That it would be fun. That's what people like him do. They try to gain your trust so that they can do terrible things to you."

"Go to hell." The voice is small, frightened, hoarse, and the words hang in the clotted air, in this small space, in the thick dark.

"I think he tried to frighten you too. I think he told you that he would find a way to hurt your mother and father if you didn't do what he asked."

There is another odor in the tortured air, and the priest recognizes it as the faint scent of urine. A thin blade of fear, cold like surgical steel in the brain, slices through the priest's consciousness. Alex Carlos has never been more dangerous than he is at this moment. Saenz decides then and there that he won't try to move any closer. He's conscious now of movement near the mobile clinic, of shadows scurrying outside the windows.

Extraordinary measures, the director had said.

There's no time to waste; he has to draw Alex out, fast.

"We talked to them. Your mother. Your father."

"You stay away from them," Alex snarls at him.

"They want to see you again. They feel bad that they couldn't help you then. But they want to help you now."

"Shut up. Shut up."

"Come on, Alex. Can't you see? You've become a little bit like him already. Is that what you wanted?" Saenz waits for a response; when it doesn't come, he continues. "I don't think so. I think the last thing you want is to be anything like him."

"I'm nothing like him," Alex says savagely from behind the curtain.

"I know you're not. So please. Come out with me now. Let us try to help. You can put him behind you, and this will all stop."

The curtain moves a third time, the plastic rings clacking against the rail as Alex draws the fabric back.

He is shirtless and barefoot, his face, torso and arms stained with blood. His jeans are matted to his thighs.

"I can't put it behind me," he whimpers.

"Yes, you can. It can be fixed."

"How can I fix this?" he screams, hurling something at Saenz's feet. Saenz flinches as it lands on the vinyl matting with a wet, slapping sound. "You tell me, Father, how do I fix this?"

Saenz doesn't have to look at it to know what it is.

"You can't bring them back, Alex; you and I know that. But you can heal yourself. Just a little bit, every day. You can regain what he took from you. You can atone for what you took from others."

Alex sits down on his haunches, clutching his bare stomach with one hand. "You really think they will let you help me,

Father? That's not how this world works." He begins rocking back and forth on his heels. "I tried to tell people, but nobody listened, nobody wanted to know. They wanted me to keep quiet. I didn't matter. None of us mattered to anyone."

"You matter. Here and now, I am telling you: what happened to you still matters."

But Alex goes on, as though he hasn't heard Saenz. "That's what's going to happen, too, when I walk out that door. Nobody wants to know the truth."

"I want to know." Saenz holds out a hand to him. "I will listen."

Saenz can tell that Alex is torn between staying and taking the hand offered to him. "Let's go," he says, as if it's a foregone conclusion, allowing a bright note of optimism to creep into his voice.

Alex rises to his feet and begins to walk toward him. Saenz waits until he is inches away and looks first at his hands—both empty—and then at his face, streaked with blood and tears, the features delicate as a bird's. And he's filled with an irrational anger: at Gorospe, at the parents, at the school—surely someone must have suspected or known something—at everything that has brought Alex Carlos to this place.

"Let me walk ahead of you, okay?" Saenz says, and Alex nods meekly.

It's only a few short steps to the door, and Saenz shouts, "We're coming out!"

He's only taken one step down from the bus when he feels it: a puff of air against his ear, followed by a burning sensation.

He turns around in time to see Alex staring down at a hole in his own left side, below the breastbone, the wrath blooming in his face, the sudden flash of a blade in a hand that was empty just seconds ago.

"WHAT THE HELL is going on?" Valdes shouts into his two-way radio, dragging Jerome behind one of their cars for cover. "Who fired that shot? Arcinas, that'd better not be any of your boys!"

The radio crackles, and then it's Arcinas, breathless, panicky. "It wasn't us, I swear! Not with our own men moving around that bus!"

"Well, who was it, then?"

Jerome looks up in time to see Saenz tipping backward into the mud and Alex Carlos falling upon him in a fit of rage.

"Gus!" Jerome shouts, and tries to get back on his feet, but more shots are fired, and Valdes drags him back down to safety.

ALEX'S SHRILL CRIES fill Saenz's ears, and he feels a cold slashing pain, first on his arm, then on his shoulder, then in a diagonal line down his chest. He falls backward out of the mobile clinic, into the mud, and sees Alex's thin figure leap out after him.

He flops over on his stomach, tries to crawl quickly away, but he feels the other man's weight on his back.

"I told you! I told you this would happen!" Alex screams, his mouth close to Saenz's ear. He's straddling Saenz's back, pulling his head up off the ground by grabbing a handful of his hair.

As he tries to push Alex off his back, Saenz can hear other voices around them shouting, the staccato popping of guns being fired.

"Stop," he tries to shout, "stop firing!" But he can only manage a strangled cry.

JOANNA DRAGS LEO forward, grabbing the rest of his equipment, battery pack and extra tapes so that his hands will be left free to manipulate the heavy camera. They find a clear spot, set up their gear quickly. They hear the sound of gunfire and now angry voices. "Leo, what's going on?" she asks him.

Leo steps aside so she can look. She sees a flurry of motion near the school gates. She pans to the right and spots what she believes to be a number of plainclothes NBI agents swooping down on the mobile clinic. A small adjustment and now she's looking at the door of the clinic, where two figures seem to be struggling with each other. Everything is happening so fast.

When she zooms in to get a closer look, she finds herself staring straight into the face of Alex Carlos, the hatred on it so powerful and terrible that she feels it almost as a kind of heat, sucked up through the viewfinder and blasting on her own face. Saenz, crawling on his belly in the mud, is trying to claw away from him, but he's very strong. He flips Saenz on his back and raises his hand high above his head.

"Jesus, no," Joanna says when she sees that he's holding a knife.

. . . BEAST YOU BEAST *you animal* . . .

Saenz hears this unnatural, high, hoarse shriek again and again as the blade flashes above him, stark against the night sky, slashing once, twice. He tries to fight him off, to shield his face and body with his arms. He manages to grab Alex's wrists, but his hands are slippery with blood, and Alex twists easily out of his grasp.

I told you but you wouldn't listen! I told you I didn't like it. I didn't want any of it. I. Didn't. Want. It.

The face above him is contorted with fury. The world begins to slow down, and Alex's screams slide lower and lower down the scale to a mere rumble in his ears.

He tries to see if help is coming, *help me now help quick*, sees a pale blur moving fast and close to the ground a few yards away from his tilted head: Jerome rushing toward him, and then a few other men, their heavy feet spattering mud.

Before he slips into the soft, welcoming dark, he sees a flash, then two, then more, in rapid succession like lightning, hears two loud, muffled explosions and Jerome's voice shouting *no, stop, wait*, and then all sound and pain and scarred yellow moon fall away.

This really hurts.

*But I've killed you at last, haven't I? All of you.
I know all your faces. Can't you see? You all look
like me. We're all the same to him, to all of them.
After we're used up, we're thrown away.*

And you were wrong, all of you.

I didn't like it. I didn't want any of it.

I. Didn't. Want. It.

*That's right. Go back into the shadows now.
Stay quiet. Give me the peace I deserve.*

*It's so cold. I'm really sleepy all of a sudden.
The pain should keep me awake, but I guess   not*

not this time

mama papa   so   sorry

so sleepy   so   quiet   it's about

time

52

SAENZ DRIFTS IN and out of consciousness. He hears hushed voices, can tell when he's alone in the room and when he's not. He struggles to wake, but in the infrequent moments when he does wake, all he wants to do is fall back asleep. His limbs feel weighted with lead, and there is a large, numb ball of *nothing* where his stomach and chest should be. Night, day—he can't tell which is which. The blinds on the windows are always drawn.

He dreams uneasily. Father Ramirez visits in one of those dreams, his bald head gleaming under the light of the ceiling lamp. In the dream, Ramirez is talking to him, kindly and reassuring, but there's something in his eyes that frightens him. The monsignor lifts up the blanket, his fleshy hands clammy, and he's still talking, talking, friendly and gentle. Saenz kicks and flails, but his limbs are heavy, so heavy, and the monsignor whispers in his ear: *It's all right. It's going to be all right. This will make you feel better. This will be our secret.*

And Saenz shouts, *Not in my Church! No secrets in my Church!* he protests, as he feels hands crawling up his legs, up his thighs. And he realizes that he is screaming in Alex Carlos's voice.

The good monsignor only laughs.

In another dream, it's Cardinal Meneses who comes to visit. He is wearing a scarlet *magna cappa* and seated on an ornate chair too large for Saenz's small hospital room. There is a fat orange cat lying at his feet, licking the toe of his shoe. Like Ramirez, the Cardinal, too, is smiling at Saenz, but it's not a very friendly smile. *Oh, but I can assure you that I sleep just fine, Father Saenz; it's your dreams that are troubled.*

"HEY."

When he opens his eyes, the blinds are open, and the wall

across from the bed is lined in alternating strips of sunlight and shadow.

"What day is it?" he asks, his voice hoarse from disuse.

"Wednesday. Four days after." Jerome holds up a drinking glass half-filled with water. "Drink?"

Saenz takes a sip of water through a straw in the glass. He swallows, then allows his head to fall back on the pillows. It's not pain—he feels pain, but it's blunted by what he believes to be massive doses of drugs—but fatigue, a sense of crushing heaviness. He looks around the room and sees a bank of monitors that are attached to him with wires and tubing.

"Alex?" he asks.

Jerome shakes his head sadly.

Saenz frowns. "I asked Valdes . . . no shooting. What happened?" His thoughts, his speech are slowed by the meds.

"Not the NBI. An over-eager policeman. Started shooting as soon as he caught sight of Alex. He took four bullets."

"Four? Four bullets?" Outraged, frustrated, Saenz tries to lift his head and shoulders above the pillows, but the pain from his wounds forces him to stop.

"Hey, hey. Take it easy." Jerome lays a hand on his shoulder and eases him back carefully to a resting position. "It all happened very quickly. The NBI agents couldn't even get close to the two of you because of the gunfire. An investigation is underway—Director Lastimosa insisted on it."

"So—all useless?" He asks the question as though he cannot wrap his mind around what has happened. "All that effort—useless?"

Jerome can't think of anything good to say, so he keeps quiet.

Saenz pounds a fist ineffectually into the mattress at a spot beside his right thigh. "But what—what to tell parents? What to say?"

A high-pitched beep goes off, and they both stare at the

source of the sound in alarm. It's emanating from one of the monitors.

"Take it easy," Jerome says, just as the door opens and two nurses rush in.

"What happened?" one of them asks Jerome.

"We were just talking."

"Heart rate and BP are up," the other one says to her.

"I think we should let him rest, Father," the first one tells Jerome.

Jerome nods. But Saenz's eyes are wide, questioning, insistent. "Who's responsible?" he asks, trying to sit up and failing. "Jerome?"

"Not your problem right now, Gus," Jerome says gently. "Your problem is to get as much rest as you can. You understand me?"

"But—"

"No buts. You're not well yet. Far from it."

The first nurse checks his IV drip. "He's right, Father. You should get some more sleep."

"Jer—"

"I'll be back tomorrow. We'll talk about it then. But only if you promise to rest."

53

THE BLINDS, HE'S learned, make a characteristic sound
when they're being drawn open or closed. He opens his eyes
and sees the director by the windows. It's daytime.

"Good morning, Father."

"Morning," he croaks.

"You came to see me when I was confined. Thought I
would return the favor."

Saenz smiles weakly. "Not very good company."

"You? Or me?" The director chuckles. "How are you feeling?"

"Been better."

"Have the doctors told you what happened to you?"

"More or less." His tongue feels thick, his mind thicker.
He holds up both hands, heavily bandaged, in front of his
face and stares at them. "Deep cuts. No major arteries or
organs hit."

Lastimosa pats Saenz's hand. "It's something of a miracle
that you're still with us."

"Fairly certain other people would use a different word."
Must have a word with the doctors about reducing the drugs, Saenz
tells himself. *Can't go on like this, without full control of my
faculties, my speech.*

"Well. Their opinion doesn't matter to me. Neither should
it matter to you." The director peers down at him. "You found
him for us."

"But gone. Finished." Saenz is shaking his head. "Shot."

"Yes." The director's face is tight with repressed anger. "I've
ordered an investigation. From what we can tell initially, it
was some rookie from the police backup unit who panicked
and fired the first shot. We'll get to the bottom of it; you have
my word. But we also have to consider that your life was in
grave danger."

Saenz nods, but the expression on his face makes it plain to the director that he's unconvinced. "But lost opportunity."

"I understand."

A deep breath, then Saenz sinks back onto the pillows, so very tired.

"But I may have something to soften your discontent, Father." The director settles himself into a chair by the windows, folding his thin arms close to his body. "When I first met you, you had just lost a battle with your Monsignor Ramirez."

Saenz's eyes open wide, fix their gaze on the director.

"Don't . . . understand."

"All these years you have been after him, Father Saenz. What has been your real goal? To defrock him? To expel him from the Church?"

"Charity," Saenz bites out. "Remove him . . . from charity. No more access to children. No more hiding or being protected."

"As I thought," Director Lastimosa nods. "Well. I will come back in a few days, Father Saenz. And if you are better, I will have a story to tell you. I think you will find it very interesting."

"Story?"

The door opens a crack and Jerome peeps in. Seeing the director, he begins to excuse himself, but the director calls out to him as he rises from the chair.

"Father Lucero. I was just leaving. Please, come in."

Saenz puts out a hand to grasp the director's cuff. "What story?"

He smiles down at Saenz. "Give it a few days, Father Saenz. I assure you, it will be worth the wait."

LITTLE BY LITTLE, Saenz's wounds heal, and his strength returns. Most of the wounds—gashes in his chest, stomach, neck and arms, a cut on his jawline and another just below his left eye—are deep. He will bear their scars for the rest of his life, but he will have a life, and it will be more or less normal. Or at least, the sort of "normal" that is normal for him.

The doctors begin to reduce the dosage of painkillers so that he doesn't feel as though he's wrapped in cotton wool from head to toe all the time. He is able to handle visitors, although he asks to limit these to just a handful—Jerome, Susan, Tato, members of his own family. He is able, first to sit up, then to stand, to shuffle to the bathroom and back, and later, to walk to and from the hospital garden, albeit slowly.

It is on one of these trips to the garden, as he's sitting on a bench in the shade of a big *narra* tree, that the director comes to see him. He walks slowly up the path in his customary *barong Tagalog*, a thick manila envelope tucked under his arm.

"Good morning, Father."

"Good morning."

He points to the bench with a bony finger. "May I sit?"

Saenz slides over to one side. "Please do."

Director Lastimosa sinks down on the bench with a slight groan, then smiles ruefully at Saenz. "You young people don't know how lucky you are."

Saenz smiles back just as ruefully. "I'm not so young anymore, sir."

They sit and contemplate the garden for a while in companionable silence. Then Saenz begins: "I seem to recall you had a story to tell me."

"And I do."

Saenz laces his bandaged fingers together and waits.

"What do you know about Eliot Ness and Al Capone, Father?"

Saenz turns and stares at him. "Eliot N—I'm not sure I . . ."

Director Lastimosa smiles. "The history books tell us that the US treasury secretary, Andrew Mellon, told Ness to gather proof Capone was violating Prohibition laws. But nobody was sure if he could be successfully prosecuted. He was a slimy one."

"So . . . the Treasury and the Justice Department took a parallel path."

"Correct. They wrangled some help from Chicago's business elite and managed to convict him of income tax evasion." The director looks as satisfied as he might have if he'd secured that conviction himself. "Eleven years in prison."

Saenz leans back on the bench. "And this has something to do with Father Ramirez—how, exactly?"

"When we spoke in your hospital room last week, I asked you: what has been your real goal in chasing after Ramirez? And you said—"

"Remove him from the charity he heads. Cut off his access to minors. Remove the veil of protection that has kept him in a position of trust all these years."

"And you have already presented to your superiors the voices of some of his victims. But they chose not to listen."

"They listened, but they did not do what was most important: to turn him over to the law and to cut off his access. So the victims withdrew, recanted."

"Then, Father, may I suggest that you, too, take a parallel path?"

"I don't understand."

Director Lastimosa takes the envelope from under his arm and slides it across the bench toward Saenz. "Are you familiar with Monsignor Ramirez's lifestyle, Father Saenz? His real lifestyle, I mean—not the one that he chooses to let the rest of the world see. If you aren't, I think you should be. He lives in a manner that is—well, let's just say he's not only turned his back on his vow of chastity but also of poverty."

Saenz opens the envelope and begins to pore over the contents: deeds to property, receipts, photographs—of expensive cars, of the facades of two homes in two separate gated communities, of a high-rise condominium in the heart of the Makati financial district. He turns to the director.

"Are you telling me Father Ramirez owns all these? How do you know? How can we prove it?"

"Let us say the monsignor is smart enough to divert money from his charity but not quite smart enough to fully conceal where it has gone."

Saenz studies the photographs again. "Money from the charity. Of course."

"Keep going," the director says, tilting his head toward the contents of the envelope.

Saenz leafs through the remaining photographs. They show four very young men and women—possibly in their late teens, at most—going about their daily business to and from the homes.

"House help?" Saenz asks.

"Hmmm. Of a sort. They were former beneficiaries of *Kanlungan*."

Saenz winces as if in pain. "So they're not really house help." He's appalled, but not surprised, that Ramirez would have the audacity to bring wards or former wards of the charity to live with him—very likely to continue harming and exploiting them.

"Sadly, no." The director stands. "You can keep those—my people have the originals. And if I may make a suggestion, you might want to pay a visit to Mrs. Veronica Urrutia when you have recovered fully. I think she and her friends on *Kanlungan*'s board of directors will be very interested to learn how the good monsignor has been spending their contributions."

Saenz is astonished. *A parallel path, indeed.* Still, after years of defeat and disappointment, he knows better than to allow himself anything more than the slightest glimmer of hope. "But this—all this has to be proven in court first."

"Oh, yes, of course. And it will be an uphill battle, I don't need to tell you. But if I know anything about human nature, Father Saenz, you may just get what you want even before any case goes to trial."

The priest rises unsteadily to his feet, his hands overflowing with the papers and photographs. "How?"

The smile on the man's face is wry but sad at the same time. "You tell a few rich people that a priest is abusing children? They may care, but they're unlikely to do anything about it. But you tell them that same priest is stealing their money? Sit back and watch how fast they move." He shrugs. "Just the way of the world, Father Saenz."

Saenz clutches the papers to his chest. "I can't—I mean . . . Thank you."

The director begins to walk away, but then he stops, as though he's remembered something. "You know something, Father? I'm a Catholic. A good Catholic, I think. Mass every Sunday, confession and Communion whenever I can. But all these years, I've been worried. About where the Church is going. About whether it still has the needs of the flock at the center of its mission. About whether it is operating within the framework of the law."

Saenz considers these concerns, so similar to those that have troubling him in recent years.

"The Church in this great Catholic country of ours is the last great, unexamined mystery. And I think you know what happens when you don't let the sunlight into dark places, Father." Lastimosa holds Saenz's gaze for a moment, then looks up at the sky. "It's going to rain soon. Better be safe inside when it comes down."

HE HAD SECOND thoughts about it, but Jerome has brought flowers anyway.

The marble headstone is small and simple, nothing but a name, a date of birth and a date of death. He stands in front of it for a few minutes, and then remembers the baby chrysanthemums and statis he's clutching behind him.

He bends and lays the flowers on the stone, beaded with raindrops from the morning's drizzle.

What a waste, he thinks to himself. *What an awful waste.*

He hears footsteps behind him, padding softly in the wet grass.

"You'll catch your death of pneumonia."

"Hey," he says, surprised at the sight of Saenz waving a black umbrella this way and that. "You're not supposed to be out yet."

Saenz smiles mischievously. "I bribed a nurse." His left hand is swathed in sterile gauze, one of many places on his body where Alex Carlos will be remembered.

"Don't tell me. Saenz money. Useful in a pinch." They both chuckle, and then he turns back to look at the headstone in silence as Saenz stands beside him. "How did you know I'd be here?"

"Just a guess. I knew the funeral was this morning." It has been several weeks since the night Alex Carlos was shot and killed, but his body was held for examination. "Thought you might not have wanted his parents to see you."

Jerome nods.

"What are you thinking?"

"I don't know." The younger priest is frowning now. "He smiled, Gus. Smiled before he died. Of course, you didn't see it; you were very close to dying yourself. Clear eyes looking past us to heaven and a smile like it was quiet in there at last."

Saenz pats him on the shoulder. This is what allows Jerome to do his work so well, and this is also what causes him such suffering. He has compassion enough for a murderer like Alex: a child so badly harmed that he grew up broken and haunted, driven to harm others in turn.

"Not everyone can be saved."

"No. Not everyone." Jerome straightens up, running his fingers through his rain-wet hair. "How did you get here?"

"Took a cab," Saenz says.

"I'll wait for you in the car, then." He turns and walks toward the curb where his car is parked.

Saenz turns back to the white headstone.

A smile like it was quiet in there at last, Jerome had said. But oh, what a long and terrible path to that quiet, and what a high price to pay for it.

I didn't like it. I didn't want any of it. I. Didn't. Want. It.

How important it was to him to have said this, the one thing he could not say all those terrible, silent years. To have said it so clearly and unequivocally, with the last breath and strength of his life.

All over his body, on his face, his chest, his arms and hands, Saenz can still feel Alex Carlos's last words.

After a minute or so, he opens his eyes and makes the sign of the cross over the grave. Then he folds up his umbrella, glad of the rain on his face as he walks over to where the other priest stands, waiting.

ON A WET green hill some distance away, Joanna Bonifacio waits for the two priests to get into Jerome's car and watches as they drive off.

Then she turns to Leo and thumps him squarely between his shoulder blades.

"Hey, Leo. That shot had better be in focus."

"Come on, Boss. When have I ever let you down?" he says, grinning as he begins disassembling the camera and tripod.

She waits for him to finish, then slides into the driver's seat, switches on the ignition, then backs expertly out of her space and forward onto the road. And the whole time, one thought is repeating itself in her sharp, predatory brain.

The ratings will shoot through the roof.

Epilogue

SAENZ IS ON his way back to the laboratory from Simbang Gabi—one of the nine pre-dawn masses leading up to Christmas—at the university chapel. A few stragglers are hanging around and chatting cheerfully outside, most of them students or faculty. They call out to him and wish him a merry Christmas. He smiles, wishes them the same and waves goodbye, then turns up his collar against the Christmas chill and prepares to cross the road.

On the other side of the road, standing in the shadow of a tree, is Cardinal Meneses.

Saenz is startled and stops where he stands. For several moments, the two men stand on opposite sides of the road, staring wordlessly at each other. A few vehicles whiz past them from either direction. *What are you doing here? What do you want from me?*

Then the cardinal motions for him to follow. He steps away from the curb and onto the grass on the other side, and Saenz crosses the road to join him. The grass is soft and dewy under his sneakers. The dawn is just beginning to break, pale lavender light touching the edges of the night sky.

"I've been meaning to speak with you, Father Saenz," the cardinal says, treading carefully through the grass. "But I wasn't sure if you'd agree to see me."

"You could have called for me."

"That would have been too . . . You would have come, but you wouldn't have wanted to."

"What makes you think I want to now?"

"Fair enough." He stops right in the middle of the clearing, looking up at the sky. "I thought I should come to tell you the news myself."

"What news?"

The cardinal pauses to clear his throat. "Father Isagani Ramirez is no longer connected with *Kanlungan*. The board voted to remove him from his post. They have also called for his resignation from the charity, pending an investigation of his activities and his conduct there."

Saenz heartbeat quickens, but outwardly he remains calm. "It's one thing to call for his resignation. It's another thing for him to actually hand it in."

"Well, then you will be pleased to hear that he tendered last Friday. And that the board accepted it without delay. It has also filed a formal complaint."

The director was right. Your rich patrons don't really care about the children. It is a veneer of piety, a façade of benevolence. At the end of the day, it all comes down to their precious money.

"Father Saenz, I had imagined that you would be happy about this, but you don't seem to be."

"Happy?" Saenz looks down at the cardinal. "Perhaps if I had heard this eighteen years ago. Perhaps if he had not been moved three times in the last eighteen years nor allowed to continue at *Kanlungan* under a cloud of suspicion. Perhaps if the complaint had not been merely about *estafa* but about the abuse of the children under the charity's protection."

Without his familiar smile, the cardinal's face looks weary, lined with care. "We did what we were advised to do. What we have always done. I have merely obeyed, Father, as we are all obliged to do." Now there is a note of entreaty in his voice. "Father, surely you understand what that means? Surely you can find some . . . compassion for your brothers who tried to do what they could, within the limits set for us?"

Saenz tries his utmost not to sound cold, but he fails a little bit. "The compassion you seek is neither mine to give nor yours to ask for."

For a brief moment, Cardinal Meneses looks as though he's been slapped, but he recovers his composure quickly. He smoothes his hand over his shirt, as though stretching out unseen wrinkles. "At any rate, the matter is out of our hands now."

"As it should have been all along."

"Should it?" He smiles cheerlessly. "I'm not so sure, Father Saenz. I worry, deeply. I worry that our standards, our principles—our very foundations—are being eroded by this . . . this openness that you seem so determined to pursue."

"Funnily enough, I worry for exactly the opposite reasons. I worry that all this secrecy, all this unwillingness to change, to evolve—to listen to reason—is eroding all that we stand for. Endangering everything that we have vowed to protect and defend."

The cardinal sighs. "We'll never see eye to eye on this, will we, Father?"

Saenz shrugs. "I think you already know the answer to that, Your Eminence." A small bow to the cardinal as a sign of respect. "And now, if you will excuse me, I have some work to attend to." He begins to walk away.

"Merry Christmas, Father Saenz," the cardinal calls out to him.

Saenz doesn't stop walking.

"Sun's coming up, Your Eminence," is all he says.

Acknowledgments

THE FIRST TIME I wrote this book—in 1996, when I was in my mid-twenties—I was angry: angry about my job, about the state of my country, about the callousness, complacency, and corruption that had dragged it there.

The second time I wrote this book—in 2013, in my forties, having moved back home with my infant son—I found myself even angrier: about the state of my country, which seemed even worse than it was in 1996, and about the callousness, complacency, and corruption that kept it there.

I couldn't have written this book a first or a second time without the faith and support of many people. So my profound thanks go to Prof. Cristina Pantoja-Hidalgo, who published the first version of the book under the University of the Philippines Press. To my agents at Books@Jacaranda, who championed my work even when I was busy doing anything but writing. To my editors at Soho, who worked tirelessly with me to make the book better.

To my parents and my sister, who helped create all that is good in me.

And to my little boy, who is teaching me how to make something good out of myself.